SYSTEMICS

Jerrel E. Phillips

DEDICATION

This book is dedicated to my wife, Kay, whose unwavering support made it possible for me to work on behalf of those on Florida's death row and to gain invaluable insight into the machinery of death that Florida calls its criminal justice system.

In the words of John Steinbeck,

Readers seeking to identify the fictional people and places here described would do better to inspect their own communities and search their own hearts, for this book is about a large part of America today.

The Winter of Our Discontent

CONTENTS

PART ONE

CHAPTER I

The small, sandy-haired boy enjoyed dodging the water as he walked along the seashore with his parents. Time and again the water approached the shoreline, only to recede back from whence it had come. To most adults it was soothing. To others it was somehow ominous. But to this little ten-year-old boy it was simply fun. No cares. No worries. Just fun. And so he ran to the water's edge, his footsteps creating a weaving path that mirrored the outline of the waves.

The boy continued to run until the sight of a figure in the distance ahead made him stop for a better look. When that failed him he continued to run in its direction. Finally, as he drew closer, he could see that it was a man sitting on the edge of the shore, his arms wrapped around his knees. The man was staring out into the Gulf of Mexico, almost as if in a trance.

"What-cha doin'?" the little boy asked inquisitively.

"Nothin' much," answered the man, somewhat startled and moderately irritated.

But when he realized that the questioner was a small boy, a smile began to cover his face.

"Just sittin' here."

"Why you doin' that?" came the next question.

"Oh, I don't know. Got nothin' else to do, I guess. Why don't you sit down here beside me?" The man was surprised to hear the words coming from his own mouth.

"Okay." And with that the little boy sat down next to the stranger and began looking out at the waves in an obvious attempt to mimic the actions of his newfound acquaintance.

The two of them wordlessly continued to look seaward. The little boy, normally not one to be particularly quiet, somehow sensed that the stranger would appreciate silence. The only sounds were the crashing of the waves and the occasional caws of the seagulls, which flew overhead. All in all, it was a tranquil setting, notwithstanding the dark-blue storm clouds that appeared over the horizon in the western sky.

The moment ended abruptly, however, when the boy's parents caught up to him.

It wasn't long before he heard his father's stern voice: "Son, what are you doing?"

"Nothin', dad. We were just sittin' here."

"Well, come along now. We've got to get on back home." The father tried not to be too scolding in front of the stranger, and accompanied his commands with a courteous nod to the man, who returned the nod as expected. For his part the little boy got up and ran over to his parents, and the three of them resumed their walk down the beach, the boy's parents scolding him because of his unwise interaction with a stranger.

The stranger watched the boy and his parents walk down the beach and longed to be that young once more. Young enough to be able to go to his parents and explain to them how everything was someone else's fault. Young enough to have no cares that would last more than a few moments in time. Oh, for those days, he thought to himself as he waved to the little boy who looked back, his parents dragging him along.

The man continued to sit on the beach and reflect on his past and his present. The future entered into his thoughts only grudgingly, for he now felt as though the future could be nothing less than his mortal enemy.

It was easily one of the hottest days of the year, especially for October. The temperature was hovering around 102 degrees, the humidity was high, and there was no rain in sight. The heat was mitigated only by looking at the Gulf of Mexico, with its blue-green water and gentle, white-capped waves. Of course, the breeze that frequented the beach helped as well. Indeed, this was the only relief that the man had. Born and raised in Florida, Mark Abramson was accustomed to the weather, but on days like today that wasn't much help. Perhaps the approaching storm clouds would bring the relief he craved.

Mark watched with amazement as the diminutive ghost crabs along the shore continuously ran to the water's edge in vain attempts to find food left behind by the receding waves. These little guys were able to advance only short distances before being repelled by the advancing water. They were, in many ways, like their observer, a man who had never been able to make any progress without being thrown backwards in failure. Just yesterday his world had suddenly collapsed yet again, when, without warning, he was summarily discharged from an otherwise stable job at Bluestone Construction Company.

Considering his ninth grade education Mark didn't expect his current prospects of getting a decent job to be very good. His opportunities would be severely limited when he had to tell people that he had been let go from his construction job because he was suspected of stealing. What's more, this thirty-three-year-old man would have to tell prospective employers about his record of having served time in State prison. All in all he now surmised that he had little chance of being able to secure decent employment.

Sitting there on the beach Mark's thoughts drifted back to other times. He thought back to when he and his wife, Susan, had first met. Those were good times. He had just been promoted to the assistant manager position at the local car wash. Indeed, he had met Susan at a lounge in St. Bartholomew one hot Friday night in July while celebrating his promotion. Somehow they made eye contact from across the bar and he knew right away that he wanted to get to know her better. She was quite attractive with sandy-blond hair and the classic, hour-glass figure, that was the envy of most. And not only was she beautiful, but she liked cars too!

In 1975 disco was it. And given the lack of disco bars in St. Bartholomew, the only thing to do was to go to Tallahassee. Mark didn't know how to ask, but somehow he gathered the courage -- and to his surprise she said yes. So away they went in an old 1969 Impala. The ninety miles didn't take long to drive that night, but it was still almost midnight when they got to town. It didn't matter, though, because there was still time before the bars closed, and plenty to do after that. On this, their first date, they closed the town. That night was a dream come true.

Susan was the one person who really seemed to care about Mark. He felt as though she supported him in all that he did. She was always trying to get him to better himself, and to an extent she was succeeding. For the first time in years Mark considered taking classes to help him finally get his GED. When he started taking the classes, he found it to be too much at first. And yet in those early years Susan never once criticized him. "Mark, you know I'll be proud of you no matter what you do," he remembered her telling him one day. He believed her then. He hoped she still meant it now.

The two were seeing seen each other almost every day, when Mark got up the nerve to ask Susan to move in with him. When she accepted the invitation he was beside himself. After their wedding in April, 1978, the couple's first home was a two-bedroom mobile home which they purchased with some money Mark had saved, along with money they had gotten as wedding presents. It was an old, yellow structure with a green awning, a 1965 model, but that didn't seem to matter. It was theirs, and it was the first real home that Mark had had since leaving his parents behind. Mark was perhaps happier then than he had been at any other time in his life.

But the good times did not last, for this young man was soon to discover how cruel life could become.

It had been an otherwise uneventful day at the car wash when Mark's friend, Jim Raulerson, pulled into the lot, and quickly persuaded Mark to go along for a ride. The two were then stopped by the police and promptly arrested for the armed robbery of PJ's Liquors. Try as he might, Mark had been unable to convince the local judge of his innocence in the escapade. The result was a six-year prison term and an explanation from his court-appointed lawyer that he had been extremely lucky to draw so little time.

Nonetheless, six years was six years, even if he did manage to gain parole in half that time.

Upon his release Mark vowed never again to see the inside of a jail cell. He also chose to heed Susan's admonition to be more careful in choosing his friends. With that Mark began what he had come to view as his second life. In spite of everything, he had begun to feel a renewed optimism that, given the chance, he could turn things around.

But now, as he sat on the beach watching the sunset, the ever-recurring doubts returned. It had been hard enough to find a job after coming out of prison. Now it might be impossible. And on top of that he now wondered if his marriage would hold up under the strain. Indeed, it was already showing signs of falling apart. No. He didn't know if he would be able to recover from this. Not this time.

CHAPTER II

Hopeful as he had been upon leaving prison, Mark had still known that tough times were ahead. He needed two things, a job and a stable marriage. His marriage had survived prison. It was now time to work on finding a job.

Mark was quite happy that Susan seemed to understand his predicament. He needed the help and comfort that she could give. But no matter how understanding she might be he knew that if he didn't find work, the marriage could only last so long. So he continued his search. He looked everywhere, but much to his dismay, he found that word of his past had already gotten around. By now everyone, it seemed, knew of his reputation and was unwilling to give him a second chance at life.

Except for Ed Baker. Ed Baker owned Bluestone and hired Mark largely because Mark had been straight with him about his past. Beyond that there was nothing Mark brought to the job that set him above the other applicants. Indeed, many of the other applicants had past experience that Mark didn't possess. Nevertheless, Baker saw Mark as someone who needed a break, and decided to give him the chance to start over.

Mark's first day on the job was rougher than expected. It was easily one hundred degrees in the shade, the humidity was high, and the breeze didn't help. The bright Florida sun pounded relentlessly as the morning mercifully marched toward lunch time.

"How long does it take to get used to this?" Mark asked Eddy, his new co-worker.

"Not long," replied Eddy. "Either you faint dead away in the first week or you live through it. I've only seen five men die out here in the past month. Your chances are pretty good, I guess."

"I hope you're kidding!"

"Yep. But it does get hot, don't it? You'll get used to it after awhile. Everyone does. Problem is, Baker won't cut you much slack. I've seen him fire a few people right off because he didn't think they could cut it."

"Yeah, but he gave 'em time to get adjusted, didn't he? I mean, he can't expect me to be perfect right off."

"I figure you got a few days. Then you'd better be up to speed. Otherwise you're out. In some ways it's better to be told up front that you can't cut it. Anyway, I'm just warnin' you. Baker don't keep people on if he thinks they're dead weight. He's fair. But he's tough."

"Well, he seemed all right to me when I was hired," replied Mark. "I thought he was pretty nice and all."

"Oh, yeah. He's nice. But he's also got his favorites. 'Suck-ups.' See Al over there?" Eddy continued, while pointing to a tall, slender, well-tanned man. "He's Baker's best friend's son. He'll be your immediate boss. He ain't no good. And he's always looking for a fight. I've seen him start fights and then rat on the other guy. Guess who always gets fired."

"Another thing, Al don't like nobody who does better than him. He'll pick a fight with anybody who stands in his way. Trouble is, the drywall he carries is smarter than he is. Get my point?"

"Yeah, I guess so. Who's that guy he always hangs around?"

"Who, the ugly one?" chuckled Eddy.

"Yeah," smiled Mark.

"Oh, that's Randy. He's another suck-up. He and Al share a place over at Fiddlers' Creek. It's a real hole in the wall. Rumor is that Randy uses the place to deal dope. Coke and pot mostly. He's always tryin' to sell the stuff around here. The grass is pretty good, but he laces it sometimes, you know. So be careful."

"Where's he get it?"

"I don't know," answered Eddy. "I got my thoughts on it, but I can't prove nothin'. Anyway, I try to stay away from the both of 'em. No good if you ask me. If I was you I'd do the same."

"Think I will," replied Mark, "Guess we'd better get back to work. Damn, it's only ten o'clock and it's already hotter 'n hell."

"Day's just begun, man," laughed Eddy. "Just wait a few hours and tell me how you like it."

Mark began to wonder what he'd gotten himself into as he began unloading the drywall off the flatbed truck. Not only was the job difficult due to the physical labor, but it was also evident that some of the people that he was now working with were people who could easily get him in trouble. Having just come out of prison, he had to be careful about his friends. He knew that. As he unloaded the drywall off the truck, he thought to himself that he was lucky to have found Eddy early. At least there was one person whom he could count on to look out for him if he needed it.

In spite of it all Mark enjoyed the hard work -- even though it was so hot. But the first day nevertheless wore him out. He was sure that he'd never make it through. Yet when five o'clock came he was still employed, and at the time, that was what mattered the most.

Time passed swiftly that summer. Mark endured the heat, which itself was no easy matter. By the end of each day he was totally exhausted, and there were times when he was certain that he would pass out from the heat. And on those days he often felt as though the job was not worth it. But he stayed. Perhaps it was the money, or perhaps it was simply the fact that he was gaining back his self-respect. But whatever it was it kept him on the job through those hot summer months, something that he never thought he'd accomplish.

Then came trouble.

Desire. Nosiness. Whatever it's called it usually leads to trouble. Mark's curiosity would be no different. It led him, consciously or unconsciously, to the corner of a construction site one July afternoon while he was on break. When he accidentally stumbled upon Al and Randy involved in a transaction, it caught Mark, as much as anyone, by surprise. It was obvious that the transaction involved drugs, but what was perhaps beyond Mark's expectation was that the buyer was a young kid -- probably not more than ten or eleven years old. Mark could only stare in disbelief at what he saw in front of him.

"What in the hell are you looking at?" snapped Al, "Didn't you see any of this stuff where you came from?"

"Yeah, I saw it," responded Mark mechanically.

"Well then, what're you standin' around for? . . . I suggest you get outta here, unless you're lookin' to buy, too."

"Hey, man, I was just leavin', okay?" replied Mark as he hastily turned to go.

"Yeah, well, I suggest we keep this to ourselves, Abramson," said Al. "You wouldn't want to lose that job of yours, now would you?"

"No, of course not. No problem, Al," was the only response that Mark could give as he began walking away from the scene.

The entire episode had lasted only seconds, but its effects would be felt for years to come.

CHAPTER III

By September the job seemed to be less burdensome. Although the temperature still reached into the nineties, the days were still cooler than usual. What was more important, however, was that for the first time since he'd begun at Bluestone, Mark was beginning to feel as though he fit in with the rest of the guys. He was now included in the gossip and the others began watching out for him, as he did for them. In addition to that, his body was becoming used to the punishing labor that it faced every day, and it, too, was responding favorably.

Soon after the weather cooled and Mark had some time off, he decided to spend a little time with Susan. He'd been out of prison for some time now and the two of them had not really had any decent time together. So on the first Friday of September he stopped by the florist on the way home, picked up a mixed arrangement of red carnations and yellow daisies and headed home prepared for a three-day weekend on the beach with his wife.

"Mark, what in the world have you done!" exclaimed Susan when she opened the front door and saw Mark, grinning from ear to ear and holding the flowers he'd just picked up.

"Do you like them?" was all that Mark could think to say.

"Of course I do, silly. But what are they for?"

"They're for you."

"But why?" pressed Susan.

"No special reason," replied Mark. "Geez, can't I buy you flowers just for the hang of it?"

"Of course you can," said Susan. "You just surprised me, that's all. I take it that things went good at work today, huh? Did you get promoted or something?"

"Nope. Didn't get no promotion," was Mark's reply. "But I did get three days off. Thought you might like to go to the beach and hang out."

"Are you kidding? . . . You really got the time off? . . . Well, sure, I'd love to go."

"Well, get packed then and let's head out," answered Mark, who by this time was getting anxious to get the weekend underway. "Eddy has a place on the island that he said we could use. And get this, he ain't gonna charge us for it! So get a move on!"

Susan didn't need to be asked twice to get ready to go. Before Mark had finished telling her to get started, she had already retrieved the suitcase, opened it, and begun throwing the essentials into it. For his part Mark got his own things together, but he was more interested in seeing to it that Susan packed her assortment of lingerie, which he hoped would be put to the test over the next couple of days.

"Do you want me to bring this, or not?" asked Susan, as she held up the baby blue teddy that Mark had given her when they got married. Seeing that his hopes had been realized, Mark nodded with a grin that provided Susan with the expected answer. Within thirty minutes the two of them were packed and on their way to Lone Pine Island. Even though the island was less than a half-hour's drive from their house, it would still be a tremendous boost for them to get away from home for awhile. Short as it was, they savored the drive as if it were a choice cut of steak -- too expensive to buy, yet too good to resist.

By six o'clock the Abramsons had arrived at the island and pulled into the driveway of Eddy's two-bedroom cottage, which, unlike the neighboring cottages, did not rest on pilings.

Mark had the door to his car open before the car even came to a stop. As soon as he was able he jumped out and, momentarily forgetting Susan, was through the front door of the cottage and initiating the inspection of the couple's newfound hideaway.

"All right!" Susan heard Mark yell as she walked through the front door.

"There's beer in the 'fridge! At least Eddy knows how to equip the place with the essentials."

Looking around, Susan was somewhat surprised that Eddy's place was not bigger, or more spacious. After all, she knew that Eddy made good money. Then again, everything that one would need was present. The kitchen, which was done in a pale blue with white appliances, was actually quite well equipped. It even had a dishwasher and a trash compactor. There were two bedrooms in the cottage. The master bedroom boasted a huge, king-size bed, full bath with a hot tub, and a complete set of oak bedroom furniture. The second bedroom, while definitely smaller, was nevertheless fully appointed with a complete bedroom set, which included a queen-size bed. The living room, as one would expect, was decorated with a misty-gray paneling, driftwood, nets, and seashells, all of which softly blended together. Perhaps the best part of the living room, however, was the unobstructed view that it afforded of the beach and the Gulf.

"Are you ready to go?" asked Mark, as if expecting an affirmative reply from Susan.

"Go where?" came the quizzical reply.

"To the beach, silly. Where did you think I meant?" responded Mark.

"I'm not going anywhere until I unpack." said Susan. "It won't take but a minute."

"Well, hurry up. The sun's goin' down."

Susan smiled as she watched Mark standing at the living room window looking out over the beach. She knew that Mark loved the Gulf almost as much, it seemed, as he loved life. Something about it seemed to relax him and to cause him to change for the better. It was times like these that she especially treasured, and that caused her to wonder why they were so seldom able to get away like this.

13

Unpacking was not one of Susan's favorite things to do; but, to her, it was necessary and she hurriedly completed the job.

"I should be ready in a couple of hours!" she innocently yelled to Mark.

"A couple of hours?" he yelled in shock. "What are you doing in there?"

"Well, I guess I could shorten it to a couple of minutes if you'd like," said Susan.

"I think that'd be a lot better," came the relieved reply.

In no time flat Susan was finished and ready to go down to the shore. By now it was almost seven o'clock and Mark was quickly becoming even more impatient.

Even though it was dusk the sand was still almost hot to the touch -- a testament to the powerful rays of the hot sun, which bore down on the island all day. Even in September there were occasionally days in which the temperature exceeded one hundred degrees. Now the sand stood alone as a reminder of the heat that had just gone, for autumn was close enough that the temperature had begun to drop perceptibly in the evenings.

Dusk was one of the best times of the day for Mark. This time of day was precious to him -- especially when he was at the coast. Among other things, it was the one time of day that he could count on being alone. The sun-worshippers had all gone inside to nurse their sunburns and most other people were not daring enough to venture out to fight the mosquitoes.

The weather was particularly beautiful on this evening as Mark and Susan strolled to the beach. There were but a few clouds in the sky, and a slight breeze was blowing from off the Gulf. The white-capped waves gently broke before they collided with the shore. It was also low tide, so that one could walk out into the Gulf for what seemed to be miles before the water came above the knees. All in all it was a gorgeous part of the country, and one that Mark and Susan felt glad to be a part of.

Susan enjoyed watching Mark as he got to the beach. She didn't mind the fact that he seemed to forget, albeit momentarily, that she was even present. After first running to the water and falling down in it, he got back up, remembered that he'd left

Susan behind, and went back to her side. "Sorry about that," was the only thing he said. It was enough.

The sand stuck to the towels as they spread them out on the beach. The task proved difficult given the breeze that blew the towels around as soon as they were positioned properly. The breeze only served to get more sand on the towels, so that eventually the job seemed pointless to them both. Nonetheless, they persisted until it was finally possible for them to lie down on them and begin absorbing the last few warming rays of the sun.

Looking down the coast one could see but a few people. Some were alone, some with partners. But all of them seemed to be walking in slow motion, not realizing that other humans were even present. It was the same way that Mark and Susan felt as they lay there gazing upon the water. Indeed, it was as if the people that they saw were not real, perhaps just figments of their imaginations.

Laying there, Mark began to think about Susan and how she had stayed by him during those times that had been so difficult for them both. She really had been good to him and he hoped that she knew how much he appreciated her. Still, he couldn't help but wonder how his life would be different without her. Perhaps he'd have a lot fewer worries and he'd have fewer rules to live by. It was the rules he couldn't stand.

Ever since he'd been in prison he'd had a very difficult time submitting to what he now saw as the authority imposed on him by society. Life with Susan seemed, at times, to be a continuation of that system. And yet, after all was said and done Susan was the one stable thing he had going for him. As he lay thinking, he realized that the rules didn't seem to be that important.

Mark raised up on his elbows and looked down the shoreline at the sun as it gradually set. It was so beautiful as it changed colors from bright yellow to a deep crimson-orange. He loved watching the sun play cat and mouse by hiding behind a cloud, only to emerge seconds later on its way toward the horizon.

"Come on, let's walk some," Susan broke the silence. "Let's walk down the beach."

Realizing the futility of a protest to this request, Mark rose slowly to his feet in response. The concession on Mark's part was not, however, altogether selfless, because walking along the shore at dusk was itself one of his favorite pastimes.

"Which way do you want to go?" asked Mark.

"Let's go this way. The sun looks so pretty right now. Besides, there aren't as many people in this direction."

As they began walking Mark watched the waves as they repeatedly rose, broke, and then crashed into the shore with sometimes thunderous sounds. As the waves struck the shore, water quickly spread inland, as if looking for some way to escape the ocean itself. But each time the ocean won the battle and called the water back from the shore.

It was amazing to Mark that something so loud could still relax him so completely. Perhaps it was the repetition that helped; or perhaps the fact that when he watched the waves everything else seemed to disappear from his mind -- even if but for an instant. It was as if there were something about the ocean and the waves that commanded his undivided attention. In return, nature provided a peace that was hard to achieve anywhere else.

Being with Susan and walking down the shore with her was heaven. He remembered the time that he had spent in prison and told himself that never again would he allow himself to return to such a place. Prison life had changed him tremendously, perhaps permanently. Sometimes he still awoke at night from dreams about the place.

The noise, that endless noise, was something that he would never forget. He would also never forget the complete isolation from the outside world (and Susan) that haunted him every day that he spent behind bars. After leading such a horrible existence it was simply enough to walk down the beach with his wife.

They walked ever so slowly down the shore until the cool evening breeze began to take its toll upon Susan. And with the breeze came what some people call the Florida state bird, otherwise known as the mosquito. For Susan this was the straw

16

that broke the camel's back. She grimaced as one of the little invaders played cat and mouse with her. Although she eventually won the war, it was not until the invaders had scored some direct hits upon her arm, thus causing momentary bursts of pain.

The pain was soon forgotten, however, as the couple reversed course and headed back in the direction from whence they had come. The setting sun's reflection upon the Gulf was even more spectacular when it came from behind the couple as they walked aimlessly in the direction of the cottage. Turning around, they witnessed the huge orange ball descending below the horizon as it hurled massive streaks of orange, red, and pink colors back up into the sky. It was as if the sun wanted to prove one last time that it had the ability to alter the appearance of the sky, and in the process cause people to wonder in awe every time that they saw it.

"You know, sometimes I just wish I could live on this island forever. Just be a beach bum, or something," reflected Mark.

"Now why would you want to do that?" queried Susan. "There's nothing on this island that pays anything. You'd die from starvation. And with my luck your life insurance wouldn't be paid up and I wouldn't even get the money from that!" Susan smiled meekly.

"Yeah, I guess you're right, but I'd die happy!"

"Oh, I see. I guess I don't make you happy then, is that it? I'm not enough for you?" quipped Susan, continuing the jest. "Is that it?"

"Well, I guess not," replied Mark as he began to run, knowing that if he didn't he stood the very real possibility of being injured.

Even though he ran as fast as he could, he was no match for the sand. It swallowed his feet with every step. Try as he did, he eventually had to admit that he could not continue the pace. So he slowed to a walk and turned around, only to see that Susan had also given up the fight and was walking down the shoreline. Taking his chances, he waited for her to catch up; not unexpectedly, she had forgiven him for the merciless statement he'd made just moments earlier.

As they strolled hand in hand back to the cottage, both Mark and Susan watched the waves moving ever onward toward the shore. The sun's reflection was only briefly interrupted by an occasional pelican, lazily floating over the water in search of a bedtime snack. Given the hour, it was time for the wildlife of the area to also call it a day and return home too. As they began the final turn toward the cottage, the sun slowly setting, Mark noticed one last pelican diving for the final catch of the day. It was a scene that would stay with him for the rest of his life.

By the time they returned to the cottage it was completely dark. Mark entered the front door and turned on the light only to find that it quickly went back out. To his happy surprise it was Susan who had decided that the light was not needed. Indeed, as the situation developed it was not needed for the remainder of the night.

The rest of the weekend passed all too quickly. The weather was perfectly gorgeous, aside from a brief shower on Saturday evening, thus providing warm days spent on the beach. When its turn came, the moon eagerly asserted its claim to the heavens; with it came the cooling breeze that made the nights even more beautiful than the days. There were no phones, no cars, no people, and no worries. As a result, the couple, in two days, were able to completely relax.

All too soon, however, Sunday evening arrived and it was time to return home.

The drive back took much less time than Mark had hoped it would. Twenty minutes, to be exact. To Mark it seemed that, just as each minute took them farther away from the cottage, each minute also took him farther and farther from the peaceful serenity that he and Susan had so happily nurtured over the past two days. Serenity was not a frequent visitor to Mark, and yet, this time he felt things would be different. His life was about to change, of that he was certain.

CHAPTER IV

Bluestone Construction usually ended its workday at five o'clock. Not because the work normally ran out, but because there is only so much heat and humidity a body can take. When conditions allowed, crews would work until sunset, but that rarely happened from June through September. So, it was not at all unusual that by seven o'clock on an uneventful Tuesday afternoon Bluestone's offices were empty. No one would return again until early the next morning.

Al, however, had different plans. As it turned out, this particular Tuesday had seen a rather decent amount of cash accumulation at the office. Most of it had been destined to for the local bank that afternoon. It would have made the trip had it not been for an unexpected flu bug that fortuitously swept through the office that day, leaving the office short of staff and the safe full of cash.

Al had never been one to engage in endeavors that required extensive planning.

So now, seeing the opportunity he had suddenly been given, he decided that it was time to act. It was time to line his pockets and rid himself of a co-worker that he had come to disdain.

The plan was not novel. It was not intricate. In fact, it was bland, and normally would not have warranted a moment's consideration by the local newspaper editor. After all, burglaries were not that uncommon in St. Bartholomew. The economy was not improving despite the best efforts of the city commissioners. The result was unemployment and an increase in crime. But the kind of crime that overtook this sleepy fishing village was typically non-violent. It was largely the result of otherwise good people who needed to eat, pay the bills, and keep roofs over their heads. Local Judges routinely recognized such problems, and more often than not put these new criminals on probation and ordered them to undertake community service to repay their debts to society. Considered in this light, the burglary that was committed upon Bluestone Construction that Tuesday night was hardly front-page news.

Nevertheless, as Al left the office that night with over two thousand dollars in cash, he initiated and consummated a plan that would have far reaching affects that he could never have contemplated.

The theft itself had been easy. The police report indicated that sometime during the evening hours on that Tuesday, the perpetrator had forcibly entered the office by way of the window, which the thief had forgotten to close after making his way inside the building. Once inside, someone who knew its combination had apparently opened the combination safe. The report also noted that the combination to the safe was listed on a rolodex card on the manager's desk, and, as it turned out, the Rolodex was open to that exact card. After removing all of the money from the safe, the burglar had simply left the office through the door. Ed Baker's secretary, Ms. Jacki Pierson then discovered the theft the next morning at eight o'clock when she arrived at work.

The Cortez County Sheriff's Department, in their report, listed the suspect as "unknown." There were no fingerprints, no tools left behind, no eyewitnesses. In short, the crime would not be solved unless and until the police got lucky, which usually meant that the thief would somehow do something stupid enough to get himself caught. So Al was confident that he had safely succeeded in improving his financial condition, while at the same time setting the wheels in motion to rid himself of his new enemy. And although this escapade was not the best of his twisted accomplishments, it was nevertheless sufficient to net the intended results.

October arrived with its clear, crisp days. Although it was not cold, it was cooler than the warm end-of-summer days that had dominated September. There was rarely a cloud in the sky, and cool breezes added to the overall enjoyment felt by most people in the area.

It was on such a day that Al decided to end Mark Abramson's career at Bluestone Construction Company.

Al had earlier decided that it would be best to put up with his enemy for a while longer in order to put some distance between himself and the theft. A month or so seemed to be in line, but it seemed to Al as though the appointed day would never arrive. When it did finally appear Al could hardly contain his joy. It was not easy to do, since he had to present himself to Ed as though he were deeply troubled at having to tell him the bad news.

"Jacki, where is Ed this morning?" asked Al in a voice that belied the jovial feeling in his heart.

"He should be in later on," she answered. " He had to make a run up to Quincy. I'd guess he'll be back in around eleven or so."

Jacki was always so pleasant. Unlike Al, she was not known to have any enemies at Bluestone. She had grown up in St. Bartholomew and had lived there continuously ever since. No question where her loyalties were. She had even married a local boy named Robert Pierson after graduating from high school, and the two of them had two children, both of whom were married and had children of their own. Jacki and Robert were also devout Baptists who regularly helped those people less fortunate than her. Indeed, if St. Bartholomew needed someone to emulate its best virtues, Jacki would no doubt be the hands-down favorite to win the prize.

Al had always wondered about Jacki. To his way of thinking she was simply too nice, too perfect. And to Al's way of thinking it was obvious that the only reason everyone was so nice to her was that she was the boss' secretary. As far as he was concerned the only reason that she even had the job was that she was a close friend of Ed's wife. But notwithstanding his unvoiced dislike for the woman, he always managed to feign a polite appreciation for all that she did around the office. It was with this attitude that he smiled as he prepared to leave the office.

21

"Will you ask Ed to see me when he gets a chance? I really need to speak with him," said Al, as he turned to go back to work at the site.

"Sure will," answered Jacki, as Al walked out of the office. I wonder what that boy's up to now, she thought to herself. But being behind in the paperwork that confronted her, there was no time to consider the question further. Her attention returned to the mundane task of sorting new invoices. Ed could deal with Al when he returned.

CHAPTER V

It was just after lunch that Ed returned from Quincy and Jacki told him that Al wanted to speak with him. Ed would have preferred to lock himself in his office and speak to no one for the remainder of the day. His trip to Quincy had not gone well at all and it now looked as if he might have to hire a lawyer to get the customer to pay him for the load of lumber that he had just delivered. It was not what he needed, especially with money being tight and the housing market continuing to be depressed with no appreciable relief in sight. But Ed knew that locking himself in his office would not help anything, and so he went out to find Al to see what he wanted. He hoped that it was good news.

"Hey, Al, Jacki says that you needed to see me," Ed yelled over to Al, who was on the frame of the project at the site. "What do you need?"

"Yeah, I'll be right down," answered Al, as he scrambled to the ground and lumbered over to where Ed was standing. "Yeah, can we talk? Inside, maybe?"

"Sure, whadda you have for me now? I hope it's good, because you won't believe what Jarvis did to me just now. Says that the lumber that I delivered to him is not choice and that he's not paying full price for it! I don't believe it! The man knows that we're not a lumber company and that the lumber was from finished sites. But no. Now he says that the agreement was for choice lumber and that's what he expects to get out of the deal."

As the two men walked into Ed's office, Al sized up the situation and realized that this was the perfect time to tell Ed about the problem that had now surfaced with Mark.

"Yeah, well, I'm sorry to hear about Jarvis, Ed," Al began in the most compassionate voice that he could muster. "But look, there's something I have to tell you. And believe me, you're going to be as shocked by this as I was. I really wish I didn't have to . . ."

"What is it, Al?" questioned Ed, now irritated. "I'm not exactly in the mood to play twenty questions."

"Well, see, it's about that money that was stolen a while back."

"What about it? Do the police know who did it? Man, I sure hope so, because we could sure stand to get that back right now."

"Well, no. It's not exactly like that," answered Al. He still couldn't tell how Ed was going to react, but he could sense that it wouldn't be good.

"Then what exactly is it like? And exactly how long do I have to wait before you tell me?"

Al, not one to be outdone in theatrics decided that now was the time to close the office door, especially with Jacki lending a noticeable ear in their direction.

"Well, Ed," Al began, walking to the door and shutting it as quietly as possible, "I found out something through the grapevine that shocked the devil out of me, and with a little checking I think I've confirmed who took the money. Mind you, I don't know if he stills has it or not. Anyway, what I heard was that Abramson, of all people, took the money. Of course, I'm sure he'll deny it. But that's what I heard, anyway."

A visibly shaken Ed sat in silence for what seemed to be hours before he regained his composure. "All right. How in the hell do you know that Abramson did anything of the sort? I mean, he's been one of my best workers since the day he started here. And if he did this he's been awfully cool about it."

"Yeah, well, that's what I thought, too," Al said. "Anyway, this guy I know tells me that shortly after the theft Abramson was down at that dive on Main Street. What do they call it? Oh yeah, the Sand Crab Bar & Grill. Anyway, he's down there putting a few down and buying drinks for his buddies. He has a few too many himself and, well, one thing leads to another and he confides in this guy that he stole the money. I didn't think too much about it and then I remembered that he stayed at Eddy's place recently and well, that had to cost money that he didn't have."

"But Abramson?" Ed responded, still shaking his head.

"I know. I know. But the man did have access to the trailer, just like all of us do. And you said something about the Rolodex being opened to the combination on the safe."

"I never said anything about that Rolodex," replied Ed, obviously sensing a problem.

"Yes you did. Yes you did," Al said cautiously. "You probably don't remember it. You were so upset at the time that it happened. Shoot, you were practically hysterical, Ed. Anyway, I'm as shocked as you are. I liked Abramson. Trusted him. Now I don't know how I can work around him when I have to be worried about whether my belongings will be there at the end of the day when I go to get them."

"Well, what do you think I should do about it?" Ed asked.

"How should I know? You're the boss. But I know if I was you I sure wouldn't have somebody like that working for me. Who knows what he'll take next?"

"Yeah, I guess that makes sense," Ed responded. "But I still can't believe it was Abramson. You know, with his record the sheriff will really go hard on him."

"A record? I didn't know he had a record. What for?" Al asked.

"Robbery or something like that. He didn't actually do the robbery, I don't think. But he supposedly knew about it. Anyway, they'll go nuts on him now," Ed replied while shaking his head. It was apparent that this was not sitting too well with Ed. And he still couldn't believe that it was Mark who had stolen the money.

"Well, you know Ed, I'm not so sure I'd even tell the police about it if I were you. Shoot, they'd have you down there in court every time you turn around. And, I don't know why, but I kinda feel like Mark needs a second chance. Don't you think losing his job would teach him a lesson? Especially if you could get your money back."

"I don't know what to think right now," Ed answered. "Tell you what. I've got a lot of work to catch up on. Do me a favor and don't say anything to anyone about this, okay? I'll handle it, but I want to give it some thought. "Oh yeah, and thanks for letting me know about it. I'm sure it wasn't easy coming in here like this."

"No problem Ed. Hey, you'd better get to work like you said. And for that matter I'd better get back outside before everyone starts wondering what in the world I'm doing in here. See you later, you hear?" Al said, as he turned to go back outside.

"Yeah, later," Ed answered. He began shuffling papers on his desk, trying to decide what task he needed to tackle first. He still couldn't believe what he'd just heard.

And yet, he had to do something about it.

Since he'd been in business there was one thing that Ed Baker did not like to do, and that was to deal with personnel problems. Especially firing someone. He had always been raised to do his best with the assurance that if he did, things would always work out one way or another. That approach had always worked for him, and he therefore could not understand why everyone didn't do the same. But obviously there would always be those who just couldn't conform, and for those people there would always be those people like Ed who would have to deal with their problems one way or another. That knowledge, however, did not really make him feel any better about this part of his job.

This particular situation caused Ed a great deal of discomfort. As he sat at his desk trying to work, he replayed the previous conversation with Al in his mind. Over and over he thought about what Al had just told him. What had he really been told?

Not a whole lot, but Al clearly seemed concerned about what he had been told about Mark. And he was right that Mark had just taken that weekend off, which had to have cost him some money -- money that he didn't seem to have. But doggone it, thought Ed. Why would Mark do such a thing? And why did *he* have to deal with it?

"Jacki!" Ed shouted into the other room. "Do you have a minute?"

"Yeah, sure, what do you need?" asked Jacki, as she began walking over to her boss' office.

"I don't know. I guess I just need some advice," responded Ed, who by now was obviously very troubled and in need of comforting as much as he was in need of advice.

And when it came to work it was usually Jacki who was able to help him out in that department.

Anyone who assumed that Ed's relationship with Jacki had begun with her employment would be grossly missing the mark. In a small town the size of St. Bartholomew, people are not afraid to get to know one another, to become friends. And Jacki had become best friends with Ed's wife. As is most often the case in small southern towns this relationship grew stronger with each passing year, to the point that Jacki was almost family. Indeed, there was very little the two families did not know about one another, so he trusted her implicitly. He knew her to be an honest person with a good head on her shoulders. And he knew that he could go to her for advice and that he wouldn't have to worry about their conversation going past that room, at least as far as her co-workers were concerned.

For her part Jacki looked upon Ed as the son that she had never had, so she watched over him every step of the way. After five years of working with him she had learned even more easily how to tell when something was bothering him. That nervous twitch he developed in his right eye, for example. Not to mention the fact that he would become very quiet and lose himself in his work. Telltale signs they were, and she saw them now.

As Jacki walked into Ed's cluttered office and saw her boss at his desk supporting his head on his right hand and staring out into space, she knew that this meeting would not be wasted time.

"What's up?" she asked.

"I don't know," Ed responded. As he got up to close the door he looked out the window at his men. Pretty good crew all in all. No slackers. And they all seemed to get along pretty well.

"Here's the problem. You know Al was in here a while ago? Well, he comes in here and tells me that he knows who stole the money from us."

"Really? Who in the world was it?" Jacki asked excitedly.

"Mark Abramson," Ed answered. "And I really can't believe it, you know. I mean, he has always seemed to be a pretty decent fellow in spite of his past. It seems to me like he's been getting things back in line. At least that's what I've gathered from our conversations."

"It doesn't surprise me one little bit, Ed," Jacki said. "The man has a criminal record. For crying out loud, he's been to jail. I didn't feel good about him from the day you hired him. Nope. Doesn't surprise me at all."

Jacki's response caught Ed by surprise. He had expected her to be as concerned about this as he was. He certainly hadn't thought that she'd be so willing to accept Al's accusation.

"Well, what do you think I should do about it, Jacki?" Ed asked, although he suspected he already knew the answer.

"What do I think? I think you out to toss him out of here right now. That's what I think. And then I think you should tell the sheriff what you know and let them deal with him." Jacki spoke as emphatically as she knew how.

"But if I tell the sheriff it'll ruin this man's life," Ed replied. "And we really don't know if he's actually done anything or not."

"Well, if you ask me, where there's smoke, there's fire. And with this man's past record I just don't think you need the trouble. I'd get rid of him today."

"Even if you couldn't prove that he had taken the money? I mean, really. This is just a rumor at this point."

"Yes, Ed. It's just a rumor now. But look at whom we're talking about. Someone with a record. A record of stealing, for crying out loud. I just think you're better off without him."

"You may be right. I don't know," sighed Ed. "I guess I'll think about it some more. Thanks for your advice, Jacki. Do me a favor, though. This is just between you and me for now, okay?"

"Anything you say, Ed," Jacki answered. "Just let me know if you need anything else. But I really do think you're better off getting rid of that guy. He's no good to you if you ask me. Anyway, I'll let you get back to work."

As Jacki left the office Ed felt no better than he had before he asked for her advice. He had hoped for a different response, although in hindsight Jacki's response was to be expected. The bottom line was that Ed had to decide what to do. And he guessed that he already knew what that was. He really did like Mark, but he couldn't just sit by and allow someone who'd stolen from him to continue working there. After all, he couldn't afford to take unnecessary risks. And keeping Mark on didn't appear to be anything but an unnecessary risk at the moment. Ed nonetheless decided to sleep on it overnight. Tomorrow would be another day.

The ride home gave Ed time to think about the situation that he faced. It just wasn't as simple as whether to fire Mark, because he also needed to decide what to do about contacting the sheriff's office. Since they had investigated the break-in they would have to be told about the fact that a suspect had surfaced. But Al was right about him having to take time to go to court. Still, Ed had always preached to his friends about the fact that people didn't stand up and do their civic duty. Too many chickens, he'd always said. So the bottom line was that if he decided to pursue firing Mark, he'd have to report this to the local authorities and let them do whatever they needed to do. In the end he decided that he really had no choice. He'd been given information by someone who supposedly knew what he was talking about. It was for the sheriff to decide what to do about it. He was a construction worker, not an investigator. It was better not to do anything hasty. So he decided to speak with the authorities and go from there.

Acting on what he thought was the rational, sensible thing to do, Ed called the Cortez County Sheriff's Office upon arriving home from work. "Hello. This is Ed Baker from Bluestone Construction," Ed told the receptionist. "Is there someone there that I could speak with about a break-in that happened on our job site a while back? I've spoken with a man who claims to know who was involved in the thing, and I wanted to give you all the information."

It wasn't long before Sergeant Anderson came on the line. "Ed, how you doin', man? I haven't talked to you since last year's Christmas party."

"Oh, I'm doing okay, I suppose. How've you been?"

"Still kickin', I guess. Marge said that you had some information regarding that theft at your site. So what's up?"

"Not sure really. I thought I'd better call and talk to whomever was handling the case. I didn't know you were involved."

"Well, I wasn't at first. But when I realized it was your place I thought I'd kind of keep an eye on things. I can pass along any information that you have."

"That's good news," replied Ed. "Maybe now something will get done. Anyway, you know I have this employee named Al Stempson, whom I've known for a while. He comes to me today and tells me that one of my employees stole the money from us. Says he heard about it in a bar or something."

"What's the guy's name?" asked Anderson.

"Mark Abramson. Ever heard of him?"

"Oh, yeah. We busted him some time ago for robbing a place in the county. It was that liquor store named PJs. He was tried and convicted. Served a few years, as I recall."

"He told me that he didn't know what was happening, and that he had nothing to do with the robbery." responded Ed.

"Yeah, well over the years I haven't met too many criminals who admitted to what they'd done. I remember Abramson claiming that his accomplice did the job and that Abramson didn't know what was going on. Said that he just 'happened' to be in the car with the money. We all got a good laugh out of that one."

"So you think he was really involved in the robbery?" asked Ed. "I mean, I've sort of believed him when he said that he had nothing to do with it."

"Listen, Ed. I deal with these types every day. They can make you think that they're the Pope himself if they try hard enough.

Do I think he was involved? You bet I do. I wouldn't trust him for anything. Especially since he tried to pin it all on his accomplice and still refuses to take any blame for it."

"So what do you think I ought to do about the theft? I mean I really don't have any proof of anything yet."

"It's up to you, Ed. Between you and me, if you want us to take it, I can bring the slimebag in here and have a little chat with him, and then we can prosecute him for it. I promise you that he won't be bothering you anymore. But if you don't want us involved, well -- I have more than enough cases to work as it is, and I won't be offended. It's your call."

"Okay. Well, I'll tell you what. Let me think about it and I'll give you a call back later. I don't know what to do right now."

"Good enough, man. And hey -- it was good to hear from you again. Tell the family I said hello."

"Will do. Say hello to your wife for me. I swear I don't know how she puts up with you," chuckled Ed. "I'll be in touch." Even as he hung up the phone Ed had decided that he wouldn't seek prosecution of Mark in spite of his prior statements on practicing good citizenship. There was still that lingering feeling of doubt about the whole thing, despite what Al, Sergeant Anderson, and Jacki had said. He hoped that his friends and colleagues would understand.

"Mark, I want to talk with you this evening before you head home," Ed stated as firmly as he could under the circumstances. It was everything he could do to keep his voice level and to control the shaking in his hands. He was amazed that he was still so nervous, even though it had been a full day since he'd decided what to do. As long as he lived he'd never get used to this part of his job.

"I guess there's no easy way to say this," continued Ed, "so I'll just go ahead and say it. I'm sure that you recall the theft that occurred here last month."

"Sure, I remember it," responded a puzzled Mark.

"Well, I've just been told that you're the person who stole the money, Mark. And while at first I didn't believe it, the fact is that

31

you do have a record and, well, I just think that it's not going to work out. Your staying here, that is."

"What are you saying? I'm fired?" asked Mark, his voice shaking. "I had nothing to do with that theft, Mr. Baker. I swear I didn't."

"Mark, I don't know for sure whether you did or didn't have anything to do with it. Personally, I hope you didn't, because I like you. But the fact remains that you've been identified as the person who stole the money from our company. And I can't have someone working for me whom I can't trust. So I'd appreciate it if you'd just get your things together and go on home."

"What, that's it? I don't get a chance to show you I had nothing to do with this? Look, man, I've worked for you for some time now. You've given me more responsibility, and now you're going to kick me out based upon what someone says and not give me a chance to defend myself?"

"I don't have a choice, Mark" Ed managed to respond.

"What do you mean you don't have a choice?" shouted Mark. "You own the damned company! You can do whatever you want."

"What you really mean is that because I've got a record you don't want to give me a chance to show you I didn't do it. Well, I'll tell you what. You don't have to bother. I can see where you're coming from."

"Mark, I know it sounds stupid, but I really wanted this to go better than this. I simply don't have a choice in this. I have to think about the company."

"Yeah, well, what about me? What about my wife? Ever think about her, Ed? Ever think about what I'm going to tell her?" Mark asked sarcastically. "And by the way, who was it that supposedly identified me, anyway?"

"I can't tell you that, Mark." answered Ed. "I think it's better that you go now, okay. We'll talk later if you want."

Five minutes and it was over. As Mark stormed out of his office Ed couldn't help but wonder if he'd done the right thing.

Regardless, it was too late to go back and change things. Time to get back to work.

The next day, as he lay on the shore and watched the shrimp boats drift out of sight, the world seemed to be closing around Mark Abramson. As he looked out at the Gulf, the memories of all of his past disappointments struck him repeatedly, without regard for his sanity. It would be so nice to be like that little boy again, he thought to himself. But that wasn't going to happen. Yesterday's departure from Bluestone was real, and it was painful. I'll never recover from this, he thought to himself. Never.

CHAPTER VI

Katherine Baker had been married to her husband for just over twenty years. And while there had been difficult times, which neither one of them believed they would survive, all in all their life together had been happy. They had first met while both were attending classes at Auburn University, where Ed was studying to become a veterinarian and Katherine was in the school of sociology. In those days of political and social unrest, both had been actively involved in protesting the war in Vietnam, Watergate, and the other issues of the day. And through their common political views, they soon discovered that they had other interests in common. So it didn't take long before Ed and Katherine became serious about each other and began thinking about marriage and their life together.

As it turned out, Ed found that his newfound attraction for Katherine also detracted from the time he could spend on his major studies in veterinary medicine. Such situations are perhaps not conducive to making the best career decisions, and as is often the case, love prevailed. Ed decided to abandon his thoughts of becoming a veterinarian and instead chose the easier route offered by the school of business.

Time seemed to fly by for Ed and Katherine, and before they knew it both were graduating from college and, not unexpectedly, setting the date for their upcoming wedding. It was a happy time for them both, and one that they would treasure forever. Their parents had enthusiastically supported their decision, which made their wedding day only that much more special. Since Katherine's parents lived in Texas and Ed's had lived all of their lives in West Virginia, it seemed only logical to have the ceremony at Auburn. It also gave their friends the opportunity to see the campus once again, and to reflect on the past four years that had brought Ed and Katherine together. And so, on October Third the two of them were married in a setting that by all accounts was ideal in every way.

The decision about where to settle down after their marriage had not been an easy one to make. For some unexplained reason, neither wanted to live in Texas, nor in West Virginia, preferring rather to see and experience other parts of the country. As a result, their first few years together took them to Colorado, Illinois, and Washington before returning somewhat closer to home in Atlanta.

In those days Ed had been less concerned about working anywhere on a long-term basis, which made it hard to generate much of an income. But the two of them made do with what they had and were quite comfortable in the life that they had made for themselves. After a few years Ed settled into the construction field and

Katherine easily found jobs in clinics in each city to which they had moved. Atlanta was certainly no different.

But the nomadic life that the two had created was destined eventually to grow old.

While living in Atlanta, Ed and Katherine had frequently heard about the beaches in neighboring Florida, so they decided one fall to take a few days off and head south. They embarked on their trip with no particular destination in mind and with no plan as to how much of the state they would try to see. The only goal was to get across the Florida line, which they accomplished in little more than four hours. Soon they had passed Tallahassee and were heading south on U.S. 98, which eventually took them to unheard of but beautiful little towns like Cortez and Lone Pine. Finally, it took them to St. Bartholomew.

Ed and Katherine had had no intention of spending their vacation in only one town, but as fate would have it, they found the people in St. Bartholomew and Cortez County to be so friendly that they decided to spend their entire vacation there. Of course, the island beaches that dotted the surrounding area made their decision considerably easier. And when they had had enough of them there was always an abundance of quaint shops to visit and seafood upon which to dine. All in all they were more than happy to spend a few relaxing days in the area before returning home to Atlanta.

It was not long after this vacation that Ed considered talking to Katherine about what he thought might be an ill-received proposition -- another move. This time the goal was Florida, and more specifically, St. Bartholomew. While in the town on vacation Ed had been quick to observe that the local housing industry seemed to be growing at a pretty good pace. To Ed, the thought of living in a town by the sea was probably about the closest thing that he could hope for in the way of a perfect life. The question was whether Katherine would share this perspective. Since he knew that she had loved their vacation in the area, he thought he would take the chance and approach her with the possibility of another move. The discussion did not take long. The answer was a surprising "okay." And with that the plans were made and it was Florida or bust.

Ed was particularly pleased with the move. Both he and Katherine found the local residents to be unusually friendly and open to helping them get off the ground with their jobs. Katherine found work as a clinical assistant in the local hospital and Ed immediately began the process of beginning his own construction company with what little money the two of them had managed to save over the past five years. Within a matter of a few months, Bluestone Construction was open for business and actively seeking new customers.

From the beginning, Bluestone had been a mutual endeavor for Ed and Katherine. Ed supplied the labor and the construction knowledge and Katherine helped manage the books after she got home from working at the hospital. She even found that through her job she was able to identify people in the community who needed a steady income in order to provide for their families. And thanks to Katherine, these people almost invariably found their way to Ed and Bluestone Construction. In those early years Bluestone could not pay much in the way of an hourly wage, but Ed nevertheless did what he could, always assuming that it would pay off later.

Bluestone naturally began as a small company that could handle most residential home repairs and remodeling. But the company's reputation as a dependable, honest, business concern soon became well known throughout the community. Not that it happened overnight; in fact, it took years. But the growth was nevertheless exceptional. Ed always attributed this to the high quality of the labor that he was able to find. People like Jacki, whom he had hired on his wife's urging. People who believed in an honest day's work for an honest day's pay. Such attitudes weren't easy to come by nowadays, and after having worked in larger cities Ed appreciated what he had come to find in his newfound home.

So, it was more than a little troubling to him when situations such as that with Mark arose, because he knew that such behavior was fundamentally out of character with the vast majority of people whom he considered to be his friends and colleagues.

For this reason, it hurt Ed to have to fire Mark. And Katherine, after all the years, knew him better than anyone, so it didn't take long for her to realize that something was bothering her husband when he returned home from work that evening. "From the look on your face it wasn't a great day at the office, was it?" she inquired.

"I guess you could say that," Ed responded after what seemed to be an eternity.

"You know that guy, Mark Abramson, who works for me?"

"Yeah."

"Well, I fired him today."

"You what?" Katherine answered. "Why in the world did you do that? I thought he was one of your best workers!"

"Yeah, well, so did I until Al Stempson told me that Abramson was the guy who stole the money out of our office last month."

"And you believed *him*? Ed, Al's one of the last people I'd believe, from what you've told me. I don't care who's son he is. You've said yourself that he's a snake."

"I know I have, but Mark does have a record, you know. And it was for robbery, Katherine. *Robbery*. So just maybe Al's telling the truth this time. And the bottom line is that I can't afford to take chances. You know that."

"I assume that Mr. Abramson had something to say about it, didn't he? What did he say?"

"He denied it, of course. But I would have expected him to do that. Anyhow, it's over now, and that's that," Ed stated matter of factly, as if just by saying it would make it so.

"I don't know, Ed. The whole thing stinks if you ask me. I mean, what does he do now? He's married, didn't you say?"

"Yeah, he's married."

"Does his wife work?"

"I don't know if his wife works." Ed responded. "And what if she doesn't? Am I supposed to keep someone on who's stealing from me, simply because he's got a family? Sounds like the Menendez brothers asking for mercy because they're orphans. The bottom line is that the business can't afford to take the chance that Abramson wasn't the guy. And besides, I decided that I wouldn't turn him in to the sheriff. So I'm actually doing him a favor. If they went after him he'd not only be unemployed, he'd be talking to his poor wife through cell bars."

"Gosh, you're all heart!" shouted Katherine, as she turned and left the room.

"Jacki agreed with me," Ed yelled into the other room. But it was too late. He could tell that it would take substantially more convincing before Katherine would see his side of things. Figuring that the day had been a total disaster, and that it was better to end it early before it got worse, Ed headed for the bedroom and lay down. With any luck the morning would bring a better day.

CHAPTER VII

The next day at Bluestone was predictably tense. Ed figured that the best way to handle the situation was to get everyone together early and explain what happened. That way there would be fewer rumors and work would resume more quickly. The decision, from a managerial perspective, was quite good, but that didn't make the news any less of a shock to everyone.

The meeting itself took very little time - five minutes, tops. Ed was vague: "Yesterday evening after discussing some matters with Mark, he decided to terminate his employment at Bluestone, effective immediately. So don't expect to see him around here anymore. Now, as to the reasons why Mark left, the only thing I can say, and will say, is that some issues arose which were very serious in nature and which do not permit me to discuss the particulars with you. That's all I wanted to speak with you about this morning, so let's all just get back to work. We've got a full day ahead."

And with that the meeting was over, and Bluestone's employees began filing out the trailer door.

As he walked out, Eddy couldn't believe what he'd just heard. It didn't make any sense at all. Just yesterday Mark had been really upbeat about the job, and everything in general. He even had his sights set on a new car. Nothing pointed to problems with Bluestone or Ed. And yet, today, Mark was no longer employed.

Eddy couldn't wait to go see Mark that evening and find out what was going on.

Al, on the other hand, was on top of the world. He knew that he'd finally gotten rid of someone who, from his perspective, had been a thorn in his side. And it had all been so easy. He alone knew the truth. Not even Randy knew, although Al didn't know if he would be able to hide his delight from Randy throughout the day. Eventually he gave in to his excitement and decided to let him in on his coup.

"Hey, Randy!" Al shouted from across the yard. "Got a second?"

"Sure, I guess." Randy answered. "What is it?"

"How'd you like that in there? Pretty scary stuff, huh?"

"Sure, it's scary. I mean, one day the guy's here, and the next he's gone. Wonder what's going on. Baker sounded pretty weird in there to me."

"You *really* want to know?" Al asked, as though he'd die if Randy said that he wasn't bothered.

"Sure. But what do you know about it, man?"

"I know that Baker fired Abramson for stealing that money from the company last month!"

"He what!?!" said Randy. "Abramson don't have it in him to do something like that. That's a lot of crap!"

"Keep your voice down, man. I didn't say that Abramson took the money. I said that he got *fired* for taking it, if you get my drift."

"Did you tell Baker that Abramson stole the money, Al?" asked Randy.

"Let's put it like this. He won't be hosin' in on our other business no more. You didn't like that, did you?"

"No I didn't like it, but jeez, man. The guy was pretty harmless if you ask me. He hasn't done anything yet, so why would he start now."

"Maybe he hasn't done anything yet, but that doesn't mean he wouldn't have, if he'd been around much longer. Besides, do you like the idea of someone like him knowing anything about that stuff? I don't."

"Sure. I guess you're right. Just hit kind of sudden-like, that's all. . . . Come to think of it, I really would have liked to have been there when 'ole Abramson got canned. I bet he needed some diapers yesterday, don't you?" A hint of laughter began to surface in Randy's voice.

"Yeah, I'm sure he cried like a baby all night! After all, he is a big bad ex-con with all that jail experience. I know I sure was afraid of him! Oooooh!" mocked Al, as the two of them walked on out to the truck to begin their workday.

Later that day, Al and Randy, not being able to get Al's victory out of their minds, broke away from the work crew for a few minutes. Time to smoke some grass. It had not taken Al long at all to convince Randy that indeed a little downtime was appropriate. And so, as they sat behind the construction site looking out at the Gulf they reveled in Al's accomplishment. Both men agreed that the set-up was one of his better ideas, and that Mark had been asking for it for some time.

The Gulf breeze felt good to both men as they sat in silence waiting for the inspiration that it would take to return back to the work site. It did not take long, however, to decide that no one would really miss them for the rest of the afternoon, which meant that they smoked more joints than either man first anticipated. This in turn led to Al's disclosure that he had also brought along some better stuff. The natural progression of events not surprisingly included what Al described as "some righteous coke," which pleased Randy to no end. As might be expected, it was not long until both men were oblivious to the world around them -- captives, as it were, to the substances they were ingesting with great fanfare and anticipation.

While Al and Randy were overjoyed at the recent events at Bluestone, Ed Baker was feeling just the opposite. The passing of the night had not afforded him the peace of mind that he had hoped for. Neither had it served to reassure him that the action that he had taken with Mark was absolutely necessary under the circumstances. And as much as he hated to admit it, Katherine just may have been right, as she usually was in matters such as these. But even so, there didn't appear to be anything he could do about it now.

As the day progressed, Ed became increasingly upset. For years he had always prided himself on being rational, objective.

After all, it was his objectivity that had benefited him these past few years in making business decisions for Bluestone. So, what happened to me yesterday, he asked himself. How could I have made such a rash decision that so drastically impacted an employee's life?

The more he thought about it, the less work he was able to do. "Why don't you just quit for the day and go on home?" Jacki finally asked him. After five hours of this his misery was bringing her down as well.

"Why should I go home? I don't see why anything will be better there," Ed answered her. "Besides, if I work it'll take my mind off things."

"Yeah, if you worked," Jacki responded. "But I haven't seen you do more than a half-hour's work all day. You act like you lost your best friend."

"Well, I guess I'm just not into it today. I think I'll take a break."

"That sounds like a good idea. Why don't you get some fresh air or something. . . . I know why don't you go over to Dairy Queen and get us both a milk shake? That way you'd cheer us both up." Jacki smiled as she made the suggestion. She knew that Ed had a weakness for milk shakes. Especially milk shakes from Dairy Queen. If that couldn't cheer him up, nothing would.

"Oh, all right. You talked me into it. I guess you're buying, right?"

"Why should I buy?" Jacki asked.

"Well, I guess because it's your idea and because this is obviously a ploy to get me in a better mood so you'll have a better day. So I don't see that much in it for me, except for more calories, which my doctor, whom *you* made me go see, says I shouldn't have. In addition to that. . . ."

"All right already. I get the idea," Jacki laughed. "I'll buy. But you'd better be in a better mood after this."

"I promise. Be back in a few minutes." And out the door he went.

As he drove down Route 98, Ed thought about how lucky he had been to find Jacki for a secretary. She knew the office better than he did in a lot of ways. And just as important -- if not more so -- she knew him better than anyone except for Katherine. Maybe the idea for the shakes wasn't so bad after all. He didn't feel that guilty as he paid for the extra-large chocolate shakes, each of them guaranteed to make one's fight with weight loss more difficult. When he arrived back at the office, Jacki could tell that he was in a better mood already.

"Well, what's that I see?" she asked him as he walked through the door. "No, I don't believe it. It's actually the start of a smile. My day's gonna get better after all. I can just feel it."

"You know, Jacki. One thing that's pretty certain. If I ever get ticked off and fire you, you'll be able to walk right into a career as a comedian. In fact, I'm surprised you haven't already tried it."

"Don't you wish!" Jacki grinned.

"Tell you what. I think I'm going to go and check out the progress at the site. That way you'll have more time to prepare for your next act!" Ed replied with a smile.

"You won't miss me, will you?"

"Not a chance!"

As he walked out the door, milk shake in hand, Ed felt better already.

Walking around his construction sites was one of Ed's favorite things to do on the job. He couldn't help but be amazed sometimes when he saw what his company could do. Take this job, for example. An eight-store strip-mall, single story. And one of the stores would be a grocery store with 35,000 square feet. It was a pretty good-sized job, especially considering that just a few years ago all he could do were a few residential remodeling jobs. He still liked building homes, but commercial was where it was at. And this job was going to help further his acceptance as a serious bidder on such projects.

As Ed walked around the half-built mall, he noticed the masonry. This mall was brick, which required some of the best masons in the area if the job were to be done right. He'd had to pay more to get them, but when he looked at the job they'd done, he knew that it'd been worth it. The layers were all evenly spaced, and the bricks were solid, - no cracks. Once it was washed down it would really be beautiful.

Inside the main store the progress was just as good. The walls were going up now. Metal studs. He was just now getting used to working with them. But it, too, was coming along okay. In fact, the rooms in the back already had been built out with Sheetrock.

As Ed walked along observing the job, he made mental notes to himself. Tomorrow would be another day, after all, and the work had to be directed if it were to be done right. It wouldn't be long before the finishing work would begin, which was his favorite part of the job. In preparing for that it was critical that the Sheetrock all line up properly. He decided that he had better look at that part of the job today.

As he looked at what would become the produce section, he was quite pleased with the work that his subcontractors had performed. None of it looked like it would need to be redone. But then again, he'd already been told that this part was okay. That being the case, he didn't spend too much time there. It was the meat department that he knew to be the problem. They had been struggling with the freezer section for days, to the point that he had wondered if it would ever come together. And as he walked over to it today, he hoped that this part of the job was also pretty much behind them.

Turning the corner to look at the freezer section, Ed was suddenly reminded of another of his problems - security. It angered him to see two men huddled in the corner of the room, obviously trying to stay out of sight. Ed knew that there were homeless people in the area who needed someplace to get in out of the weather, but that didn't mean that they could stay in his building. He had enough problems as it was without risking thefts or, worse, fires from carelessness. So it wasn't in the most charitable tone of voice when he began telling the two men to get out of his store.

"All right, you two. Let's get out of here, before I call the police! I've told you guys before that this place is off limits!" Ed's voice continued to rise as he walked toward the two. "Go on now. I mean it!"

"Hey Ed, it's just us." Al responded nervously. "We were just leaving, man. Taking a break."

Ed stopped dead in his tracks. He immediately recognized the smell of joints. And then he saw the pipes. "Wait just a minute. What are you two up to in here?"

"Let me handle this, okay," whispered Al to Randy.

"We were just taking a break, Ed," Al then responded. "It's okay, isn't it?"

"Depends on what you call taking a break. What do you have there, anyway?"

"Just some new smoke, man." Although he was trying to act nonchalantly, the nervousness was apparent on Al's face and in his eyes, which seemed to have unusual difficulty looking at Ed.

"Look, Al. Don't treat me like a fool! I know what you're doing. And you're not gonna do it on my time, or on my site.

"Now pick up your stuff and get out of here before I call the sheriff!"

"But Ed, it's just a little wacky weed. No big deal," Al answered him as if trying to lighten the atmosphere.

"You heard me. Get out! . . . And I suggest you do so now, while you still can."

As Ed yelled at the two men, he noticed Al nervously moving his feet. Then he caught sight of the baggie filled with powder.

"Al, I seriously suggest that you two pick up your stuff and get out of here right *now*." Ed said in an amazingly calm voice.

Al, sensing that the tone in Ed's voice signaled not calmness, but rather an effort to avoid a fight, looked at Randy. "Come on, man. Looks like we're not supposed to be having a good time around this place. Let's leave the man alone."

"Yeah, sure." Randy's shaky voice replied. "No problem, Ed. Listen, we didn't mean no harm or nothin', okay?"

"No, it's not 'okay'," replied Ed. "Just get out of here . . . NOW!"

With that Al and Randy began getting their stuff together as quickly as possible. Then, as he was looking around to make sure he had everything, Al realized that Ed had seen the baggie. As if to acknowledge that Ed's suspicions about the substance were accurate, Al bent down, picked up the bag quickly, and walked past Ed at a fast pace while putting the baggie in his pants pocket. "See you later, Ed," he mumbled as he brushed past him.

As he dutifully followed behind his buddy, Randy looked at Ed and, as if searching for a positive answer, asked him about his job. "I hope you won't hold this against us, Ed," was the most he could say, however.

"Don't expect any favors. Right now I think I ought to call Anderson and see what he thinks."

"Who's Anderson?" Randy asked.

"He's Ed-here's law buddy. Ain't that right, Ed?" said Al, already knowing the answer. "Yeah, ole' Ed here is real tight with the cops cause he don't never do nothin' that ain't pre-approved."

"Get out of here!" Ed yelled, as he turned and walked away.

Upon returning to his office Ed went straight to his desk and tried to bury his thoughts in paperwork. Best to forget what he had just seen. Or so he thought.

"So what in the world happened to you?" Jacki asked as she entered the room and saw Ed staring into space.

"Nothing."

"Nothing? Bull. You look like you just came from doing battle over that building permit," Jacki responded. But her attempt at humor was not appreciated.

"It's nothing. All right?"

"Well, it must be something. I've worked with you too long, Ed. Remember me? I'm Jacki."

"Yeah, I remember you. Now, tell you what. Why don't you just get back to work and leave me alone!" Ed responded.

Realizing that something was clearly wrong, very wrong perhaps, Jacki elected to heed Ed's advice. Almost in tears, she turned and walked away. "Do you want the door open or closed?" She asked on the way out.

"Closed," was Ed's laconic response.

As Jacki walked away she heard him dial the phone and then ask for someone, but she didn't know whom. It wasn't long before she heard Ed's obviously agitated voice coming through the walls. Not being one to pry, she tried her best to avoid hearing whatever it was he was talking about.

As the clock struck three, Ed's door opened and he emerged, still clearly agitated.

"I'm going to see Mark Abramson. I don't know if I'll be back today or not," was his only statement to Jacki as he walked out the door.

Jacki, not knowing what to think about the events of the afternoon, once again tried to immerse herself in work. Too many accounts receivable needed to be updated, and with the end of the month approaching, she knew that if she wanted to avoid overtime, she had best be getting to work. It wasn't that she minded the overtime. To the contrary, she could really use the money. Nevertheless, she didn't want Ed to have to pay it. So she once again attacked the paperwork with renewed vigor.

Barely a half an hour had gone by when the office door opened and in walked Ed. Obviously still upset, he walked straight to his office without saying anything.

"Did you find Mark?" Jacki asked quickly.

"No, he wasn't at home," was Ed's uninformative response. "I'll get him later. I think I need to speak with him tonight. Look, I've got a lot to do. I may be in here awhile. Feel free to leave at five, okay?"

"Well, okay. But if you need me to, I can stay," Jacki answered.

"No, that's all right. But thanks anyway. And by the way, I'm sorry for getting short with you earlier." And with that Ed walked into his office and closed the door. He was still in his office when Jacki left for home at five thirty.

CHAPTER VIII

I t had been a long and tortuous day for Ed Baker. As he sat in his office, alone with his thoughts, he wondered what had really happened last month when the office in which he now sat had been burglarized. For Ed the question was not only *who* had stolen the money, but *why* had they done it. After all, to his knowledge he had done nothing to cause anyone to want to hurt him. No, the only thing that made any sense was that whoever stole the money had done so because they needed it, not because they wanted to get even with Ed for anything. And when he thought about that, he knew that almost anyone could be a potential suspect, because the whole county was hurting economically. Mark Abramson was hardly the only person who may have needed the money. Yet, Ed couldn't ignore the fact that Mark had a criminal record for having stolen before. Nevertheless, he felt that he still owed Mark an opportunity to explain his side of things. That is, if Mark would still talk to him.

As the phone rang, Ed anxiously waited for Mark to pick up on the other end. But he still wasn't too excited about the prospect of having to discuss once again, this issue with this employee, whom he had summarily fired the day before. When he heard the phone suddenly engage, his heart almost stopped.

"Hello," Susan's soft voice broke the silence.

"Hello, Susan. This is Ed Baker, from Bluestone. How are you today?"

Immediately Ed told himself that he must be one of the most idiotic people in Cortez County.

"How do you think I'm doing, Ed?" Susan answered as coldly as she could. "Did you call to insult my husband a little more?

Because if you did, he ain't here. So you might as well find someone else to hurt."

Sensing that she was about to hang up, Ed shot back, "Susan, look. I don't want to get into it with Mark again. As a matter of fact, I wanted to talk to him about what happened yesterday. I thought about it some more, and I just think that he and I should talk about all of this. Is he there?"

"I've already told you he isn't."

"Well, when he gets home would you tell him that I'm at the office and I'd appreciate it if he would give me a call? I really would like to talk to him." Ed tried to be as pleasant as he could, in spite of what he sensed was an overwhelming amount of hatred coming over the phone.

"Yeah, sure. I'll tell him you called. Bye, Ed." As she hung up the phone it was everything Susan could do to keep from crying. But she knew that the tears wouldn't help. They wouldn't help her, and they wouldn't help Mark, wherever he was.

The office seemed to be closing in on Ed as the evening wore on. Still, he didn't feel like going home. Going home would involve answering more questions, explaining more actions, and generally trying to justify to Katherine why he had done what he had done. So he called her instead, and promised to call it a day just as soon as he could finish that last bit of paperwork that he had told himself he was going to complete. Katherine went easy on Ed, letting him believe that he had given her a satisfactory explanation for this bit of overtime, when she knew that he simply wanted to be alone.

The office. It seemed to be choking Ed the longer he stayed. But at the same time it was one place where he could think. Really think. And tonight he suddenly felt like he needed to be alone. Not because he was upset with Katherine, or anyone else. But rather, because the Ed Baker he knew would never have tossed an employee out into the street without first giving the employee an opportunity to defend himself. Ed now realized that something had happened to him. Something perhaps that he really didn't want to face -- yet he knew that he must.

49

When Ed and Katherine had first met at Auburn both had been exceedingly idealistic. As he thought back to those days now he remembered conversations they had had. Katherine was always the more caring of the two, more committed to trying to heal the inequities that she knew existed in society. It didn't take long for her zeal, her passion for caring about other people, to infect Ed. Both of them, from that time forward, had consciously tried to do whatever they could to help those people they met who were less fortunate than themselves.

Atlanta had given Ed and Katherine the perfect opportunity to come face to face with the less fortunate members of society. What they had observed was a city of tremendous opportunity. It was vibrant, constantly on the move, never sleeping. But this growth and opportunity did not belong to everyone. Indeed, it seemed that for every successful businessman there must have been at least one unlucky soul who was barely able to put food on the table for his or her family. Yet, from Ed and Katherine's standpoint, their fellow citizens did very little to help change the plight of these people whom they believed needed their help. It was the eighties, and the republican revolution was in full swing. To the Bakers, that meant that unrelenting greed was acceptable conduct to most of the people they came in contact with.

Seeing the poverty and despair had solidified Ed's decision to do what he could to help those who were less fortunate (or so he thought). This meant that whenever he could, he used hiring opportunities to take chances on people whom he knew needed a break and who most likely would not get that break from anyone other than himself. It was not by accident, therefore, that many of the people Ed hired were intensely loyal to him as a boss. He had gone out on a limb for them and they knew it. The least they could do was to give him an honest day's work for an honest day's pay.

When the Bakers moved to St. Bartholomew, they found plenty of opportunities to further their self-professed need to help their fellow citizens. It wasn't that people were always looking for handouts. To the contrary, they found their new neighbors to be justifiably proud people, even when unemployed. These were not people who relied upon others to get ahead. They had been taught that a rugged individualism was preferable -- even if it meant that you went to bed hungry at night while others who were equally unfortunate eagerly got by on government handouts.

It seemed rather simple to Ed that the easiest way to help his friends would be to give them jobs in his new company. And this he did. It didn't take long for word to get out that Ed Baker would give you a job when perhaps no one else would. And as far as Ed was concerned, that was just the way he and Katherine wanted it. Bluestone was still growing and everyone was benefiting from it.

As Ed sat in his office that night, he thought about those days in the past – about where he had come from. It had taken him a long time to get where he was, and he was proud of his past. His concern was not that he had traveled a road that most of his competition would just as soon have ignored. No. His concern was that somewhere in all of this, he had detoured from that road, and in the process had become only a shell of his old self. He now wondered how he could get back on track. He sensed that it was time for a mid-trip correction.

As Ed reminisced about his past, he couldn't help but recall that Mark Abramson had come to him as a man who needed help. Mark couldn't get a job because of his past record, and at the time it was perhaps because of that sordid past that Ed had taken a chance on Mark. Ed couldn't help but ask himself how he had gotten to this point – the point where he was using that same record against Mark. Someone who, until that time, had been one of his best employees. He now wondered if the problem was not with Mark, but rather with himself.

"My gosh," Ed mumbled to himself. "How'd it get to be eleven o'clock already? Katherine's going to have a fit."

As he got up from his chair he shook his head. He hadn't solved any of the problems of the world on this evening. And Mark hadn't called him back. Oh well, he guessed that he'd just have to keep trying to get in touch with him and see if he couldn't at least get something out of him. While putting on his windbreaker and walking to the door, he told himself that it would eventually work out.

On opening the door, he breathed in the cool night air and decided that it would be a good night to go for a quick ride over to Pinewood and back, thus affording him the opportunity to look out over the water. The moon was full and high in the clear sky, and Ed knew that meant that the view would be spectacular. An additional fifteen minutes wouldn't make any difference to Katherine, who would most likely be asleep by now anyway.

The night air with its slight breeze felt good on Ed's skin, and helped to make him feel better about everything. It would all work out. Of that he felt certain. So he locked the door and with a light step began walking to his truck.

"What's up, Baker?" the voice asked.

As he turned to answer, Ed suddenly saw the knife coming at him. With no time to react, he then felt the knife piercing his flesh. And try as he might, his attempts to fend off the attack were predictably unsuccessful. No chance to appeal to the attacker's sense of decency. No realistic chance to scream for help, for even if he had, no one would have heard it.

The knife felt cold at first -- then hot, as it penetrated Ed's intestines. As if it somehow knew the job it was expected to perform, it then moved upward toward his diaphragm. Then it withdrew, as if its mission were over. But as soon as it retreated it received another command to return to the field of battle and engage the enemy once more. And not having an alternative, the dagger obeyed its commander and repeated the carnage until the job was done.

As Ed lay on the ground he could feel the life racing from his body. Slowly at first, but then faster, so as not to give him time to say the things he wanted to say, or to think the things he wanted to think. All he could do was to think about Katherine and the life that they would have had together. And then, as the life-blood continued to stream from his body, his grip on consciousness began to ease until he finally, mercifully, surrendered to an inevitable death.

PART TWO

CHAPTER IX

I t was early in the morning when Katherine awoke on the living-room couch to a snowy television set. Thinking that it wasn't too late, she was shocked to find that her watch said four thirty in the morning.

"Where is Ed?" she mumbled to herself. But once she regained some cognitive ability, she remembered that he had been pretty upset over the whole affair with Mark.

She knew Ed well enough to know that he may have decided to take a drive and forgotten about the lateness of the hour. Sooner or later he'd come sneaking in the door, trying to be as quiet as possible so as not to wake her and incur what he always wrongly assumed would be her indignant wrath. With that in mind, she decided that it made no sense to get up when she could get another couple hours of sleep. It wasn't long until she drifted back to sleep, safe in knowing that when she awoke her husband would have returned and would be cursing the fact that he would have to turn right back around and head to work.

One thing that Jacki had always prided herself on was the fact that she needed little sleep, and so had no trouble getting up for work every morning. Such a quality came in pretty handy in a job like hers, because she was expected to open up the office at 6:00 every morning.

This morning began like all the rest, with the slight exception that it was a Friday morning, which meant that an activity-filled weekend was approaching. Lots to do, and this weekend all of it involved things she really enjoyed -- craft shows, some boating, and going to the church social on Saturday night. Not everybody's cup of tea, perhaps, but it was her life and she enjoyed it. So it was with a little less dread that she arose from a somewhat restful sleep, showered, dressed, sat down to eat breakfast, and glanced at the paper before leaving for the day. As she looked at the paper, she marveled at the violence that always seemed to occupy so much of the news. What is it with people these days, she thought to herself. Doesn't anyone have any sense of morals anymore? Not wanting to get too depressed about such things, she quickly moved on to the comics. At least she could get through them without having to be reminded about what she continued to see as an increasingly hostile and misguided world. Better to live in a perpetual state of ignorance and leave the problems to those poor "city people," as she called them, who had no choice but to deal with them in order to survive. Soon she was once again engrossed in the continuing saga of "Hagar," who always seemed to her to bear a little too much resemblance to her father -- what with his omnipresent potbelly and blissful state of simplicity.

Jacki's wanderings through the comics ended abruptly, however, when her cereal bowl crashed to the floor. "Rufus!" she yelled, as her fourteen-pound cat skittered across the table with milk dripping from his whiskers. "You're gonna get it when I get hold of you!" But she knew that, in keeping with past such episodes, Rufus would hardly endure any harsh punishment. He was part of the family, after all, and no matter how much he fretted her, the bottom line was that usually he made her laugh. So Rufus once again sat on the edge of the table, licked his paws and whiskers, and glared at Jacki for having the audacity to suggest that he should somehow restrain himself when it came to partaking in a bowl of cereal that she must have poured for him.

"Now look what you've done!" he heard her mutter to herself as she got up from the table and recognized that, as usual, most of the milk had landed in her lap. As if he really cared.

After hurriedly changing clothes, Jacki grabbed a slice of bread and a cup of coffee. As she rushed out the door of her house, she was still muttering to herself, confident that no one could hear some of the statements she was making about the cat that she had repeatedly threatened to get rid of. Rufus, seemingly oblivious to it all, watched as she left him once more.

Her Plymouth station wagon, now ancient in most people's eyes, didn't help her much on days like this, when Jacki needed to step on it a little in order to make it to work on time. But one thing that she did have to say for the car; it always got her where she was going. It was just that now it took a little longer doing it. Today was no exception, which contributed to her heightened state of anxiety, begun earlier by Rufus. Even so, Jacki knew that if she were late Ed would hardly say anything to her. He never had in the past. No, the anxiety was not caused by Ed, but by Jacki's own sense of responsibility that many of her friends admired and wished that they possessed. Well, they could have it on days like today, because on such days it was more of a curse than anything else. At least that's what Jacki told herself while following an equally old Ford Pinto which seemed to be resisting its owner's efforts to coax some more rpm's out of the already over-taxed engine.

Pulling into the office parking lot Jacki was not surprised to see Ed's truck. She just hoped that today he would be as understanding as he had been in the past. Sure he will, she thought to herself, but I still need to do something about that infernal cat.

As she turned off the ignition and prepared to leave her car, Jacki for no reason suddenly felt something come over her as if telling her that she should go no further.

But she knew that she needed to get a start on the day. So whatever it was that came over her would just have to wait. She had work to do. She locked the car door and began walking to the office door.

Her mind relentlessly refused to let her forget the sight of Ed's bloodied body as it lay there beside his truck. What she didn't remember for some time, however, was her actions immediately subsequent to the discovery. Gone from her immediate consciousness were her many screams and convulsions. Gone was the recollection of having bent down over Ed's lifeless body and caringly closing his eyelids. Gone was the memory of having rushed inside to call for help. It would take months of hard work before these events would resurface and allow her to put part of the awful puzzle back into place. Yet after those extensive efforts paid off and enabled her to put some certainty back into that terrible morning, she concluded that it had been a mistake to summon those memories back from her subconscious. Not surprisingly, she also found herself looking back upon that moment in her car when life was still promise-filled, and she wondered what it was, who it was, that had tried to save her from viewing the carnage that lay on the other side of Ed's truck.

The Cortez County Sheriff's Office responded to the scene after receiving Jacki's frantic and largely incoherent call for help The first to arrive, Deputy Francis Smith, initially had some serious reservations about the call. After all, murders were something that happened in big cities, not in places like bucolic St. Bartholomew. Francis, or Frank as he was called, had been incredibly lucky since joining the sheriff's department. He had never had to investigate a murder in Cortez County, and probably couldn't even remember when the last murder had taken place, or even who the victim was.

Frank's response to the sight of Ed's mutilated body was therefore one of uncharacteristic shock and a feeling of being overwhelmed by the circumstances. But when all was said and done, there were certain fundamental requirements expected of any law-enforcement officer who responded to a scene such as this. And Frank undertook those responsibilities admirably well under the circumstances. His first instinct was to take Jacki by the hand and lead her away from the scene, a task which he had little trouble completing since Jacki had no desire to remain any longer than necessary by Ed's bloody body. Then, with laudable consideration for the need to preserve the scene, Frank began to cordon off the area while awaiting the arrival of his backup and the medical personnel. By the time the more experienced people arrived to begin the investigation, Frank was satisfied. He had done what was needed in order to give them the opportunity to begin the arduous job of looking for the details that hopefully would solve the first murder to plague their town in over a year.

The local sheriff's office began the job of processing the crime scene with a dogged determination that was often not seen in larger metropolitan areas, which had come to take violent crime for granted. The Sheriff himself arrived at the scene within minutes of being notified and began setting up the team that would undertake this initial aspect of the case. If the case were to be solved and successfully prosecuted it would be critical to handle the crime-scene investigation very carefully. Otherwise, they could run the risk of contaminating the evidence, in which case a judge could refuse to allow it to be introduced into evidence against the suspect.

It wasn't long before the area was being scoured for tire tracks, pieces of clothing, and footprints. Anything that could possibly shed light upon how the brutal crime had been committed was carefully considered. Unfortunately for the investigators, however, there were no usable tire tracks to be found. Tires would leave an impression in the ground that could be preserved by the use of plaster molds and then compared against the tires on the vehicle that a possible suspect might have been driving at the time. But the sand proved to be an unwilling assistant in their attempts to identify any such tracks, since Jacki had driven into work that morning and unknowingly driven over the same area that any suspect would also have used.

Plenty of footprints could be found, but to the dismay of the investigators, the footprints, just like the tire tracks, had been destroyed in the panic that ensued immediately after Ed's body was discovered.

The investigators searched faithfully for items left behind by the assailant. But once again there was nothing. Whoever had committed this act, the detectives decided, must have been a professional -- or at least smart enough to be sure to leave nothing behind, not even the murder weapon.

After giving up on the crime scene around Ed's body, the detectives decided that the photographers should nevertheless photograph every inch of the area. One never knew what might turn out later to be critically important, even though at the moment it might seem to be insignificant. A rather sizable investment in Eastman Kodak was made by the sheriff's department in hopes that it would pay off down the road.

With a paucity of clues having been left on the ground, the detectives decided that their best hope for a break in the case might well lie with Ed himself. Deputy Smith had been careful not to disturb Ed's body, knowing that it would be critically important later in the case. So, when the photographer arrived, he was able to preserve the uncensored horror of Ed's bloody and beaten body for the future.

After the photography session had been completed the coroner, Doctor Sharon Smith (who happened to be Deputy Smith's wife), was now allowed to begin her task of removing the body to the morgue. Dr. Smith, knowing that it could be important later, first rolled Ed's body over onto its stomach, so that the photographer could get some shots of Ed's back as it appeared at the scene. The detectives then searched the outside of Ed's clothing for any other clues that might have been left behind. Anything would be a help, but their search, again, was futile. Dr. Smith and her assistants then placed Ed's lifeless body on a stretcher, put it in the ambulance, and left for the morgue, where the autopsy would be performed.

It did not take long before frustration set in for the detectives handling the case.

William Langdon, or Bill as he was known to his friends and colleagues, had been assigned the lead detective role by Sheriff Whittaker. Bill had been with the department for well over fifteen years and had handled practically all of the murder investigations at the department for the past seven years. Standing a little over six feet, two inches tall and weighing almost two hundred and forty pounds he made an imposing impression. Add his mustache, nearly bald head, and ever-present sunglasses, and it was easy to see how he was able to cajole his suspects into admitting their guilt in whatever crime he happened to be working on. He was the Sheriff's obvious choice to head this investigation, which everyone knew would be a high-profile case that *had* to be solved.

Bill's partner on the case, not expected to return to town until later in the day, would be Don Richards, a detective with half the experience as Bill. Don Richards not only had less time on the force than did Bill, but he also had about half as much body weight, making the two a rather comical sight when they were seen walking together. And as if to irritate Bill intentionally, Detective Don Richards not only had jet black hair, but he had enough hair that he often tried to get away with wearing it in a ponytail. "I need it for undercover work," he would tell his friends (and his boss) when asked. But Don was not to be taken lightly. Unlike Bill, he had a Bachelor's Degree in criminology and had worked at the FBI, having received special training at Quantico, Virginia, where he concentrated on solving serial crimes and other particularly difficult types of homicides. After graduating at the top of the academy, he had served for five years in New York before deciding that he didn't really like trudging around in the snow and cold rain all of the time. So he picked a spot on the map and moved. The spot happened to be St. Bartholomew, and after his move he vowed never to go north again.

Realizing that the crime scene would not likely yield any significant clues to assist him in solving this case, Bill turned his attention to Jacki, who by now had managed to control herself to the point of being able to speak coherently once again. He knew that Jacki could prove to be crucial in helping the investigation, and so, he knew had to treat her with kid gloves.

"Ms. Pierson?" Bill began. "Can we talk for a few minutes?"

"Bill," Jacki responded, "you know better than to call me Ms. Pierson. And of course we can talk."

"Okay, Jacki. Tell you what, why don't we do this. Can you tell me when you got here this morning and when you realized that Mr. Baker had been attacked?"

"Yeah, well, it's pretty much like I told that Frank," Jacki began slowly. "I drove up around six o'clock. I was running a little late because Rufus, you know my cat Rufus, don't you?"

"Yes, Jacki, I know Rufus."

"Well, Rufus spilled some food on me and I had to change clothes and, well, I really didn't like what I had to wear. But I really didn't have much of a choice . . ."

"Jacki, I don't mean to be rude, but we really need to stick to the case, if it's okay with you. I've got a lot of work to do today and it's pretty important that I follow up on any leads as soon as possible so that we have a better chance of catching whoever did this. Okay?"

"Sure. I understand," Jacki answered, although she wasn't at all happy about having been interrupted. "Well, I was late for work, as I said. I pulled into the parking lot, got out of my car, and the next thing I know I'm staring at Ed's body lying there on the ground. I really don't know what happened next, although I guess that I called you-all."

"Now, Jacki, when you first saw Ed, do you know whether he was still alive?"

"Oh, no, he wasn't alive. I could tell that for certain."

"And how long was it before you called us?"

"Shoot, I don't know. Just a few minutes, I guess. It took a while before I was able to talk halfway decent, don't you know."

"Did you move Ed's body at all before we got here?"

"Of course not!" Jacki almost yelled. "What sort of sicko do you think I am, anyway, Bill Langdon? I ought to tell your mother on you for asking me a thing like that. That's what I ought to do!"

"No, no, Jacki," an obviously startled Bill replied. "I didn't mean that you did anything wrong. It's just that some people react differently when they find something like a dead body lying around. Sometimes they do things that they wouldn't ordinarily do. And if you had done anything like that, it's okay; I just need to know now, before we get underway with the investigation. You understand, don't you?"

"Yeah, I guess so. I still ought to tell your mother on you, making it sound like I'm some sort of sicko or something. How would you like it if someone asked you something like that? I worked for Ed for a long time, Bill. I've been through enough

61

already this morning without having to defend myself for something I didn't do!"

"Okay. Okay! I'm sorry. Really I am, Jacki. Tell you what, looks like we've covered about everything that happened out here. Mind if we go inside and continue this?"

"That would be good, I think." Jacki said, as the two of them began walking into the office.

As Bill entered the office behind Jacki, he couldn't help but feel Ed's presence. This was the part of the job that he hated. No matter how many of these cases he handled, he always felt like the victim was somehow with him when he went to places that the victim had frequented. In some ways it comforted him, but in other ways it was unsettling. This time was no different, because he knew that this office was Ed's pride and joy. It was in some respects his life. To have to enter into it now and begin the task of going through Ed's belongings would somehow just not feel right, no matter how necessary Bill knew it would be.

As they walked into Ed's office, Bill waited for Jacki to sit down and then he pulled up a chair and tried to make himself comfortable. "Jacki, why don't you tell me about Ed. I really didn't know him that well, but from what I do know he hardly seems like the sort of guy who would end up being murdered."

"You're telling me!" Jacki answered, her voice quivering. "What do you want to know about him?"

"Well, why don't we start with the obvious. Do you know if he had any enemies?"

"No he didn't have any enemies. None that I know of, anyway. He didn't hurt anyone, or mistreat anyone."

"Now, Jacki. Between you and me, Ed had to have made somebody mad at one time or another. We all have."

"Not Ed. No sir. Ed didn't have any enemies. And by the way, Bill. I'm sorry for yelling at you out there. I'm just pretty upset by all of this." Jacki decided that it was probably a good idea not to let Bill think she was still upset with him.

"No problem, Jacki, as long as you're not going to tell my mother on me. I really don't want another spanking, you know." Bill laughed at his own response.

The thought of Bill's mother taking his mammoth frame over her knee and beating his rather large backside suddenly made Jacki laugh, but just for a second, lest it seem somehow inappropriate in the midst of such serious business. "It's a deal," she managed to answer, relieved that maybe they could talk as friends and not be as formal.

"Well, then. If Ed didn't have any enemies, why would he wind up like this? Tell you what. Have you had a chance to look around here since you got to work?"

"No, I haven't. Why?"

"What I was thinking was this. How about it if you look around and tell me if you see anything out of order, or missing."

"Sure. I suppose I could do that."

Jacki didn't take long before she came to the conclusion that everything was where it should be. The safe was okay; it hadn't been disturbed. All of the equipment was there. Nothing ransacked. "No, Bill," she reported. "Everything looks okay from what I can tell. Sorry."

As he moved around to Ed's desk, Bill decided that the next step would be to go through it, although he realized it would be difficult for Jacki. "I'll tell you what," he said. "Do you mind if I go through the desk here? You know, see if there's anything there?"

"Well, I guess it's okay. If you think it'll help . . .. Oh, my gosh, there are some of our employees coming to work. I totally forgot about that. I'd better explain this to them somehow. I totally forgot about work. Ed and I were going to do some office work early this morning until we got a shipment of lumber in from Port St. Joe. He'd told everybody else to come in later today. No sense in paying them to sit around and do nothing."

"I'll tell you what, Jacki. Do you mind if I go out and tell them what happened? I may need to talk to some of them anyway."

"Sure, be my guest. It'll save me from having to do it. I'll just find something to do in the meantime."

As Bill went outside, Jacki tried to sit down at her desk and catch up on some paperwork. She quickly realized, however, that it was useless. So she went back into Ed's office to sit. Maybe she would feel closer to him in there. Maybe she would wake up and the nightmare would be over.

But Jacki felt funny sitting behind Ed's desk. It was the first time she had allowed herself to be so bold. Just didn't seem right. Nevertheless, today she needed to be there. She needed to be as close to her boss as she could and this was the obvious spot to choose. His desk was predictably neat, just like its owner. And although everything was in its place, it was still clear that Ed had been working last night. Jacki didn't know whether to laugh or cry when she thought of the times that she had teased him about being so fastidious with his workplace. "You're worse than my mother," she repeatedly told him, as if he would change. Not that she wanted him to; but she had constantly been told by her mother that she needed to pick up after herself, and it had struck her as somehow ironic that she worked for a man who could run her mother a close second in the neatness department. Jacki did notice more files on the desk than when she had left yesterday evening. He must have been balancing some books. And there was the note with Mark's phone number on it. I wonder if he ever got in touch with that lowlife, Jacki thought to herself.

Word of Ed's death began to spread as the residents of the sleepy fishing village began their workday. It didn't take long. Indeed, since everyone knew everyone else word spread faster than a bad case of poison ivy. It wasn't long before the usual curiosity seekers began coming to the scene to try to catch a glimpse of the deceased, of his blood, and of the detectives who were hard at work on their behalf.

As he began his work, Bill quickly realized the enormity of the task ahead of him. There were the employees to interview, the autopsy to observe, and reports to write. There was just no way for one person to get it all done. But, he knew he had to, so he continued to plod along. He would talk to the employees for now, since "old Doc Smith," as he liked to call her, would be ready to begin the autopsy. But not too long into his interviews he looked at his watch and suddenly remembered one highly important task -- someone had to go tell Katherine what had happened! She couldn't hear it from someone other than their office. So, here was one more job to add to his ever-growing list. And this job was one that he really didn't like to perform.

As he turned to see if someone could keep his potential witnesses there while he went to see Katherine, Bill spotted Sergeant Anderson over with the technicians. "Fred, I didn't know you were here," he shouted to his colleague.

"Yeah, they called me over when I got in today. You know, I never thought I'd see anything like this in Bartholomew. Don't know why -- just figured that it couldn't happen here."

"It's happened before, you know," Bill replied, though he didn't know how this would help to ease the hurt that he saw on Fred's face.

"Yeah, I guess it has. But it's never happened to someone I knew before . . .. And it sure hasn't been this bad before, at least not the cases I've been involved with."

"You think so?" asked Bill. "What about that Hill kid a couple of years ago. That was pretty bad, as I recall."

"Sure it was bad. But you know, they just killed that boy. Whoever did this seems like he had a pretty big ax to grind. You know?"

"You're right about that," Bill said. "I don't know how many there were, but I bet I counted at least ten stab wounds on Ed's shirt. Lord knows what the total number will be when the M.E. is able to check things out more thoroughly. You know, I just can't see Ed having any enemies like that. He seemed to be pretty easygoing to me."

"He was," Fred agreed. "But you know, he did have some real characters working for him over the past few months. I guess that was to be expected in his trade, though. Come to think of it, he had called me a few days ago about one guy that was working for him. Guy by the name of Mark Abramson. You remember him?"

"Abramson. Abramson." Bill thought for a while, but nodded his head as he drew a blank on the name. "For some reason the name sounds familiar, but I can't put it with anything. Should I be able to?" he asked Fred.

"Well, he was that kid that we busted a few years back for doing that robbery. Remember? He was convicted and served a few years. Three I think. He came back here to live. Married. Lives in a trailer over on the north side of town. Real nice wife.

"Anyway, a few days ago, Ed called me because he had heard something about this guy Abramson telling someone that he had been the one who committed the B & E on Bluestone's office a while back. Abramson worked for Ed at the time. Ed called me because he wanted to know what to do about firing the guy, whether we would prosecute him, that sort of thing."

"What did you tell him?" asked Bill.

"Told him we'd look into it, if he wanted us to. But I kind of got the idea that he liked the kid. Wanted to give him a break, you know."

"So did he say he was gonna fire him?"

"No, he didn't. I never heard from him again after that. Don't know what he decided to do about the whole thing."

"Interesting. Might be worth checking out. Better than what we've got so far, which is nothing. Hey, Fred. Would you mind doing me a big favor? I really hate to ask, but I kind of need some help."

"Yeah, sure. What is it?"

"Would you go tell Katherine for me? She knows you better than she does me, and I really think it might be easier coming from someone she's a little closer to."

"You would stick me with that. Can't say as I blame you. Also can't say I didn't see it coming. Sure. Any idea where she's at?"

"No idea at the moment," said Bill. "I was going to go over to her house first. Hopefully we can catch her before she leaves for the day."

"Well, I guess I'd better head over there. . . . This ought to be a real fun time. Sure you don't want to go?"

"Naw. I'd better stay here and try to sort things out. Thanks a lot, Fred. She'll appreciate it in the long run."

"Yeah. See ya' later. I don't know how long I'll be, okay?"

"Sure. Take as long as you need."

Bill watched as Fred pulled out of the lot. I sure don't envy him right now, he thought to himself.

As the doorbell rang Fred prayed that somehow he'd find the strength that he knew it would take to get through the next few minutes. Those few minutes began sooner than he had anticipated, as Katherine opened the door almost immediately after his finger released the doorbell.

"Fred!" Katherine said, as if somewhat shocked to see him standing there. "How are you doing?"

"I'm okay, I guess, Katherine," Fred responded in about as even a tone as he could muster under the circumstances.

"Well, what in the world brings you out here so early, anyway?"

This doesn't help any, Fred thought to himself. She seems to be in a pretty good mood.

"I came to see you, Katherine," was the only response that he could elicit at the moment.

"And what in the world for?" she asked. "And shouldn't my husband be present for this? I mean, you know how such a rendezvous can look," she said with a smile.

"Katherine, can we go inside and talk for a moment?" Fred was serious. "It's been a long morning already. I kind of need to take the old load off, if you know what I mean."

"Well, sure, Fred. Come on in. Now, what's on your mind this morning?"

As they sat down on the couch in the living room, Fred couldn't help but look around and think to himself that this room was about to be changed, possibly forever. This furniture, all matching in soft-brown, early-American tones, was about to look somehow different. Katherine and Ed had bought it only a few months ago and had been so proud of it. And as he looked across the room at the lazy-boy, which was Ed's favorite chair (even if it was way past its prime according to Katherine), Fred knew that very shortly Katherine would barely be able to look at it.

"Katherine, I have to tell you something. I don't know how to do this right. I guess . . ."

"Ed. Where's Ed? Where's my husband?" Katherine suddenly screamed, as she realized that something was very wrong with the entire situation. "Where is he, Fred? You didn't come here for no reason, did you?"

"No, I didn't, Katherine," Fred answered. "Katherine, Ed passed away this morning."

"What do you mean, 'passed away'?" she asked, her voice starting to tremble.

"Where's my Ed?"

"Katherine, I don't want to have to tell you this, but Ed has been murdered. We don't know exactly when. And we don't know by whom. But Jacki found him this morning when she got to work."

"Excuse me!" Katherine yelled, as she got up and ran out of the room. As Fred sat there he could hear her sobs emanating from the bedroom. He had never felt as helpless in his life. It was as if all of the training had been for naught.

After he could stand to wait no longer, Fred decided that it was best to go check on his friend. He didn't want anything to happen to her on top of everything else that had occurred this morning. As he knocked on the bedroom door, he heard a faint "come in" in response, so he figured that she wanted his help.

"Are you all right?" he asked her as he opened the door, while at the same time realizing how stupid a question he had just asked.

"He hated this wallpaper," Katherine mumbled, her lower lip quivering. "He really hated it. And I wouldn't change it."

"Well, if I know Ed, he probably just said he hated it to see how you would react."

"No, he hated it. Fred, are you sure it was Ed? Tell me you're not."

"We're sure, Katherine. There's no doubt."

"How did it happen?"

"Katherine, that's not important right now," Fred answered, hoping that he could get out of this one.

"It's important to me, Fred!" Katherine struck back. "It's important to me!"

"Okay, okay. He was stabbed outside of his office. . . . We don't know exactly when it happened. And like I said earlier, we don't know who did it."

"Did he . . . Did he feel any pain?"

"I don't know, Katherine. I'm not a doctor. I hope he didn't, you know."

"Where is he now?"

"He's been taken to the coroner's office. There'll have to be an autopsy, since foul play was involved. You understand, don't you."

"I don't know. Do I have a choice?"

"No. We have to do this so that we can document the crime for the trial, whenever we catch the SOB and get him in a courtroom. Without an autopsy, Katherine, the guy could get off. And nobody wants that."

"Yeah. I guess you're right. . . . Fred, I don't mean to be rude, but do you think that I could maybe be alone?"

"I don't know if that's such a good idea, you know," Fred stated matter-of-factly.

"Let me have someone come stay with you."

"No, that won't be necessary."

"Yes, it will. I'm not about to leave you totally alone right now, Katherine. I'd be worried sick."

"Tell you what," Katherine offered. "I'll call Bonnie and ask her to come over. Is that all right? Will you feel better if I do that?"

"Yeah, I'll feel better. But I'll tell you something else. I'm going to post a patrol car outside of your house for a little while so that . . ."

"I'll have no such thing!" Katherine shot back. "I don't need someone sitting outside of my house every hour of the day and night!"

"Now, Katherine, listen to me. We have no idea who did this to Ed. And we have no idea *why* he did it either. Now I know Ed.

And there's no way he'd let me leave you here without protection. Don't you think we owe that much to him?"

"Not fair, Fred Anderson," came the meek response. "You win. But please don't make it too long. Just catch the guy who did this. Promise me that."

"I promise, Katherine. You have my word on that. We've already got most of the squad on it. . . . Tell you what. Do you mind if I use the phone? I'll go ahead and call to get someone over here, and then I'll be able to get out of your hair sooner."

"That's fine. Go right on ahead."

After calling Bill and arranging for someone to come over to guard Katherine, the two of them sat and talked for a while until Fred could see that Katherine really wanted to do nothing more than contemplate the full extent to which her world had just been turned upside down. Granting her unspoken wish, he quickly let himself out of the house to wait while the new widow began the process of placing into unseen compartments in her mind all of the memories of her husband that she could summon at the moment. It would be a never-ending task that he knew she would repeatedly perform for years to come.

CHAPTER X

"**N**O! YOU CAN'T DO THAT! PLEASE, DON'T! PLEASE, MISTER, NO!" The yelling. The endless yelling. Stop it. Stop beating that man!

And yet the beating continued. As did the tortured screams of the man who lived down the cellblock from Mark. The guards hated the man because he had assaulted a police officer in Miami. It had been a hot summer night when the breeze off of the Atlantic seemed to play hide and seek with the residents. The officer involved was making what he had expected to be a routine stop when the man had suddenly and without warning begun to pistol-whip him to within an inch of his life. The man had been on PCP at the time and, unbeknownst to the officer, had over a pound of cocaine in his car when the officer pulled him over for a faulty taillight. When the officer was found later that night he was barely breathing.

Fortunately for the Dade County Sheriff's Office, there were many witnesses to the beating. Many of the witnesses themselves possessed lengthy criminal records, and most of them had open cases with the state attorney that they wanted to avoid. They were therefore, motivated to do the right thing, which enabled law-enforcement personnel to apprehend this man whom they were intent on either putting behind bars or sending to the funeral home in order to help the local economy.

Night after night the man screamed in prison. And night after night Mark lay on his cot and listened to it. Earplugs helped only to an extent. No matter how much he wanted it to, nothing ever eliminated the noise completely.

The screaming never stopped. Even after Mark was paroled and sent back home to start his life over he continued to have nightmares about the man. And the worst part of it all was that since he never saw the beatings, his imagination was left to fill in the details of the horror he heard. So, night after night he was doomed to awaken in a cold sweat brought on by his recurrent dream about the man and his pain.

The yelling. The endless yelling. Stop it. Stop beating that man!

CHAPTER XI

The knock on Mark's door came early in the morning on the day following Ed's murder. The knock was loud. It was authoritative. It was intrusive, and unwelcome. It was not, however, unexpected.

As Mark opened the trailer door, he looked up into Bill Langdon's piercing, black eyes. Langdon had arrived at the trailer that morning with Don Richards. Both men were anticipating their meeting with Mark, because they assumed that it would end in the case being solved.

Mark had heard about Ed's murder over the radio the day before. The news came as a shock to him, as it had to most people. But for Mark the news also carried ominous overtones with it. He knew that his recent termination, together with his criminal record, would place him at the top of the list of people to interview about the crime. To make matters worse, he and Susan had fought like pit bulls after he told her that he had been fired. To his surprise, the argument had been short-lived, leaving him with the impression that Susan would support him. The next day, however, had brought on another onslaught of her wrath, during which she had threatened to leave. One thing led to another and he had stormed out of the trailer, gotten into his car, and driven around for most of the night that Ed was killed. He now realized that this lack of an alibi would hardly put him in a good position should fingers start pointing at him.

"Mark, we'd like to talk with you, if you have a few minutes," Don Richards began.

"Depends on what you want to talk about," came the angry, and somewhat unexpected, response from Mark.

"Hey, calm down, man," Don quickly replied. "We just want to talk to you about what you've been up to lately. No big deal, okay?"

"Is this about Ed Baker getting killed?"

"Yes, as a matter of fact it is. But why would you think that anyway?" Bill now chimed in, sensing that his subject was getting nervous about the topic of conversation.

"I don't know," Mark answered. "I just figured that since I used to work there and all, that you'd be talking to everyone that knew him."

"Yes, that's what we're trying to do," said Don. "By the way, do you mind if we come in? It's kinda awkward standing out here."

"Shouldn't you have a search warrant or something?"

"Now, why would we need a search warrant, Mark? We told you that we just wanted to talk to you about Ed. Chill out, man." Don tried to put his most compassionate face on, lest he risk losing Mark's story. By now he was also satisfied that he should be taking the lead on the case. Past experience told him that his long hair and smaller frame made him a more approachable figure than his partner, especially when the two of them were working a suspect together.

"Well, I guess you can come in." Mark was uneasy about the entire situation, but nevertheless unlocked the screen door and opened it for the two men. He instinctively knew that they were coming into his home in order to find evidence to help in placing the blame for the murder squarely on his shoulders.

"Nice place you got here, Mark," Don began. "Are you married?"

"Yeah, I'm married. Why do you ask?"

"Well, I know that when I was single I never kept my place looking this nice. Took my wife to do that. Boy, she let me know pretty quick that she expected me to keep the old place looking neat as a pin. Looks like your wife has the same approach, huh?"

"Pretty much so. But she's pretty good to me, so I put up with it."

Sensing that Mark would at least be somewhat open with them if they kept the conversation light, Don decided that he'd continue on down the path that he had begun.

"So, what's your wife's name?"

"Susan."

"Where's Susan now, if you don't mind my asking."

"I'm not real sure, you know. I haven't seen her this morning."

"Gee, I hope there's nothing wrong. A little trouble in Mudville, is there?"

"No. . . Well, I don't know. Maybe there is."

"Nothing serious, I hope," Bill decided to interject, acting as sympathetic as he could so as not to unsettle his suspect.

"Thanks," Mark instinctively responded. "I hope it's not, either. But she seems pretty steamed this time."

"Aw, I wouldn't worry too much about it," Don reassured him. "You know how women are. I'm sure it'll all be over this afternoon. What did you say it was about? I forgot."

"It was about me getting laid off at Bluestone."

"Oh, that's right. Man, I guess that must have hit you both pretty hard. Anything we could do to help?" Bill really had to struggle to get these words out with a straight face.

"Naw. Nothin' no one can do right now. She'll just have to cool off."

"So Mark, why in the world did you get laid off anyway?"

"Lack of work, mostly."

"Lack of work? But I thought that Bluestone was doing pretty well." Don glanced over at Bill as he tried to continue to keep things on an even keel. Sure enough, he could see that big old vein starting to pop out on Bill's forehead. Don knew that he wouldn't be able to control himself much longer. That was Bill's one weakness. He didn't particularly like to deal with suspects, and sometimes it showed.

"Well, it was doing okay," Mark calmly answered. "But things on my end were getting kinda slow for right now. So Ed laid me off until it picked up again."

"What is 'your end', Mark?" Don asked.

"Sheetrock."

"Well, Mark, that's funny. Everyone else we talked to said that they had more work than they could handle."

"Comes and goes. Depends on what section they're working on."

"Yeah, I guess you're right. Well, so what are you gonna do now? Must be pretty tight moneywise."

"You might say that. Especially since Susan don't work."

"Yeah, but at least she pretty much supports you in all of this, doesn't she? I know she's mad now. But it'll blow over."

"I guess it might. But I'm not sure this time. She's pretty steamed."

"Well, shoot, man. It's not like it's your fault or anything," Don continued to draw him out. "I mean, what else could she want from you? Especially when she's not working herself!"

"I hadn't thought about it like that," Mark answered with a smile starting to show on his face. "Now that you put it that way; where does she come off hassling me about all of this?"

"That's right!" Don continued the charade.

By now Bill was thinking of calling ahead to have himself checked into the psych ward at the hospital lest he go nuts listening to all of this. He hadn't seen this much manure since last week when he was helping his uncle out on his hog farm. And it smelled better at the farm.

"I mean, I am the one that brings home the dough. All she does is spend it!"

"Right again!" Don happily chimed in. Then, growing suddenly calm, he said, "By the way, Mark. The reason we're here is this: we're doing routine visits with people who knew Ed. Asking questions. You know, cop stuff."

"Yeah, sure," Mark eagerly replied.

"The only thing we needed to know is whether you know if Ed had any enemies. Had he had any fights lately? Did you hear anything? And, well, I'm kind of embarrassed to say this, but we were kind of hoping that since you had been in prison before that you might know people who know people. Know what I mean?"

"Yeah, I figured you be wantin' to talk to me."

"So, have you heard anything?"

"No, man. I honestly haven't."

"What about enemies. Did Ed have any?" Bill asked.

"Not that I know of. He was a real likable guy, Ed was. I can't imagine who would have wanted to hurt him, you know."

"Okay, that's all we needed to know," Don stated, as he began rising from his chair. "We won't bother you any more. Tell you what, though. If you do hear of anything, how about giving us a call. Okay?"

"Sure."

"Well then, here's my card. Might even be a reward for any helpful information."

Don looked at Bill as he turned his attention to him and asked, "You don't have anything else, do you, Bill."

"Nope, not a thing. Mr. Abramson, it's been a pleasure talking to you. Hope everything with your little missus works out for you."

"Thanks. I do too." Mark moved over to the door, opened it, and breathed a sigh of relief as the two men walked out and back to their car.

"Thanks again for your help, Mark," Don yelled back as he was getting behind the wheel. As both he and Bill closed their doors, he backed the car up and left, while Mark, standing on the porch steps, continued to be thankful that he wasn't in the car with them.

"Now, let me ask you one question," Bill stated matter-of-factly to Don. "Why in the world did you just leave that scumbag standing there when you know that he was lying to us about being laid off? Are you getting soft in your old age? Or is it senility?"

"Because it wasn't time yet, that's why. And besides, you're lead on this case. You could've taken him in if you wanted. So why did you leave him there?"

". . .'Cause. I'm hungry and I didn't feel like looking at his stupid face for another three hours today. Plus, I was having too much fun watching you play the man's best friend. I bet he's sitting back there wondering how in the world he dodged that bullet."

"Yeah, he has to be. And while he's doing that we're gonna find his old lady and find out where he was during the night. What do you want to bet she has no idea where he was?"

"I'll be amazed if she even remembers his name, from the sounds of things!" Bill chuckled. "But before I let you totally screw up the case I want to get something to eat. If it's all right with you that is."

"Burger King?"

"Burger King."

And off they went.

And as they expected, Mark found religion for the balance of the next few hours.

The lunch hour passed quickly and soon it was back to work for the two detectives. By now both men had come to the conclusion that they had spent the morning with Ed's murderer. Now the key would be to find the evidence that would enable them to obtain the indictment they wanted.

Given their concern over Mark's version of Bluestone's early termination of him (neither detective had heard of anyone being laid off at the company), they decided that it would be a good idea to nail down the truth about that. It was with somewhat high hopes that they rang Jacki's doorbell that afternoon.

As the door opened, Bill and Don stared into Jacki's red, swollen eyes. Bad timing. But knowing they had to wind things up quickly, the detectives nevertheless decided to push ahead with the purpose of their visit.

"Hi, Jacki," Bill said, hoping that he could get through this interview in a hurry.

"Hi," came the response.

"Don and I had a few more questions to ask you, if you don't mind."

"No, of course. Come on in. Boy, you guys must work all the time, to be out here on a Saturday."

As the two men walked into Jacki's home, both were impressed by the organization. Everything in its place. And not even a speck of dust was to be found.

"Cleanliness is next to godliness" was Jacki's oft-repeated expression. "Come on in the living room and have a seat," she said to the men. "Would either of you care for some iced tea? I was just fixing myself a glass."

"No, Jacki," the men responded in unison.

"Well, do you mind if I get myself a glass, then?" She walked into the kitchen and began preparing the beverage that, as a southerner she'd come to equate with one of life's little necessities.

"Jacki," Bill said in the direction of the kitchen. "You remember that guy, Mark Abramson, don't you?"

"Sure. Why?"

"Well, what we were wondering was this: do you know why he left Bluestone?"

"Sure I do," Jacki answered as she walked back into the room and took a seat in her favorite chair. "Do either of you recall anything about a break-in at our company? It was about a month or so ago."

"No, I don't remember anything ---"

"Yeah, I remember that," Don interrupted. "Fred told me about it right after it happened. Somebody got some money. Couple of thousand or so, I think."

"How'd they get in?" Bill asked.

"Well, if I remember correctly, that was the thing that no one could figure out. There wasn't any sign of forced entry. And the money had been taken out of a lockbox."

"It was a safe," Jacki corrected him. "And the safe had a combination and all."

"So what does the break-in have to do with Abramson? I mean, from what I heard no one ever found out who was responsible for that." Don's interest began to perk up at the thought that just maybe they were about to find the piece to the puzzle they'd been hoping for.

"Yes, they did know who took it. It was Abramson," Jacki replied with an obvious air of satisfaction. "Ed had found out about it a week or so ago. He told me all about it."

"What did he tell you?" Bill anxiously responded.

"Well, let me think. I want to get this right, you know. Let's see. Yeah. He said that another employee of his, this guy named Al, told him that Abramson had taken the money."

"So, what did Ed do when he found out about it?"

"Fired him, of course." Jacki stated matter-of-factly. "He should've done it a long time ago. And I told him so, too."

"Why do you say that, Jacki?" Don asked.

"Because. He had a record, you know. You can't trust those guys for nothing. He was bad news; and Ed should never have hired him."

"So when did he fire him, Jacki?"

"A couple of days before he was killed. It was in the evening, when Abramson came in from off of the job site."

"What happened?" Don continued the questioning.

"Well now, I don't really know. You see, I had already left for the day. Ed just told me that he was going to fire him. Then the next morning he told me that he'd done it. He called the employees together that morning and told them that Abramson was gone."

"How did they take it?"

"Okay, I guess. I mean, they were kind of shocked and all, but they got over it."

"Did they think that Abramson had taken the money?"

"I don't know. See, Ed didn't tell them why he fired the guy. Just told them that he was gone. To tell you the truth, I don't think anybody missed him. He was bad news as far as I was concerned. I know that."

"What about this guy, Al," Bill chimed in. "Who is he? What's his last name?"

"Stempson is his last name. He's one of Ed's employees. Been with us for a while. I think Ed knew his father or something."

"Any idea how we can get in touch with him?" Bill continued.

"Yeah, I can get his number for you. No problem."

"Getting back to Abramson," Don asked, sensing that they finally had the break that they had hoped they'd get. "How did he take getting fired?"

"I have no idea. Guess he didn't like it too much. I mean, who would? But I never seen him after Ed got rid of him. By the way, what was his record for, anyway?"

"Robbery," Don answered. "He held up a store with a gun."

"Should've known. Do you guys think he killed Ed? I mean, you must if you're this interested to come out here on a weekend and all."

"We don't know right now, Jacki," Don said. "But I do know that you've been a lot of help. I'll tell you what. If you think of anything else about this guy Abramson, please call either Bill or me and let us know, okay?"

"Yeah, sure."

"And another thing, Jacki. How about it if you don't tell anyone about our talk, okay?"

"Yeah. Whatever you say. . . . Come to think of it, you don't think I could be in danger do you? I mean, if that lunatic finds out that I've talked to y'all there's no telling what he might do."

"Don't worry about that now, Jacki," Don reassured her. "He won't know a thing about our talk so long as you don't tell anybody."

"Don, we'd better be getting along, don't you think? We've taken up a good bit of this nice lady's time." Bill sensed that they had gotten about all of the information they could. Bill had never been one to hang around an interview and discuss milk and cookies. To him it wasn't productive and therefore wasn't part of the job description.

Don, on the other hand, counted the opportunity to meet with people and get to know them as one of the best parts of the job. In fact it was a critical part if he were going to maximize the amount of information he could get. So, he never passed up an opportunity just to talk about whatever the witness wanted to discuss. And besides, it irritated his partner, which he secretly enjoyed watching from time to time. But today was Saturday after all, so he decided to give Bill a break.

"Yeah, Bill, you're right. I guess we'd better get on along." As he stood up and prepared to make his exit, Don felt the joints in his knees start to give way. Catching himself on the edge of the chair, he remarked with a smile, "Bill, I think I'm gonna trade both of these knees in for two pretty ones like Jacki has there."

"Now, Mr. Richards, you don't mean that!" Jacki blushed, as the remark caught her off guard.

"I certainly do, Jacki," came Don's response. "But we better not say anything about this to your husband."

"You wish!" Bill chuckled. "Guess what, I'm goin' for the gusto on this one, buddy!" Seeing that Jacki had a bit of a worried look on her face, he quickly added, "Just kidding Jacki. I like to yank his chain every now and then."

"Thank goodness! You know how he can be sometimes!"

"Yeah, I know. Just like a husband, right."

"Right."

"Well, we'd better go now. Thanks for your help, Jacki," Don replied. "Give our regards to your husband. And we'll let you know if we have any other questions, okay?"

"Fine with me," Jacki answered. "I just hope that you catch the guy who did this, that's all."

"We'll try our best," Bill responded, as the two men walked out of the door and to their car. Both were growing increasingly certain by this time that they had identified Ed's killer. The only thing left to do was wrap up the loose ends.

The loose ends began with confirming Jacki's version of the circumstances under which Mark had left Bluestone. The process didn't take long. A quick review of Mark's personnel file confirmed, in Ed's own handwriting, that he had terminated his employee for stealing from the company. According to Ed's notes, Mark had been furious when told that he was suspected of the theft. His notes further reflected that Mark had denied having taken the money, and that he had asked for an opportunity to show that Ed's information was wrong.

Nevertheless he had been let go. Furthermore, the termination had taken place less than forty-eight hours before Ed's death.

Next on the list was Al. He had not been particularly difficult to find. He was at home when the call came, and, although nervous at the prospect, readily agreed to speak with both detectives. The interview went smoothly from all points of view. Al retold his well-rehearsed story that Mark had been overheard bragging about stealing the money. To add flavor to the soup, Al, on a lucky hunch, also told his questioners about Ed's initial disbelief that Mark had been the culprit, but that he had eventually confided in Al that he had suspected Mark all along. Finally, Al "explained" how he himself had often felt afraid of his former co-worker, who everyone knew had a hot temper.

The coroner had completed the autopsy on schedule. To no one's surprise, the cause of death was stabbing. To be more precise, the immediate cause of death was determined to be asphyxiation cause by the severing of his windpipe. But, as the coroner was quick to conclude, by this time he had sustained fourteen other stab wounds, so death would have occurred eventually either with or without the final, sickening act of dismemberment. The murder weapon was believed to be a double-edged knife — probably a hunting knife.

Needless to say, the single most important piece of evidence sought after by Don and Bill was the knife that had been used to end Ed's life. A search of the area had failed to turn up anything. So until it was learned who had committed the crime, the detectives decided to forego a further search until more promising leads developed. Cortez County, as everyone knew, was a large county. To search it entirely would be impossible, even assuming that the murderer and his weapon were still present.

With Jacki's information and the confirmation found in Ed's paperwork, Don and Bill decided to conduct an intense interview of their prime suspect. It was Sunday morning when they headed back to Mark's trailer.

Once again Mark heard the familiar knock on his door. Looking out of his window, he recognized the cars from the day before. He knew instinctively that the detectives' return could not mean good news. But sitting on his bed, he knew that regardless of what lay ahead, he would have to face it. It was with a forced sense of bravado that he made his way to the front door of the trailer that he and Susan had worked so hard to make into a home.

"Yes, Don, can I help you?" Mark asked with an equally forced smile on his face.

"Mark, would you please step outside for us?" came Bill's response.

Stepping outside, Mark quickly sensed that this was not a social visit. "What's up guys?" he queried, though he knew from his past experiences that he was unlikely to receive a full answer to his question.

"Mark, we'd like to ask you a few more questions about Ed. And we'd appreciate it if you'd come down to the station with us, so that we all can be a little more comfortable." Bill's response took Mark by surprise, not only because of the request, but also because of the tone of Bill's voice.

"Do I have a choice?" Mark asked. "I mean, I've already told you all that I know."

"Well, Mark, we'd like to go over some of what you told us. After all, we want to make sure that we understand exactly what you were saying yesterday." Bill's answer came quickly and with a tone that told Mark that this man was getting tired of waiting.

"Do I need an attorney?" Mark asked.

"Why would you need an attorney, Mark?" Don answered. "You're not under arrest. And you don't have anything to hide, do you?"

"No, of course not. . . . Look, if you want, I'll go to the station with you. It won't take too long will it?"

"Not at all," Bill replied. "Do you need to get your wallet or anything?"

"Yeah, I guess I'd better. I'll just be a minute guys." As Mark turned to get his wallet, Don followed him. Bill liked his partner and his instincts for dealing with suspects. Better to go with this dude, Bill thought, than to have him come back out with a shotgun and blow us all away.

A few moments later, Mark reappeared at the door with Don close behind. As they pulled out of the driveway, Mark did not see the other unmarked squad car sitting by the side of the road, where another detective sat calmly reading the morning paper.

The ride took less than ten minutes. Even so, Mark was surprised at the memories, nightmares, really, that it brought back from his prior arrest. As he sat in the back of the car, he was truly glad that he had made a new life for himself. Even if Ed Baker had tried to ruin it for him.

Entering the station gave Mark the same feeling and the same sense of dread that he had experienced during the ride. Hopefully this won't take too long and I can get the heck out of here, he told himself. But those thoughts were quickly dispelled when Bill led him to what he recognized from his past dealings in this place as the interrogation room.

"Have a seat, Mark," Don said, though with a voice that had suddenly become less friendly and more akin to that of a drill sergeant who was about to get warmed up for a new set of recruits. "Mark, you don't mind if we record this, do you? We just want to make sure there's no misunderstanding over what is said. Yesterday, well, Bill and I kind of got confused about things. So we thought we'd better be more careful this time."

"No, I don't care," came Mark's response.

"Mark, as we said earlier, we want to talk to you about Ed and about Bluestone Construction. Now, tell us again about your relationship with Ed."

"There's not much to tell. I worked for the man for a little over a year until he laid me off. He was a pretty good person as far as I'm concerned. I mean, you know, he gave me my first job after getting out of prison. I was really thankful for that. And he was a pretty good boss, you know?"

"So how'd you feel when he laid you off? I mean, didn't that make you kinda mad?" Don continued the questioning while Bill sat beside him, calmly taking everything in.

As Mark looked around the room, he was taken by the bleakness of everything around him. The cold green walls. The dirty, white linoleum floor. The single, cheap, gray steel table and chairs. Why is it that all of these rooms are drab, he thought to himself. How could anyone stand to work in this every day?

"How'd I feel?" Mark repeated Don's question.

"Yeah, how'd you feel?" came Don's response.

"I guess I was sorta mad at first, you know? I mean, most people would be mad. I'd worked a long time for the man and never given him a moment's trouble. And then he up and lays me off."

"Why'd he do it?" Don asked.

"From what I can tell it was because the company was short on jobs, you know?"

"Funny, I heard that Bluestone was really doing well. In fact, I heard that Ed was hiring more people so that he could finish all the jobs that he had on time."

"Well, like I told you earlier, I do Sheetrock, and that part of the job was slow. I guess this was a temporary sort of thing."

"You mean, like maybe he was gonna call you back?" Don asked.

"Yeah, I guess he might of."

"So, when was the last time you saw him?" Don continued.

"Gee, I don't know. I guess it was a couple of days before he died."

"Are you sure?"

"Yeah, it had to have been. He fired me on Wednesday, and was killed on Friday, right?"

"You tell me," shot back Don. "Was he killed on Friday?"

"That's what the paper said. I'm just going by what the paper said." Mark was starting to get concerned about the direction of the questions. These guys didn't want him for what he could tell them about someone else.

"Mark, let me ask you this. Routine question, okay?"

"Yeah, sure."

"Where were you on Thursday night?"

"I was at home with my wife."

"All night?"

"Yeah."

"Was anyone else there?"

"No"

"What did you do?"

"Nothin'. Just drank some beers, watched some TV, and went to bed."

"What did you watch on TV?"

"Murphy Brown."

"Wrong. Comes on Monday nights, not Thursdays. You sure it wasn't 'Murder She Wrote'? Geez, can't you lie better than that?"

"What kind of beer?" Don continued.

"Miller."

"How many?"

"I don't know. I wasn't counting. Enough, I guess."

"Enough for what, Mark? To get up the nerve to kill Ed Baker?" By this time Bill had heard enough and he was getting tired of fooling with this guy. "We know you killed him, Mark. We know it just as sure as turkeys get nervous at Thanksgiving. So why don't you come clean and tell us how you did it, and why you did it. That way we can all get on with our lives."

"Look, man. I know what you think, but I didn't kill Ed Baker. I liked Ed. I already told you that."

"Garbage! Absolute garbage! And I'm getting real tired of you dishing it out, man! Tell me again, why did Baker fire your butt?"

". . .'Cause he didn't need me no more. I've already told you once."

"You're lying to us man. He fired your stinkin' butt because you stole from him and he found out about it, that's why! Now, why don't you cut the crap and for once in your lousy stinkin' life tell the truth? Ed Baker made you mad. He fired you. And you decided to take care of things in your own way, now didn't you?" Bill, by now, was practically yelling at the top of his lungs. So much so that he didn't hear the deputy enter the room.

"Detective Richards, can I see you for a minute," the deputy whispered to Don in the only calm voice that had been heard for some time.

"Sure," Don answered, as he began walking outside with the deputy.

When they were outside and the door was closed, the deputy delivered his message, "Detective Richards, Sergeant Anderson called in. He said that a Ms. Abramson did return to the home. He talked to her and she said that she didn't see her husband at all on Thursday night. He apparently stormed out of the house after getting in a fight with her. She has no idea where he went."

"Where's Fred now?" Don asked.

"He said to tell you that he's going somewhere with her, probably bringing her here to get her statement. He said he'd catch up with you later."

"Thanks deputy."

As Don turned to walk back into the room, he did so with renewed confidence that Ed's murderer was sitting before them.

"Tell you what, Mark," Don said as he entered the room. "I'm not real sure what you said about where you were on Thursday night. Would you mind telling me again?"

"Like I said before, I was at home with my wife. I was there all night. We watched some TV and then went to bed."

"I thought you drank some beers."

"Yeah, we did."

"Miller. Right?"

"Miller."

"Is there any doubt in your mind about that?"

"No."

"None whatsoever?"

"None."

"You know, Mark, we've been here for some time now. And frankly, I'm getting a little bit hungry. Why don't we all settle down for a bit? Do you want something to eat? We'll buy."

"I don't know. Maybe a burger or something."

"Okay. You got it," Don answered as he turned, opened the door, and summoned a deputy to get lunch for the three of them. Then, as he looked at his partner, he continued, "Mark, tell you what. Bill and I here have some things to go over. How about if you sit tight and we'll be right back. You comfortable?"

"Yeah, I guess."

"Okay, we'll be right back."

As they walked out of the room, Don advised Bill that Susan had not substantiated her husband's alibi, and that she had no idea where he had been on the night of the murder.

"I say we go ahead and book the maggot right now," was Bill's quick response.

"I'm tired of looking at his maggot face."

"Well, before we do that we'd better talk to Whittaker. I don't want to do anything on this without his approval. I mean, your maggot friend in there could be getting ready to take the big ride on Sparky, and we don't want to see it fall apart on us."

"Yeah, sure. Is he in?" was Bill's only response.

"I think so. We might as well catch him while we have a chance."

The meeting with Sheriff Whittaker was brief. After all, it didn't take long to explain the crime itself, together with the evidence that had been gathered. Whittaker, though still somewhat hesitant without having found the murder weapon, nevertheless approved of the arrest. On the other hand, Don and Bill left the meeting with no doubt in their minds that someone in the department had better find that weapon as soon as possible. No one wanted this arrest to backfire on them.

As they returned from meeting with the Sheriff, they found Mark wolfing down the burger, fries, and Coke that someone in the department had brought back. As he watched Mark eating the last bit of his lunch, Don wondered how he would feel if he were given the news that he knew Mark was about to receive. In most ways an arrest was very gratifying to him, but he didn't arrest many people on a charge of first-degree murder. Somehow it was different. Especially since the potential sentence could be death.

The decision of who would get to do the honors was not in doubt. Bill always wanted to do it, especially when he was the lead on a case. This would not be an exception. So, as he walked up to Mark, who was sitting at the table in front of him,

Bill instinctively grew more somber and more serious.

"Mark Abramson," Bill's stern voice boomed. "You are under arrest for the murder of Ed Baker. Stand up please and turn around."

"WHAT?" Mark's shaken voice answered in return. "You've got to be kidding, man! You've got to be kidding!"

"Turn around, please, and place your hands against the wall. You know the routine." As Mark turned around and felt himself being patted down by Don, he heard Bill read the familiar warnings to him. "You have the right to remain silent. You have the right to an attorney. If you cannot afford an attorney, one will be appointed for you. Anything you say can and will be used against you in a court of law. Do you understand these rights?"

"I didn't do nothin', man!"

"Do you understand these rights?"

"I didn't do nothin', man!"

"One more time! Do you understand these rights?" Bill was yelling by this time.

"Yeah, I understand them, jerk!"

"Okay," Bill responded. "Now that we understand each other, I'm going to let that nice deputy over there finish up with your processing, after which you'll be shown to your new living quarters for awhile. But don't get too used to them, because you'll probably be moving over to Starke soon. And I understand that the accommodations over there aren't nearly as nice."

Bill soon realized that he shouldn't have made the latter statement until he was out of his prisoner's spitting range. "Ingrate!" was his only response as he and Don walked away.

CHAPTER XII

The events of the past few days had nearly overtaken Katherine. Suddenly she found herself having to call relatives and tell them about the horror that had invaded her life, and theirs. The call to Ed's parents was by far the one that she dreaded the most; still, for some strange reason she felt closer to them at this moment than she had felt in all of the years since her marriage to their son. She knew that they would take the news especially hard, so she first called her father-in-law's brother, who lived near Ed's parents. She hoped that he could go to the house to lend support when the news was delivered. The call, as expected, was very painful. She hoped that it was the only such call she would ever have to make in her life.

No sooner had she notified the relatives of Ed's death than she received the coroner's call asking her to what funeral home she wanted the body released. The question, although it should have been expected, nevertheless took her by surprise. For no particular reason she told the coroner's office to deliver Ed's body to Mayfield's Funeral Home on South Elm Street. She soon found herself at Mayfield's (she would later be unable to recall how she got there), where she was faced with the overwhelming task of choosing a casket, burial clothes, funeral spray, music, burial vault, and the day and time of Ed's funeral. "How can this be happening?" she repeatedly whispered to herself. "How can this be happening?"

When she returned home Katherine found that the town that she and Ed had chosen to adopt as their own had turned out en masse. Word of Ed's death had quickly spread throughout St. Bartholomew, and it was not long before the townspeople had banded together and arranged to bring food to Katherine and the relatives who were expected to arrive. Katherine would later recall that she thought there would be no way that all of the food could be eaten. But at least she had one less thing to worry about that day.

Friday finally came to an end. Katherine fell asleep that night, knowing for the first time in twenty years that when she awoke she would never again be able to talk to, or see, her husband and best friend.

The news of Ed's murder soon spread across the region. By the end of the day on Friday it had spread as far north as Tallahassee, where it was carried on the local television stations, and as far west as Pensacola. While such was less predominate in those cities of more substantial populations, fear began to reach down into the smaller communities that surrounded St. Bartholomew. The fear spread like a cancer until it had infected practically everyone in the vicinity. The fear would continue until the madman who had committed this senseless act was found, brought to trial, and convicted. But even if he were convicted, many said that the area would never again be the same. Never again would people feel comfortable helping strangers, or leaving their doors unlocked, or walking the streets alone late at night. Life would be different from this point on.

The little boy sat in church with his parents that Sunday morning. It was a clear fall day. It was the third day after Ed's murder and the church was filled with a congregation longing for sustenance in order to be able to make it through the days and weeks to come. It mattered not that the church was located in Shelbyville, a small coastal town twenty miles to the west of St. Bartholomew, the cancerous fear had spread that far.

As the little boy sat in church, he thought to himself that today might not be as boring as all of the past Sundays had been. Though only ten years old, he could sense that there was an unusual amount of fear on the faces of people around him. He saw that same look of fear on the pastor's face .

It was not long before the singing had concluded and it was time for the sermon. On most days this was the time that the little boy dreaded the most. The sermons frequently touched on sin. And on the devil. And on hell. And they were highly effective on this ten-year-old, inasmuch as he was convinced of his need to walk the straight and narrow lest he be thrown into the pit of fire. Nevertheless, he normally found himself during this time daydreaming about things that a ten-year-old prefers to consider. The adults could figure out all of the "hell stuff" (as he called it). But today as the singing concluded, he resolved to listen to the pastor's message, simply because he assumed that it would be more interesting given the events of the past few days. He would not be disappointed.

"Friends, as we meet here today a great evil has overtaken our neighborhoods. It has overtaken them just as surely as it overtook cities much larger than ours. Cities to the far north of our fair town. As I am sure everyone in this room knows, a man by the name of Ed Baker was stabbed to death while leaving his office just this past Thursday. Ed Baker had done nothing to deserve such a brutal, senseless death. Indeed, he had worked late that night to further the interests of his company, which in turn would have given continued employment to those citizens who live in this area. And I need not remind you that good employment is not easy to find in this depressed economy.

"Ed Baker was a good man. To those who knew him he was a kind man. A man of few words, but a man who, when he did speak, spoke the truth. Mr. Baker was a giver of himself. He was known frequently to assist in charitable causes such as the Red Cross disaster relief operations, as well as helping to feed the homeless. He also stood shoulder to shoulder helping his friends build houses to be given to those in our community who are less fortunate than we are.

"Now I am not saying that Ed Baker was perfect. He was not. He was a sinner just like you and me. But he tried to do the right thing by his fellow man -- not because he thought that it would benefit him financially, but because in his heart he believed that he should give back to his community.

"Our thoughts and our prayers go out to Ed's family. He will be sorely missed by all whose lives he touched."

The sentiment was touching, to the point that there was barely a dry eye in the house that bright, sunny morning. But the minister continued: "Let us contrast the loss suffered by our society when Ed Baker was taken from us with the harm that continues to threaten us by the continued presence of the person who committed this abominable act. Friends and neighbors, as surely as we sit here this morning there is an evil among us. A man, possessed of the devil, has invaded our fair community. We must resolve to do whatever we can to assist our police officers to find this individual and to bring him to justice -- justice that is sure, that is swift, and that is certain. For whoever committed this horrible act deserves not to walk among us anymore. Indeed, he deserves not to live anymore. For he has broken that most critical commandment which is found in Exodus 20:13, 'Thou shalt not kill.' And so, he must pay with his own life, whenever he is found."

The congregation was captivated by the message that they heard that morning. A message that continued past the noon hour, which was, as most ministers will tell you, the point at which attention spans began to fade. But today was unlike other days. The congregation cared not what the hour was, because their community had been injured, its innocence lost. It had been a heart-wrenching week. A week that even young children would remember for years to come, the little boy included.

The church service ended that Sunday morning with prayers for Ed's family and friends as well as for the men and women who were so diligently trying to find the person who ended his life. It was a service that was repeated in churches throughout the region, to the relief of the people who, prior to Ed's death, had lived, worked, and played with an innocent but false sense of security.

Ed's body had rested in Mayfield's Funeral Home since the coroner had delivered it there on Friday evening. The funeral had been scheduled for Monday morning in order to allow family from outside of the state to travel to the small Florida town. And once the family arrived there was the inevitable family night which, on this date, was scheduled for late Sunday afternoon and evening.

Katherine, though heavily medicated in order to make it through the Sunday-evening event, was nevertheless astounded at the way the evening had turned out. On the one hand she had not been prepared for the casual nature of people's dress. It was indeed hard to spot anyone other than family members who was clothed in attire that would suffice for church services on Sunday morning. Why, it seemed as though no one was any more creative than to wear blue jeans and a clean shirt. Man, woman, it made no difference. And were it not for the solemnity of the occasion it would have been almost comical to compare the visitors with their well-worn jeans to the family members who, to a person, were immaculately dressed in full suits and the finest jewelry.

But Katherine, who was more acquainted with the ways of many northern towns in these situations, was equally surprised by the sheer volume of support that was shown during this night. People whom she had never seen before came to pay their last respects to Ed. And what is more, it was obvious to her that the support was heartfelt and genuine. In fact, even a casual survey of the visitors revealed that hardly an eye was dry. It did not take long, therefore, for Katherine to remember that *this* was the real reason that she and Ed had moved to this town years ago. It was not for the glamour, or for the ability to gain more toys. Rather, it was to return to what both of them had felt really counted in life: a close-knit community in which the residents cared about each other and would help each other in times of need. This was clearly a time of need, and Katherine quickly thought to herself that Ed would have been overjoyed were he able to see just how genuine these neighbors were in sharing their nonmaterial wealth.

Sunday evening quickly passed and Monday morning just as quickly came on the scene. It was not an arrival that Katherine looked forward to. Indeed, her one prayer was that God would somehow enable her simply to get through the day. She was, after all, about to bury her husband and best friend of sixteen years. This deed would require all of the strength that she could summon. Her hope was that she could handle the situation in a manner that Ed would have wanted.

As she rode in the limousine from her house to the funeral home, Katherine looked out of the window at the simple houses on her left. These were houses that were inhabited by simple people with simple dreams. And though they were simple in many ways, they were rich in others. She and Ed had spent many an evening talking about such things, and over the course of their years in this place she had come to see the value in this way of life, something that she admittedly had trouble comprehending at first. But now, as she passed these houses she thanked God for allowing her to experience life with these people.

To Katherine's right was Apalachee Bay and in the distance, Lone Pine Island. This too was a scene that she and Ed had often taken in together. On this day the sky was powder blue with only a few wisps of clouds coming in off of the Gulf. Calm winds meant that the whitecaps on the bay gently made their way to the shore. Blue herons, ever vigilant in their quest for more small fish, patrolled the shoreline with their long, spindly legs as the pelicans occasionally flew by looking for the larger mullet that schooled further out in the bay. Too often this had become a routine site for Katherine. Today it was hardly routine. It was, in some ways, her strength.

As the limousine pulled up to the funeral home, other family members and friends descended on the vehicle and made their way to Katherine's door. The door opened slowly and Katherine, dressed in the only black dress she owned, just as slowly exited from the car. And then she felt her legs begin walking toward the chapel door as if on their own. Perhaps if I don't go in there all of this will go away, she thought to herself, but she knew that that would never happen. But a few short seconds later, therefore, she was inside the chapel standing in front of the closed casket where she knew her husband now rested.

The chapel itself was small, much smaller than Katherine had expected. At the same time, however, it was very comfortable and intimate, as was appropriate for times like these. Ed's casket sat at the front of the room bedecked with a huge funeral spray of white carnations and red roses. On either side of the casket were freestanding lamps, which, in turn, were surrounded by at least forty floral arrangements -- more arrangements than Katherine would ever have expected. So many arrangements, in fact, that the local florist had been forced to call in favors all over the county to fill all of the orders.

More important than the appearance of things was the fact that so many of the townspeople had elected to attend the funeral. The chapel itself was completely full, which necessitated the opening of the doors on three sides of the building to allow latecomers an opportunity to participate in the service. These numbers did not include the law-enforcement officers, who also attended in their full dress uniforms. All in all it was obvious to the family that Ed's death had deeply affected the entire community in ways beyond their wildest expectations. It was a tribute to Ed and it was a tribute to the town.

Katherine sat by her mother as they listened to the minister give a simple message that counseled the family to remember that Ed's earthly body had died, but his spirit, his soul, lived on, and would live on for all eternity. For that reason, the minister reminded them, Ed's death was not entirely a cause for grieving, but also a cause for celebration, since he now lived in a better place, a place that was free from pain, free from suffering, free from sin. He would be missed. That was a certainty, as evidenced by the crowd attending the service. But, Katherine was reminded, even the fact that Ed was sorely missed was evidence of how much good that he had brought to his friends and family during his days on earth. And so, the minister concluded, Katherine must look to the good that could come from his death, because as surely as Ed had done good things with his life, so must his memory continue to do good in death.

As the minister concluded his short message, the mourners were invited to join hands as they sang Amazing Grace to the melody played by the minister's wife at the piano. "Amazing grace, how sweet the sound that saved a wretch like me," the group sang in a slow, soulful manner, as though at any moment adults and children alike would break down in uncontrollable tears. "How precious did that grace appear the hour I first believed." As the verse ended the minister began humming the tune that was known to all. It was not long before the entire room was filled with the melodic sound of voices that looked to God for strength to continue on in a town that had somehow been radically changed that Thursday night past. As the piano slowly ended the song, the minister read various scripture passages, concluding with the Twenty-third Psalm. With the final benediction the service was concluded, and Katherine realized that in just a few short minutes she would be saying good-bye to her husband forever. As her knees began to give way, she held onto her mother for the support that she would need for the immediate journey ahead.

Ed Baker was laid to rest in a small community cemetery overlooking St. Bartholomew Bay. It was a simple plot that was bedecked with flowers of all types. A headstone would follow in the weeks to come. For now, however, the spot was well known to practically everyone in the county. It was the spot that they now visited on occasion when they needed to remember the horror that had visited their town. For Katherine, however, it was the spot where she now went in order to find the strength to make it through each day. The horror was, for now, something that she could not allow herself to recall. There would be time enough for that in the days ahead. At present she needed to do nothing more than sit with her husband so that the two of them could once more look out at the bay while the pelicans watched over them from above. Ed would like this, she would repeatedly think to herself. And then the familiar tears would fall.

CHAPTER XIII

The grand jury proceedings normally began at nine o'clock on the first Monday of every month, unless, of course, there was no need to call the jurors together. On this Monday, however, the same day as Ed's funeral, the prosecutor decided that the proceedings were indeed necessary. And out of respect to Ed, he decided that they should begin at one o'clock in order to permit mourners to attend the funeral services. Besides, neither he nor his colleagues expected that the jurors would require much time in order to produce the indictment that was requested against Mark Abramson. Of that everyone was confident.

The assistant prosecutor who would be handling the case was a distinguished-looking gentleman of some forty-five years of age. Though he lived and had an office in Tallahassee, he had served the small coastal town for eighteen years, having arrived on the scene shortly after graduating from law school twenty years earlier. His arrival in St. Bartholomew was brought about through his father's longtime friendship with the State Attorney, Samuel Thornton, whose office was in Tallahassee.

In his eighteen years of practice as an assistant prosecutor, Andrew Smallwood had always loved the challenges of the job that he held. He had begun in the misdemeanor section of the office, where he had handled traffic cases. About the time that he was getting comfortable with what others considered to be petty cases, he found himself involved in more difficult DUI trials, and then onto more serious misdemeanors. In a matter of a few short years, he was in front of circuit court juries advocating felony convictions for hardened criminals for whom he was seeking long-term incarceration. All in all it had been a rather quick journey from his humble beginnings. It had been a journey that he had not expected to take, especially since he had intended to practice in the more lucrative area of corporate civil law upon his graduation from law school. But despite the comparatively lower income that he realized as a government attorney he had come to believe that he was actually making a difference in the community. Admittedly, such a feeling was little consolation in the beginning as he watched his former classmates driving their expensive cars. But as he grew older he began to feel that the sense of accomplishment he felt each day when another criminal had been taken off of the streets. It far outweighed what he considered to be the more slavish existence that he would have had working seventy-hour weeks in a richly appointed office.

By contrast, Andrew looked around his small, wood-paneled, office with its three by five-foot window overlooking the parking lot three stories below. His desk was the usual government-issue gray metal; that is, during those few times that one could actually see its top. He'd been offered larger and nicer desks in the past and always turned them down for this old sawhorse, as he called it. The floor wasn't any better. It was covered with files and wadded up pieces of paper, the latter having once been destined for the wastebasket that was strategically placed in the center of the adjacent wall, requiring Andrew to raise his skill level as a would-be basketball star. For now the floor was covered and he wasn't about to apologize to anyone. He was up to his eyeballs in cases and now he had this new murder case to worry about. He'd had his share in the past few years (all of them in Tallahassee), and he'd won all of them, he was proud to say. And even though this case offered him the opportunity to get some good publicity, he didn't need either at the moment. But then again there never seemed to be an opportune time to take on another murder case. The things would drain you if you let them. Especially if the case deserved the death penalty. With any luck this new case would be relatively easy, he thought to himself as he sipped his Sunday-morning coffee.

Andrew studied the case file that contained the detective's reports of their investigation into Ed's murder. It was a gruesome killing, he thought to himself. A lot of rage. A lot of blood. The photographs would be dynamite in front of a jury.

The question of motive seemed to be easy to answer. Clearly Mark had been upset over the loss of his job. He had a prior felony conviction and would therefore have had a difficult time replacing the job that he had just lost. What's more, if Ed had decided to press charges for the theft, Mark could have been facing some serious time. Put all of that together with his lack of an alibi, and Andrew felt pretty confident that he could secure a first-degree murder conviction. He'd had harder cases in the past. Sensing that he wouldn't have too difficult a time convincing a grand jury to indict Mark, Andrew decided to work for only a few hours that Sunday and take the rest of the day off. Tomorrow wouldn't be that difficult. Maybe I'll buy some plants for this place this afternoon, he thought to himself as he closed his briefcase and walked out the door to go home.

When Andrew got home he had a message from Thornton. "Sam called just now," his wife informed him. "He said something about Abramson's story didn't check out and they had arrested him for Baker's murder. The grand jury will still be meeting tomorrow afternoon to consider the case. . . . But I guess you knew that."

"Thanks, honey. Want to go out shopping? I've got some time on my hands." As they walked out of the house a few minutes later Andrew felt good about tomorrow's proceedings in St. Bartholomew. By the end of the week his name would be back in the papers and on television as the prosecutor responsible for bringing another murderer to justice.

The drive to St. Bartholomew had been soothing for Andrew. It was a beautiful, clear October day with no rain in sight. The sort of day in Florida that could almost make you think about swerving to avoid an armadillo in the road. Then again, maybe it's not *that* nice, Andrew thought, as he chuckled to himself. Nevertheless, the weather and the water did present a perfectly bucolic setting that would take most people's breath away. Andrew again considered himself lucky to be able to live and work in such a place. It almost took away the thoughts of the unpleasant business to which he would have to attend in a few short hours. Hopefully it would be over soon and then he could enjoy the rest of the day.

Driving down the meandering, two-lane road, he spent almost as much time watching the pelican-patrolled water as he did watching for oncoming traffic. I wonder what it would be like to glide over the water like that every day, he asked himself. Don't know if I could do it, but I'd sure like to try for a day or two. But for now there were more pressing duties awaiting him, so he put such thoughts out of his mind, stepped on the accelerator, and turned his thoughts to the business at hand.

As he pulled into his parking space at the courthouse, Andrew caught a glimpse of the small crowd of people that had assembled on the front steps. Not already, he thought to himself. I guess we're gonna be getting some press today. He didn't even question how the crowd had found out about the upcoming proceedings. In a town this size, it would be impossible to keep quiet something this big.

"How is everybody today?" he asked the group as he bounded up the courthouse steps. "Y'all should be out on the bay taking advantage of this gorgeous weather."

"Mr. Smallwood, Mr. Smallwood," came the local reporter's inevitable voice. "Can you tell us what will be happening inside this afternoon? We understand that a suspect has been apprehended."

"Yes, Mr. Jennings. We do have a suspect in custody. The grand jury will be convening shortly to consider the charges. We will be asking that the grand jury return an indictment for first-degree murder." With each case Andrew was becoming more adept at handling the press. And with each case he was learning to like it more.

"Do you intend to seek the death penalty, Mr. Smallwood?" another voice in the crowd asked.

"We are looking at that, and many other issues at this time," came Andrew's reply. "If the circumstances warrant it, you can be assured that our office will seek to fulfill its duty to the people of Cortez County."

"Andrew, we understand that the suspect's name is Mark Abramson."

"Yes."

"What can you tell us about Mr. Abramson?"

"Nothing at this time, I'm sorry. I really must be going in now. . . . Thank y'all for your concern. Our office will keep you updated as events warrant." And with that Andrew went up the stairs in the deliberate fashion that signaled the determination of a seasoned professional who knew what he wanted and was about to get it. As the doors swung shut behind him the crowd quieted down, secure in their belief that the case was in good hands.

The grand-jury room was in reality nothing more than a large conference room that no one ever used. As such, the room had become the obvious choice to house these meetings, which frequently concluded with indictments being issued for citizens thought to be guilty of crimes that, for the most part, were inconsequential compared to those committed in the urban areas of the state. Today's proceedings would be different, however. And no one was particularly happy at the prospect of being asked to consider such weighty charges.

"Ladies and gentlemen, my name is Andrew Smallwood," began Andrew. "I am a prosecutor in this judicial circuit and today it is my duty to bring before you certain charges that my office, the Office of the State Attorney, is asking that you file against a particular individual whom we currently have in custody.

"Now before we get started let me sort of give you an indication as to what will be happening this afternoon. First, this is not a trial. You will not see a defense attorney, and you probably will not see the accused. What will happen is that I will be calling some witnesses to the stand to describe to you certain events that have unfolded in our fair community. They will tell you what they observed, and after that I will ask you to bring back what we call an indictment, that is, formal charges, against the accused. Assuming that you do your duty and bring back such an indictment, your job will then be finished. The accused will be held for trial at which time a new jury will be called to consider his actual guilt or innocence.

"Now, during this proceeding feel free to ask questions of the witnesses. This isn't particularly formal. The main thing is that you good people get all of the facts that you need to help you understand what happened and why we think that the accused we have arrested is the person who committed the crime. And, oh yes, should you feel that you need additional information and want to hear from other witnesses, well then, you just tell me, and I'll have that person subpoenaed to testify.

"One other thing. These proceedings are entirely confidential. You'll notice that this nice lady, Margaret, will be taking down everything that's said in here, but that's just so that in case anything out of the ordinary happens we'll have a record of it. But other than that, there will be no discussion of what happened in this room. No press. The accused won't be privy to it. Confidential. So feel free to ask whatever questions you'd like. Okay? . . . Good. Does anyone have any questions at this time? . . . Very well then, we'll get started. The State will call Detective Bill Langdon."

As Bill Langdon walked into the room that he knew all too well, he carried himself slowly, resolutely. It was obvious from looking at him that this was not a job that he seemed to relish.

"State your name and occupation for the record please," began Andrew.

"Bill Langdon. I'm a detective with the Cortez County Sheriff's Department. I've been there for about fifteen years now."

"Mr. Langdon, did there come a point in time at which you were asked to respond to Bluestone Construction?"

"Yes there was. It was last Friday, I believe."

"And what did you find when you arrived there?"

"I found a very gruesome sight. I pulled into the driveway of Bluestone Construction and there were already some other squad cars there -- maybe three or four. Anyway, somebody came up to me and told me that I should prepare myself, because it wasn't a very pretty sight.

"Anyway, I got out of my car and walked over toward the front of the building and there lying on the ground was Ed Baker, whom I later learned was the owner of Bluestone Construction."

"And in what condition was Mr. Baker when you found him?" Andrew continued.

"Dead, to be blunt about it. He'd been stabbed several times."

"And how did you know that?"

"Because his clothes were riddled with tears in the fabric. There was blood all over his clothes and on the ground where he lay. When I unbuttoned his shirt there were several stab wounds on his body. Over ten, I'd say."

"What did you do next?"

"Well, we photographed the body and the area. Then we had the coroner's office take the body away. After that we went inside and began going through the office. I spoke with Ed's secretary, Jacki Pierson. She didn't really have anything to add, other than she was the one who found Ed's body. She found it when she arrived at work that morning and then called the authorities."

"Did your investigation continue?"

"Of course. Actually we got kinda lucky."

"How is that?" Andrew inquired.

"Well, when I came back out of the office I saw a buddy of mine, Sergeant Fred Anderson, going over the crime scene. Fred, I mean Sergeant. Anderson, knew Ed. He told me that Ed had called him a few days ago and asked him what to do about one of his employees. The guy was a Mr. Mark Abramson. Seems that someone had told him that Abramson had broken into his office a while back and stolen some money from the company. Anyway, Ed called Sergeant. Anderson because he was unsure of how to handle it. You see, Abramson has a past criminal record for robbery. And Ed was afraid that if he turned Abramson in

Abramson would go to jail. Ed didn't seem to want that. So he told Fred that he would handle it himself."

"What did he mean when he said that?"

"I think he meant that he would fire him."

"And did he?"

"Well, at the time I didn't know, but I've since learned that yes, he did fire him. From what I can tell Abramson took it *real* bad. I guess it left him out in the cold, because with a criminal record and then being fired for stealing there's no way that he'd be able to get a job around here."

"So what did you do after learning about that?"

"Well, by that time my partner, Don Richards, was back and we went over to talk to Mr. Abramson."

"What did he tell you?"

"Well, he told us that Ed had laid him off because of a lack of business. Said that his wife was pretty steamed at him. Stuff like that. He was pretty nervous. And drunk."

"You say that he was drunk?"

"Very much so. And nervous."

"So what did you do next?"

"Well, if memory serves we next went back to see Jacki Pierson. She confirmed that Abramson had not been laid off because of a lack of work. In fact, they had more work than they knew what to do with. She said that Ed had fired Abramson because Abramson had stolen from the company."

"So what did you do after learning that?"

"There wasn't a whole lot to do at that point. We went to talk to a guy who worked with Mr. Abramson. The guy's name is Al Stempson. He confirmed for us that Mr. Abramson had confessed to breaking into Ed's office and stealing the money."

"And what happened next?" Andrew continued with his methodical presentation of the case.

"Well, we went by and picked up Mr. Abramson. He voluntarily accompanied us to the station downtown. We again asked him about why he left Bluestone and he again started telling us that he was laid off due to a lack of work. Well, we sorta lit into him at that point and let him know that we knew that he'd been fired. We asked him where he'd been the night that Ed was killed."

"And what did he tell you?" asked one of the jurors.

"Good question," Bill responded with a nod of approval. "He told us that he'd been at home that night watching Murphy Brown with his wife. Well, we knew right away that that was a lie, because Murphy Brown comes on on Monday nights, not on Thursdays."

"Did his wife confirm that he was with her, though?" asked Andrew.

"Actually, while we were talking to Mr. Abramson, Sergeant. Anderson found Mr. Abramson's wife. And *no,* she did not corroborate his story. In fact, she said that they'd had an argument that night and that he'd left the house in a rage. She had no idea where he was all night."

"Detective Langdon, did Mr. Abramson ever confess to this murder?" asked another juror.

"Actually he did. It kinda surprised Detective Richards and myself, because usually these guys sorta dummy-up, if you know what I mean. But with Mr. Abramson it was as if he had a guilty conscience and he finally had a need to confess. I think he felt better afterwards."

Hearing this, Andrew got a sick feeling in the pit of his stomach. He was in a bind and he knew it. But the remedy wasn't obvious. It was clear that Abramson was the right guy. He already had given the jury more than enough information to bring an indictment. As he quickly thought it all through he decided that they had heard enough. "Thank you, Detective Langdon," he said. The State next calls Doctor Sharon Smith to the stand."

Sharon Smith's testimony took less than ten minutes. It was not difficult to describe the fourteen stab wounds that she had found on Ed's body. Neither did it take long to tell the jury that Ed died from asphyxiation, which came from his throat being slit by the sharp, piercing blades of the knife. The autopsy photographs were next given to the jury for review. And with that unpleasant job done, Andrew asked the jury for an indictment of first-degree murder against Mark Abramson.

The grand-jury proceedings had taken a little over ninety minutes from start to finish. Andrew was not at all unhappy with the timing. Neither was he uncertain about the grand jury's decision. It, like the proceeding itself, did not take long. Within thirty minutes he had been given the jury's decision. Mark Abramson would stand trial for the first-degree murder of Ed Baker. Mark, Andrew thought to himself, would also be the first person from Cortez County to go to death row in decades. And he would be the one to bring it all about, he thought to himself as he drove back home to begin preparations for the trial to come.

CHAPTER XIV

Two days after his arrest, Mark found himself facing an indictment for the first-degree murder of Ed Baker. As he sat in his cell he stared out through the bars, past the aisle that went past his cell. On the opposite side of the aisle was a nondescript, yellow cinder-block wall. It was thoroughly clean, rendering it impossible to kill any time trying to read the pathetic handwriting that otherwise might have been left by someone who, like himself, had nothing better to do than count the hours as they slowly passed. And yet, Mark found that he spent most of his time staring out through those bars at that wall. At least it reminded him that there was something beyond this seven by seven-foot box that they called a cell.

And so, Mark Abramson, Inmate number 478D, stared endlessly at the wall that was little more than three feet beyond those bars. He was not unusual. They all stared at it when they were first brought to the jail. It held an attraction for them, much as though it were the embodiment of their dreams. Dreams of going beyond their cells and living life as they used to -- only better. But still, after a while they all, Mark included, realized that while the wall was three feet from them, it might as well have been three miles away. Their freedom was just as much out of their reach. And there was nothing that they could do about it.

It was Bill Langdon who served the indictment on Mark. It was a simple, unceremonious process that took less than a minute. Upon handing the formal charges to Mark, the obviously pleased detective turned and walked away leaving the prisoner to read the grand jury's official statement asserting that he was a cold-blooded murderer. As Mark read the indictment, the import of the charges began to settle upon him. This was real. It meant that he would soon be fighting the most important battle of his life; and if he lost this battle his life would be over.

"Guard!" he began to yell. "Guard!"

"What?" came the anonymous response.

"Come here a minute, will you?"

"Why?"

"Because I have a question, that's why."

"So ask it. I don't have time to come down there."

"Come down here right now, you bum! I pay your salary you know!"

"First of all, I ain't no bum. And second of all, you *used* to pay my salary. But not any more!" chuckled the voice, obviously proud that it had gotten in the last word.

"Come on, man," responded Mark, quickly deciding that a more conciliatory tone was perhaps appropriate. "All I wanna know is when my arraignment's gonna be."

"How should I know?" came the voice's reply. "I ain't no judge."

"I hope you ain't no judge! But you gotta know something."

"Uh, huh. I know everything. That's because I'm so important that ain't nothing gonna take place in this town without me knowing about it. Uh, huh. Matter of fact, I'm so important, I think I'll just head on home and rest my poor bones. See you later, son. My shift's over."

"Aw, come on, man," replied a more frustrated Mark. "Don't do this to me. All I wanna know is when the stinkin' hearing is."

"I'm telling you, Abramson, I have no idea. Contrary to your hasty assumption, I am not the information center for greater St. Bartholomew. Got that?"

"Got it."

"Now, as soon as I know when your precious hearing is gonna be held, then I'll be sure and give you the good news. But in the meantime, I'm headin' outta here. I'll see you tomorrow. Got that?"

"Got it. . . . Sorry to be so pushy. Guess I'm pretty strung out."

"Yeah, well you'd better do yourself a big favor and get used to it. You got a lot of time to kill in there. And with your charges, I don't expect that they're gonna let you have free reign of this place. . . . But I guess you figured that out already."

"Kinda thought so."

"All right, then. You get some rest and I'll see you tomorrow."

"All right."

The voice left.

As Mark sat in his cell, the approaching second night of his incarceration was signaled by the presence of overhead lights in the aisle outside of his cell, as well as the single incandescent bulb inside. Nighttime was in some ways a blessing, since it meant the end to a day that had been tortuous. It was in other ways a curse, since it meant that all too soon a new day of pain would assault his consciousness.

"NO! YOU CAN'T DO THAT! PLEASE, DON'T! PLEASE MISTER, NO!"

The yelling. The endless yelling. Stop it. Stop beating that man! Slowly but perceptibly, the memories began their return to Mark's new life. It had been months since he had suffered from the memories of his last incarceration. He had tried relentlessly to put those memories out of his thoughts so that he could get on with his life and enjoy the time that he had with Susan. Now, however, sitting alone in his cell, he knew that all of the old memories would flood his thoughts, just as the flood waters would slowly build in the local rivers until eventually they were released to cause untold misery on anything and anyone in their paths. And sitting in his cell with nothing to do, Mark knew that he would be as helpless to stop those recurrent thoughts as he would be to stop a determined river from overflowing its banks.

He began to remember in particular the screams that permeated his wing the night his friend had been bludgeoned to near death. It had been officially listed as an accident that had occurred when the friend had fallen down some stairs at the end of the wing. So many people had fallen down those same stairs. Each time the injuries were massive. Each time there was no one around to witness the unfortunate accident. Upon leaving that place he had considered himself fortunate that he had never encountered the stairs. He had vowed to never be placed in such an exposed position again under any circumstances. Now he began to consider that such circumstances might well return to his world.

As the night marched on he began to weep on his cot, quietly though, lest he be heard and suffer the consequences he knew he would face. Experience had taught him that. Experience had taught him many things that he had tried to forget. As he drifted off into sleep he could only hope that sleep would be merciful and if but for a moment return him to his home and the way of life that he had begun to take for granted. Experience had also taught him that it would often be futile to hope for such peace. Experience had eventually worn him down to the point that hope had been lost. But this was a new trip, and despite his circumstances he determined that he would challenge his past in every way possible. So, on this night he pursued sleep until it transported him to places he could otherwise not expect to see in his immediate future.

"Abramson, you have a visitor," boomed the guard's voice in front of the bars on his cell. "Front and center. You know what to do."

"Who is it?" Mark asked. "It's nine o'clock in the morning."

"It's your wife, I think," responded the guard. "That is, if her name is Susan."

"Yeah, that's her," smiled Mark. "Today is starting off better already. Power of positive thinking, I guess."

"Well, that's nice. But you know what? I've got count to finish and too many stupid forms to complete, which unfortunately is going to prevent me from taking your self-help course, much as I'm sure it would benefit me. So what say you come on out and we'll go on down and see your next of kin. Okay?"

"Yeah, sure. . . . Just a minute though, okay? I need to straighten up a little."

"Uh, huh. I can see your point. And while you're doing that I'm gonna call Vidal Sassoon to come over and give you a nice haircut. Any particular style you'd prefer? Now get your butt out of that cell now! Otherwise you'll have all day to sit here and comb your hair any which way you'd like."

"All right, all right. I'm coming," came Mark's answer. "Geez, you don't have to be a butthead about it." And with that he walked out of the cell and down the aisle, combing his hair and straightening his clothes as he strolled along.

As they entered the holding area Mark quickly was reacquainted with prison procedures that he had repeatedly tried to forget. Just as he knew would happen, he heard the terse orders telling him to begin what he knew would be the strip search that he also knew would become routine before long. The routine would be a part of his life until he heard the jury's "not guilty" verdict months down the road.

"Okay, Abramson. Hands against the wall. Feet spread," came the guard's voice. And to Mark's amazement his pat-down search was initiated and completed in just twenty seconds. With this obnoxious procedure completed he now saw the gate open and he was ushered through it and into the visiting room, where his wife waited for him, still in a state of disbelief.

As Mark hurried to Susan he could feel the tears begin to well up. You can't do this, he thought to himself. You have to be strong for her. But regardless of the inner commands that he tried to impose upon himself, the tears began to come as he reached out for her and then began to squeeze her in a bear hug that she thought might just render her breathless.

"Honey, how are you?" was all that Mark could say at first. "Thanks for coming. I didn't know if I'd see you again. What with everything that's happened."

"Now, why in the world would you think that?" Susan responded.

"Well, as I recall, the last time I saw you there were pieces of furniture flying through the air in my direction. It kinda left me with the impression that things weren't really all that great, you know?"

"Yeah, well. We can talk about that later. Mark, what in the world is goin' on? Everyone is saying that you killed Ed. It's in the paper and everything. The phone's ringin' off the hook."

"Look Susan, it's gonna be really rough for a few months until this all gets straightened out. I need you to hang in there, okay?"

"I'll do what I can, Mark. You know that. But what are you gonna do? Have you talked with a lawyer yet or anything? When do you get outta here?"

"I don't know. I mean, I won't know when I can leave until I have the arraignment and a bond hearing. Should be soon."

"What about a lawyer? Mark, you've got to get a lawyer."

"I know. I know. But until the arraignment I don't think I'll get anyone. At least not through the public defender's office."

"Why do you want one of their people, Mark? You said the last time that they were worthless, remember?"

"Yeah, I know that, but unless you can find someone on the outside to take the case, I don't know what choice I'm gonna have."

"Well, I guess we'll just have to find someone then."

"Yeah, with what? Susan, this ain't gonna be cheap. It's gonna be more than we got. A lot more."

"How much?"

"I have no idea. But it'll be at least a couple of thousand."

"Well, we can get that together. It won't be easy, but if we try we can do it. Now don't worry. We're gonna get the best person we can for this. You'll see. Now, you just try to relax and don't worry about all of this. It's gonna be okay."

"*Don't worry?* Exactly how am I supposed to do that? Susan, I'm about to be charged with murder! Don't look at me and tell me not to worry!"

"Okay, Okay! You know what I meant, Mark. I know you're upset. Land, I'm upset enough, and I'm not the one in here. All I'm saying is we're gonna beat this thing, no matter what it takes. Okay?"

"Yeah, I guess so. I'm sorry I yelled, but man, I'm scared. You know, last night I could hardly sleep for the longest time.

All of those old feelings started coming back. Susan, I don't know if I can handle this again. I really don't."

"Sure you can, honey. It's gonna be all right. Just one thing, though. The next time you get tired of my cooking, just tell me. You don't have to go to this extreme to avoid it." A smile came over Susan's otherwise stressed face.

"Right now I'd give anything to have your cooking," Mark replied with a grin. "Why don't you bring me some pork chops with apple sauce. And limas too while you're at it. And, oh yeah, don't forget to put one of your files in it."

"Yeah, I sure will. In fact, I'd better head on back so I can get it started. I see they're moving people outta here."

"Has it been a half hour already?" asked Mark. "It sure doesn't seem like it."

"Well, it has. So I'd better be getting ready. I'd forgotten how fast these visiting times could fly by."

"Yeah, it doesn't take long, does it?" said Mark, as he began to stand up from the table. "But it won't be long before I'm back home. You'll see."

"Now listen, honey," Susan replied, "I know it's hard, but try not to worry about all of this. I'm gonna do everything I can to find someone to help you. Do you hear me?"

"Yeah, whatever you say," came Mark's response. "Look, I guess we'd better say good-bye, before I wind up gettin' in trouble and you're not allowed to see me anymore."

As he kissed her, Mark held Susan as tightly as he'd held her in a long time. She was, at this moment in time, the only thing that mattered to him. She was also his only hope somehow to find a way out of this nightmare. But he also knew that this would be a very difficult time for both of them, as evidenced by the tears that began to fall down her cheeks as she kissed him and then turned to leave.

Watching Susan walk toward the door, Mark regained some of his own composure. "Susan, one more thing. Thanks for not asking."

She smiled, nodded, and began to run as she left the room.

115

CHAPTER XV

"**M**ama, what's it mean when somebody's a rained?" the little boy asked his mother. "How can somebody be rain?"

"What in the world are you talking about, son?" replied the mother, obviously tired of the seemingly endless questions that flew from her son's mouth most hours that he was awake. I thought all of the questions were answered long ago, she thought to herself as she exhibited an outward appearance, as all mothers must, of intense interest.

"It says here in the paper that this guy was rain," came the predictable response. "What does it mean?"

Reaching for the paper the mother, who by this time in her life was more skilled at deciphering cryptic speech than experienced CIA agents, asked the boy, "What is it that you're reading?"

"There," came the response, as if it should have been obvious to mom. "Right *there* it says that that guy was rain."

As she looked at the article the boy's mother realized the mistake and instantly managed to hide the grin that she felt beginning to overtake her face. "It's not rain, son, it's *arraigned*," she finally replied.

"What's it mean? Arraigned."

"I'm not sure, son. I think it means that this guy did something wrong, and the judge told him about it, and he's gonna have a trial. You understand?"

"Yep, I understand," replied the little boy. His question answered, he returned to one of his pastimes, reading the paper just like his parents did every day. Although he didn't understand much of what he read, it still made him feel more grown up. It was important to feel grown up. After all, he was ten years old. It wouldn't be long before he'd be going to work just like his dad, and going fishing just like his dad, and just being a man like his dad.

My word, thought the boy's mother to herself. What's this world coming to? As she read the paper the headline read, *Killer Charged With Murder Of Ed Baker, Pleads Innocent.* The article indicated that Mark Abramson had been formally charged at his arraignment with first-degree murder, and that the State was seeking the death penalty. Beside the article was Mark's photograph, taken at the jail on the day of his arrest.

I hope they fry that maniac, the mother thought to herself. Anybody who would do that to someone doesn't deserve to live.

The arraignment had taken no more than 10 minutes. The courtroom was packed, as expected, for everyone wanted to catch a glimpse of Ed's killer. How would he walk? Would he look sorry for his actions? What about his appearance? How could he even hold his head up after what he did? All were questions of no particular importance, but questions nonetheless that would not go away until they were answered.

Mark, his arms and legs bound in chains, was led into the courtroom by no less than six sheriff's deputies. As he shuffled into the room that morning he immediately surveyed the crowd in order to answer questions of his own. Where was Susan? Would she talk to him? Would she hug him? Where was Katherine Baker? Where was the prosecutor? Where was his attorney? What would the crowd be like? Would they understand? Surely they would. It was all a mistake.

Looking out at the people in the courtroom Mark immediately saw Susan, who was sitting on the front row. "Where's my lawyer?" Mark whispered to her anxiously. "Who'd you get?"

"Mark, honey, I can't find anyone that we can afford. I'm sorry," came Susan's tearful reply. "I'll keep trying, though. I won't give up."

"Excuse me, ma'am," interjected a sheriff's deputy. "No conversation with the inmate. And please step back, away from the railing."

"But I was just talking to my husband," shot back Mark's wife. "That's not a crime, is it?"

"Susan, it's all right," Mark said. "We'll talk later, okay."

"Okay," came the muffled response of a seriously upset Susan Abramson. "Twenty-thousand dollars, Mark!" she finally whispered. "And that's just the down payment!"

As Mark shook his head and turned around he looked at the deputy standing beside him. "Hey, John," he asked, "any chance at getting these shackles removed? I can't hardly move. And they hurt."

"Not unless the judge orders it," was the only response.

Mark turned back to Susan, rolled his eyes, shrugged his shoulders, and moved back to his seat at the table in front of him.

"All rise," came the familiar call from the short, stocky bailiff. "The circuit court for the second judicial circuit, in and for Cortez County, Florida is now in session. The Honorable Samuel F. Pinkston presiding." And as Judge Pinkston entered the courtroom the bailiff concluded his announcement with the stern warning to "be seated."

Judge Pinkston was by reputation a stern man who had been raised in what was once rural central Florida, not far from Orlando. It was an area where simple values were what counted. A man was judged by whether he kept his word, not on how much education he had attained. Nevertheless, young Samuel had excelled in every school that he had attended, and as a result he was readily accepted into the law school of his dreams at the University of Florida. There, too, he had stood out in his class, graduating in the top five- percent. Samuel was a voracious reader who thrived on the challenges presented by the rigorous curriculum at law school. He read and reread cases, memorized their citations and their holdings, and could perorate on them at will when called upon to do so in class. Given his well-known affinity for criminal law, it was no surprise when he went directly from law school to a practice as an assistant state attorney in central Florida, where he stayed until he and his new bride moved to her old homeplace in St. Bartholomew. Following a short career as a prosecutor in Cortez County, where he had won eighty-seven percent of his cases, he was the odds-on favorite to be appointed to the vacant circuit court judgeship where he had served the good people of Cortez County with enthusiasm and distinction. A cautious jurist, he had never been reversed on appeal -- a record that he cherished and eagerly flaunted when given the opportunity.

At the age of fifty-five Judge Pinkston now found himself presiding over his first murder case. And as this well-seasoned, gray-haired professional looked out over the packed courtroom, which was also adorned with two photographers and a courtroom artist, he began to sense that this case would be different from any of his past cases. He also thought to himself that for the next hearing he would have to wear his robes, something that he was not accustomed to doing in the normally informal court cases that typically occupied his time. How was this going to look in the papers?

As the judge peered down over the bench in Mark's general direction, he exchanged what he guessed would be the first of many glances with what was by now a famous criminal defendant. As he slowly put on his glasses, he picked up the file that had been placed on the bench for him. "This is the case of the State of Florida versus Mark Abramson. Case Number CF-19A61. Are you Mr. Abramson?"

"Yes sir, I am." replied Mark.

"Young man, please stand when you address the court." shot back the visibly upset judge, sensing that this would let everyone know who was in charge.

"Yes, your honor. I'm sorry," said Mark, while rising from his seat.

"Mr. Abramson, you are charged with the crime of first-degree murder, to wit, the murder of Mr. Ed Baker. Now this crime carries with it the potential sentence of death if convicted. Now Mr. Abramson, do you have an attorney?"

Mark stared ahead, his eyes beginning to glaze over.

"Mr. Abramson! I said, do you have an attorney?"

"Sir," came the trembling response out of Mark's mouth. "My wife's been looking for an attorney for me, but she can't find one yet. We can't afford any of them that she's talked to. I guess I'll need some time to find one."

"Well, Mr. Abramson, we're not going to wait around for you to shop around. This court has a heavy enough caseload as it is. If you're telling me that you cannot afford an attorney then I'll go ahead and appoint the public defender's office to represent you."

"But sir, I'd really like to find my own . . ."

"Mr. Abramson, listen to me. I'm not going to wait around for you to go shopping! Understand, the charge against you is serious. My advice to you is to have an attorney who knows how to handle these types of cases. They're complex. The public defender's office has plenty of people who have experience in these types of cases, and I'm sure that they can help you. So you work with them, you hear?"

"Yes sir," Mark replied, his voice gaining some strength.

"Very well, then. I will not take a plea from you until you've had an opportunity to speak with your attorney about the charge against you. We'll continue this matter to two weeks from today. That is all."

"Your honor?" Mark asked. "I would like to ask you to set a reasonable bail for me. I've asked around and it's my understanding that I'm entitled to be released on a reasonable bail."

"Denied," quickly responded judge Pinkston. "This is a capital charge. The State is seeking the death penalty, Mr. Abramson. By statute there is no bail in these cases." And with that he stood and walked from the bench.

"All rise!" shrieked the proud bailiff, as he watched his favorite judge exit the courtroom.

"Mark, I'll be over to see you later," yelled Susan, as the deputies began once again to surround Mark and direct him out of the courtroom. She saw only a nod of Mark's head and realized that he was in a state of disbelief over what had just taken place. Was he really unaware of the fact that the State wanted to impose the death penalty on him? From his response she could only conclude that indeed he had been caught by surprise. Once again she felt her eyes begin to well up with tears that she knew she would not be able to contain. Wanting to be alone, she quickly picked up her purse, turned, and began to leave the courtroom only to realize that most of the spectators were staring at her while whispering to each other. Although she could not hear what was being said, she instinctively felt that she was the target of a hatred that she had never before encountered. Once they get to know Mark it'll all be different, she thought to herself. But until that time came the tears would continue to fall. For Mark and for her.

CHAPTER XVI

Ninety miles away from Mark and Susan's home was Tallahassee, Florida's capital. This small, sleepy town had in recent years become a bustling city. True, it wasn't a metropolis, but then the citizens didn't want it to be. In fact, many if not most of them had deliberately chosen to live there because of the friendly, hometown atmosphere. It was also a beautiful town, especially in the spring when the azaleas were in full bloom and the air was fragrant. There were few inhabitants who weren't somehow inspired by the majestic, moss-cloaked, oak trees that line the streets. And under the great oaks were rings of pink, red, purple and white azaleas. It was all so beautiful.

For Joel Cummings, Tallahassee had always been a town that had fulfilled all of his needs. It was a good place to grow up and to raise a family. Since the crime rate was low you didn't need to fear walking the streets at night. The townspeople were friendly, also. And they were proud of their town. Furthermore, the schools were some of the best in the state, and since he leaned toward an academic environment, he felt right at home there.

It wasn't just the academic life that Joel liked, however. The schools also provided a lot of entertainment -- mostly football. On Friday nights the air smelled of high-school football. It was everywhere. And anybody who was somebody went to the games. Joel was always amazed at the attendance at these games. It didn't seem to matter whether the weather was clear or pouring down rain, warm or below freezing -- the people always came. Perhaps they liked to hear the crashing of the helmets or the tearing of the jerseys. Or perhaps they liked to see and hear the marching bands. Of course, one could also not discount the number of youth who went to the games because it provided them with an opportunity to engage in amorous pursuits forbidden by their parents. In that light the games became a sort of mating ritual.

But possibly the biggest reason for the games' popularity was that they provided the citizens with a chance to escape, if just for awhile, the pressures of everyday life. At the same time the games allowed them to take out their frustrations vicariously through the youth on the playing field. Regardless of their reasons, however, the people who attended the games all agreed that they got their money's worth. The rivalries were intense, both between the football teams and the bands, and it was most often the case that the winner of the city championship would also be a serious contender for a statewide title, both in sports and in music.

Joel had attended many of these games while he was in school, and thus considered himself to be an insider. He didn't play football; he didn't play in the band, either. But he sure knew who played on his school's team. And when the team played out of town he was often one of the fans in "hostile territory." Joel loved the games. It was the one time that he and his girlfriend could be together, away from teachers and parents. While they most often went to the games with friends, the evenings always seemed to end with them being alone -- just the way they liked it. It was a sort of heaven for Joel, a heaven that he wouldn't recognize or appreciate until years later. Everyday life would see to that.

A Tallahasseean by birth, Joel was educated exclusively within the city line. He had attended elementary, middle, and high schools in Tallahassee. And when the time came to go to college, he drove the short distance down Tennessee Street to Florida State University. It was there that he began his studies in sociology, psychology, and the humanities. Joel loved exploring the human psyche, and he found more than ample time and opportunity to do so at the university. For the first time, it seemed, he was allowed to delve into theories that ranged from creationism to Darwinism, and everything in between. He learned of yin and yang, the two opposing "forces" found in man that function together while at the same time being diametrically opposite. He also learned of the early European schools that developed the yin and yang theories into their own refined viewpoints of the universe. The disturbing fact for Joel however, was that many if not most of these theories seemed to contradict the teachings upon which he had been raised and nurtured as a boy. And he knew that if he expressed support for these theories outside of the university setting, he would come into conflict with many of his elders. None of the townspeople whom he knew would support or condone thinking that encouraged individuals to develop *both* sides of the personality. They all believed that man was only to develop the rational side of his existence, while at the same time suppressing the side that cried out for frivolity and sensuality. Joel nevertheless continued in his studies of the philosophies and, to his satisfaction, he excelled in them. Four years later, he graduated with a degree in the humanities and a different outlook on life.

Joel quickly became less than the typical citizen of Tallahassee. Not only was he educated in a field that seemingly contradicted much of what he had been taught at home, but he had also traveled rather extensively. For the most part his travels had taken him northward to the larger cities such of Washington, Philadelphia, and New York. He had worked part-time jobs in most of them, usually as a waiter, and had found that there were many new and challenging things going on in the world. These jobs enabled him to meet people from almost every walk of life and to see how different people struggled with what he had come to see as the two opposing forces within each person's life. He also found, to his relief, a tolerance for opposing viewpoints. Suddenly he could voice his views on such topics as the criminal justice system, prison reform, the death penalty, welfare, et cetera Not only could he voice them, but he could do so without being afraid of being ostracized from his community. To Joel the change was welcome and, as a result, the tolerance he had previously possessed for his hometown began to wane.

But not everything that Joel saw in the north was pretty. He also saw true poverty for the first time. The poverty bred hatred and the hatred violence. It seemed as if there were murders everyday. And the situations all seemed to be the same. Fights arose over either domestic arguments, drugs, or a need for money. The results were often tragically the same: death. And often at an early age. It all seemed to be so senseless, and yet there seemed to be no cure for it. This poverty and violence was new to him. While he had read about it and seen it on the news, it was different actually to experience it for the first time.

Joel saw another type of violence, also -- a violence committed upon the poor by those in power. To someone as naive as Joel the solution to the problem of poverty was simple: feed, clothe, and shelter the poor with money from the more fortunate in society. But in real life, however, the solution was hardly ever so simple. The transfer of money would mean that the businessmen, the doctors, the lawyers, and the politicians would have a little less. And while it seemed simple enough to have the underprivileged elect politicians who would carry out such plans, Joel discovered that the underprivileged didn't vote. So, the poverty relentlessly continued.

After a few years of seeing the other side of life, Joel decided that it was time he do something with his life. After leaving Tallahassee and Florida State, he quickly discovered that his bachelor's degree was not enough. In order to earn a comfortable living he would have to go further in school.

It was not as if this realization were shocking to him, though. To begin with, he had always liked, and even loved, school. He felt safe there. And in Tallahassee it was evident that the available jobs were primarily with the university or in government, either of which would demand a specialized degree to enter into the workplace as a professional. Joel's only concern, therefore, was not whether to go back to school, but what to study when he arrived.

It was at this point that Joel, perhaps unconsciously, began to draw from his boyhood teachings in the church. He thought back to all that he had been taught about the need to help one's fellow man. To be there when your neighbor is in need. And he remembered the scenes of poverty to which he was exposed in the northern industrial centers of the country. Those scenes had touched him and made him wish that he'd had the tools to help, to make a difference somehow. The more he thought about it, the more he was persuaded that law school was the road for him to take. It would be law school and the practice of law that would enable him to make a difference. It would be law school that would sharpen his thinking and enable him to stand up for himself. And so, after much deliberation, Joel mailed his application to the Florida State University School of Law. It was time to return to his roots.

Joel was readily accepted into the law school. And once he began his studies there, he became truly fascinated with the law and its varied nuances. It was constitutional law that intrigued him the most, however. For the first time he began to see the Constitution as a living, breathing, document that stood as a shield against oppression. And he also saw that in spite of all of the decisions surrounding this miraculous document, much still needed to be done. Activists were still needed to ensure that the document would remain a shield and not be used as a sword against the poor and the oppressed.

The years seemed as but a moment for Joel, and after three years of hard study he graduated. Then it was on to the bar exam, which he was required to pass before he could practice law. After two arduous months of study and preparation, the time finally came for him to take the exam. For two days he sat, wrote, thought, and created answers designed to impress nameless graders who held his future in their hands. When it was over he was exhausted and spent. He wondered how he would ever be able to wait the two months it would take before he got the results. But the day finally came, and he learned that he had passed the exam. Six weeks later he was admitted to practice law in the State of Florida.

Joel decided that he wanted to work for himself. It would be risky, but he also felt that it would be the most rewarding. When Joel began practicing he had no choice but to take any case that walked in the door. Nevertheless he continued to aspire to the practice of constitutional and criminal law. He had always

126

enjoyed criminal law in law school and he had done well in it. He felt as if it, like constitutional law, was an area in which he could contribute and perhaps do some good. But for now he would continue to be a generalist, working out of the small office in which he shared a conference room, copier, and secretary with Philip Miller, the attorney next door. He and Philip had talked of becoming partners one day, but their interests were not the same; Joel wasn't sure the two of them would get along that well on a daily basis anyway. Sharing space gave them the best of both worlds. Not only did they manage to cut costs, but they could also bounce ideas off of each other when they needed to, without the formalities and pitfalls of partnership hampering them. It was just the arrangement that Joel needed; he began to settle into his new life quickly and with great anticipation of events that he could not even begin to imagine.

CHAPTER XVII

In the years since he had opened his law office, Joel Cummings had managed to build up what for him had been a satisfying general practice. Nothing special. Just a small boutique office that turned out what he believed was top quality-work. As time had passed he had handled an increasing number of criminal cases, which had meant that he had seen more and more courtrooms. And he loved the resulting litigation. It was the main reason he had chosen law as a profession. The rush that he felt every time he was in court was unlike anything else he'd ever done. And yes, he was good at it -- if he did say so himself.

As his caseload had grown, Joel had of necessity moved into an office of his own. It was small. Just himself and his secretary, Marge Roberts. Marge had only been with him a few months, but she was already invaluable to him. She handled an ever-increasing number of the routine office tasks, which left Joel more time to handle his cases. Other than Marge, Joel was on his own, with the exception of a somewhat green law clerk who doubled as an investigator when necessary. Ronald Braithwright, or Ron as he preferred to be called, was in his third year of law school at Florida State and worked for Joel whenever he was able. He too was becoming an indispensable part of Joel's practice.

Joel was understandably proud of his accomplishments since graduating from law school. Unlike many of his colleagues, he had managed to find work actually practicing law, and now had his own law firm, which, though not profitable yet, was on its way to providing him with a comfortable living in what he expected would be a rather short period of time. As far as his practice itself was concerned, he had been forced to spend the usual amount of time handling divorce cases, personal injury cases, wills, et cetera You name it and I've handled it, he often thought to himself. But that was to be expected of a young lawyer. And he was willing to put in the time handling the grunt work that the established firms didn't want to be bothered with. Anyway, he had achieved admirable results in an increasing number of criminal cases, even though a significant number of those cases were DWI charges.

This young upstart was nevertheless surprised when he picked up the phone on a clear, blue Wednesday morning and heard an unfamiliar voice ask, "Is this Mr. Cummings?"

"Yes. This is Joel Cummings. To whom am I speaking?"

"Mr. Cummings, this is Judge Samuel Pinkston in St. Bartholomew. I believe you have handled a case or two in my courtroom during the past year."

"Yes, your honor, I have," came Joel's cautious reply. What in the world have I done now, he thought to himself. My career was going so well. I knew it had to come to an end.

"Mr. Cummings, I'll get right to the point. The reason I'm calling is that I have a case down here, a criminal case, to which I intend to appoint you."

"Yes, your honor. What type of case is it, if I may ask."

"It's a capital case, Mr. Cummings. Your new client is a man by the name of Mark Abramson. . . . Mr. Cummings. Are you there?"

"Yes, your honor. May I ask why I have been appointed to this case?"

"You may. It's really very simple. I had initially appointed the public defender's office to the case, but they have advised me that they already have an overwhelming number of capital cases for which they are responsible. Due to the overload they were required to conflict out of the case, which left me with a defendant who needs an attorney. You, Mr. Cummings, are his new attorney."

"Your honor, where is Mr. Abramson being housed?"

"The Cortez County jail, I believe. He should have the paperwork on his case. The case is really just underway. The indictment has been returned and he has had an initial appearance. I have not yet taken a plea, but I assume the plea will be not guilty."

"That's correct, your honor."

"Now, how could you say that when you haven't even spoken with your client, Mr. Abramson? Of course, if he chooses to plead guilty it would save everyone a lot of time. But that's your-all's decision. Bottom line is that I'll have a formal arraignment early next week. Good day, Mr. Cummings."

"Good-bye, your honor." As Joel heard the click in the receiver and then the dial tone, he instantly wondered what he had done to deserve this. Was it an honor? Or was it punishment? The times that he'd been in front of Pinkston had been pretty short and uneventful. Be that as it may, his world, he sensed, had suddenly been turned upside down. At least for now.

"Marge! Do you have a second?" Joel yelled from his office.

"What's the matter?" responded Marge, somewhat used to Joel's not infrequent outbursts of insecurity. "Has the coffee gotten too cold again?" she asked, as she rose from her desk and began the short trek into her boss' office. "I don't know what I'm going to do with you. I've told you I don't know how many times that if you put the little cup on the little hotpad the coffee will stay nice and warm for you." Well, I'll be, she then thought to herself as she entered the inner sanctum and found Joel sitting at his desk, staring out the window. Maybe it's not the coffee this time.

"Marge, come in and close the door please."

"Why? There's no one in here but us, Joel." came the secretary's flippant retort.

"Oh, yeah. Okay. You're right. Have a seat."

"I'm not sure I want to, the way you look. Was there something wrong with the mayonnaise on your sandwich again, Joel?"

"No. Listen, Marge. Do you know who was on the phone just now?"

"Yeah, Judge Pinkston."

"How do you know that?"

"Because, he told me that's who it was when I answered the phone. You know, that's what I do. I answer the phone." said Marge.

"Well why didn't you tell me it was Pinkston on the other end of the line when you put him through?"

"Because it's fun to watch you sweat, that's why. . . . Actually, I think I did tell you, but you weren't listening, as usual."

"Well, whatever. Do you know what he wanted?"

"Yeah," Marge matter-of-factly replied.

"How do you know that?"

"Because I was listening to the conversation."

"You what!?!" came Joel's immediate response. "When did you start . . ."

"Gotcha!" came the secretary's timely answer, before things could get out of hand. "No, I wasn't listening in on your conversation. What did he say?"

"He called to tell me that he was appointing me to a capital case! Some guy named Abramson. Mark Abramson, I believe is what he said. The case is in St. Bartholomew."

"Abramson," Marge said. "Isn't that the guy that stabbed some construction worker a few weeks ago?"

"Shoot, I don't know," said Joel. "I was so surprised by the call I didn't think to ask Pinkston about any particulars."

"If it's the guy I'm thinking of," Marge began, "it was a really gruesome killing. Stabbed the guy a number of times. Pretty bloody. The victim was supposedly pretty well liked."

"Aren't they all?" quipped Joel. "Doesn't matter whether they sold cocaine to little kids so that the Mafia could increase its profits. By the time the press gets ahold of it the guy's a saint."

"A little cynical now, aren't we, Mr. Liberal of the Month?" joked Marge. "I think you may be wrong about this victim. From what I read he really was a pretty decent human being. . . . One thing's for sure -- St. Bartholomew is really in a stir over it."

"I can imagine that they would be," said Joel. "They don't get this sort of thing down there too often."

"That's right. Why do you think everyone likes to go there? Besides the fact that it's gorgeous?"

"True. And now I get to be the guy who comes in and tries to defend the jerk that did this. It should be a real blast, is all I can say."

"So how did you get this thing, anyway?" asked Marge. "I mean, don't they have people down there to handle their cases for them?"

"I'm not sure," came Joel's response. "Pinkston said something about the PD's office conflicting out due to workload. But that sounds like a load of crap to me. The PD's office has five times the manpower that I do. Not to mention the fact that I've never handled one of these things in my life."

"Well, guess what, boss? You are about to get some experience. . . . I can see it now. There. On the wall. Next to the portraits of F. Lee Bailey, Roy Black, Edgar Bennett Williams, will be the true star -- Joel Cummings!"

"Yeah, well, guess what, Ms. Roberts? Somebody's gotta type all the pleadings, do all of the filing, organize the case, schedule appointments . . ."

"Uh-huh. In other words, you expect this place to function like a team, is that it?" smiled the admittedly proud secretary.

"You got it," Joel responded. "It ain't gonna happen any other way. Now, as much as I'd like to continue down this path to stardom, I think it would be more profitable if you could find out when I can visit with my new client."

"When do you want me to set it up?"

"As soon as you can. If past experience is any guide, Pinkston won't give me any time to prepare."

"What about Simmons and Wright? They're both in need of your attention, you know."

"I know that, Marge," said Joel. "But they'll have to wait a little while longer. I guess I'll just have to fit everything in somehow."

The drive to St. Bartholomew had mellowed Joel somewhat. As he drove to meet a client that he'd been given responsibility for less than twenty-four hours earlier, Joel let himself daydream about how he expected the case to unfold. It would not be easy.

He knew that. But if he applied himself and focused on the issues that would be presented to him, he felt confident that he would be up to the challenge. So the further he drove along the winding coastal highway, the better he felt about everything. He'd driven this road countless times before, and while it wasn't always perfect, on cool autumn days like today when the sun sparkled on the dark blue water, he always came away feeling better about his life. Today was no exception.

Joel was nevertheless thankful to be able to get out of the car as he pulled into the oyster-shell parking lot at the jail. As strange as it sounded when he told others of his feelings, on the two previous occasions that he'd been here visiting clients he had sort of enjoyed himself. As jails go, the structure wasn't imposing or threatening. Its red-brick exterior was spray-cleaned at least once a year, leaving the structure rather pleasant looking when viewed against the calm, blue water of the St. Bartholomew river behind it.

Walking into the jail, the attorney went first to the receiving window. In a matter of minutes after showing the receptionist his membership card to the Florida Bar, he was escorted to a pale blue visiting room, where he was left alone to await the arrival of his new client. The room was probably no more than nine by ten feet in size, with an old, metal table in the middle and two metal folding chairs around it. Its concrete walls, while not adorned with pictures or other such decorations, were nevertheless interrupted once by a small window that overlooked the river. Joel, as if being pulled by a magnet, gravitated to the window and stared out at the river. He daydreamed about sailing while he waited for Mark. Not here. In Tahiti, perhaps. Maybe this coming summer if he could get the time, he thought.

His ruminations were soon interrupted by the metal door opening in order to allow the entrance of inmate number 478D.

"Mr. Abramson?" Joel asked the disheveled looking man standing in front of him. "My name is Joel Cummings. I've been appointed by the court to represent you in your case."

As he began slowly walking toward the table in front of him, Mark looked at the attorney from head to toe, slowly, ever so

133

slowly, as if he wanted to gauge the extent to which he should consider even speaking with the man. Then, raising his eyebrows, he nodded his head, motioning for the attorney to ask the guard to leave the two of them alone.

It was the first test that Joel was given on the case. He had failed, and sensing as much, immediately looked at the guard and casually advised him that Mark and his attorney wished to be left alone. In return the guard removed the handcuffs from Mark's hands, secured his leg irons to the security clamp on the floor, and then exited the room so that the two men could talk.

"That's better," continued Joel. As he smiled at Mark he was immediately struck by what he perceived to be distrust on the part of his new client. "Mr. Abramson, as I said earlier, I have been appointed by the court to represent you in your case."

"When did that happen?" questioned Mark. "I don't remember any hearing where that happened. No one asked me about it."

"Well, I don't believe that there was a hearing, Mr. Abramson. Apparently the court first appointed the public defender's office to represent you, but they declined the representation, because of their caseload. It was at that point that I was appointed by Judge Pinkston." Sensing that he needed to move forward with his new client, Joel continued. "Now, it is my understanding that your arraignment will be coming up soon -- probably next week. So the first thing that we need to consider is your plea."

"I didn't do it," answered Mark somewhat caustically.

"Mr. Abramson, please understand, I'm not here to judge you. It is entirely irrelevant to me whether or not you committed this crime. Okay? My job is to defend you to the best of my abilities so that you get the best result possible in your case. Understand?"

"Yeah, sure. I understand. Now understand me. I didn't do it." replied Mark. "Just tell them that."

"I understand that, Mr. Abramson," said Joel, "but before you decide how to plead I believe that you should let me see what I can do to cut you a deal with the state attorney's office. Now my guess is that . . ."

"Listen, man, did you not hear me the first two times? I DIDN'T DO IT! That's all they need to hear! . . . And I ain't gonna plead guilty to something I didn't do! Period. . . . Now, do you understand me, or not?"

"Mr. Abramson, . . ."

"Do you understand me, or not, Mr. Attorney?" shouted Mark while rising from the table and looking Joel square in the eye.

"I understand you, Mr. Abramson. I understand. But please understand *me*. I have an obligation to you to explore all possibilities of your case. Now, if you're telling me that I am not even to talk to anyone about a plea bargain, then that's what I'll do. But I have to advise you that I don't think it's wise."

"It's not wise, huh?" said Mark. "Well, let me tell you something, Mr. Attorney. It's *my* butt that's on the line right now. Not yours. And if I lose this thing they want to *kill* me. So, no, maybe I'm not being real *wise* right now, because I've got a lot on my mind. Things like, what kind of guy have they got to represent me. Things like, *if* I win will I have a family left when it's all over. Things like, *if* I win will I be able to get a job. Things like, if I *lose* what will it be like to be strapped into a chair and have two-thousand volts of electricity thrown through my body. Sorry, Mr. Attorney, but I guess I'm just not being real *wise* at the moment."

As Joel looked at Mark, he could see the rage and the pain that his client felt. But most of all, he could sense utter fear like he had never seen before in any of his clients. It was unlike anything that he had experienced to this point in his short career. And yet, "I see," was the only response that came out of his mouth.

"Mr. Abramson," Joel continued, regaining his composure, "Please don't misunderstand me. I know how you feel . . ."

"You know how I feel?" shouted Mark. "How could you possibly know how I feel? You can get up and leave anytime you want. The last time I checked, I don't have that privilege."

135

"Bad choice of words, man," came Joel's response. "Tell you what. Whatta you say we start over, okay? Mr. Abramson, my name is Joel Cummings. I've been appointed to represent you in your case." As Joel then reached out his hand to his client, he noticed what he thought was a faint smile begin to appear on Mark's face.

"Mr. Cummings, my name is Mark Abramson, and I'm the person you've been appointed to represent. And in case you haven't heard, I didn't do it." Mark began to chuckle guardedly as he looked at Joel's reaction to him.

With the tension in the room somewhat abated, the two men then began the task of trying to piece together the events that led up to Mark's confinement. Mark, to his credit, related those events for Joel as accurately as possible. For his part, Joel, though he became more skeptical of Mark's innocence as the meeting progressed, did his best to keep an open mind through it all.

Several hours flew by while Mark told Joel what he could remember about his arrest and the events leading up to it. It was not a pretty picture. These were events that Joel felt certain would lead a jury to convict his client of Ed Baker's murder.

"Mark, all I can say is that I'll do my best," was the only assurance that the attorney would give his client. "But now keep in mind, I'm not saying I don't believe you," ventured Joel cautiously, "but what would help tremendously would be if you could give me some names, even one name, of someone who could give you an alibi. That way, if the person were credible, you'd have a really strong case. So I want you to do some thinking about that and see if you can't think of someone you met during that night who would be able to come into court and testify for you. You know, suppose you stopped for gas or bought something. A clerk might remember you. . . . Mark, it's really very important."

"I know it is, Mr. Cummings, but I swear to you that I can't think of a single person. But as I said earlier, talk to Susan. She'll be able to tell you where I was part of the time."

"Yeah, I'm sure she will. And I certainly want to talk to her about a lot of this. But you're the only one who knows where you were that night so I'm afraid you're probably the only one who can help on that front. Another thing, though. I haven't seen the murder weapon. Did the detectives say anything to you about matching your prints on it or anything like that?"

"No. They didn't say nothin about it at all."

"Well they do have it don't they?"

"I don't know. I assume they do. But if they did they didn't say nothin' to me about it."

"I'll talk to them about it then," said Joel. "I am kind of surprised that they didn't say anything to you about it, though. What about Ed Baker? What sort of a person was he? Was he well liked, or a jerk, or what?"

"Well-liked, from what I could tell," Mark said. "Mr. Cummings, I don't know of no one who would want to do him any harm. He was a really nice man."

"Except to you, that is."

"What do you mean by that?"

"What I mean, Mark, is that the nicer he was to everyone the better the State's case is against you. After all, he had fired you only a few days before this happened. Now I'm willing to bet that Mr. Baker, nice as he may have been, still had a few enemies around here. It's pretty hard to be in business as long as he was and not make someone unhappy. What we have to do is to find that person."

"How're you gonna do that?" asked Mark.

"In the first place the police should have done it, so we'll start there," replied Joel. "Depending on what they tell us, we may have to do our own investigation on that point. One thing I am curious about is this guy Al Stempson -- the one you said was doin' drugs. He would seem to me to be someone that Ed Baker would be pretty loath to have working for him."

"Yeah, if he knew about it," Mark said. "But I don't think Baker knew about it. In fact, I'd be willing to bet that he didn't, because I heard Baker was tight with Al's dad. Best friends, I think. So I don't think Baker would have done anything about it even if he'd known about Al. From what I can tell Ed really was pretty good friends with Mr. Stempson. And he also really seemed to like Al, for what it's worth. That surprised me, I guess."

"Why?"

"Well," Mark answered, "I just thought that Al was a real jerk. He and I didn't get along at all. Especially after I spotted him dealing drugs. . . . I guess I should've turned him in to Ed right then, but I didn't. I just chose to stay out of his way."

"Okay," said Joel. "I'll tell you what. We've covered a good bit of ground today. I've got to take a look at the police files, and I also have to talk to the state attorney on the case to see where they're going with it. I need to talk with Susan, too. . . . So for right now you just try and relax. I know it's not gonna be easy, but try and keep calm. I'll be back to see you in a few days. In the meantime, if you can think of *anything* that you think will help me out on this, please write to me and let me know. . . . Okay?"

"Okay," answered Mark, "and Mr. Cummings, thank you for helping me out."

"It's my job, Mark, but I'm glad to be able to help you anyway." The two men stared at each other from across the table for a few seconds until Joel reached for his briefcase, began to close it, and then stood up to leave. "Listen, you take care of yourself, Mark. We'll do the best job we can. I assure you that."

As Mark nodded his head in response, Joel motioned for the guard stationed outside of their door. As the door began to open the two men shook hands and Joel walked briskly out of the room, through the bars, and into the parking lot. Once outside he exhaled deeply and said a prayer for God to watch over him as he began to handle what he realized would be the most important case of his life. He would need the help, because as exhilarated as he was, he was also scared too death. He only hoped that his client had not sensed the concern that he had for his well-being. As he pulled from the parking lot, Joel looked out again over the gently flowing river and began the drive back home. The ninety-mile drive would give him time to think about the case, whether he wanted to or not.

CHAPTER XVIII

"**Y**our client's gonna fry," boomed the voice of Andrew Smallwood over the phone into Joel's unsuspecting ear. "But other than that, what can I do to help you, Mr. Cummings?"

"Judging from your statement, I suppose you already know that I've been appointed to represent Mark Abramson in his murder case."

"Yes, I had heard. Good to have you on board."

"Very well. I'm calling now to introduce myself and to advise you that we are making a formal demand for discovery in this case. My written demand will be delivered to you this afternoon."

"Why sure, Mr. Cummings. I'd been expecting it. So how do you propose that we proceed?"

"If memory serves," said Joel, "your office has an open-file policy. So I guess that I'd like to schedule a time to drop by and review the evidence. Whenever would be convenient for you, of course."

"Of course. But I do have to tell you that in death cases we try to be a bit more accommodating. So normally what we'd do is simply copy whatever you want and send it on over to you. That is, if you know what it is you're after."

"Everything. I think that my written demand will make that pretty clear."

"Of course. I'll tell you what then. Give me a couple of days and I'll have my staff run photocopies of everything for you. Now, what about the photographs. Do you want photocopies or duplicates of the originals?"

"I'd rather have duplicates."

"Sure. . . . I thought you said that this was your first death case?"

"I never said that, but it is. What difference does it make?"

"None, really. It's just impressive to see someone so thorough, when he's just getting his feet wet. Doesn't always happen, you know."

"Well, thank you. I'll take that as a compliment."

"Please do -- it was meant as such," was Andrew's response. "I'll get those files over to you right away. Anything else?"

"No. That'll be all for now. Thank you, Mr. Smallwood."

"Don't mention it. Now listen, if you don't have these files in two days you give me a call. You hear?"

"I sure will. Good-bye."

"Good-bye, Mr. Cummings."

Well, at least someone's gonna be okay to work with, thought Joel to himself as he stared out of the window of his office.

The next voice that Joel heard on the phone was that of a pleasant-sounding female who, judging from the inflections, he supposed was in her late twenties. "Hello, Mrs. Abramson," Joel said into the receiver. "My name is Joel Cummings, and I've been appointed to represent your husband in his murder case."

"Yes, Mr. Cummings. Joel said that you would probably be calling. What is it you'd like to know?"

"Well, I guess there's a lot that we need to discuss. And given the sensitive nature of this matter I'd prefer to do it in person, rather than over the phone. Do you have any idea when that might be arranged? In case Mark didn't tell you, I'm in Tallahassee."

"I can come up there whenever you'd like, Mr. Cummings. Today, if you need me to."

"That would be fine, Mrs. Abramson. Let me turn you over to my secretary, and she'll give you the directions to my office. It's been a pleasure speaking with you."

"Thank you, Mr. Cummings," said Joel's wife.

The drive to Tallahassee was one that Susan had taken on enough occasions for it to become rather boring. This time she was more than willing to get out of town, however, what with her husband's recent notoriety and the effect that it had already had on her ability to lead a comfortable, anonymous life. So on this day she drove the two hours at a leisurely speed and tried to pass the time by thinking of anything other than the events of the past few weeks. Those thoughts only led to questions about what would happen in the future, and the future was hardly something that she wanted to contemplate at the moment. But after the two-hour drive, Susan located Joel's office and once again reality began to settle in. She could feel herself tense as she walked the short block from the car to the office door. And despite the fact that she would have in many ways preferred to have turned and run, she opened the door and walked in a deliberate fashion to the receptionist's desk in front of her.

"Mr. Cummings, this is Susan Abramson," announced Marge while escorting Susan into Joel's office. "Can I get you two anything? Coffee or tea, perhaps?"

"Nothing for me, Marge. Susan, would you care for anything?" Joel managed to say while trying to get over the sight of his client's very attractive, obviously upset wife -- a wife who had clearly been trying to hide her tears from these strangers.

"Just some water, if that's okay," said Susan.

"Thank you for coming up to see me," said Joel in an effort to get the conversation off the ground. "I know that it was quite a distance to come."

"Yes, it is kinda far, Mr. Cummings, but . . ."

"Please call me Joel," interrupted the attorney.

"Okay, . . . Joel. I just figured that it was pretty important to see where everything is in all of this. I don't really know what's going on."

"Well, let me see if I can clarify things for you, Susan. As you know, Mark's been arrested for the murder of Ed Baker. The State has charged him with first-degree murder." Joel hesitated a moment, then continued, "and they've indicated that if he is convicted they intend to seek the death penalty. That's why it's very important that everyone work together in all of this."

"Mr. Cummings . . . I mean, Joel, do you think the State really will be able to convict Mark? He swears he didn't do it."

"It depends, Susan. . . . Ah, thanks, Marge. Susan, here's your water."

"Thank you, ma'am," Susan nodded to Marge.

"Now, as I was saying," Joel continued. "It depends on what kind of case the State can put on. But I have to tell you that based on what I've heard so far, it looks to me like they have a pretty good case of *circumstantial* evidence against your husband. They will be able to show a jury that Mark was fired by Mr. Baker and that within a few days Mr. Baker was savagely stabbed to death. And mind you, Mark doesn't have an alibi for the time when the murder supposedly occurred. Put that with the fact that Mark had a prior record and it doesn't look too good."

"But they don't have anything that really puts him at the crime scene, do they?"

"No, Susan, they don't. And that's exactly what we're going to have to drive home with the jury. I think that's a big flaw in the State's case."

"So what do you need from me?" asked Susan.

"Well, number one, I need you to tell me everything that happened during that time period. *Anything* that you can think of I need to know, no matter how insignificant it may seem to you. *Especially* anything that might shed light on where Mark was on the evening of Baker's death."

"See, that's just it," replied Susan. "I don't have any idea where Mark was. We had had a fight, because I got upset when he told me about losing the job. He stormed out of the house and I didn't see him again that night."

"Did he ever tell you where he went?"

"Naw. He just said that he went out for a drive. . . . Mr. Cummings, that's not really unusual. He'd done that before. That's why I didn't really think anything about it. Except for being mad at him, that is."

"Tell me this," said Joel, "can you think of anyone else who might have done this to Ed Baker? Someone must have had it in for him pretty badly to do something like this. I mean, this murder was brutal, Susan. It wasn't as if someone just drove by and shot him once or twice. He had multiple stab wounds, and I've heard he was strangled. And from what the police could tell he hadn't been robbed. . . . So it would seem that someone went there for the express purpose of killing him."

"But Mr. Cummings, I don't know of anyone who disliked Mr. Baker. I hate to say it, but the only person I know of who had anything against him was Mark, and that was only after he got laid off. But believe me, Mark is not a killer. I know him, and he could not have done this to Mr. Baker," her voice trembled.

Joel could see that Mark's wife was becoming increasingly upset under all of the pressure. Her eyes were becoming moist with tears and he could sense that it wouldn't be long before she would break down. Why in the world don't they teach you how to handle things like this in law school, he thought to himself. I'm not up to this.

Indeed, during his entire law school career, Joel had been taught to be strong and never, under any circumstances, to show any vulnerability. That was fine for dealing with a judge, and in fact it had worked to his advantage many times when he was in court. But it did little to help him now. And he didn't have time to take another course so he could figure out what to do. No, this was on-the-job training of the most delicate kind. Why couldn't she ask him to recite the facts of *Marbury versus Madison,* or something like that? Then he could respond with full force and show her how skilled an advocate he could be for her husband.

"I'll tell you what, Susan," Joel quietly said. "Do you know what you can do for Mark that will help him the most right now?"

"No, what?" she answered.

"Be there for him whenever he needs you," continued Joel. "It may get a lot tougher on him before it gets any better. And he's going to need to know that he has someone he can lean on when those rough times come."

"Why wouldn't I be there, Mr. Cummings?" asked Susan, as if the alternative were unthinkable.

"I'm not saying you won't be there, Susan," Joel continued. "But believe me, in criminal cases I've seen it happen over and over that families split up and the defendant is left holding the bag when he needs someone the most. Now in many cases the defendant truly brought it all on himself, one might say. But that's not always the case. And *especially* before and during trial it is critical that the public and the jury see that everyone is behind Mark Abramson. It'll do more to help his case than you might know. So promise me that you'll provide some moral support for him, okay?"

"Okay. Is there anything more, Mr. Cummings?" asked Susan. "I'd kinda like to be getting back home now. It's getting late, and lately there's been a lot of fog on the coastal road at night."

"No, of course. I didn't mean to keep you." As Joel got up from his chair he looked at Susan as compassionately as he could. "It's going to be all right now. There's no need to worry. It won't help -- and believe me, Mark will be able to sense that you're worried. So you be strong for us all. And be careful heading back home. Thanks again for coming by."

As he walked her out to the door, Joel looked over at Marge and saw that she appeared to be as upset as Susan was. When the office was again empty of visitors, he turned to his secretary and said, "We've got a lot of work to do, Marge. But I'm not at all sure that it's going to make any difference in the final analysis unless we come up with a smoking gun."

The arraignment had taken less than five minutes. Mark was brought into the courtroom, where he sat beside his counsel and did as he was told. He did not look at the spectators, except for a brief moment to be sure that Susan was there. Her smile let him know that he was not alone in the room, which was otherwise packed with people whose main goal at the moment was to get a good look at the man who killed one of their own. But other than that there was little for them to see. Judge Pinkston, in his usual manner, quickly took the bench, read the title of the case, and noted for the record that all counsel were present, as was the defendant, who was present with his attorney, Joel Cummings.

"We're here today to accept the defendant's plea in this case," barked Judge Pinkston. "Mr. Abramson, have you had an opportunity to consult with your attorney?"

"I have, your honor," answered Mark, as he stood beside his attorney.

"And what plea would you like to enter to the charge of first-degree murder for the death of Ed Baker?"

"Not guilty, your honor," was Mark's answer.

"Very well, then. Have the parties entered into discovery?"

"We have, your honor," said Andrew Smallwood. "Mr. Cummings has provided me with a written demand for discovery, and I am in the process of getting that together at this time. I expect to have it to him within a couple of days at the most."

"Okay. Mr. Cummings, I assume that you will comply with the State's discovery requests as well."

"Of course, your honor."

"Okay then. Why don't we do this. I'm going to set this case for a status conference in one month. We'll see where we are then. In the meantime the defendant will remain in the county jail. That's all for now."

As the judge rose from the bench and exited the courtroom, Mark turned to Susan and told her that he loved her. He was then escorted out of the door and back to the jail to await the next stage of his case.

"The nerve of that man to say he didn't do it," someone in the audience yelled for Mark to hear as he was being taken away. The crowd collectively mumbled its approval of the remark as Susan and Joel made their way out of the courtroom as quietly and uneventfully as possible.

On Tuesday morning when the mail arrived, Marge anxiously opened one package. Given its size and the fact that it came from the state attorney's office, she rightly assumed that it had to be a copy of the police file on the Baker murder. Marge, like her boss, had been on pins and needles waiting to see what information the state attorney had that could be so damaging to a client whom Joel wanted to believe was innocent. Most seasoned attorneys and their support staffs quickly learned not to put too much hope in the client's innocence. Rather, they knew to look for the strengths and weaknesses of the case – to be professional and detached. That is what would win most cases. But Joel Cummings was hardly a seasoned attorney, and at this stage of his career he wanted to believe that the person he was representing was innocent of this horrendous murder. Not only did it add to the excitement of it all, but it also made it much easier to sleep at night.

"Joel, the discovery's here!" yelled Marge into her boss's office. "Look's like quite a bit of stuff. The photos are here, too."

As he rose from his desk Joel felt his heartbeat increase. This stuff was exciting. Real Perry Mason type law. Never in his wildest dreams would he have believed that he would be doing this sort of thing so soon after graduating from law school.

"Here, let me see it, Marge," said Joel as he walked to her desk. "Any good pictures in there?"

"Yeah, but you don't want to see them if you just ate," Marge said. "They're pretty bad."

"Tell you what," said Joel, "how about getting Ron in here and we'll all sit down and go over this stuff together. When's he supposed to be in today, anyway?"

"He should be in within the hour, I believe," answered Marge. "I believe he was going Christmas shopping at the mall for a few hours first."

"Well, I've got news for him," mumbled Joel. "He better get it out of his system pretty quickly, because I've got a feeling that we're about to become very busy. Let me know when he comes in, will you? In the meantime I'm going to take a look at what we've got here."

"Sure boss. Whatever you say."

As he pored over the sheriff's case file, Joel was struck by the thoroughness of the detectives' work. None of the cases he'd seen thus far in his practice had been worked this thoroughly. But then again, those were not murder cases, or "death cases" as

Smallwood seemed to like to call them. What's more, the fact that the case had been so exhaustively analyzed meant that it would probably be that much more difficult to win.

"I hear that we got some goodies today," Ron said, breaking the relative quiet of the office. "How's it look? Anything good?"

"Yeah, if you're Andrew Smallwood it looks fanfriggentastic," was Joel's immediate response. "Man, I've been reading this stuff for the past hour and I haven't seen one thing that's particularly helpful. At least nothing we didn't already know. Hey, Marge, how's about coming in here so we can get started on this beast, okay?"

"On my way," came the anticipated reply. "I thought you'd never ask."

After a few hours of looking at mundane police reports and disgusting autopsy photographs, the three members of Mark's legal team were tired. Tired and frustrated. On the one hand, it was obvious that the authorities had meticulously worked the evidence they'd found at the crime scene. The position of the body, the blood at the scene, the lack of robbery as a motive, and the failure to locate the murder weapon, -- all of it had been well documented. The autopsy appeared to be equally thorough. Ed's body was photographed from head to toe. The severed windpipe was photographed at close range, as were the fourteen other stab wounds to the victim's body. Of course, in typical police fashion, a ruler had been laid by each stab wound before the picture was taken so that the jury could get a feel for the size of each wound. Cause of death was asphyxiation. Cause of the conviction would be juror horror.

On the other hand, it became equally apparent that there was no evidence that directly linked Mark to the victim. No footprints, no fingerprints, no blood on any of his clothes. And, of course, he had consistently denied any involvement to detectives Langdon and Richards. With nothing but indirect, or circumstantial, evidence to support their case, Joel sensed that his client's future would ultimately depend upon the strengths of the arguments presented by each side. It just might be possible to win, he thought to himself. But at the same time he had to acknowledge to himself that the circumstantial evidence was strong, so much so that he himself wasn't predisposed to believing his client.

"Ron," he said to his assistant. "I want you to interview every witness listed by the State. That includes the detectives. And if possible I want you to speak to Mrs. Baker as well. Surely her husband made some enemies while he was in business. Nobody is that clean."

"When do you need it?" Ron asked.

"In two weeks, if not sooner," answered Joel.

"But Mr. Cummings, Christmas is right around the corner, and I was planning to go out of town on break. You know, we talked about it. I was going back home to see my family."

"In two weeks!" shot back an obviously irritated Joel. "I know what we discussed. But I also know that I've got a status conference coming up with the judge, and if experience is any guide he's gonna want to move ahead with the trial. And besides that, there's a man sitting in a cell in St. Bartholomew who I dare say would love to be able to go home to *his* family about now, but he's not going to get the chance, either. In fact, if we don't do our job right he's *never* going to see his home again. So don't give me excuses. Do I make myself clear?"

"Yes sir," said Ron. "I'll get right on it. Sorry to bring up about the break. I didn't mean anything by it."

The status conference with Judge Pinkston gave Joel another opportunity to head to the coast for a change of scenery. With his caseload on an ever-constant increase, matched only by the increasing demands of Mark's case, Joel was soon feeling overwhelmed by the responsibility. Thank goodness I don't need a lot of sleep, he thought to himself.

Judge Pinkston's status conferences were informal and cordial. But they were not to be mistaken for social events. The judge expected all attorneys to be present and to be prepared. He also expected all parties to abide by his orders, regardless of how unfair one might consider them to be on occasion. Joel, having previously tried two other cases before the judge, was thus well aware of his obligations when he arrived for the conference on that chilly January morning.

"Mr. Cummings, how do you do?" Judge Pinkston greeted the young attorney. "As you can see, Mr. Smallwood is here, so I suppose we can get started. This shouldn't take too long, I guess."

"I wouldn't think so, your honor," replied Joel.

"Well, what do you boys have for me today?" inquired the judge. "Where are we on this case? Any plea agreements in the making?"

"My client is not interested in a plea agreement, your honor," said Joel. "We don't feel the facts are sufficiently strong to justify a manslaughter conviction, much less a conviction for first-degree murder."

"Okay, I suppose that's your client's prerogative," stated the judge rather abruptly. "But I would guess that the state attorney's office would see things differently."

"We would indeed, your honor," answered Smallwood. "We feel quite strongly that this is a first-degree murder case, your honor. Just look at the brutality of the killing. But it is for just that reason that we would concur with Mr. Cummings that a plea agreement is not in order. The people of the state of Florida demand justice in this case, and that is best served by a trial on the merits."

"All right, all right. Tell you what. You boys save it for the jury, since it sounds like that's where we're headed. And since that's the case I guess we need to set a trial date. How long do you fellows think you'll need?"

"Probably two weeks, I'd think," said Joel.

"No way," countered Smallwood. "Judge, I think we can get this done in a week, max."

"Now Mr. Smallwood," replied Pinkston. "This man is on trial for his life. You wouldn't be telling me that you don't think he should be given his day in court, would you?"

"No, judge, that's not what I'm saying, but . . ."

149

"Very well, then. The trial will be set for the two-week period beginning the first full week of March. That's the third, I believe. . . . Now, are there any motions outstanding at this time?"

"None for the State, your honor," said Andrew.

"Your honor, we have none either," added Joel.

"Your honor, there is one thing I'd like to mention, if I may," said Andrew. "I've been hearing a lot of talk from defense counsel about how his client isn't guilty, he wasn't even at the scene of the crime, et cetera Well, if that is the case I would expect him to be claiming that he has an alibi. But so far I haven't seen a notice of alibi and, as your honor is well aware, the Florida Rules of Criminal Procedure require that such a notice be filed. So at this point I guess I'm forced to move the court to exclude any evidence of an alibi."

"What?" a startled Joel shot back. "What are you talking about, excluding an alibi? You very well know that my client intends to claim an alibi. And you've known it since the first day that we spoke about the case!"

"Judge, the rules are the rules," Andrew pressed. "I move the court to exclude the alibi."

"Judge, I agree that the rules are the rules, but if you exclude the alibi my client has no case. I was unaware that I had to file a formal notice."

"Well, Mr. Cummings, I suggest that you read the Florida Rules of Criminal Procedure, and that you read them soon, because this is a criminal case, and in my courtroom we follow the rules. Now, I'll tell you what, I'm going to deny Mr. Smallwood's motion, but don't let me catch you doing this again or I might not look so kindly on your client's cause. Do I make myself understood, Mr. Cummings?"

"Yes, your honor, and I apologize to the court. I'll file the formal notice as soon as I get back to my office."

"Very well, then. Is that all gentlemen?"

"It is," replied both men in unison.

"Then you fellows have a nice day."

As he lay on the bunk in his cell that night, Mark stared at the ceiling and did something he'd tried hard not to do. He contemplated the future. His future. He had learned from his first incarceration not to think about such things, but after this arrest he had caught himself doing it again. Nevertheless he had successfully taught himself to stay away from such excursions of the mind. But try as he might, the thoughts always returned when something happened on his case.

This night was no different. Joel had come by to see Mark after the status conference and had relayed the judge's decision to begin the trial on March Third. It was little more than six weeks away. Six more weeks and hopefully this would all be over.

But then again, March Third could signal the beginning of the end for the prisoner. After all, as his mind kept reminding him, he had believed in the system once before when Jim had gotten him mixed up in that robbery. It was clear, he thought, that Jim was the only person responsible for that crime. But Mark had paid for it with three years of his life. No, he couldn't, he wouldn't, be overconfident this time around.

Still, as he lay on his bunk listening to the incessant talking of cellmates, Mark knew that he had to be at least somewhat optimistic if he were to stand any chance of winning. He would need to help his attorney. And equally important, he would have to be strong for his wife. He could do it; he'd done it before. Just keep focused. That's all it would take.

"Hey, keep it down!" yelled Mark from his bunk. "Some of us are trying to think down here."

"Think about what, man?" was the answer he received from another ward of the State. "You got nothing to think about besides walkin' that big walk. 'Cause you ain't gettin' outta here, man. Ain't gonna happen no way, no how."

Sure it will, Mark thought to himself. Sure it will. And then he drifted off to a better place, beyond the limitations of his four cell walls.

Five miles away Susan lay on her bed and looked out the window at the night sky. It was so pretty this time of year, when the air was cold and the everything seemed clearer. You could easily count the stars when the moon wasn't full. And if you listened real hard, sometimes you could even hear the waves beating against the shore. Most nights she, like her husband, managed at least partially to succeed in thinking about things other than the case. But tonight, again like Mark, she couldn't clear her mind of the approaching trial. What would it be like? Would Mark hold up well? What would happen to him? And most of all she found herself wondering what her husband was thinking about at that time.

As Susan looked out the window and saw the tall pine trees reaching to the sky, with their needles swaying in the wind she felt as if she also had no choice but to go wherever the current events led her. She sensed from past experience that there would be little that she could do for Mark. He was caught up in the system now. And as she had heard all too often, once the system has you it doesn't let go. So if that were the case, the awful possibility existed that her husband would be convicted of Ed's murder. And regardless of the jury's decision on his fate, it was equally clear that she and her husband may never again have a life together. "No, you can't think like that," she found herself mumbling. But try as she might the thought persisted. And with that thought came the equally troubling admission that she might not be strong enough to get through all of this. Was she expected to give up her life too?

No, I have to think positively, Susan continued to tell herself. Mark is innocent. He has a good lawyer who seems to care about him and who wants to do the right thing by him. It's all a big mistake and once the jury sees Mark and comes to understand his ways, they'll know for certain that he is not the right man. It has to work out that way. It has to.

But not far from Susan's home another woman lay on a bed and looked out at the same clear sky. And like Susan, Katherine Baker's thoughts also traveled far beyond the confines of her home. Katherine also thought about her husband. But unlike Susan, Katherine's thoughts were not allowed to contemplate life when her husband returned home. To the contrary, her thoughts were captive to demons that insisted on Katherine's living -- and reliving -- her husband's murder every night. The slashing, penetrating knife continued on its mission until its victim finally surrendered to its seeming omnipotence. And with each victory of the knife Katherine's mind traveled from the blade to the hand holding it, to the arm, the shoulder, the neck, and ultimately the face of Mark Abramson. It was a face that laughed and writhed with unbelievable pleasure at the unspeakable horror that it was witnessing. And then, almost as if on cue, she would see the face in that courtroom, where it uttered the words that she detested with every fiber in her body: not guilty!

Katherine Baker had never understood how someone could be so preoccupied with something as horrible as the murder of a loved one. Now, with Ed gone but a few short months, she could not understand how anyone could ever be freed from the pain and anguish inflicted by such an event. Her life was over. It had ended with the last futile breath that her husband took at the hands of his assassin. She only hoped that she would live to see the day when Mark Abramson's life was ended with the same measure of pain that her beloved husband had felt at his hands.

It was indeed a cold January night upon which the moon kept vigil over these three souls, and wept for the troubles that were sure to come to each tortured soul, when the sun pierced the stillness of the night sky.

Back in his office the next morning, Joel looked at his calendar and wondered how he would ever be able to prepare for what he knew would be the most important trial of his life. He had first met his client little more than a month ago and already the judge was forcing him to go to trial in a month and a half. He had never before seen a case move through the system so quickly. So why then didn't you oppose the court's decision to go to trial so soon, he asked himself. Instead, he had sat by like a lamb and even agreed to the rapidity with which his client's journey toward justice would proceed. "Ron!" he yelled to his assistant, "we'd better talk when you get a chance."

"What is it, boss?" inquired the young law student, who had been dutifully pouring over police records.

"You heard me say this morning that we go to trial beginning March the third, didn't you?" asked Joel.

"Sure did. And it looks to me like we'll be in pretty good shape. I've reviewed all of the sheriff's reports and talked to everyone who would talk to me. It doesn't look to me like there's much left to do."

"Okay. Whom have you talked to again?" Joel asked. "I thought you were having trouble with people."

"I have been. Really the only people who would talk to me are Susan Abramson, the two detectives, and the medical examiner. No one else would even return my call."

"Have we gotten any new information?"

"No. The sheriff's reports seem to be pretty much accurate. Everything checks out. And I haven't been able to locate anyone who can give me an alibi for Mark."

"What about the murder weapon? Was it ever found?"

"Nope."

Thank God for small favors, Joel thought to himself. At least one thing's going our way. "Were you ever able to talk to Katherine Baker?" he asked his assistant.

"No, I tried a couple of times, but it's useless."

"Okay, then. I guess we really have no choice but to go into depositions cold. I'd really hoped that we would have at least some idea what they were saying before they appeared. Just keep trying."

"We'll do, boss," said an obviously confident Ron as he turned and walked out the door.

"Joel, it's Susan Abramson on line two," yelled Marge. "She sounds upset."

So what else is new, thought Joel to himself as he picked up the receiver. "Susan, how nice to hear from you. What's on your mind?"

"Nothing really," came the concerned wife's reply. "I was just wondering if anything new has developed in Mark's case. Have you been able to find anyone who can give him an alibi yet?"

"Not yet, Susan, but we're still trying. We're doing everything that we can. Believe me."

"No, no. Don't misunderstand me, Mr. Cummings. I didn't mean to suggest that you weren't doing everything possible. I was just wondering if maybe something had turned up. Kinda hoping that it would, you know."

"I know, Susan. But so far we're running up against brick walls. I'm hoping that we can get some more leads when we take some of these people's depositions."

"When's that again?"

"They start early next week, and I expect that they'll go most of the week." answered Joel. "I'll let you know as soon as I hear anything new, okay?"

"Okay. I'm sorry to bother you, Mr. Cummings. I know you're busy." said Susan, who had obviously been crying as she sniffled into the receiver.

"What was that?" asked Joel. "I thought we had an agreement to call me Joel and not Mr. Cummings. And there you go again breaking our agreement." Hopefully some levity will help, he thought to himself.

"Yeah, I know," came the shaky response on the other end of the line. "But I just have a hard time with it. I'll try and remember next time."

"Okay then. I'll tell you what. I'd better run along for now. But in the meantime you try not to worry, okay Susan? It's going to be all right. I promise."

"Okay. I'll try. Thanks again, Mr. Cummings. You have a nice day."

"Good-bye Susan," answered Joel as he hung up the receiver. "She's going to take it really bad if Mark is convicted," he mumbled to himself as he returned to the file.

As he drove back to St. Bartholomew on Monday morning Joel felt uneasy about the proceedings that would be underway in little more than two hours. He had taken plenty of depositions in the past, but for some reason this time it felt different. It was the magnitude of the case, he guessed. Try as he might he was increasingly having to deal with the thoughts of what would happen if his client were convicted.

Much to Joel's liking, the press had at least been relatively quiet in the weeks following Mark's arrest. Of course there had been the obligatory articles reporting the results of the few hearings that had been held to date, but nothing out of the ordinary. Actually the press coverage had been rather even-handed, at least more so than expected. Maybe things wouldn't be so bad after all, he thought.

The neutral press coverage helped Joel confidently enter this week of depositions. He would need the confidence, because the week promised to be filled with work. So much so that he had decided to stay at one of the local motels each night, rather than returning home. His office staff, that is to say Marge, would just have to get along without him. She wouldn't like it, especially since she'd already been overtly concerned about the lack of time spent on other cases. But with a case of this magnitude there was little choice. And he had juggled things around with amazing dexterity thus far. Just a little while longer and all of this would be over and he could return to what he now realized was a relaxed, though in many ways inconsequential, law practice. For now, however, it was time for him to show a certain assistant state attorney that he was no pushover.

His confidence notwithstanding, Joel was glad when the week ended. He had begun the last day, Friday, by checking out of the small motel that had in many ways become his home. I could get used to life down here, he thought to himself as he looked out over the St. Bartholomew River that meandered past the motel parking lot. But he knew that behind the dutiful smiles that had greeted him that week were feelings of reluctance at having to give aid and comfort to him. He was the guy who was charged with the responsibility of helping the man who had so brutally butchered a valued member of the community. So as he placed the paid room receipt in his coat pocket and walked to his car, Joel was not at all unhappy to be closer to the return trip to Tallahassee.

The depositions that Joel had hoped would provide him with the tangible leads to show real progress in the case had instead proven uneventful. The detectives had almost gleefully recounted their investigative steps, all of which were meticulously documented and seemingly unassailable. Jacki Pierson had likewise been of little help. She had provided substantial details about finding Ed's body, but nothing that could give Ron anything new to look into. The evidence technicians dutifully retraced their collection of all of the evidence, including Ed's blood, photographs, fingerprints that provided dry leads, as well as their overall observations at the crime scene on that last tortured day of Ed's life. And finally, Katherine Baker described her last conversation with her husband and then the visit from the authorities, during which she learned that Ed's life had been taken from her at the hands of a vicious killer, whom she now knew to be Joel's client. The hatred was palpable in the room through much of the two hours that Joel spent with Katherine on that Friday. He was truly glad when he was able to tell her that he had no further questions to ask her at that time. And with that he again walked out into the sunshine, got into his car, and drove over to the county jail to see his client one more time before returning to his home to prepare for the trial.

"Hello, Mark," Joel said to his client has he walked into the visiting room. "It's a little bit cold in here today, isn't it?"

"Yeah, I guess so," answered Mark, who for the first time since he had known Joel was beginning to feel uneasy about the possible outcome of his pending trial. "It's hardly ever the right temperature in here. . . . But then again, I guess they ain't real concerned about little things like that, you know."

"I guess not," answered Joel. "Are you all right, Mark? You look pretty ragged around the edges today. You're not getting hassled in here are you?"

"No. No real hassles. I'm just getting a little bit shaky, I guess. The closer this thing gets the more nervous I seem to get, you know."

"Yeah, I guess I can understand that. But look Mark, the case is going fine. There were no surprises from the depositions, and that's the main thing."

"Well, that's good . . . I guess. But if there were no surprises then I guess that means there also are no more leads, huh?"

asked Mark showing concern. "I mean, when you started this week you said that you were going to find where the weaknesses were in their case. I take it that if the depos only told you what you already knew, then we're still left with nothing. Or am I missing something?"

"Yes and no, Mark," said Joel. "You're right we don't have any fresh leads. But at the same time the State still doesn't have a murder weapon, and they still have no one to place you at the scene. They have no direct evidence linking you to the crime. And that's a real problem for them."

"That's nice, I suppose," replied Mark. "But I guess we still have no one who can give me an alibi. Correct?"

"Correct. My investigator has looked everywhere, Mark. We are simply going nowhere with that."

"So then, I have to testify," stated Mark matter-of-factly. "I've been thinkin' about that for a while now, Joel, and I really think that there's no choice about that."

"Mark, you can't," said Joel. "We've gone over this before. If you testify you're going to open yourself up to a vicious cross-examination, and in my opinion you'll probably do more harm to your case than good. I really don't want you on the stand."

"Well, what am I supposed to do then, man? I might as well just invite them to convict me. Hell, I'll just go ahead and plead guilty right now and get it all over with! I mean, if I'm supposed to give up I just as well do it right!"

"Now Mark, we're not giving up. . . It's just that . . ."

"It's just what, man? It's just nothin'. It's just that I don't have a case and I'm gonna take the fall for somebody else, just like I did with Jim. But this time I won't be back out in a few years. This time I'll be in it for life, or worse!"

"Mark, listen to me. In the first place you're not gonna be convicted, okay? But even if you are convicted they're not gonna get the death penalty on you. They have no evidence linking you to the crime. And no jury's gonna send someone to death row if they aren't sure that the guy did it. And in this case there's no way that the jury can be sure, even if they do convict you. So just calm down now and we'll get through this."

"Calm down? . . . Calm down?" Mark looked at Joel with a look that telegraphed his disbelief. "Listen to me, *lawyer*. I'll calm down when I'm good and ready to *calm down*. And until you're sittin' where I am right now, I never want to hear you tell me to *calm down*. Do you understand?"

"Yeah, I understand, Mark," answered Joel. "Tell you what. I've got to be heading back now. Why don't we both think through things again. See if there are any new angles that we haven't thought about, okay? . . . And Mark, trust me. We're doing everything that we know to do in order to win this thing."

"Uh-huh. . . . Tell you what, Mr. Cummings. I'll be more than happy to trade places with you any day of the week. 'Cause if this is the best you can do, then I'm worse off than I thought." Mark stared at his attorney for a few seconds to let the words hit their target, and then yelled to the guard as he rose from his seat. "Hey, guard, we're done in here. Take me back."

The look Mark gave Joel was one of utter hatred. It was one that Joel had never seen before in any of his clients. It was one that he hoped he would never see again. Regardless, he managed to stretch out his hand to his client as if to signal that all was forgiven. But not surprisingly, the distraught client walked through the door and back down the corridor to his cell without so much as acknowledging that the attorney was present. Joel picked up his notes, threw them in his briefcase, walked out of the room, and headed for his car with the express intention of forgetting, at least for the moment, the name of Mark Abramson. With the windows rolled down and the stereo blasting, he pointed the car north and depressed the accelerator.

The next morning came all too soon for Joel until he slowly remembered that it was a Saturday. Not that he would have much, if any, reprieve from work. But at least he wouldn't be hounded by the incessant ringing of the phone. And he also wouldn't be restricted by having to do battle with the clock. Given the state of his office and his schedule, these little amenities counted for more than he ever would have thought possible. And what the heck, as long as he was going to take advantage of those creature comforts he might as well go for it all and eat breakfast at less than warp speed.

As Joel lazily puttered around in his kitchen he couldn't help but dwell upon the argument he had had with Mark the previous afternoon. I wonder if I would feel any different if I were in his position, he thought to himself. Standing there bent over the counter measuring the tomatoes, peppers, and onions to be added into his omelet, Joel tried to think about what life must be like for his client. How would it feel to be on trial for your life? He had to admit that it was pretty heavy stuff. Just thinking about it made him uncomfortable.

After finally preparing what by anyone's standards would be a fine breakfast, Joel sat down and polished it off while listening to the radio. No point in reading the paper; there's hardly ever anything good in it anyway, he thought to himself. Besides, I need something upbeat in my life. So he let the music into his thoughts -- quite a difficult ticket to come by lately, as anyone who knew him surely was aware.

It was not long into his hard-won excursion into relaxation that he was brought back to reality by a knock on his front door. It was not an unusual knock. Pretty typical, actually. But it was a knock nonetheless, and at this moment it wasn't welcome. Compounding the irritation was the knock's failure to go away. And so, sensing that there was really no choice but to acknowledge the knock's supremacy, which he counted as almost equivalent to that of the ring of the telephone, Joel acquiesced to its demand and opened the front door.

"Well, it certainly took you long enough," said Marge. "I didn't get you up or anything, did I?"

"No, not at all. I was just eating breakfast."

"Good. . . . I started to call first, but I figured you might be asleep."

"So you decided to come right on over and wake me up in person, is that it?" asked Joel, with a slight smile on his face. "Or could it have been that you really were just nosy about what happened with the last of the depos? . . . Come on in while you're trying to figure out an answer."

"Guess you're right. I didn't come all the way over here to wake you up personally. . . ."

"Ahh, what a shame. I haven't been personally awakened in a long time."

"You know what I mean, Mr. Igit," Marge shot back. "What I was going to say was that I would like to know what happened the last two days in St. Bartholomew. Did we get anything good, I hope?"

"Hardly," Joel answered. "Katherine Baker imitated an iceberg through most of her depo. She gave me nothing. To hear her tell it, her dearly departed Ed was a virtual saint. You can expect the Pope to invest him within a matter of days. And since Ed was so perfect, no one would have wanted to harm him in any way. Except our three-eyed client, of course."

"But of course," said Marge.

"The rest of the depos were as productive as Baker's. Bottom line, Marge, is that we have no leads that I can see. Nothing. The only thing I thought was interesting was that the detectives seemed pretty squirrelly when talking about Mark's statement to them. They danced around it so many times I was getting motion sickness. But I don't see any basis to suppress anything. Like I said, I just didn't get much."

"Could have been worse," suggested Marge. "At least nothing pointed to Mark's guilt. . . . I assume."

"No, nothing except what we already knew," sighed Joel. "You know, Marge, I almost feel like it would be easier if we knew the guy did it. But the way this is shaping up, everything is circumstantial, there's no direct evidence linking him to the crime, he steadfastly denies any involvement, and I don't think I can prove that he's telling the truth."

"You don't have to prove anything, remember that," said Marge. "You've told me over and over that it's the State's burden to prove the defendant's guilt. . . . So believe in what you've been telling me. How 'bout it?"

Joel looked at Marge and smiled. "Thanks," he said. "I appreciate what you're saying. And I guess I really do believe what I've been saying about that, but it sure doesn't seem like that's the way everything works. . . . By the way, you want a cup of coffee? I just made it."

"Sure, why not?"

"Why don't we sit outside on the porch?" said Joel, as he reached for a cup. "It seems to have warmed up some from what it was yesterday. It was pretty cold down there with the sea breeze and all."

As they walked to the door and onto the porch, Marge couldn't help but notice that something seemed to be bothering her boss. For the first time since he had taken this case, or any case for that matter, he appeared to be defeated. It wasn't like him. "So what's bothering you?" she asked.

"Whadda ya mean?" came the anticipated reaction. "Nothing's bothering me."

"Oh, yeah? Well, why then are you staring off into space like you're trying to communicate with extra terrestrials? Did I not comb my hair this morning or something?"

"Well, I was kinda wondering about that," he quietly replied with a smile. "But no, it's not your hair. . . . At least that's not all of it."

"Okay, wise guy. And push me much further and the term will become more derogatory. Am I going to have to pry this one out of you? Or are you going to give it up peacefully?"

"I don't know, Marge," said Joel. "I've just been thinking about all of this. About Mark. And you know, I really don't think I'm up to it. I mean, this guy's future is literally on the line right now, and here I am, four weeks away from trial, and I don't have squat. In fact, I've got less than squat. And the forecast is for continued squat with a mixture of crap thrown in for good measure. . . . I just don't know if I can do this or not."

"Whadda you mean, 'I just don't know if I can do this or not'?" bristled Marge. "In case you don't recall, you've been the one out front on this case since you got it. You've organized us all and you've gotten the job done so far. . . . It's not your fault if the evidence isn't there, Joel. How many times have I heard you say that you take the case as you find it? Huh? How many times? . . . So what's really going on?"

"I don't know," Joel said. "I guess I'm just getting stage fright, that's all. . . . You know, I don't think it'll be long before we start getting some pretty nice weather around here. I think I saw a robin the other day. Scooter must've seen something too, because he was sitting in the window for the longest time swishing his tail. He doesn't usually do that unless there's enough meat on the bird to make it worthwhile. . . . So I figure it must've been the robin."

"Yeah, diversion, Cummings. I love hearing about Scooter. But unfortunately I don't think your cat has much to do with this case. At least I hope he doesn't."

"I don't know -- sometimes I think he could be a help. Marge, did you ever want something so bad, but knew deep down that it wasn't going to happen?" As he walked to the side of the porch Joel looked out over the yard, its live oaks draped with Spanish moss glistening in the morning sun. "I never told you, Marge, but all my life I wanted to handle one of these cases. All my life. I mean, it's like the most thrilling work that I can think of. The stakes are huge. . . . And so here I am. I have the case and there's not a thing I can do right. And if I screw up, my client could die. . . . You know what he told me yesterday, Marge?"

"No, what?" answered Marge, realizing that something had in fact happened to cause her boss's sudden anxiety.

"Mark told me that if I can't do any better than this then he'll lose the case. Marge, the man looked at me like he hated my guts."

"And so, you automatically figure that he's right and you're wrong, is that it? Well, let me tell you something, Joel. In the first place, you're the one who's been through school and knows how to handle these things. Not your client. You're the one who's seen all of the evidence. And you're the one who's tried cases. Now listen to me, you've worked your butt off for Mark Abramson and he should be grateful for it. But if you listen to him and it causes you to screw up, he'll be right. He will lose the case. So you'd better get back in control and try this case like you know how. . . . Besides that, I suspect that your client is pretty scared about now. Think about it, Joel. You said you were getting stage fright. And you've been through trials before. Don't you think Mark Abramson has to be terrified? I would be. And that probably explains why he said whatever he said. So don't let it get to you. You'll probably hear a lot worse before the trial is over."

"Yes, mother."

"Don't 'yes, mother' me, Joel. You know I'm right. So just get it together and move on. You have a client who's depending on it."

"I know that, Marge, but you know, what if we lose? What then?" Joel said as if his secretary was bound to have the answers.

"What then?" answered Marge. "Well, I guess if nothing else you'll know you did your best. That is, assuming you do your best. If you continue to throw these pity parties then you'll lose the case *and* know that you did your client a disservice. Now, I don't think we want that, do we?"

"No, I don't guess we do," said Joel. "So I guess we'd better get to work, huh?"

Marge looked at him and shook her head. "I suppose *we* could get to work, if that's what you want to do. But as long as you're listening to me, let me give you some more advice. Why don't you take the day off. Shoot, take the whole weekend off. Seems to me like Joel Cummings needs some time to sit back on his porch and look for that robin he saw the other day. And besides that, Scooter seems like he's pretty starved for attention."

"I can't do that, Marge, there's . . ."

"There's too much work to be done. Yeah, I know. I've heard it before, Joel. And it seems to me that since I've known you there's always been too much work to do, but despite that the work has always gotten done. So I suggest that you forget about it for a while and think about Joel first. Do you understand?"

"Yes, mother. I understand," answered Joel as sarcastically as he could manage.

"And one other thing," said Marge, "I'm *not* your mother. But if you like I'll get her over here. I know where she lives, Joel, so you'd better listen to me now."

"All right. All right," came the sought-after response. "But it's only because Scooter is lonesome."

"Fine. Whatever. I don't care what the reason. Just stay away from that office today so I don't have to go visit you at a mental institution when all of this is over. Gosh, what am I gonna do with you? Huh?"

"Right now you're gonna let me sit and relax by myself so that I'm well rested on Monday," quipped Joel.

"Fine. I guess you're right. Once again I've solved another problem. You know, I don't understand why I'm so gifted. It's been this way all my life," said Marge as she walked back through the house toward the front door. "But I guess some things are just not meant to be understood by mere men."

"Yeah. That's it, Marge. It's a gift. And I guess I should be grateful for it, huh?"

"It's taken you this long to figure that out?" answered Marge. "I thought you were brighter than that, Joel. Maybe you *had* better keep working this weekend, after all." Smiling as she said it, she turned and walked to her car. "When you win that really big case that actually pays you a fee, I want a raise so that I can dump this old rolling wreck, Mr. Bigshot Attorney."

"We'll see, Marge. Take it easy. I'll see you on Monday." Joel closed the door, walked back to his coffee, and looked back out at the birds in the yard. "Scooter, where did I lay those depo files, anyway?"

Scooter didn't respond.

CHAPTER XIX

Two weeks before the trial was to begin, Joel was busy immersing himself in the final preparations. Jury selection would be the first hurdle, perhaps the most important. And as he had already discovered, Joel's task in this phase of the trial would be substantially more complicated than in any routine DUI case. The more he reviewed the law the more he realized that it would take at least two days just to pick a jury. Worse than that, he wondered if they could even find a jury that was impartial. Everyone in this small town, it seemed, knew the victim. Small consolation, but at least most of the investigation is completed, he thought to himself.

But the investigation wasn't complete.

"Joel, we have to talk," an obviously excited Ron said to his boss while opening the office door and walking to Joel's desk.

Turning toward the door, Joel said something inaudible into the receiver and then looked to his assistant. "Just a minute, Ron. I'm on a call."

"Joel, we really need to talk," came the response as Ron shoved papers under his boss's hand. "Better read it."

As he hung up the phone, Joel sensed that he'd better pay attention to Ron. He had learned over the past few months that Ron, as most law students are want to do, was prone to believing that everything was a major problem. Fact was that most of the time the problems were non-existent, or insignificant at the worst. Ron was no exception. But the tone of Ron's voice this time left little doubt that something serious had in fact occurred. So Joel decided that he'd better listen to his assistant. As he quickly realized, Ron's excitement was justified.

"Who the hell is Jonathan Walker?" yelled Joel. "Where the hell did he come from?"

"As you can see," answered Ron, "he's currently housed at the Cortez County Jail with our client. He came from under a rock. And he says that our client, Mark Abramson, confessed to him that he committed the murder!"

"Where did you get this affidavit?" asked Joel.

"Smallwood's office just delivered it. They said that they had just obtained it, but who knows? Isn't that Langdon's signature as the witness?"

"Yeah, looks like it. Listen, get your things. We're heading to St. Bartholomew."

The drive to St. Bartholomew went quickly since Joel wasn't overly concerned about being stopped for speeding. He figured that was the least of his worries at the moment. "Ron," he said to his assistant, "we've got to get this trial continued. There's no way we can walk into that courtroom now and put on a case for Abramson. . . . What I need you to do is prepare a motion for continuance. I need to file it with Pinkston's office tomorrow."

"Sure, but how are we going to get it down here?"

"Somebody's gotta drive it down, I guess. Don't worry about that. Just get it done, okay?"

"Sure."

"And it goes without saying that, depending upon what this new witness tells us, we're going to need a full background check on him. I want to know everything about him, including what he had for dinner yesterday and what he plans to have tomorrow. Understand?"

"Yeah."

"And Ron, we're going to have to have a pretty serious conversation with Abramson. The last time I met with him he was really wired. Wanted to fire me. So this isn't going to be that comfortable. I need you to take very careful notes."

"Okay. . . . Whom are we gonna see first, Joel?"

"Walker. That way we'll be able to deal with Abramson better."

Gaining admittance into the jail was getting to be a piece of cake for Joel. By this time he felt like most of the guards were family, he'd seen them so often. Today was no different, and soon he and Ron were waiting in the visitor's room for the new witness.

As he strolled into the room, Joel could tell right away that Walker had been waiting for them. He was a tall man with a bulky frame. Bad haircut. Bad teeth. Bad complexion. And as he walked to the table he glared at Mark's representatives as if to let them know that this would not be easy.

"Mr. Walker, my name is Joel Cummings and this is my assistant, Ron Braithwright. We represent Mr. Mark Abramson, whom I believe you may know."

"I might."

"Well, Mr. Walker. We have been given what I believe is an affidavit supposedly signed by you. Let me show you the affidavit." As Joel gave a copy of the affidavit to the man, he asked, "Is that your signature, Mr. Walker?"

"Yeah, I think it is," Walker answered.

"And to whom did you give this affidavit, Mr. Walker?"

"Some dude."

"Was it the state attorney?"

"Might have been."

"Was it a deputy Langdon?"

"Might have been."

"Could you tell us how you came to know Mr. Abramson?"

"No."

"Why not, sir?"

"Because, everything I have to say is on that piece of paper. Don't got nothin' else to say."

"So you won't tell us anything else about what's in the affidavit?"

"You're smart, ain't you? Figured that out real quick."

"Mr. Walker, do you understand that if I have to I can have you subpoenaed to give a deposition in this case and you'll have to talk to me then?"

"Whatever you want to do man. I've got plenty of time on my hands."

"Okay, sir. I guess we'll be seeing you later. . . . Guard!" yelled a frustrated Joel. "We're through in here." As Joel turned around to face this new witness he could tell that this man would be extremely hostile to Mark. It was only a question of how much damage he could cause. As Walker left the room Joel looked at the guard with raised eyebrows. "He's a real piece of work, isn't he?"

"You're too kind," said the guard. "You want me to bring Abramson in now?"

"Sure. We might as well make everybody happy today," Ron said. "Why keep the party to ourselves."

As Mark was escorted into the room, he looked at his attorney with sheepish eyes. Their last encounter had been less than friendly, and given the time to think things over, Mark had decided to go a little easy on the man who on second thought was his main hope of survival. His heart nevertheless began to sink when he looked at the two men in front of him. Their countenances were entirely too serious. I hope I didn't irritate him too much, Mark thought to himself.

"Hello Mark," Joel began. "You're looking pretty good today. You look a little more rested than the other day."

"Somewhat, I guess. It's pretty hard to ever get much rest around here, as loud as it is."

"Mark, the reason we're here is that we have something to go over with you. We need your help."

"Yeah, sure. What is it?"

"Do you know a guy named Jonathan Walker?" Ron asked.

"Don't believe so," answered Mark.

"Are you sure?" asked Joel. "Tell you what, when you were brought out here do you remember passing a guy, an inmate, going back to his cell from here?"

"Sure. You mean Waddles?"

"Who? Waddles?"

"Yeah. Big guy. We call him Waddles 'cause he waddles everywhere he goes. Sure, I know him."

"How do you know him, Mark?" asked Ron.

"Just from being out in the exercise yard with him. Plus I see him every now and then at the cafeteria. . . . Why?"

"Mark, there's no easy way to put this," Joel said solemnly. "He's given an affidavit to the state attorney. He says in the affidavit that you told him one day in the yard that you killed Ed Baker. He says that you told him you used a knife and that the police would never find it. . . . Mark, are you listening?"

The room was silent. As Ron and Joel looked at their client, they could see that this news had struck Mark like a bolt of lightning. He was quiet at first, staring straight ahead as if trying to pierce the wall in front of him.

"You're kidding me, man. You're kidding. . . . Tell me you're kidding!" the client finally pleaded.

"We're not kidding, Mark," Joel responded. "Here's a copy of the affidavit. You can read it for yourself."

"I don't care what it says!" shouted Mark. "I have never talked to anyone about my case. *NEVER!* And I ain't never confessed to anyone, 'cause I didn't kill that man. . . . I didn't kill that man, Mr. Cummings!" Suddenly the shouting diminished, then slowly changed to a quiet sobbing. "I didn't kill that man, Mr. Cummings. I ain't never killed anyone. You've got to believe me. You've got to . . ."

"Mark, listen to me. It's gonna be all right. We're gonna get to the bottom of this. But in the meantime I want you to keep your cool, okay?" As Mark nodded his head, Joel continued, "Now I'm going to speak to the guards and ask them to have you moved to a cell away from the other men. It may take a while, but . . ."

"I don't want to go into solitary, man," said Mark.

"I know you don't. But listen to me, Mark. It's for your own good. If you're in solitary it'll prevent anyone else from coming up with this kind of story. And it'll also keep you and Walker from seeing each other. I don't want you to say *anything* to him at all. . . . Do you understand?"

"Yeah. I understand. But I still don't want to go into solitary."

"I know you don't, Mark. But like I said, it's for your own good. . . . Now, one other thing. I'm going to have to ask for a continuance. I've got to depose Walker now, and we've got to get to the bottom of this whole mess. It's in your best interest, Mark."

"Okay. Whatever you say," answered a resigned client.

"Okay then. Now, you keep it together. If you need anything you call me collect. But I don't want to talk about the case over the phone, because the phones are probably monitored. If you want to discuss the case write like you have been. Okay?"

"Okay."

"Good. We'd better go now. We've got a lot of work to do."

As Mark rose and began to walk out of the room, Joel could tell that his client had just been emotionally flattened. It would take time for him to get over this. "We're through here, guard," Joel said as he and Ron also began their exit.

"I believe him," intoned Ron as they got back into Joel's silver Ford Taurus.

"Believe who?" asked Joel.

"Abramson. If he's lying he's one heck of a good actor. Nope, I believe him."

"I know," said Joel. "I'm afraid to say it, but I do, too."

It didn't take more than twenty-four hours for Judge Pinkston to consider the defendant's motion for continuance. He understood the defendant's predicament and the consequent need to conduct further investigation of the facts surrounding this new evidence. But Judge Pinkston was nevertheless a firm believer that a conscientious defense team should require little time to investigate a single issue such as this. Accordingly, although he granted the request, the trial was postponed only until March Seventeenth. Mark's defense team had just over three weeks to prepare their case.

In light of the surfacing of Jonathan Walker, Joel decided that further preparations would be largely worthless until they had a handle on the damage Walker could inflict. As such, his deposition was quickly scheduled -- with the considerable assistance of the state attorney, of course. So, Joel and Ron found themselves back down in St. Bartholomew four days after they originally learned that someone had given birth to a man by the name of Jonathan Walker.

The deposition of Mark's newest enemy took little time. Walker recounted the facts as stated in his affidavit. Upon hearing Mark confess to the crime, he had decided that the proper thing to do would be to bring this evidence to the attention of local law enforcement. He had done this by contacting detective Langdon. Walker told Langdon of a day when he and Mark were in the exercise yard along with several other prisoners. He had taken a liking to his fellow inmate and had begun swapping stories. As they began to talk they eventually got around to discussing their current charges, his being battery and Mark's being murder. To his shock, Mark admitted to him that he had stabbed Mr. Baker in order to get even with him for firing him. It was a chilling recitation of the crime, according to Walker. Mark seemed to be bragging about the crime, possibly in an effort to look tough. He, Walker, expected nothing in return for his testimony. He hadn't even asked for anything. He just wanted to be a good citizen.

Ron's investigation into Walker's past yielded little additional information. While the twenty-three-year-old Walker had been arrested seven times in the past, he had only been convicted five times -- once for shoplifting, three times for cocaine possession, and once for burglary. All total he had spent two years behind bars.

As the trial grew closer, the mood at Joel's office became increasingly desperate, then pensive, then simply despondent. Barring a miracle, the three members of Joel's defense team could see no way that their client could avoid a conviction. Their challenge, they each decided, was to be as upbeat as possible in front of Susan and Mark, and to do everything in their power to prevent what seemed to be inevitable.

The day before the trial began, Joel moved his office to a rented, one-room office in St. Bartholomew. Marge had insisted that she be allowed to accompany Joel and Ron on this journey. The other clients would simply have to understand. So after packing a small U-Haul truck with the essentials, they converged on the small town as quietly as possible. If Andrew Smallwood thought he would get by without a fight on this case, he was wrong, they thought to themselves. This client would receive their best efforts.

As the clock marched relentlessly toward the Seventeenth, Mark and Susan both became increasingly anxious. It was now less than twenty-four hours before the trial was scheduled to begin. Twenty-four hours before Mark would be displayed to the citizens of St. Bartholomew and be judged by them.

Convincing herself that her husband would soon be returned to her and that they would then be able to resume their lives, Susan in many ways looked forward to the approaching days. After all, Joel had repeatedly told her not to worry about the case. That was his job. Susan also knew that the jury would be able to see through the lies that Walker would be telling. And if they didn't believe him, they had no other reason to believe that Mark had done this. She'd tell them herself, if necessary. In the final analysis she believed her husband. He simply was not capable of committing such a horrible crime. Not the Mark she knew.

As she walked into the visitor's room that afternoon, Susan was feeling more confident than she had in weeks. The nightmare was soon to be over.

"How you doin', honey?" she asked Mark as he slowly walked into the room toward the wooden chair next to her.

"Well, I'm still here," came Mark's mumbled response. "So I don't know how I am. How are you doing, anyway?"

"Well, I'm still here," quipped Susan with a smile. "Are you ready for tomorrow?"

"I don't know. Cummings was in to see me today. He and that guy, Braithwright. We worked on the trial all morning."

"That's good, isn't it?" asked Susan. "I mean, that's what you're supposed to do."

"Yeah, I know. It's good that we went through this stuff again. . . . Spent a lot of time on deciding what kind of people we want on the jury. Cummings says that's critical. . . . I don't know, Susan. I guess it's going okay."

"Boy, you sure don't sound like it's okay. What's happened anyway?"

"Nothin' really. It's just that everything seems to be so lopsided against me, Susan. We don't have *anything* that shows that I didn't do this. *Nothing.* It all boils down to how many holes we can poke in the State's case. It was hard enough before, but when this jerk Walker came up with his story . . . Well, I just don't know how we're gonna do it, that's all."

"Mark, listen to me," cajoled Susan, taking her husband's hand in hers. Mark's hand was clammy and cold -- surprisingly so. "You're gonna have to be strong through this. You're gonna get through it. I know you are. And when it's over we're gonna go somewhere away from here. As far away as we can. Just the two of us. And we're gonna forget that this ever happened, okay?"

"Susan, right now I'd settle for just seeing our home again. For crying out loud, I'd be real happy just to see Lone Pine Island again. . . . You remember that time we spent the weekend over there? That was so nice."

"Yes. it was," said Susan. "That reminds me, Eddy stopped by the other day. Said to tell you that he's pulling for you, Mark. He said that everyone felt the same way, that you didn't do this."

"Well, that's nice of him, but he hasn't bothered to come by."

"Yeah, he said that he hadn't been here. He said that he just couldn't bring himself to come over. I don't think he knows what to say, Mark."

"Whatever," Mark said. "You know, Susan, I was thinking about that weekend on the island. We really had a good time, didn't we? . . . The place was so deserted and the water was so calm."

"Yeah, it was real nice, Mark. I never will forget you chasing that sandpiper down the beach. You acted like you really thought you'd catch him. . . . Do you remember that?" Susan asked her husband, who suddenly seemed as though he were miles away.

"Mark?" she said, as she picked up his hand and gently put it in hers. "Are you okay?"

"I guess," Mark answered. "I was just thinking back to those earlier times. Whatever happened to us, Susan? How did this happen?"

"Waddya mean, 'how did this happen'?" questioned Mark's wife. "Things just happen, that's all. And we're gonna get through this, honey. Just be patient."

"Susan, do you think I killed Baker?" asked Mark suddenly.

"What kind of question is that, Mark?" asked Susan. "You know I don't think you could have done that. . . . You know it."

"And you're not just saying that? . . . Susan, I need to know. For real."

"For real. I know you didn't do it," said Susan, squeezing her husband's hand. "And I don't want you to ever ask me that question again. You hear?"

"Sure," Mark said matter-of-factly. "I just needed to know, that's all. . . . Listen, it's getting late. I guess you'd better go so you don't get home too late."

"Yeah, I guess you're right," said Susan, looking at her watch. "I didn't realize it was five o'clock already." As she stood up from her chair she put her arm around Mark's broad shoulders. For so many years he had been the one who had to be strong. Now she realized that it was she who would have to provide that strength. Just let me get him home, she thought to herself. He'll be back to his old self in no time. "Listen, honey, you get some rest tonight, you hear? You're gonna need to be on your toes tomorrow." Mark embraced her for what seemed like minutes until the guard interrupted them. And as he turned to walk away, she quickly took a Kleenex from her purse and wiped the tear from his cheek. "I love you, honey," she quietly said.

"I love you," said Mark. "Please don't forget it." As he raised his handcuffed hands to wave to her, he repeated the plea and began walking down the corridor. "Please don't forget it," she heard him say. The words came back to her over and over during the night. I never will, she thought to herself. I never will.

175

The case of the State of Florida versus Mark Abramson began promptly as scheduled at nine A.M. on March the Seventeenth. The courtroom was packed, as anticipated. Sitting in the front row of the audience on the right side of the courtroom were Katherine Baker and Ed's relatives. Seated throughout the courtroom were numerous supporters of Katherine. To her left and also seated in the front row was Susan. She was alone. If there were any supporters of her and her husband, they were quiet. This was not an occasion to show intense loyalty to the defendant. That much was evident from the moment people began gathering at the courthouse parking lot for what would clearly be the social event of the season.

Suddenly the side door to Susan's left opened and she saw her husband shuffle through the door, accompanied on each side by two heavily armed sheriff's deputies. What in the world do these people expect, she thought to herself as she looked at Mark trying to move forward with his feet in manacles and his hands handcuffed to waistchains. His new blue suit, white shirt, and blue tie really looked nice, even with the security measures imposed on him by the deputies. In fact, it would have been easy to mistake him for the defense attorney were it not for such things. And to her relief, once seated Mark's handcuffs were removed, enabling him to look more human.

Minutes seemed to crawl along now until Susan saw Ron and Marge make their way through the back door with boxes upon boxes of materials. The two members of the defense team walked deliberately to the front of the courtroom and greeted Mark with appropriate smiles for a brief second. Then each turned to Susan and nodded to her as if to say, don't worry we'll take care of everything.

Not long after his assistants' arrival, Joel entered the courtroom just in front of Andrew Smallwood and the prosecution team. Joel followed Ron's and Marge's lead as he approached Mark, shook his hand, and whispered words of encouragement to him.

"All rise," intoned the bailiff in a loud voice that resonated throughout the courtroom. On cue, the door beside the judge's bench opened, allowing for the brisk entrance of the man who would preside over the business at hand. "The Honorable Judge Samuel F. Pinkston, presiding!" continued the bailiff. "Be seated."

"This is the case of the State of Florida versus Mark Abramson," announced the judge. "Let the record reflect that the defendant is present with counsel, Mr. Joel Cummings. The State is represented by the Honorable Andrew F. Smallwood. Are the parties ready to proceed to trial?"

"We are, your Honor," answered both attorneys in unison.

"Very well, then. The first matter of business is jury selection. I believe that you each have copies of the jury panel summoned for this case."

"We do, your Honor," chimed the attorneys.

"Okay, let's get started," said Pinkston. That said, Mark's trial began to unfold in the orderly fashion that all knew would characterize a trial presided over by this no-nonsense judge.

As expected, jury selection took the entire day. The spectators who had come to be entertained soon realized that this would not be the action-packed event that they had expected. No, it was nothing like the shows that all of them had repeatedly watched on television each night. Why, after six hours of listening to what seemed like endless drivel, they had not once seen anyone point an accusatory finger at the defendant to seal his fate. No, all they heard were endless questions about whom the prospective jurors knew, had they read about the case in the paper, did they believe that the defendant was innocent until proven guilty, et cetera.

For Mark, however, the day was sobering. Over and over he had heard questions placed to the jury about their feelings on capital punishment. Disturbing to him were their responses, because with the exception of four men, all thirty of the other prospective jurors repeatedly said that they believed in the death penalty and would have no trouble imposing it if the defendant were found guilty. "They're like robots," Mark whispered to Joel.

The questions continued, and each time a juror indicated some trouble with the death penalty, the prosecutor was quick to tell him that theirs would be only an "advisory opinion" to the judge. It was the judge who would actually sentence the defendant. So they needn't be overly concerned about the impact of their decision. "I thought the judge is basically required to follow the jury's recommendation," Mark asked his attorney. "He is," was Joel's response, "but the jury isn't allowed to know that. I've already told Pinkston I think they need to know it. He won't let me tell them."

Day One ended with a jury being chosen to hear the State's case against Mark Abramson. Nine men and three women. Twelve jurors in all. All twelve firmly believed in the death penalty. All twelve were glad that they didn't actually have the final decision over this man's life or death. It would be easier to sleep that way.

Day Two began with the eagerly awaited opening statements of the attorneys. For each man it was the first opportunity to explain his case to the jury. Andrew Smallwood began the presentations with a passionate assessment of the evidence that he anticipated he'd lay at the feet of the twelve jurors he wanted to persuade. His presentation was masterful in putting together the pieces of what was a very complex puzzle. The skill and persuasiveness with which he accomplished the task were indeed impressive. He concluded his statement confident in the knowledge that he had set the tone for convicting the defendant, while at the same time advancing his own chances at one day becoming the next state attorney for that district.

Joel Cummings, on the other hand, was equally impressive in his summation of the facts. Those facts, he contended, hardly pointed to his client. Rather, taken as a whole they did nothing more than paint his client in a bad light. Beyond that the jury would hear no facts that directly and conclusively linked his client to this horrible crime. His client had been in jail before when he was wrongly charged of a crime. This was nothing more than another feeble attempt on the part of the State to convict an innocent person. Joel spoke eloquently, passionately, as if his client's life depended on it. When he concluded his opening statement, he retired to his table satisfied that he had put the best spin possible on a weak case. The look that he saw in his client's eyes told him that Mark was equally satisfied.

The good feelings felt by both counsel at the conclusion of the opening statements soon dissipated. It was now time to show the jury, as well as the audience, just how horrible a crime the defendant had committed. So the prosecutor began the presentation of witnesses. First came Jacki Pierson to retell the discovery of Ed's mutilated body. It was a gripping tale and hard-hitting in its impact on the jury, particularly when Jacki was shown and identified a photograph of Ed's body lying on the ground in a pool of blood. As Jacki concluded her testimony, the tears began to flow genuinely as she recalled the last time that she saw her beloved boss. To Joel's single question she replied that no, she had not seen Mark near the area when she arrived on that morning. In fact, she hadn't seen him for some time. Nevertheless, she knew that Mark was furious with Ed for having fired him.

The next witness was Bill Langdon. It was the detective's job to describe the crime scene and the significance of the evidence gathered at that spot. Recounting these events in admirable fashion, he next told the jury of his interrogation of the defendant. It was a routine event undertaken only after the defendant had been advised of his rights. The defendant denied any involvement in the crime at first; but, Langdon continued, he finally admitted that he was at the scene!

Hearing this for the first time, Joel jumped to his feet, asked for the jury to be excused and excoriated the prosecution for introducing new evidence into the trial, evidence that he'd never heard of before. "Mr. Cummings, are you saying that the prosecution didn't tell you about this admission?" Judge Pinkston inquired.

"I am, your Honor, and I move the court for a *Richardson* hearing to inquire into the violation!"

"Very well, then, let's look into this," was Pinkston's response. "Mr. Smallwood, did your office advise defense counsel that Mr. Abramson had given a statement to the detective?"

"We did, your Honor," Andrew sheepishly replied.

"And did you, Mr. Cummings, review that statement?" continued Pinkston.

"I did, your Honor."

"Did you depose the witness about that statement, Mr. Cummings?" asked Pinkston.

"He did, your Honor," interrupted Smallwood. "But he never asked detective Langdon about that part of the defendant's statement! I would direct the court to page seventy-six of the detective's deposition, which was taken on January the Sixteenth."

"Your Honor, I didn't ask about it because I had no reason to believe it existed!" snapped Joel. "How can I ask about something I didn't even know existed?"

"Mr. Cummings, that's why they're called *discovery* depositions, to give you an opportunity to discover what the other side knows. Now, if you didn't ask the right questions, that's not the prosecutor's fault here. So I don't see how I can rule in your favor on this. I find that no discovery violation occurred. Bailiff, bring in the jury and let's continue -- hopefully without further interruptions."

Langdon's testimony took little additional time. He had accomplished the task he had set for himself. Joel's cross-examination, passionate as it was, was unsuccessful in illuminating the duplicity in the detective's story. As Langdon stood down from the witness stand, he walked briskly between the opposing camps, looked at Mark and winked. I've got you, and you won't get away until I say so, he seemed to be saying.

The rest of the day's testimony was comparatively uneventful. The coroner confirmed the cause of death being a severed windpipe, together with multiple stab wounds. Detective Richards explained how they had searched Ed's office and found papers indicating that he had fired the defendant shortly before his death. The papers indicated that he had fired Mark because Ed believed that Mark had stolen money from his company. His belief was bolstered by the fact that Mark had a prior conviction for armed robbery.

As Mark sat through the first day of trial, his thoughts increasingly ran to his home, his wife, anything but the courtroom. It's over, he thought to himself. There's no way I can overcome this. There's just no way. The daydreaming was mercifully interrupted by the court's announcement that court would be in recess until the next morning. The next witness was scheduled to be Jonathan Walker.

Day Three. To no one's surprise Walker testified as expected. The defendant, Mark Abramson, had bragged to him about murdering Ed Baker. Mark had even enjoyed the killing, Walker added, while shaking his head as if in disbelief that anyone could be so evil. Walker's shock and outrage at the defendant's actions were visibly shared by the audience most of whom gave intermittent glances toward the defense table in order that they might get one more look at the monster who had extinguished the life of one of their own.

Joel's cross-examination of Walker attempted in vain to secure an admission from Walker that the prosecutor had promised him leniency. The witness, who by now was adept and well prepared for such questions, heroically stood his ground and refuted the allegations brought by the man who was defending the monster.

"The State calls Susan Abramson," announced Andrew Smallwood, to the shock of many in the courtroom.

"Mr. Cummings," whispered Mark anxiously, "what's going on? They didn't say anything about calling Susan, did they?"

"She was on their witness list, Mark," answered Joel, "but we weren't sure whether they'd call her or not. She was aware of it."

"Why didn't anyone tell *me*?" asked Mark. "It would've been nice to know."

"We didn't want to get you upset," said Joel. "It's gonna be all right."

"Ms. Abramson, I just have a few questions for you," began the prosecutor. "First, were you with the defendant on the night that Ed Baker was killed?"

"No."

"Do you know where he was that night?"

"No. But I know that he didn't . . ."

"That's all I needed to know, Ms. Abramson. Thank you. Your witness, Mr. Cummings."

"I have no questions," said Joel.

As Susan stepped down from the stand and walked past Mark, she looked over at her husband and felt the tears begin to come. Her pace quickened as she neared the door at the back of the courtroom. Stepping out into the parking lot she ran to her car, opened the door, and began sobbing uncontrollably.

Inside the courtroom Smallwood called his last witness, Katherine Baker. Katherine, like the witness before her but for very different reasons, was fighting back the urge to cry. She responded to prosecutor's questions describing the last time that she had seen her husband. She had expected him to return that night. To her shame she had fallen asleep with the lateness of the hour, only to awaken the next day with the realization that Ed had not returned home. It was not until Sergeant. Anderson, a friend of Ed's, came to the house and told her about Ed's death that she realized her husband would never return home. Her final act as a witness was to identify Ed's mutilated body in a photograph taken by the coroner.

"I have no questions of this witness," said Joel.

"Then the State rests," announced Smallwood.

"Okay, I believe that'll be all for today," announced judge Pinkston inside the courtroom. "We'll resume tomorrow morning at nine o'clock with the defense case, Mr. Cummings."

Back at the jail that night, Joel, Ron, and Mark discussed Mark's testimony for the following day, while Marge met with Susan in an attempt to console her. "It's not over by a long shot," Marge found herself saying to the distraught wife. "Mark will take the stand tomorrow and tell his side of this. When he gets done the jury will know that he couldn't have committed this crime."

Day Four. As Mark took the stand he felt himself shaking. Every eye in the courtroom was on him. He could feel the stares. He could sense the hatred in the room. He could sense that he was the target of that hatred. He knew this was his one chance to change peoples' perceptions of him. It was a chance that he demanded of his attorney after Langdon's lie to the jury about his confession.

After running through the usual questions to ease his client's mind, Joel began to get to the point. "Mr. Abramson, where were you on the night that Ed Baker died?"

"My wife and I had been arguing because I lost the job. I got mad and went outside and just decided to go for a drive. So I got in my car and headed out of town. I drove and drove for a long time."

"How long?"

"I don't know -- hours."

"Was there anyone with you?"

"No."

"What did you do then?"

"I went back home. By then it was almost dawn."

"Mr. Abramson, did you kill Ed Baker?"

"Most certainly not. I could never do that."

"Do you have any idea who might have done this?"

"No."

"Did you at any time tell Detective Langdon that you killed Mr. Baker?"

"No, I did not."

"Did you at any time tell Jonathan Walker that you killed Mr. Baker?"

"No, I did not."

"I have no further questions, your Honor," said Joel, as he walked to his seat.

"So, are you telling us that you weren't upset about losing the job, Mr. Abramson?" began Andrew Smallwood.

"Of course I was. Anyone would be," answered Mark.

"And you know of no one who saw you that night?"

"No. I told you. I was in my car, alone."

"And you are telling us that Detective Langdon is lying, is that correct?"

"Well, I know I didn't tell him I killed Mr. Baker."

"And you are telling us that Mr. Walker is also lying, is that it, Mr. Abramson?"

"Yes, he's lying. I never even talked to him before."

"So everyone is lying but you, is that it, Mr. Abramson?"

"I know I'm telling the truth."

"Even though you know that if you're convicted of this brutal crime you could face the death penalty? You wouldn't lie to avoid the electric chair?"

"No, I wouldn't," snapped Mark.

"Then I guess you're just a saint, Mr. Abramson," said the prosecutor jokingly. "I have no further questions of this witness, your Honor."

"Call your next witness, Mr. Cummings," demanded judge Pinkston.

"The defense rests," announced Joel.

"Does the State have any rebuttal witnesses?" asked Pinkston.

"The State does not believe that it needs to present a rebuttal case, your Honor," replied Andrew.

"Very well, then. Tell you what. We'll recess for the rest of the day to allow counsel and me time to get the jury instructions straight. Court will resume tomorrow morning at nine o'clock." Judge Pinkston surveyed the courtroom as he stood to exit. The room was packed. It was clear by now that tensions were high. He was glad that this thing was drawing to a close.

Day Five: A day for conclusions.

As the prosecutor rose to address the jury, he knew that the game was his to lose. He could sense it. So he elected to be brief. Just review the evidence in a summary fashion. The evidence pointed to one man, and one man only: Mark Abramson.

Joel's summation was equally direct and equally brief. "When all is said and done," Joel told the jury, "you have no evidence directly linking Mark Abramson to this crime. The reason for that is simple. He didn't commit the crime. And what about Walker? Well, despite what he says, he expects to be helped in his case. And as for Langdon? He has a vested interest in securing a conviction. He wants a promotion. Ladies and gentlemen, when you review all of the evidence, I am confident that you will find my client not guilty."

The rebuttal argument by the prosecution was shorter still. "Ask yourselves, if not Abramson, then who?. . . The only liar in the courtroom was Abramson. He had the biggest motive of all to lie. He wants to save his own skin."

As the jury was given their instructions, Mark thanked Joel for the job that he had done. "We're gonna be okay," Joel answered. "Just remember, it takes a unanimous verdict. I think they have doubts."

But forty-five minutes after being sent to their deliberations, the jury indicated to the bailiff that they had reached a verdict. Counsel's presence was secured, and Mark was hurriedly brought back into the courtroom and seated in his chair to await the arrival of Judge Pinkston.

"All rise," boomed the now-familiar voice of the bailiff, as Judge Pinkston strolled into the courtroom with a somber look on his face.

"Be seated," the judge began. "Counsel, I have been informed that the jury has reached a verdict. Are you ready to receive the verdict?"

"Yes," both men responded in unison.

"Very well, then, bring in the jury. And while they're on their way, I will advise those of you in the audience. When the verdict is read there are to be no outbursts of any kind. Do I make myself clear? . . . Okay. Now, ladies and gentlemen of the jury, have you reached a verdict?"

"We have your honor," said the jury foreman.

"Please give the verdict to the clerk," said Pinkston, who then took the verdict, read it, and gave it back to the clerk for delivery to the foreman. "Will the defendant please rise."

Mark felt his feet almost buckle as he rose to stand beside his attorney.

"Mr. foreman, what is your verdict?" asked Judge Pinkston.

"We the jury, in the matter of the State of Florida versus Mark Abramson, find the defendant *guilty* of murder in the first-degree," announced the foreman.

"Mr. foreman, is your verdict unanimous?"

"It is, your Honor," said the foreman.

"Your Honor, we'd like to have the jury polled," Joel said, his voice trembling.

Mark felt his knees give way as he heard each juror announce his agreement with the verdict. As he sat down, his head fell into his hands and he began to weep from the depths of his being.

"The court will recess for the remainder of the day. This case will resume tomorrow morning at nine o'clock to begin the penalty-phase aspect," said Judge Pinkston. And with that he rose and walked hurriedly out of the room.

"Mark, listen to me," said Joel. "We're gonna fight this. Do you hear me? We're gonna fight this. . . . I'll be over to see you tonight, so we can prepare for tomorrow. . . . Okay?"

As Mark nodded his head, the guards approached and chained his handcuffs to his wastechain. He began the now familiar shuffling toward the door, staring all the while over his shoulder at his wife, who sat in the first row crying. She was leaning over in Marge's arms like a small child, seemingly oblivious to the snapping of camera shutters around her and the requests from reporters to tell them how she felt at that moment. The prosecutor and his team finally drew attention from her as they left the courtroom for the courthouse steps, where they could answer all of the questions that would be posed to them about their victory.

Day Six: Judgment day.

The day began like the rest for Mark, except that he was now kept in a cell that was far removed from the other prisoners. He was now under heightened observation by the guards, since he now posed a distinct escape risk. Nevertheless, the sun came up just as it always had. But this day would be different from all the rest.

Joel and Ron had visited with Mark the night before. The strategy for the next phase was simple. The State would likely put on evidence of his prior conviction, in order to argue that the prior violent felony of armed robbery justified the death penalty. They would also argue that Ed's murder was so vicious that it was what Florida called heinous, atrocious, and cruel. Such murders could also be punished by death. Likewise, the State was expected to argue that the length of time between the job termination and the killing showed that Mark had planned this murder. The murder would then arguably have been cold, calculated, and premeditated, without any pretense of moral justification. If the State were successful in this argument the death penalty would again be justified.

For its part the defense would show that Mark was a good person who had a family and who wasn't deserving of death.

It was unusual to hold court on Saturday, but the judge wanted to move things along. As Mark shuffled once again into the courtroom to the piercing stares of the audience, he checked to make sure that Susan was in her spot, which she was. He nodded to her, then turned and sat down at the now-familiar wooden table.

Upon seating himself, the judge explained to the jury that this aspect of the trial would be held to determine the defendant's punishment. It was sort of a mini trial. Each side could present evidence, then there would be final arguments and instructions, at which point the jury would deliberate. Explanations completed, the prosecutor rose to begin his case.

"Your Honor, the defense has graciously agreed to stipulate to the entry of this certified copy of the defendant's prior criminal conviction. So I will give that to the clerk and ask that it be marked as State's exhibit A, for identification. Your Honor, I would also move its admission into evidence."

"No objections," said Joel.

"Very well, then," said Judge Pinkston. "It will be admitted. Call your first witness, Mr. Smallwood."

"The State has no witnesses your Honor. Instead we will rely on the testimony presented at the previous stage. We therefore rest at this time."

"Okay, defense, call your first witness," the judge said to Joel.

"The defense calls Susan Abramson," said Joel in a voice that sounded more authoritative than he felt.

As Susan walked to the stand she passed her husband, looked at him, and winked. Both knew that their lives were about to change. Susan's only hope at the moment was that she could help her now-defeated husband. Her testimony was detailed and recounted her life with Joel. He had been a kind and considerate husband, always providing. And while there were times that he was without work, he had always done what he could to find more employment. She did not believe that he killed Ed Baker. In fact, if he were released right now, Mark would be welcomed back home with open arms.

"No questions," said Andrew Smallwood when asked if he wished to cross-examine the witness.

Mark was the next, and final, witness. Once again he denied the killing. In a voice that trembled with every other word, he recounted his life with Susan. His life had been great. It had been full. He knew that if given the chance he could benefit society once again. He was truly sorry about Ed's death, but he wasn't the man who had caused it.

"Just one question," Andrew said when asked if he had any questions of the witness. "Tell me, Mr. Abramson, would you lie to save yourself from the electric chair?"

"No," answered Mark.

"Then you're a better man than most, sir," said Andrew, hearkening back to Mark's prior denial during the guilt phase of the trial. "We have no further questions, your Honor."

As Mark stepped down from the witness stand, he heard his attorney announce that the defense had no further witnesses, to which the prosecution agreed.

"Court will recess until two P.M.," Judge Pinkston said from the bench, "after which we will hear closing arguments and I will instruct the jury."

At the resumption of the proceedings, Mark sat in his chair and stared at the twelve people who would decide his fate. He noticed that none of them would look at him. Their faces were somber, intense, angry. It was evident that they did not enjoy their jobs. It was equally obvious, however, that they were very upset at Ed's death, and at Mark for having committed it.

Tuning back in to the proceedings, Mark heard the prosecutor conclude his remarks. "And so I implore you, ladies and gentlemen, when you consider the evidence in this case, together with this defendant's predisposition to commit acts of violence, there is but one punishment sufficient to answer the acts he's perpetrated. Death. *Death* is the only punishment that will remove him from our community with certainty. *Death* is the only punishment that is called for by a statute that asks you to weigh his crime against those things that the defense suggests, call for mercy. And so, I leave it to you twelve members of the community to recommend to the court that this man pay the highest punishment for butchering Ed Baker. Thank you."

"Ladies and gentlemen," Joel began, "there is simply no way that putting my client to death will bring back Ed Baker. And the statute is clear that if you do not sentence my client to death he will spend the rest of his life in prison. That's not a fate that any one of us would want for ourselves. And I suggest that it is sufficient punishment for this man. In addition, it would allow him at least to serve his community in some small way by doing odd jobs to pay for his way, so to speak. Finally, I ask you, how will killing my client bring any peace to this community? Will it bring back Ed Baker? No, it will not. Will it cause his widow to grieve any less? I suggest that it will not. Will it lessen Susan Abramson's pain? No it will not. No, all it will do is to feed the bloodthirsty appetites of those in the community who clamor for the blood of anyone whom they deem lower than themselves. Ladies and gentlemen, I know that you will give this matter your fullest attention. I pray that you will spare my client his life and let this community begin the process of healing these wounds that have bled too much already. Thank you."

As Judge Pinkston instructed the jury in the law, Mark once again watched them. They were serious in their jobs. That was clear. "Joel, tell me again," he whispered to his attorney, "does it have to be unanimous to get the death penalty?"

"No," said Joel. "The State needs seven out of twelve votes for death. If it's a tie the sentence is life." He kept his voice as low as possible while the judge concluded his instructions.

As the jury left the courtroom, Judge Pinkston recessed court. "The attorneys will remain on call," he admonished Joel and Andrew. "Guards, why don't you keep Mr. Abramson in the holding cell for now."

Mark stood once more while his guards secured the chains and led him from the courtroom. Susan watched her husband exit while she wondered to herself if life would ever be worth living again.

"Susan, why don't we go across the street for some coffee," Joel asked. "I think we all could use something to drink about now. . . . Marge, can you carry her things for her?"

"Sure, Joel," Marge replied. "Come on, Susan, let's get out of this place while we can, okay?"

"Okay," said Susan, "whatever you say. I couldn't stand to sit in here another minute."

As the four exhausted friends left the courtroom, they each looked out across the parking lot to the bay to their left. The water was so beautiful and calm. The shrimp boats floated in the far distance while the oyster boats were closer to shore. "Quite a life, I guess," said Ron to the group.

"Yeah, quite a life," said Joel. "But you know, they have no idea how lucky they are. And they have no idea just how much power the State has over their lives. It's really scary when you think about it. . . . Oh well, let's get something to drink."

Sitting in the restaurant the group couldn't help but realize that they were the subject of people's continuous glances. "We'd better get used to it," said Marge. "I've got a feeling we're not real popular around here."

"I think you're right," said Joel, as he sipped his iced tea.

The minutes turned into an hour, and then turned into two hours. And then the minutes stopped when the waitress informed Joel that his presence was needed in the courtroom. Joel quickly rose and walked out while Ron took care of the bill. "We're right behind you," said Marge, putting everything onto her luggage cart for the short trip back across the street. "Susan, you stay right by my side now, you hear?"

"Sure," came the meek response. "Where else am I going?"

Back in court it was again announced that the jury had reached a verdict. Everyone was present when Judge Pinkston returned to the courtroom in his usual, determined manner.

"Okay, we're back on the record in the case of the State of Florida versus Mark Abramson. Mr. Abramson is present with counsel. The prosecutor is also present. I've been informed that the jury has reached a verdict on the penalty to be imposed. Is everyone ready to proceed?"

"We are, your Honor," came the usual unified response.

"Very well, then, bring in the jury. And I caution you again that there are to be no outbursts."

As the jury returned Mark once more watched them closely. No one would look at him. All eyes stared straight ahead.

"Have you reached a verdict, Mr. foreman?" asked the judge.

"We have, your Honor," came the answer.

"Very well, then. Please hand your verdict to the court."

Once more Mark watched the foreman give the paper to the clerk, who gave it to the judge. After reading it with an expressionless face, Pinkston returned it to the clerk, who dutifully delivered it to its temporary custodian.

"Will the defendant please rise?" boomed Judge Pinkston's voice.

Mark rose slowly and began to face the jury, not noticing the guards moving up behind him. "Joel, thanks for all you've done, man," was all that Mark could think to whisper to his attorney.

"Mr. foreman, what is your verdict?" asked the court.

As the foreman began to read the verdict, Mark, for the first time, noticed the jurors look in his direction. "We the jury, by a vote of twelve to nothing, impose the sentence of death on the defendant, Mark Abramson."

Amid the hushed murmurs in the courtroom came a soft whimper from behind Mark. It continued and grew louder and then became uncontrollable, despite Marge's efforts to console Susan.

"Guards, please remove the defendant," yelled Pinkston from the bench. "Ladies and gentlemen of the jury, the court thanks you for your service to the community. You are advised that you are not obliged to speak with anyone about this case. However, if you wish to discuss it you are free to do so. You are now excused. The court also thanks counsel for both sides on a case that was well tried. Mr. Cummings, you did an admirable job under trying circumstances. Court is now adjourned and we are off the record."

"I hope your client rots in hell!" came a sudden voice from the crowd. "And why don't you go with him!" someone else joined in.

"Ron, let's get everything together and get out of here. Pronto." As he looked around, Joel realized that amid all of the confusion Mark had been removed from the courtroom without Joel even saying good-bye to him. My gosh, he thought to himself, how could I have let that happen?

With that, Susan and the three members of the defense team turned and began what seemed to be a much longer journey to the door. But this time they were surrounded on both sides by members of the audience who had elected to stay and savor the moment, and to get one last look at the scum who had dared to defend the man who killed Ed Baker.

Thirty days later Joel returned to that same courtroom to hear Judge Pinkston formally sentence Mark for the crime of murdering Ed Baker. Judge Pinkston, as he was required to do by statute, had itemized the factors that he believed justified the death sentence. Mark had committed a prior violent felony, the murder itself was heinous, atrocious, and cruel, the murder was cold, calculated, and premeditated. In mitigation of the sentence, Judge Pinkston found only that Mark was married at the time of the murder. After weighing the factors in as scientific a fashion as possible, Judge Pinkston found that the jury's decision was appropriate.

"Mark Abramson, it is the sentence of this court that you be transported to an appropriate facility of the Department of Corrections and that you remain incarcerated at said facility until such time as you shall be put to death as provided by the laws of this, the great state of Florida. May God have mercy on your soul. Bailiff, you may take the prisoner away."

PART THREE

CHAPTER XX

Two years, eight months, seventeen days. Practically twenty-four thousand hours. Babies had been born and had begun to walk and to pull their kitty cats' tails. Seven space-shuttle missions had flown. Congress had stood for election and the presidential race was beginning to encroach upon the nightly news. Two years, eight months, and seventeen days of changes for everyone, it seemed, except death-row inmate number G904892.

Mark's conviction and sentence had been appealed directly to the Florida Supreme Court. As required by law the appeal had been filed within thirty days after Judge Pinkston's death sentence had been issued. The appeal had been handled by the appellate division of the public defender's office -- the same public defender's office that previously had chosen not to help Mark because its caseload was too heavy. It was no lighter now. After meeting with their client for thirty minutes, and corresponding twice, the office filed an admirable brief that raised seemingly all possible legal issues. Fifteen, to be exact. The Florida Supreme Court, as was customary in death cases, had granted oral argument, and had used the opportunity to explore the appellant's claim that the late disclosure of the jailhouse informant had prejudiced the defense. But after much spirited discussion and seven months of deliberation the court had denied that claim, and all others presented, in a seven-page opinion. The conviction and sentence would stand.

In cases where a life was at stake, custom dictated that a further appeal would be taken to the United States Supreme Court asking for review of the conviction and sentence for alleged federal constitutional errors. That court, after six months' deliberation with no oral argument, had now declined to hear

Mark's appeal. The decision was unanimous and succinctly stated, in the court's two-sentence paragraph denying what is known as certiorari.

As Mark opened the latest envelope from his attorney he could tell it bore bad news. The decision from the United States Supreme Court was enclosed. If the news had been good he would have undoubtedly received a telephone call. No. This was the long anticipated letter from his lawyer advising him that the High Court had denied certiorari and that the law now considered his conviction to be final. He had been on the row for over two and a half years. Since being sentenced to death he had spoken with his attorneys for three hours and had received five letters from them discussing his case. He now had two years to file a motion for post-conviction relief, a 3.850, as it was typically called. That motion would be handled by yet another attorney who worked for another agency of the state. Mark, the letter said, should be hearing from them soon. The attorney wished him the best of luck in his appeals.

Sitting in his seven-by-seven-foot cell Mark read and reread for hours this latest letter, together with the denial of his appeal. He had now been on the row long enough to know the ramifications of being turned down at this stage. It had been an uphill battle before. Now the task seemed practically insurmountable. He finally put the letter aside and decided to write to Susan to let her know of his latest defeat.

As Mark began this latest in what had been a string of letters to the outside world, he asked himself yet one more time whether he would ever be able to have a normal relationship with his wife. It had not gone unnoticed that he heard from her less and less as time progressed. It was to be expected, he supposed, but after his sentencing in St. Bartholomew he had hoped that they would stay together.

"Mark," Susan had told him in the Cortez County Jail, "no matter what, I'll always be here for you. Don't you ever forget that!" The words had poured out of her mouth that day almost as rapidly as the tears had fallen from her eyes. Susan would never know how much those words had meant to her husband, who, by this time, had no need for any material possessions. Those words were, in fact, more valuable than anything he had ever owned. As he was being transported to the Union Correctional Institution in Raiford, he kept repeating those words to himself over and over. Indeed, the words were so precious that he hardly even focused on the landscape as the van made its way to what could be his last home.

The thoughts of his life with Susan and their dreams together had also made his acclimation to UCI, as it was known, somewhat easier. It had not been easy. While he had managed to block out of his mind what was happening to him with every strip search that he endured, it never became acceptable to him. And the level of security on the row was beyond anything he had ever imagined. He was allowed to wear only his standard-issue prison garb, blue trousers with a yellow T-shirt, which signified a death-row inmate. He was strictly limited in the amount of personal possessions he could have with him, and he could only get replacements from a prison canteen. For the first four weeks after his arrival, he had been placed on suicide watch, just in case he had decided to cheat the state out of its opportunity to kill him legally. He was then moved to his cell which, like all the rest, looked out onto a corridor in the front with solid concrete walls on the remaining three sides. By rule he, like all others, would stay in this cell twenty-three hours a day, except for two days each week when he would be entitled to exercise outside on a concrete pad known as the yard. On two other weekly occasions he would be allowed to shower. This was to be his life until the State decided that it was his turn to die. While unlikely, that could come soon. He would have to wait.

Sitting on his bunk Mark stared at the blank page before him. It was always hardest to begin these letters because for the past year he had wondered, really wondered, if he was losing his wife. At first she had written to him almost daily. The letters had been filled with every sort of detail and minutia that Susan could think to include. And there was always the perfume that she had used to scent the paper. But over time the daily letters became weekly letters with fewer details, as if they were written out of an obligation. And for the past year Mark had grown accustomed to receiving still fewer reports from home. As seldom as once a month and more distant than ever. Nevertheless, Mark had faithfully continued his efforts to maintain communication with his spouse. So it wasn't long until the blank page before him was filled with the latest news of his life, such as it now was.

"Hey, Blondie, what're you up to now?" the voice of Mark's neighbor interrupted his chain of thought.

"Shut up, man, I'm writin' a letter back home. I gotta concentrate," replied Mark.

"Why you doin' that?" asked the neighbor. "You been pretty quiet over there."

"Yeah, well," began Mark, "I just heard from my lawyer. I just got denied by the Supreme Court. I guess I'm about to graduate."

"Guess so," said the neighbor. Frederico Gonzalez had been Mark's neighbor since Mark had arrived on the row. He was old -- sixty-two to be exact -- and he had been on the row for fourteen years. He was a man of considerable stature at six-foot-three inches tall, and he weighed two hundred and fifty pounds. His size had helped him stay out of trouble since he had arrived on the row, and when he coupled that with the fact that he possessed an IQ of over one hundred ten, he had been able to achieve some degree of respect. His seniority had also brought him the respect and admiration of his buddies on the row, and Mark was no exception. Frederico, or Billygoat, as he was known to his friends, had miraculously survived three death warrants against him. But his time was now running out and he knew it. He therefore used what time he had left to help his friends fight for their own lives whenever they could. "Don't dwell on it, Blondie," was the advice that he chose to give Mark on this day.

"I'm not," answered Mark. "I'm just writing to my wife. I thought I'd better let her know about it . . . if she still cares."

"She still cares, man," said Frederico, "but I keep tellin' you, with time, no matter how much they care, they eventually give up. That's why you have to be strong."

"I know. I know," Mark said. "But I'm still gonna write."

"Sure. And when you do, tell her I said that I could use a good rib-eye, if she wants to cook me a meal someday."

"Dream on, Billygoat, dream on," responded Mark. "She ain't fixed me no rib-eye in three years or more, so you can just stand in line. . . . Now, just leave me alone and let me finish this letter," he chuckled. "I don't have all day, y'know." With that he returned to his letter. It was not a simple matter, writing such letters, because he had learned to think carefully about every word he selected for inclusion. It helped pass the time. Every such word must also be spelled correctly, and the letters must be written with style. All things considered, this letter, like all the rest, might take him three hours to write. Three hours less time to think. Three hours less time to live.

As the sun rose over Raiford on a foggy, cool morning in April, the plane circled the prison and landed in what passersby on the two-lane road would likely consider to be a lush, green pasture. It was a pasture indeed, but when necessary it also doubled as a landing strip for small aircraft. On this day the twin-engine Saab landed as it had done many times before, deftly avoiding the cattle grazing nearby. As its wheels touched down the small plane pulled up closely to the administration building. The passenger door opened and two men stepped from the plane, greeted only by several white egrets who maintained a vigil over the area. The egrets watched the two visitors with suspicion.

It took little time for the smartly attired men to walk the short distance from the plane to the single-story, red-brick administration building of the Florida State Prison. Once inside they were ushered directly to the superintendent's office, where they stayed for no more than a few minutes before emerging once more from the building and returning to the plane. The egrets watched as the propellers slowly began to turn. The right one first and then, as if suddenly awakening from a deep sleep, the left one followed. The plane turned, moved forward, and eventually rose back into the skies and headed westward.

Later that day news traveled from cell to cell and tier to tier on death row at UCI.

"Carouthers got a warrant! Do you know when the date is?" were the news and question of the day. "No idea," was the universal response. That night the row was quiet for the first time in months. Everyone seemed to have the same thing on his mind: what would happen to Carouthers, and who would be next? What would they do when their time came? Their questions were at least partially answered the next morning when they read in the paper that Carouthers' execution was scheduled to be carried out in fourteen days.

He had been on the row little more than six years, and yet it was his third death warrant.

There was little expectation that he would survive it.

"Hey, Billygoat, what's the deal with the warrant?" Mark asked his neighbor. The question was always the same. It did not need to vary because Frederico knew what information was really sought.

"It's serious, man," said Frederico. "I talked to Carouthers in the yard a few months ago. He said he was worried then, because his case was just sitting there with nothing going on. He didn't think that he had any real issues left. . . . But who knows? With the warrant being only two weeks it sounds pretty serious to me."

"I guess he's over there now," said Mark. "I heard they had to drag him out of his cell to take him over to the watch."

"Yep. They probably did. Can't say as I blame him none."

Two weeks later, as night fell on the row, orders were given to lock down the institution. All inmates would remain in their cells until further orders from the superintendent. Those orders came two days later, but only after a white hearse left from the death chamber at Florida State Prison bearing Carouthers' charred body. The egrets watched the hearse depart the grounds and looked to the sky once more. For now the skies were clear.

Time continued to pass slowly during the hot and humid summer months that followed Carouthers' execution. It was a time of relative calm, in part because the Florida Supreme Court took its annual, month-long summer recess, which meant that no warrants would be signed until the Court resumed session in late August. Life on the row had therefore calmed down, except for the expected flare-ups brought on by the intense heat that beat down on the prison.

Mark's days were no different from those of his neighbors. He awoke each morning at five o'clock, ate breakfast, and then tried to read for a few hours. Sleep followed until lunch was brought to his cell. Then more reading, more sleep, followed by dinner. The high point of his day was mail time, which usually came an hour or so after his dinner was served. It was the one time that he might have some contact with the outside world. The letters were not exactly plentiful lately, so when they did come they were savored even more.

"Mark, I thought I'd better get this into the mail to you as soon as possible," wrote Susan on one occasion. "Eddy stopped by yesterday evening late. You remember Eddy, don't you? Well, it may be nothing, Mark, but he said he overheard that guy Al and his friend Randy talking the other day. Eddy said it sounded like Randy was upset or something. He said he thought he heard Al tell him something like he should just shut up and you'd take the fall for it. Who knows what it means, Mark, but I just thought you should know."

As Mark finished reading the short letter from his wife, the excitement rolled over him in waves. I knew something had to happen, he thought to himself. I knew it.

Sitting in his cell and looking out at the corridor on the other side of the bars, Mark began once more to daydream. Could it be that there was hope after all? He couldn't allow himself to think like that, he thought to himself. Better not to dream. Not any more.

Nevertheless, it didn't take him long to put a plan together. Out came the legal pad and pen. After writing to Susan to tell her to find out what she could about all of this, he turned his attention to the law offices of the Death Penalty Litigation Project, or the Group, as it was called on the row. It was the state agency that Mark understood would be responsible for handling his post-conviction appeal. The letter didn't take long to write. A simple introduction and then the facts of what Susan had told him. He finished it up with a request that someone contact him as soon as possible to discuss looking into the matter. As he handed both letters to the guard for mailing, he couldn't help but believe that finally his prayers had been answered. There would be an end to this after all.

But Mark soon discovered that while there might be a happy ending, it would take some time to arrive. The long anticipated beginning step toward that ending arrived a year after he had written to his new lawyers. It arrived late one Thursday afternoon in the form of an envelope. The envelope was white and in the upper left-hand corner was an ornate script that announced to all that the contents of the envelope had originated in the law offices of the Death Penalty Litigation Project. It was the first such envelope that had been addressed to Mark, and it arrived seventeen months after his appeal had been denied by the United States Supreme Court.

Mark nervously opened the envelope, removed the single sheet of crisp and equally impressive paper, unfolded it, and read the short communication: "Dear Mr. Abramson: You're case has been referred to our office for handling of your post-conviction motion. This is to advise you that we are in the process of obtaining your appellate record at this time and will begin reviewing the same, after which we will be in contact with you. Thank you, Judd Klingbeil." What is that supposed to mean, Mark thought to himself. "Hey, Billygoat, I got a question for you!" he yelled to his neighbor.

"What now, Blondie? This advice ain't free, you know."

"Yeah, well, bill me. What kind of crap is this, anyhow? I get a one-paragraph letter from some guy in the Group. It says that they're gonna pull my record and read it and then they'll be in touch. Man, I only got seven months before my 3.850 is due, and these guys haven't even gotten my record yet! I wrote to them a year ago and told them about what Susan said."

"Now aren't you glad you wrote to them again like I told you to do?" answered Frederico. "And just think, it only took three letters to get that response. I'm telling you kid, you've got to keep on these guys or else it's all over. Don't let up. Write back and ask them to give you an exact date that they'll be out. I'll bet you won't get it."

"Yeah, well, you just wait and see. 'Cause I'm gonna make 'em answer me and give me a date. I'm not puttin' up with that."

"Uh-huh. Heard it before. Tell you what: we'll talk in a few months. Then tell me what it is you're puttin' up with."

"What am I supposed to do in the meantime, man? I haven't heard from Susan in three months now. I don't know what she's doin' or if she even knows I'm alive. Now I get this garbage from this guy, Klingbeil, saying he'll be in touch. It's been seventeen months since they should have gotten started on my case. Seventeen months." As he slowly plunged back into thought Mark continued his conversation with his friend. "I'm dead, aren't I, Billygoat?"

"Naw, man. Not yet. Just keep the heat on. I'm serious about that. Keep the heat on. Elsewise you're gonna be in trouble. Listen to me on this one, Blondie. I mean it. I've seen guys get carried out of here in a box because they left things to those guys in the Group. Trust me, ain't no one cares about your case like you do. No one."

As he lay on his bunk and stared at the ceiling above him, Mark knew that there was truth to what Frederico was saying. He, too, had seen guys simply pass the time and do nothing on their cases, relying instead on what had ultimately turned out to be empty promises. Those guys were now either dead or without hope and waiting to die. I've got to keep up the pressure he thought to himself as he drifted off to sleep. I can beat this thing. I know I can.

Mark's crusade to play an integral role in his case was laudable, if not naive. He firmly believed that he would have to have Susan's full support. It was therefore with a renewed fervor that he intensified his letter-writing to his wife. With every letter the urgency increased. "Susan, please write back as soon as you get this letter so that I'll at least know that you got it. I desperately need your help." The message was always clear and could not have been misunderstood.

It was for that reason that Susan sat at the kitchen table late one night and responded to Mark's latest plea with a sincerity that she had thus far avoided. "Mark, honey, writing this letter is probably the hardest thing I've ever had to do in a long time. No, it's the hardest thing I've ever had to do. It's time that I told you what's going on. You see, honey, a couple of years ago I had to sell our mobile home in order to make ends meet. I tried to avoid it by working two jobs, sometimes three, but things just never went right. That's why I got the post-office box. Anyway, it's gone, Mark. All of it is gone. I've been living in a small apartment here, and it's been okay, but there's only so much of it I can take. So, I've decided that it's time for me to make a change.

"Mark, I think I'm going to move over to Pensacola for a while. You know, go see some friends of mine and try to get my head back on straight. It's just that around St. Bartholomew everybody knows me and looks at me funny. I've heard that some people think I was with you when Ed died. Not that I think you did it for a minute. It's just that people around here are sure you did, just like they're sure about everything that goes on. I can't take any more of it, honey, so that's why I've got to leave for a little bit.

"I know you need help with your case. And with Eddy. I've called him practically a dozen times so far and he hasn't called back once that I know of. Why don't you give his name and address to your lawyers. They should be able to track him down.

"Mark, I'll write to you when I get settled in over at Pensacola. I love you, honey. I always will. But I just can't take it anymore. Love, Susan."

It took Susan almost an hour to get through the letter, what with the tears that continued to fall from her cheeks. Why did all of this have to happen, she asked herself. What did we do to deserve this?

Four days later Mark read Susan's words over and over, searching for any hidden meanings that might lie within. It was as if they leapt from the page armed with daggers that pierced his skin as they searched for his heart and soul. Doesn't she know that she's all I've got, he asked himself repeatedly. Or does she just not care? Whatever the answer to the questions, the result was the same. He was now broken, alone. As he lay on his bunk and stared at the dimly lit corridor in front of his cell, he began to sob uncontrollably. "Trust me, ain't no one cares about your case like you do. No one," he remembered Frederico saying. How right you are, he thought to himself. How right you are.

The next morning when he was called out to the yard, Mark told the guard to leave him alone. He had work to do. It wouldn't take long, but it was work nonetheless. Once more he found himself sitting on the floor, legs outstretched with his legal pad awaiting the words that would eventually form the letter that he would write to the Florida Supreme Court. The letter was short and polite. In as succinct a style as he could elicit, Mark advised the Court that his 3.850 was due in four months and that so far he had not even seen a lawyer from the Group. He had tried on at least five different occasions to get them to do something on his case. He was tired of being jerked around. So, in as respectful a tone as he could muster, Mark Abramson asked the Court to drop all of his appeals. He'd finally had enough. If the State wanted to kill him then he was ready.

"Guard!" he shouted when the letter was ready to be mailed. "I've got something to go in the mail." As the overweight guard slowly arrived at the front of the cell, Mark handed him the sealed envelope in an almost ceremonial fashion. "Be sure and deliver that one, okay, Paul? It's real important."

As he looked at the envelope the guard noticed the addressee. "Not another one, Abramson. Why do you guys always think that the FSC is going to care a wit about anything you write to them? You'd think you'd learn by now."

"They'll care about this one," said Mark. "I've decided to drop my appeals. No need to take up space any more."

"You sure about this, son?" Paul asked, suddenly concerned. "That's pretty serious stuff you're talking about. Maybe you should give it some more thought before you send it out."

"Send it!" Mark burst out. "If you really care about me you'll just send the damned thing and let me get this over with!"

"Suit yourself," said the guard. "But I think you're making a mistake."

"Might be," Mark said. "But at least I'll be in control of something in my life. It's been a long time since that's been the case; and right now it feels pretty good."

Mark watched as the guard turned and lumbered down the corridor, envelope in hand. As he stood with his hands on the cell bars he took in a deep breath and exhaled slowly. I've finally done something for myself, he thought. I can't believe it took me this long.

CHAPTER XXI

"NO! YOU CAN'T DO THAT! PLEASE, DON'T! PLEASE, MISTER, NO!" The memories that had returned after Mark's arrest had only increased the torment of his soul. Never would he be able to rid himself of those screams in the night. Not until his own screams had been heard and silenced that is. Soon. Perhaps soon.

As Mark sat alone in his cell contemplating the enormous ramifications of his decision to end his appeals, he took out another piece of paper and began writing to Susan. As he began writing, delicate and precious memories began to return. Memories of his life with Susan, their home, their walks on the beach together. They had had their own little world. It hadn't been perfect, but it had been theirs, until it was destroyed like a fighter jet blown from the sky by a heat-seeking missile. There had been no warning, and to this day there was no indication from whence the missile had come. Mark had now come to realize that he probably never would know why he had been chosen to pay for Ed's murder. He told himself that it made no difference. The only issue now was how he would deal with it. Susan can help me, he thought to himself as he struggled to put the words on paper. He held back the tears that so often returned when his mind drifted back to what now seemed to have been carefree days with his wife.

As Mark sat on the cold floor of his cell trying to decide how best to explain to Susan why he had decided to give up the fight, he looked around his cell. This is what I've been reduced to, he thought to himself. A cot, a sink, a toilet, some books and magazines, and a bunch of legal papers that don't talk about the fact that I didn't kill that man. That's it. "Susan," he whispered to himself, "I just thank God that you can't see me like this. I never want you to see me like this. Never."

It had taken years, almost four since his conviction and sentence, for Mark to reach this point. It was a long time by some standards. By others it had been rather soon in coming. But it came nonetheless. And when it did it broke Mark Abramson. Never again would he be the person he had been before, and he knew that. His primary concern now was how to end his current circumstances while causing as little pain to his wife as possible. It would not be easy. Of that he was certain.

What Mark did not count upon, however, was the sudden, unexpected visit to his cell by a minister who had been asked to look in upon him. Brian Connors was a man who had just recently become involved in counseling inmates at the prison. He sported a small build and walked bent over, his torso wracked with pain and crippled with arthritis. Yet despite the pain this mild-mannered man of sixty-seven made bi-weekly trips to the prison to provide a shoulder to cry on when needed. He was not an ordained minister, just a person who cared. He was paid nothing for his services. His influence was calming and his reputation was impeccable, so he was allowed to visit with the inmates on the row at their cells, a privilege accorded to only a few.

"Hi, there," said Connors as he walked up to the cell door.

"Hi," said Mark. "What do you want?"

"Nothing particularly," said Connors. "My name's Brian Connors. I've just been visiting with folks along the tier here, and since we haven't met before I just thought I'd say hello. I hope this isn't a bad time."

"I don't know that there are any good times around here, to tell you the truth. I was just starting to write a letter, but I . . ."

"Well, let me run along then. I don't want to bother you, Mr. Abramson,"

Connors answered. He had been talking with inmates enough to know that pressure didn't work if he was to ever become a friend in the true sense of the word. "Maybe we can talk some other time." Connors slowly turned away from Mark's cell and began walking down the corridor.

"No, Mr. Connors, that's okay. I didn't mean you couldn't stay. It's fine with me if you stay. We don't get a lot of visitors back here, you know. . . . By the way, my name's Mark Abramson."

"Good to meet you, Mr. Abramson."

"So what do you do here? I guess you're a guard of some sort, huh?"

"Now why would you say that?"

"Because this is the row, man, and they don't let just anyone back here. They won't even let my lawyers back here. So I know you got to be somebody important."

"No. I'm nobody important, Mr. Abramson. In fact, I couldn't be farther from important. I'm just here to talk to anyone who wants to talk. I'm a lay-minister of sorts, I guess you'd say."

"Yep, should've known it. A padre," said Mark. "Well, tell you what, Mr. Connors. I don't feel like buyin' that stuff today. You're just wastin' your time and mine, so why don't you just save us both some time." Mark began to stand up from the floor as he saw the old man's smile turn into a look of obvious disappointment.

Brian once again began to turn and walk away. "I understand, son. But just in case you change your mind, here's my card with my address on it. I'd be happy to hear from you if you ever want to write, okay?"

"Sure, padre," responded Mark, reaching his hand through the bars to take the card from Brian's hand. "Maybe tomorrow or sometime later I'll feel more like talking. It's been a kinda rough week."

"I understand. If you ever want to visit, just let a guard know and they'll tell me when I'm out here the next time. I come over here a couple times a week usually. Take care of yourself, Mr. Abramson. You'll be in my prayers."

"Yeah. Thanks for coming by, padre," said Mark. As the man slowly walked down the corridor and out of sight Mark watched and in some ways, wished that he had asked him to stay. But not now. No, for now he had a letter to write.

"Abramson, you've got a legal visit." Mark heard the guard before he came into view. "Let's get ready."

"What do you mean, legal visit?" asked Mark. "I don't have no lawyer."

"Well, this guy thinks you've got him," chuckled the guard. "So, I guess you'd better go see what he wants."

"What's his name?"

"Klingbeil. Judd Klingbeil."

"Man, I don't wanna talk to that guy. You tell him that for me, okay?" asked Mark.

"Why don't you tell him for the both of us," answered the guard. "I ain't relaying no messages for you. I ain't no secretary. Now, come on. Hands against the wall and spread 'em. Let's get this over with."

Mark, as he knew to do, turned and placed the palms of his hands against the wall of his cell. When the pat-down was over he stood while the guard secured his arms to his waistchains and bound his legs in chains. "This better be good," he mumbled to the guard as he shuffled out of his cell and down the corridor to the visiting room where the attorney waited for him.

"Mr. Abramson," smiled Judd Klingbeil to Mark as he was escorted into the visiting room. "My name is Judd Klingbeil. I'm an attorney from the Death Penalty Litigation Project. Here's my card. I came here today to discuss your case with you. Now, the first thing I need to do is . . ."

"Now, hold on there just a minute, Mr. Klingbeil," Mark interrupted, "as I suspect you already know. I've decided to drop my appeals. I sent my notice in to the Supreme Court over three weeks ago. I'd think that you'd've gotten a copy of it by now."

"We did," said Klingbeil, "and that's part of what I wanted to talk to you about. You see, Mr. Abramson, we feel your case has substantial legal issues that need to be raised. Those issues won't be heard if you drop your appeals. So it's in your best interest to withdraw the notice that you filed with the FSC."

"I have no intention of dropping anything, sir," answered Mark.

"But, Mr. Abramson, I don't think you understand the critical importance of what you've done. If you are allowed to proceed with your action . . ."

"Wait just a minute," interrupted Mark again. "What do you mean, if I'm allowed to proceed with my action? It's my case, and my life. I'll proceed as I want to proceed."

"I'm sorry, Mr. Abramson, but that's not necessarily the case," said Klingbeil. As he paused for a moment Mark couldn't help but notice that the man would not look at him when he was talking. He seemed to be continuously staring at notes that he'd made on a single legal pad that he had laid in front of him on the table separating the two men.

"The law in Florida is pretty clear on this point, Mr. Abramson," Klingbeil continued. "In order for the FSC to determine if your sentence is proportionately correct, your appeal has to be prosecuted. Since our firm is responsible by law for handling your case, that means that we must proceed."

"What if I fire you?" Mark shot back.

"Mr. Abramson, I don't believe that the FSC will allow that to happen."

"So let me get this straight. I have no say in whether I appeal my conviction. Even if I want to drop my appeals, you people will go ahead and appeal anyway. Is that it?"

"Yes, I guess you could say that's it," said Klingbeil. "Now, would you like to get to work now and help me to get started preparing your 3.850?"

"When's it due?"

"In four months. That's why it's imperative that we get started as soon as possible."

"Why is it so important now, sir?" Mark asked sarcastically. "I wrote to you people months ago and begged you to get moving on my case because my wife had heard from a friend of mine that he'd heard something strange. I hear nothing for over a year and then I get a letter from someone saying that you're going to start reviewing the record."

"Yes, I remember. I wrote the letter," said Klingbeil.

"Well then, sir. Have you read the record?"

"No. But we're working on it."

"So how exactly do you think I can help you now if you don't even know what my case is about? . . . Tell you what, why don't you go back to your little office and find someone who knows what he's doing, who knows my case, and send that person back. Then I'll talk."

"Mr. Abramson, you don't understand, I am . . ."

"I understand plenty, sir. I understand that it's *my* life on the line, not yours. I understand that I wrote to you idiots months ago with new information and begged you to do something on my case, and all I got was one stinking letter saying you're going to start on my case. I understand that I heard nothing after that, and that I decided it was in my best interest to drop my appeals. And now I understand that I can't even do that, because you have to appeal my case anyway, even though you don't know what the heck my case is about! I understand plenty, mister attorney. I understand plenty."

"Now, don't get upset," said Klingbeil. "It's not productive."

"No, it's not," said Mark. "Tell you what. Answer me this. Who was the victim in my case?"

"I don't recall his name. It was a man, though."

"How did he die?"

"I'm not sure. Was he shot?"

"Oops. You're wrong."

"Did I know him?"

"No, I don't think you did?"

"Oops. Wrong again. Today's not your lucky day, mister attorney. One more question. What kind of case is this?"

"It's a capital case, Mr. Abramson. Now, are you through playing games?"

"Maybe. . . . Tell you what, I'll quit playing games when you quit playing games. Okay, mister attorney? I mean, it is my life after all."

"Okay, you've made your point. Now, why don't we get down to work? It's obvious we have a lot to do. Why don't we get started by you telling me about yourself."

"Why?"

"Because we need to know as much about you as possible. We need to know all of the facts that we can."

"Don't you want to know about the case?"

"Yeah, well, if that's where you want to start then it's okay with me. Why don't you tell me how all of this developed, what happened at trial, et cetera."

"All right. If you really want to know. How long do we have, anyway?"

"I've got two hours today."

"Okay. Well, I have no idea what happened to Mr. Baker-- Ed Baker. He's the victim. You see, I used to work for him." As Mark proceeded to explain the details of his case as he knew them, his attorney sedulously took copious notes. The more he wrote, the more comfortable Mark became with the man, and the more that he opened up. Finally, after an hour and a half of what seemed to be non-stop talking on his part, Mark remembered to tell Klingbeil about Eddy. "You see, Mr. Klingbeil, Eddy apparently overheard these two guys talking, and one of them, Al . . ."

"Al who?"

"Al Stempson. He worked with me at Bluestone. Anyway, Al supposedly told this guy Randy to shut up and I'd take the fall for something. I don't know what they were talking about, but obviously Eddy thought it was important. That's why I wanted you-all to contact him."

"What's Randy's last name?"

"I don't know. Eddy might, though."

"Okay, we'll talk to Eddy. Any idea how I can get in touch with him?"

"No, except you might talk to my wife. She should know."

"All right. Tell you what," said Klingbeil, as he reviewed his pages of notes. "I think I have plenty to get started on for now. One other thing, before I go. Mark, I may want to send one of our investigators out to see you to get more facts. Normally they would have met with you first, but since I was going to be out here anyway I thought I'd stop in. So if one of them comes by to see you it is critical that you talk to him and cooperate, okay?"

"Yeah, sure."

"And one other thing. I may want to have you talk with a mental-health professional. Did you talk to a psychologist or psychiatrist before the trial?"

"No. I didn't. Why do you want me to talk to a shrink?"

"Because we need to see if there is anything in your past that would have provided mitigation that the jury could have used to justify not giving you the death penalty. It's pretty standard stuff, Mark. I'm surprised that your trial attorney didn't do it."

"Well, I don't know about that, but I don't want to talk to no shrink."

"Mark, listen to me," responded Klingbeil. "It's important that you cooperate with us on this. We can't afford to leave any stone unturned. As you no doubt know, when your 3.850 is filed it must contain all issues that you intend to raise in your post-conviction appeal. Anything that is left out is prevented from being raised later. It's called a procedural bar. It means that neither the state courts nor the federal courts will let you raise the issue later if you didn't raise it in this 3.850. So we have to look at everything. It's important, Mark. It's very important."

"And what if I don't agree?"

"If you don't agree then it seriously hinders our ability to represent you on your appeal. We need your help, Mark. I need your help."

"I'll think about it."

"Good enough. For now, anyway. . . . Look, I've got to go. Thanks for talking to me. I'll be back in touch, but it may be a while. You'll probably hear from our investigator first."

"Okay." As he stood up Mark extended his hand to shake the hand of his new attorney. The man now seemed sincere, and it impressed Mark. It wasn't what he expected. "Mr. Klingbeil, I'm sorry for being so rude earlier. I really do appreciate your help.

And I guess I will go ahead and withdraw the notice that I filed with the Supreme Court."

"Don't worry about it, man," responded the attorney. "We'll withdraw the notice for you." As he turned to walk out of the small, five-by-seven-foot concrete room, Judd Klingbeil was obviously relieved that he had convinced Mark to cooperate with him. "See you later, Mark," he said to his client with a smile. "We'll be in touch."

As Mark walked back to his cell he felt a calmness descend upon him. He had gotten his point across to the lawyer; of that he was certain. Maybe there would be a light at the end of the tunnel after all. "Hey, Billygoat," he yelled to his neighbor, "I'm back in the fight. Decided to fight on!"

"Glad to hear it, man," came the answer. "Did you hear? Rumor is that the governor's office is about to sign another warrant. This week, supposedly."

"Any idea who?"

"No. Just heard it's gonna happen. Guess we'll find out soon enough."

"Yeah, guess so." As he lay back down on his cot, Mark replayed in his mind the discussion that he had had with Klingbeil. It really did seem to be productive. Maybe I'm not ready to die after all, he thought to himself. There's still some life left in me. As he dozed off to sleep his thoughts shifted back to the island and the times that he and his wife had strolled the beaches for hours on end. Arm in arm they had walked along, talking of their plans for the future. They'd had dreams back then -- good dreams. Maybe he could still dream those dreams, he thought. As the rolling waves in his mind crashed to the shore, Mark slowly fell into one of the deeper sleeps that he had experienced in months.

Klingbeil's prediction was accurate. It was an investigator who paid Mark the next visit. The investigator's name was John Winston. A tall, gangly man, twenty-four years old, with long, stringy hair, Winston's appearance hearkened back to the sixties. He was wearing blue jeans and a dress shirt that had obviously seen better days. He smelled of cigarette smoke and his eyes were bloodshot from a lack of sleep.

"Hello, Mark, my name is John Winston," said the investigator as he smiled at Mark and shook hands. "Mr. Klingbeil asked me to come by and see you about your case. So if it's all right with you I'd like to discuss some matters with you."

"I guess that would be all right. But first I'd like to see some identification, if it's okay with you."

"Why, sure. In fact, that's a real good idea. You never can be too cautious, you know." As he handed Mark a business card confirming that he worked for the Group, Winston nodded at his client, as if to signal his approval at Mark's caution.

"What was it you wanted to talk about?" asked Mark. "I thought we covered everything when your boss was here. Or at least we got things started."

"That's basically true from what Judd told me," said Winston. "But one thing he didn't have time to get into was the penalty-phase aspect of your trial. It's my understanding from reading the trial record that there really wasn't much evidence presented to the jury. What I wanted to talk to you about was your background and what your trial attorney discussed with you prior to the penalty phase of your case."

"Why is that important?" asked Mark. "I thought we put on evidence for the jury to look at. It was mitigating evidence, or something like that."

"Yes, that's correct. Did your attorney explain to you what was going on there?"

"Kinda."

"Well, let me explain it for you, then." Sensing that his show of intelligence would help him later, Winston continued. "Once you were convicted of murder it was up to the State to show that there were what are called aggravating circumstances present. Those are things that the statute says justify the death penalty. Then, after the State puts on evidence of those things, the defense has an opportunity to present evidence of what are called mitigating circumstances. Those can be pretty much anything that shows that you weren't wholly to blame for the crime. Say for example if you'd had an accomplice, or you'd acted under mental duress, or you'd had a bad childhood. Also, if you had done some particularly good things in the community in the past that could be a mitigator. It's really pretty much anything that shows the jury why they should let you live.

"Now, from what I can tell from reading the record, it looks like your trial attorney really didn't give the jury a chance to get to know you, so to speak. And it was his job to do so. If he didn't do it, then he was ineffective in representing you and it may be grounds for getting your sentence reversed."

"Uh-huh," Mark mumbled.

"So what I need to know, Mark, is this. What-all did you tell Mr. Cummings about your past?"

"Not a whole lot, I guess. Just the usual stuff, you know. . . . I thought he did a pretty good job, actually."

"Well . . . why don't we put that aside for now and let me get some background information from you. Is that all right? Some of these questions are going to be pretty personal, Mark."

"Sure, I guess. What sort of questions?"

"Well, why don't we start at the beginning? Where were you born? Pretty easy, huh?"

"I was born in Montgomery, Alabama. Why is that important?" Mark asked the investigator, who sat across the table and began taking notes.

"It's important because we need to know as much about you as possible. Now just bear with me on this, Mark, because it'll probably take some time. Now, where did you go to elementary school?"

"Eastside Elementary School."

"Middle School?"

"Florenceton Middle School. I went there through the eighth grade."

"And what about high school?"

"Carlton County Senior High."

"What were your grades like? Did you graduate?"

"My grades were okay. C's mostly. And no, I didn't graduate."

"Why not?"

"Got tired of it. I dropped out when I was 16."

"I bet that made your folks pretty mad," said Winston. "I know mine would have been furious if I had done anything like that."

"Yeah, mine were pretty upset. They kicked me out of the house."

Winston paused for a moment and looked at his client. It was clear that this wasn't easy for Mark. But this was just the sort of stuff that needed to come out as far as Winston was concerned. "Man, it's gettin' kinda hot in here, isn't it?" He always liked to change the subject a little at this point. "Think I'll roll up my sleeves."

"Yeah, it does seem to be getting a little warm. But that happens in here a lot. Cold one minute and hot the next."

"Kinda like torture, I guess," added Winston. "These jerks really ought to be fired. . . . Tell me, Mark. Now I know this may be hard to talk about, but did your father or mother ever hit you?"

"Whadda you mean, hit me? Sure, they spanked me."

"By the way, what are your parents' names?"

"Why do you need to know?"

"For our records, Mark. I forgot to ask you earlier."

"Keith and Shelby."

"Nice names. Now tell me, Mark, did they ever hit you a little harder than you thought they should have?"

"What do you mean?"

"You know, like use a belt really hard or something?"

"No. . . . And I don't like where you're going with this. My parents were good people, Mr. Winston. Yeah, they were strict, but they should have been. And maybe if I had listened to them I wouldn't be where I'm at now. So I don't want to hear any more about my parents, okay?"

"Mark, now listen to me. I understand how you feel. Believe me, I do. But now is not the time to protect them. If they did something to you we need to know about it, because it could

219

save your life. . . . Tell you what. Why don't we move on to something else for now? Would that be better?"

"Yeah, that would be better. I don't want to talk about this no more."

As the conversation moved on to the rest of Mark's life, he began to relax for Winston, which allowed Winston to obtain significant bodies of information about Mark's job history, his marriage to Susan, and his prior conviction. The interview was a tedious and time-consuming affair, but one that Winston had conducted with over twenty other clients. It had gone pretty much as planned. It finally began to wrap up after four hours of seemingly endless questions and monotonous answers.

"Mark, there are just a few other things I needed to ask you about," said Winston. "In these types of cases it is our normal practice to have our client examined by a psychologist. It's a pretty standard interview. You'll be given a series of pretty stupid tests and the psychologist will ask you many of the same questions about your past that I did. It's just so that we can get a psychological profile on you so that we can determine how best to present your case to the court. I'm going to ask a Dr. Steven Goldfarb to come see you. You'll like him, Mark. He's really nice, and he's thorough. He'll probably spend about a day with you. I just wanted you to know about it in advance. Do you have any questions?"

"What if I don't want to see this guy? I mean, I'm sane, and I'm not stupid. I really don't see any point in meeting with the guy."

"Mark, look. I need you to cooperate with me. It's just so we can get a handle on your case. We're trying to save your life, Mark. We've handled a lot of these cases and we know what to do. This is routine stuff that is a critical part of the process. So how about it? Will you help?"

"If I have to I have to. That's what it boils down to, doesn't it?"

"I'd like it if you consented because you wanted to help, Mark. It's not going to work if you fight us." As Winston looked across the table at his client he managed to make eye contact and gave Mark the most sincere look that he could manage. "Whadda ya say?"

"Well, I guess it can't hurt to talk to him. Just let me know in advance."

"Sure. I'll go ahead and set it up. Thanks Mark. . . . Oh. I almost forgot. I need you to sign these releases to allow us to get all of your records. Medical records, school records, prison records, et cetera."

When Mark finished signing the forms for the investigator, he pushed his chair back from the table, signaling his desire to end the meeting. As he looked out the plate--glass window of the interview room, he motioned to the guard to come get him. "Thank you for coming to see me, Mr. Winston. It was a pleasure speaking with you." As he held out his arm to shake hands, the door opened and the guard indicated it was time to leave. The two men shook hands, Winston patted him on the back, and Mark motioned for the guard to take him back to his cell. As he walked slowly, deliberately, down the hall it dawned on him that in the nearly four hours they had spent talking, there was no discussion of the crime or of the investigation into it. That'll probably be the next visit, Mark thought to himself. At least we're making some progress, anyway.

Mark's kind disposition toward his new attorney and investigator didn't last long. It had been two months since he and Winston had met for the marathon session. During that time he had heard nothing from anyone at the Group.

His patience was growing still thinner when he was suddenly called out of his cell to meet with Dr. Goldfarb. Despite his request there had been no advance warning. The doctor, as expected, had spent almost a full day with Mark and examined in excruciating fashion the details of his life, especially his home life as a child. The doctor then proceeded to conduct silly sounding tests on his patient. Upon concluding the meeting the doctor abruptly told Mark that he had enjoyed the meeting and quickly left the room. I'm nothing but a number to these idiots, he thought, as he slowly walked back to his cell, tired and discouraged.

Another month slowly passed without any word from the Group. Then came a letter from Klingbeil informing Mark that the 3.850 would soon be ready for his signature and filing with the court. The attorneys in the office were very impressed with the progress that had been made on the case, and they were sure that Mark would be equally impressed. I'll believe it when I see it, was his reaction.

"Hey, Billygoat, I think you were right about my attorney," he said to his neighbor. "I've never felt less in control of anything in my life. Now I get this letter and they say my 3.850 is almost done and that it's really great. Thing is, I have no idea what's in it. It is still my case, isn't it?"

"Nope," was the neighbor's only response. "It stopped being your case the minute that judge said 'May the Lord have mercy on your soul'. Trust me, man, it ain't gonna get any better."

And it didn't.

Two days before the deadline for filing his 3.850 Mark received another callout.

"Abramson," came the now-familiar voice of the guard. "You've got a legal visit. So let's get moving."

"Who is it?"

"It's Chief Justice Rehnquist, I think. He's come to offer you a seat on the High Court. You need to be fitted for your robes, though," he chuckled. Then, after a pause, he continued, "I don't know who it is. Some investigator, I think. Anyhow, he's from the Group."

Fifteen minutes later Mark was again ushered into the visiting room where all legal visits were conducted. "Hello, Mr. Winston," he said. "What brings you by?"

"I've got your 3.850, Mark," smiled Winston, obviously proud of the purpose of his visit. Pulling the 3.850 out of his briefcase as if unveiling a great work of art, he continued. "As you can see, it's quite impressive. Two hundred eighty-six pages! We've really got 'em on this one, Mr. Abramson. Judd says it's one of the best cases he's seen."

"So what are the claims?"

"Well, I don't have a lot of time, but we can go over it a little. Mostly what I need you to do is to sign here saying that you're filing this motion for post-conviction relief. Then I'll go on to St. Bartholomew and file it in the circuit court. The deadline is the day after tomorrow. But I guess you knew that anyway." Winston grinned a knowing grin as he completed the last sentence. "Here, just sign on this last page and we'll be off and running."

As he dutifully signed his 3.850, Mark couldn't help but be impressed with the thickness of the document. It was obviously the product of a sizable amount of work. "It looks good," he said to Winston as he handed him the document.

"And it is good, Mark," Winston replied. "By the way, this is your copy and these are the appendices that go with it." As he finished the sentence Winston pulled three bound volumes of documents out of his briefcase and gave them to his client, along with the motion itself. "Why are your eyes getting wide, man? You didn't know there was this much stuff out there, did you?"

"Not about this case I didn't. No sir. I had no idea."

"Oh, there's quite a bit. Let me tell you briefly what's in all of this. First, we found that the State had withheld a sizable number of documents from you prior to trial. Mark, the records that they withheld deal with the investigation, but they also deal with the snitch, Jonathan Walker. Seems that Walker got one heck of a sweet deal for testifying against you. He got his charges nol prossed – dropped, in other words. The man walked out of jail a free man the day after you were sentenced to death! What's more, the State knew about it at least a month before your trial. Cummings had no idea. That's claim one. It's what we call a *Brady* claim, after that case, *Brady versus Maryland*.

"The next claim is against Cummings. We filed it because the man didn't do his job. It's a claim for ineffective assistance of counsel. Bottom line is that he should have found out about Walker. Plus, he didn't conduct much of an investigation into the other parts of the case. That guy he had as an investigator was still in law school, for crying out loud! So that's the claim under

Strickland versus Washington. We feel it's a pretty strong claim as well.

"The next claim alleges that Cummings screwed up in your penalty phase by not presenting the mounds of mitigating evidence that existed in your case. It's another *Strickland* claim.

"The rest of the claims are pretty standard. Boilerplate types. To tell you the truth, it's unlikely at this stage that we'd get relief on them, but we wanted to preserve them for a later appeal."

"What about Eddy's information?" Mark asked. "How did that turn out?"

"Went nowhere, Mark. Sorry. . . . Look, I'd better run. Thanks again. Read all of this over and let me know when you're done. We'll discuss the details then."

"Well, what happens next?"

"Good question. Then I've really got to be heading out. We've asked for an evidentiary hearing before Judge Pinkston. Under the law he has to give you that unless he can conclusively deny relief based upon the records themselves; that is, if they show that you're not entitled to relief. No way that's the case, so I expect that you'll get that hearing. Then he'll have to rule on the 3.850 after the hearing is over."

"How long will it take before we know about the hearing?"

"No idea. First thing he'll probably do is to order the State to respond to the motion. Then after they do that, he'll decide. It'll probably be at least two months before he tells us when the hearing will be. Okay? Look, I've really gotta go. Enjoy the reading, Mark. Let me know what you think."

With that, Winston left Mark with four stacks of documents -- over a thousand pages in all. Mark, still in somewhat of a daze, picked them up, cradled them in his handcuffed arms, and once more began the long trek down the hall back to his cell.

As he sat cross-legged on the bunk in his cell, Mark anxiously put the appendices to the 3.850 on the bunk beside him. He situated each volume just right -- side by side for easy access. Then, as if he were engaged in a ceremony, he began reading the 3.850 itself.

The reading was slow. Boring at first. And he didn't understand half of it. But then again, he had plenty of time to figure it out. To his relief, however, it began to get real interesting when he began reading about the deal that Smallwood had negotiated with Walker. According to other inmates who had talked to Winston, Walker had admitted to them that Smallwood gave him a "get out of jail free card" in exchange for testifying against Mark. What's more, Walker admitted to other inmates that he had never heard Mark say anything about the murder or his involvement in it. Court records showed that Walker had been freed the day after Mark was sentenced to death. Judge Pinkston was the presiding judge. As he continued reading, Mark learned that Walker had also given Winston an affidavit admitting that he had lied on the stand.

"Man, Billygoat, we got'em now!" an elated Mark announced to his neighbor. "The only guy to testify against me has just been proven to be a liar! They gotta give me a new trial when they see this!"

An obviously half-asleep Billygoat mumbled something unintelligible in response, so Mark continued to read.

The exhilaration he experienced from his early reading soon became a distant friend. For he soon discovered that his attorneys had launched a full-scale attack on his trial attorney, a man whom, until now at least, he had basically liked. The argument, he soon learned, was that Cummings was in over his head. He and his staff were inexperienced. And while he had tried to do the job, the truth was that he had failed to conduct an adequate investigation. If he had been competent, the pleading stated, he would have found on his own that Walker was a fraud.

The sadness that Mark felt at seeing Cummings pilloried soon turned to anger, however. As he continued to read he learned that the Group maintained that Cummings's problems in the guilt phase of his trial were far overshadowed by his outright incompetence in the penalty phase. That aspect of the case was fraught with errors because, as was asserted by Dr. Goldfarb, Mark had been physically and mentally abused by his parents as a small child! "WHAT?" he yelled upon reading the allegation. "Where in the hell did they come up with this crap?"

"Okay, okay. I give up. What's going on, man?" mumbled Billygoat.

"Listen to this, Frederico," began Mark. "'It is Dr. Goldfarb's belief based upon his examination of Mr. Abramson that he was mentally and physically abused as a child. The abuse itself is believed to have been so pervasive that the Defendant has repressed his memory of the assaults. Dr. Goldfarb further contends that the abuse was suffered at the hands of both parents. Significantly, while both parents acknowledged that Mr. Abramson was raised in a strict home, and while both admit to themselves having been the victims of abusive parents, neither will answer any direct questions about their child's formative years. It is also important to note that Mr. Abramson's sibling, a one-year-old boy, died from what were deemed at the time to be natural causes.' . . . Do you believe this garbage, man? How can they print this stuff? I didn't tell them they could do that!"

"You signed the pleading, didn't you?" asked Frederico.

"Yeah. So what?"

"Well read it. It's not only them saying that this is what happened. It's also you, my friend!"

As he reread the signature page of his pleading, Mark's stomach rose to his throat. Frederico was right. His signature attested to the truth of everything contained in the pleading. "Man, I'm going to stop this," was all he could say. "I've got to stop it before my folks see this."

"Oh yeah, how're you gonna do that? When's the motion due?"

"Day after tomorrow," replied Mark.

"So you're stuck," chuckled Frederico. "Sorry to laugh on you, man, but it happens every time. . . . Look. You can't pull back on that pleading now, because if you do you'll lose all of your appeals. And besides, from what you said earlier there's some good stuff in there. That stuff about the snitch is pretty good. So I don't see that you've got any choice."

"Well, what am I supposed to do, just sit here and watch my family get paraded around like a bunch of freaks? It ain't right, man. It ain't right. I've got to . . ."

"What you've got to do," interrupted Frederico, "is to get ahold of your parents and set this straight with them. Otherwise you're gonna have trouble with them."

"Yeah, well, I'm also gonna fire these jerks," Mark announced.

"No you're not, man," was Frederico's immediate reply. "Why don't you get it through your head. This ain't your case no more. You ought to know that by now. You've tried to fire them once already and no one would listen to you. I keep telling you it ain't no use."

Frederico's last statement hung in the air, as a sea fog that had suddenly rolled in off of the bay only to overtake everything in its path. Both men knew that what he'd said was true, but neither wanted to discuss it. Frederico nevertheless broke the stillness. "Mark, listen to me. I've tried to fire those jerks at least five times. Five times, man. And every time the courts just ignore it. See, I'm supposed to be crazy as a bedbug, so anything I say is just ignored. And since I'm crazy I obviously can't represent myself. So as far as the courts are concerned I need those guys."

"Yeah, well, sometimes I think I'm saner than they are," said Mark. "Man, this sucks. There ain't no way out of it, is there?"

"Tell you what. If you find it, then let me know. 'Cause I've been looking for it for a long time."

"Well, I'm gonna find it," Mark responded. "And when I do, you'll be the first one I tell."

Once again it was quiet. Mark returned to his reading. Frederico returned to his nap, interrupted at times by what he could tell were the muffled cries of a man who at any minute could give up. Frederico had been there before. He therefore accorded his naïve neighbor the courtesy that had been denied him years ago. He allowed him to continue on his own until Mark, like he, was transported by sleep to a better world.

"Guard!" shouted Mark when he awoke. "Next time you see that Connors fellow, how about tellin' him that I'd like to talk to him."

"Sure," answered the guard, as Mark turned over on his side and tried once more to end the day.

CHAPTER XXII

It was the lead story in the St. Bartholomew Press that Sunday morning. The headline announced that almost five years after he had been sentenced to death, Mark Abramson had once again asked the court to overturn his conviction and sentence.

"KILLER SEEKS TO AVOID ELECTRIC CHAIR" was the attention-grabbing headline of the day. The story was predictable. Short on facts and long on disjointed discourse about the horrible nature of the crime. It had, after all, been the worst crime ever to haunt little Cortez County. People would never forget it entirely. They would share the widow's angst until the killer paid for the crime with his life. Until then it could not, it would not, be business as usual around town.

Winston's prediction about how the case would proceed had proven true. Judge Pinkston had received the defendant's motion, reviewed it, and ordered the State to submit a written response within thirty days. The State dutifully filed its response, which included a particularly sarcastic and scathing attack on the Defendant's allegations that evidence was withheld. The factual allegations were, the State maintained, insufficient to entitle the Defendant to any relief whatsoever.

The State's protestations notwithstanding, Judge Pinkston decided that an evidentiary hearing on certain of the allegations was indeed in order. So, Mark's hearing was scheduled for mid-September, almost nine months after his 3.850 had been filed. For the first time in five years he would leave his cell at Raiford and return to the place he had called home for so long.

As he rode in the back of the prison van and looked out the window, he drank in the views of the Gulf of Mexico, views that, while not entirely forgotten, needed to be restored to his mind's eye lest the memory of them one day die from neglect. It was truly beautiful, this part of the world. The water calmly made its way from distant, unknown places changing colors from the azure blues of the south to the dark, forbidding blues of the open sea. But once it arrived on the North Florida coast it had once again metamorphosed into a beautiful emerald blue-green color that gave the region its name, the Emerald Coast. And on a day like this day the water glistened in the bright sun, beckoning the curious mixture of tourists and migratory birds to savor the beauty of the sandy white beaches. Those same beaches had once been home to Mark and Susan.

Contemplating the simple, unpretentious majesty of the area was not, therefore, entirely risk free for this former resident of St. Bartholomew. But at least it made him feel as though he were still alive. Such feelings had been stripped from him the moment he had heard twelve members of that jury say that they each believed that he was guilty of killing Ed Baker. So in spite of the fact that he would obviously have preferred to have been able to stroll the coastline once again with his wife, Mark, for now, was grateful once again to be able simply to breathe in the area's warmth and beauty. He would savor the moment, short as it was, for who knew how long it would be before he would be able to enjoy it again?

Mark's questions about his future were soon to be answered, however. What Mark had not fully comprehended was that almost no resident of St. Bartholomew, or of Cortez County for that matter, ever wanted to give him the opportunity to return to his home. The idea that he would once again stroll his favorite beach was even more ludicrous. As the day approached for his evidentiary hearing to begin, the community became increasingly hostile to the thought that this murderer would be temporarily returning to their midst. Neighborhood watch groups met to finalize plans to ensure their assigned areas were kept safe from harm. Flyers were passed out around town reminding folks that the hearing would begin promptly at nine o'clock on Tuesday morning, and that a show of support for the prosecution was critical in their fight to see justice carried out. The local radio stations played their part by encouraging callers to provide them with their views of what should be done to this monster who would soon be harbored among them. The suggestions differed in specifics but not in outcome: Abramson should die as soon as possible. It was an abomination to spend another tax dollar on keeping the vermin alive. It was indeed a restless community that awaited the arrival of this defendant who wanted an opportunity to free himself of the sentence that had been placed around his neck.

Forty-eight hours before the hearing was to begin, Andrew Smallwood worked steadily and deliberately to ensure that Mark would never be freed from captivity. The conviction had been wholly justified: of that Smallwood was convinced. Sure there were some problems with Walker's testimony, but regardless of whether he was now wavering, it was still clear that the right man had been convicted. There would be no apologies from this prosecutor.

"Bill, this is Andrew Smallwood," detective Langdon heard as he picked up the receiver. "I wanted to check with you about Walker. Have you talked with him again?"

"Yeah, I talked to him this afternoon, as a matter of fact. He's back in the jail over here. Mad as ever."

"About what this time?" asked Andrew. "Aren't the accommodations suitable?"

"I don't think that's it," chuckled Langdon. "He's just upset because he got picked up again. He swears he didn't burglarize that store in Miami. And he's not at all happy about having to testify this week."

"Is he sticking to his story?"

"So far he is. Man, he's sure not happy about it, though. I think he really regrets giving Klingbeil that affidavit."

"It does complicate matters some. But I guess it's not surprising that he would turn on us. . . . Let me ask you something, Bill. Is there any possibility that we can do anything for him with those guys in Miami-Dade?"

231

"Like what?" Langdon asked. "You're certainly not thinking of trying to get him another deal are you?"

"Why not? If the guy disavows the affidavit, says he was pressured into signing it or something to that effect, we could maybe do something for him. . . . We need this death sentence to stand, Bill."

"Sure we do, but let's suppose we could work out something down south. How can we trust this dude to keep his mouth shut? He's already talked once."

"He won't," answered Smallwood. "We can see to that. All we have to do is condition the favor on him keeping quiet. Shouldn't be too hard to do. If he gets convicted no judge is gonna have any mercy on his sorry butt. Not as many times as he's gotten a break."

"Well, do you want me to talk to him again?"

"Yeah, why not. Explain to him that if he testifies in accordance with his affidavit, the prosecution in Miami is not going to look very kindly on him down there. This guy is only out to save his own skin. He'll jump at the chance to walk. In the meantime I'll call some friends of mine in Miami and see what we can get going. Thanks a lot, Bill. . . . Are you ready for Tuesday?"

"I've been ready, man. It's been too long. We need to get the show on the road."

"I agree. Listen, I'd better go. Talk at you later." As he hung up the phone Andrew felt proud of his latest brainstorm. One way or another he'd maintain control of this hearing. Of that he had no doubt.

"Abramson, you've got a visitor," said the guard who appeared at Mark's cell door.

"Hey, Carl, good to see you, man," said Mark with a genuine smile on his face.

"It's been a long time."

"Yeah, I guess it has," the guard responded. "How you been doin'?"

"Still kickin' I guess," Mark said. "But it gets pretty difficult sometimes, you know. I'm just looking forward to this hearing right now. I think things could really turn around for me this time."

"Yeah, maybe. Listen, you ready to go? These folks are waitin'."

"Uh-huh. Who is it anyway? Not more lawyers."

"Nope. Not lawyers. It's your parents, Mark."

"My parents?" asked Mark, who was clearly shocked by the news. "They want to see me?"

"Yeah, I think so. See, there's no one else in here that they're related to. So are you coming out or not?"

"Sure. Let's go."

As Mark walked into the familiar visiting room at the jail he couldn't help but be tense at the prospect of seeing his parents again for the first time in so many years. He had seen neither of them since before he was indicted for the murder. It was as if they didn't exist. No cards or letters. No phone calls. Nothing. But then again, he hadn't tried to contact them either. The fault went both ways, he figured.

Upon entering the room Mark was struck by the appearance of both Keith and Shelby. His father's hair was now almost completely white. He had aged so much.

Wrinkles now replaced the previously tight, tanned skin on his face, and underneath his clothes it was obvious that his once muscular body had turned soft with age. He stood before his son physically bent and emotionally broken.

Mark's mother was no better off. It was clear to her son that in spite of her forced smiles she was suffering from the current situation. She was dressed immaculately as ever, and her now silver hair was neatly permed and perfectly coifed as always. But she, like her husband, had borne the weight of the past years and had not escaped from under it without being changed in spirit. It was doubtful that she would ever fully recover, regardless of the outcome.

"So, mom. Dad. How are you? I'm sort of surprised to see you here."

"Don't I even get a hug?" asked Shelby with a partially hidden smile. "It has been a while, son." As the mother and her son embraced, tears began to fill her eyes. It had been far too long since the two had seen, or even communicated, with each other. She held him tightly, as if by doing so she could single-handedly transport him from this place to the safety of their home.

"Mom, how are you doing?" was the only thing Mark could manage to say. "How are you holding up?"

"Your mother's not doing well, son," said Keith. "This has been really hard on her. Me, too. But we'll get through it." After an awkward pause, the father continued.

"The question is how are you holding up, son?"

"Oh, I don't know. Some days are better than others, I guess. But mostly they're all alike. I'm getting by."

"I guess you're glad to be back here," said Keith. "In spite of everything, I mean."

"Yeah, I guess I am. But dad, no one has been here to see me. Not until today, when you all came. What's going on?"

"Mark, I imagine that they don't know how to handle it. There's a lot of bad feelings out there. People are pretty upset. They're mad."

"Well, they were mad before the trial, but people still came by. . . . At least some people did."

Avoiding the awkward reference to their failure to visit their son, Shelby stood up and walked to the window overlooking the town. "Yeah, but this time it's different, honey. These people are acting downright mean. I don't know how else to put it. It may be that people are scared to come see you." Then, sensing the hurt that the statement had unexpectedly caused, she added, "Of course, it may be that people just haven't had time to get here. You just got in town yesterday, didn't you?"

"Yeah, yesterday evening. That's probably it."

The conversation continued for over an hour. Small talk, really. Each of the three family members was ill at ease with the situation. It was not something they had experienced before, seeing a loved one behind bars. It was foreign to them, and they suspected it always would be. The guard's interruption to let them know that they had only five more minutes was at some levels a welcomed intrusion. When visiting hours came to a close each of them embraced one more time and walked stoically out of the room, promising to resume the meeting the next day. No words were spoken about the allegations of abuse, which were central elements of Mark's request for a new trial. No one knew how to begin such a conversation. Perhaps tomorrow, each of them thought to himself. Perhaps tomorrow.

While the boy and his parents sat in the sparsely appointed visiting room, others sat in the sanctuary of the First Church of Shelbyville and listened to the Sunday sermon.

The service was heavily attended, as were most on Sunday mornings. Today's service was not particularly different from those past. It was simply that the members sensed a need to be together since the community was about to relive once again the horrible events surrounding Ed Baker's death. They were consoled by the pastor who, as he had done in years past, reminded them that even though this evil had permeated the county, they would be able to survive it, only if they would remain faithful to his teachings on the subject. The murderer would pay with his life. God had demanded it, and they must support the State's effort to see that God's will would be carried out. As the service concluded the congregation filed out of the beautifully adorned sanctuary and through the heavy, oak front doors. As they milled around outside many heads nodded in agreement that the murderer had been allowed to live far too long. If there were to be justice, his execution should be carried out now, not next month or next year.

Listening to the adults discuss this topic of the day, the boy wondered what had driven them to speak so strongly against a person who had at one time lived among them.

Yes, he had done wrong. But didn't the Bible also say to forgive one another? Or did that just apply to certain people, or to certain offenses? It had always seemed disingenuous to the boy, this idea of the death penalty. People always said that the

Old Testament required it. And they were right. But the New Testament teachings of Christ were hardly supportive of such behavior. What's more, the boy didn't understand what these people wanted. Did they want to go back to the ways of the Old Testament and execute kids for disobeying their parents? It just didn't make sense to him that one should pick and choose which portions of the Bible to follow. Perhaps someday he would be able to figure it all out. Today, however, he just wanted to get back home.

As the car pulled out of the church parking lot, fifteen-year-old Steven Morada contemplated the events of the day. He just couldn't understand the thinking of many of the people he knew. "Mom," he finally asked his mother, "what do you think about this guy who killed Mr. Baker?"

"What do you mean, son?" asked his mother, somewhat surprised. It wasn't like her son to discuss such serious topics with her.

"Well, why is it that everyone wants to see him executed so quickly? I mean, the paper said something about him claiming that he's innocent, or something like that."

"Yeah, well you can't believe everything you read, Steve," replied the mother.

"Besides, what would you expect the guy to say? He's gonna be fried pretty soon."

"But what if he's right? What if he didn't do it? What then?" the boy persisted.

"If he didn't do it the prosecutor wouldn't have charged him with it, son," answered the mother. "Besides that, he had a trial before a jury. He had his chance to tell the jury his side of things and they didn't believe him. So he has no right to complain if you ask me."

"Yeah, and the paper said that he's claiming that some of the witnesses lied."

"Steve, what else is the man going to say? Huh? If the witnesses had lied the jury would have seen it. That's what trials are all about, son."

"I just don't think it's right, that's all," Steve said. "If that one guy lied the way the paper said, it seems to me that the prosecutor is wrong to go after this dude."

"Steve, that's nonsense. Besides, you heard the pastor just now. We have an obligation to support the State. If we don't then we might as well be criminals ourselves. This guy killed Ed Baker and he should pay for what he did. Instead of that he's living the good life on our tax money. It's wrong, I say. And if you think about it some more you'll see what I mean."

"What's wrong, mom, is that everyone I know is licking his chops waiting to see the guy killed. I think half of the people in Cortez County would line up to be chosen to pull the switch if they had the opportunity. Why don't they just get a life or something?"

"Steve, don't talk about your neighbors that way," snapped the boy's mother.

"These are good people you're talking about."

"And these good people were volunteering to drive vans to the hearing so that they could watch the freak plead for his life, mom. For crying out loud, Reverend Perkins is leading the whole procession! It's like the man is obsessed with killing the freak or something. I don't see where they're such good people."

"They only want to see to it that this county is safe for us to live in. And don't talk like that about the pastor."

"Doesn't sound to me like it's too safe for this guy who's gonna get fried," smiled Steve, relishing the opportunity to contradict his mother. "Sounds to me like they all think they're better than anyone else and that they can't make a mistake. That's what I think."

The boy's mother was perplexed. Here, after months of pleading with her son to talk to her, she was now looking forward to him shutting up. Who had put these thoughts in his head anyway, she asked herself. "Steve, I don't know what the answer is," she finally muttered. "All I know is that the man was tried by a jury and found guilty. And I know that the man he killed was a good man. He was decent and honorable and he didn't deserve to die like that. No one does, except for that guy Abramson."

"Yeah, mom, whatever you say," said Steve, as he turned his head and looked out the car window at the houses as the car sped past on its way back home, its occupants now silent in contemplation of events past and events yet to come.

It was late on Monday evening that Andrew Smallwood completed the last witness preparation. He had arrived in St. Bartholomew that afternoon and begun to set up shop in his office in the courthouse. The office was leased by the state attorney's office so that its prosecutors would have a place from which to work when they attended hearings in the small city. It was not extravagantly equipped, but it at least had the necessities. Enough to get you through with minimal discomfort. And that was all that Andrew asked for.

Now confident that he was prepared to defend against Mark's accusations, Smallwood closed the door to his office and walked one block to the jail. By now he was well known to the staff at the jail, and so it was with minimum difficulty that he gained admittance to the facility and made his way to the visiting room where he awaited Jonathan Walker.

"Mr. Walker," he said to the inmate as the man slowly entered the room, "I wanted to come by to see you before the hearing, because I don't know if I'll have an opportunity to speak with you after the hearing begins. Has Mr. Langdon spoken with you yet?"

"I've seen him a few times," stated Walker matter-of-factly. "He says that you're gonna help me out. Is that true?"

"Depends on what you mean by help you out, Mr. Walker."

"What I mean is, do I get out of here or not?"

As Andrew looked over the man who sat across the table from him, he knew he was in control of things. This deal could be clinched with little difficulty. "That's a somewhat difficult question to answer, Mr. Walker," began Andrew. "It depends on your testimony at the upcoming hearing. If you are truthful in your testimony, then I believe my office can help you. I've spoken with the authorities in Miami and they assure me that they would look very favorably upon your assistance to my office."

"And so, if I testify truthfully, as you say, I can expect to walk. Is that it?"

"That's essentially it."

"And what do you consider to be truthful testimony, Mr. Smallwood?"

"I think we all know what the truth is, Mr. Walker. The truth is that Mark Abramson butchered that victim. Now you might not have known the victim, but a lot of people around here knew him real well, and they want this man to pay for what he did."

"And so you want me to testify so that this dude takes the rap for killing Baker. Is that it? Is that the truth, Mr. Prosecutor?"

"That's essentially it. Now listen to me, Walker," Andrew shot back in a low, determined voice. "I can be a lot of help to you if you tell the truth on that stand. There was never a deal and you know it. The fact of the matter is that you heard Abramson confess to the murder. And now he's pressuring you to change your story. That's the truth, Mr. Walker. And nothing but the truth."

"And if I tell the truth, sir? What then?"

"Well, then I'll do whatever I can to help you out down south. I don't think you'll have to worry."

"But there are no guarantees, is that it?"

"Right."

Walker thought about the choice for a while and then smiled. "Guess I don't have much choice but to tell the truth, sir," he said. "I'll see you at the hearing." As he stood from his chair and extended his hand to Smallwood, Walker nodded his approval of what would be a joint undertaking. "Don't worry, Mr. Smallwood," he finally said, as he turned to go back to his cell. "Just get some rest like I'm going to do. You'll probably need it."

"Yeah, I think you're right. And thanks, Walker. We'll take real good care of you. Don't worry about it at all."

As he exited the jail Andrew's thoughts were on anything but rest. The adrenaline was pumping and sleep would be impossible for now. What the heck, he thought to himself. It's a nice night out. Time to go for a walk. Tomorrow will take care of itself.

Five years after he had been convicted and sentenced to death, Mark found himself being led into the same, forbidding courtroom that he had come to fear in the past. Nothing had changed. It was decorated with long, flowing crimson draperies that covered the windows. The many wooden benches that provided seating for those spectators in the audience were covered with matching crimson velvet cushions to maximize the comfort of those people who chose to sit through what were often long and boring hearings. But it was the front of the courtroom that drew the attention of all who entered that hallowed place. The judge's bench was elevated almost a foot above the rest of the floor, forcing those who had to address the court to look up to the judge, as if in supplication. The bench itself was nine feet wide and made of solid mahogany. To the judge's left sat the judge's clerk. To the right was the witness stand. In front of the bench behind yet more mahogany furnishings sat the court clerk, court reporter, and court bailiff. Ten feet beyond those personnel were the prosecution and defense tables. All in all it was an imposing place for anyone to be. It was designed that way and it achieved its purpose. The place evoked no fond memories for Mark as he sat behind the counsel table next to his lawyer.

As Mark looked around the courtroom, he slowly took in each face in the audience. He absorbed them as though they were rays from the sun. He wanted just enough to be able to remember them later, but not enough to cause him harm. He remembered the lethalness of the stares from the trial. It was not necessary to repeat it now. And yet, he continued to survey the audience, hoping beyond hope that he would see his wife. Only when he was satisfied that she was not in the audience, did he turn back around and prepare himself for what lay ahead.

Mark had little time to wait before Judge Pinkston, looking older and heavier than he had at the trial, entered the courtroom and assumed the bench. "This is the State of Florida versus Mark

Abramson, Case Number CF-19A61," resonated the jurist's voice through the courtroom. "The record will reflect that the Defendant is present with his collateral counsel, Judd Klingbeil. The State is represented by the Honorable Andrew Smallwood from the Office of the State Attorney. We are present today for an evidentiary hearing on the Defendant's Rule 3.850 Motion for Postconviction Relief. Mr. Klingbeil, is the defense prepared to begin?"

"We are, your Honor," said Klingbeil.

"Very well, then. You may call your first witness."

"The defense calls Jonathan Walker," announced Mark's attorney, as he looked at Mark and winked in a gesture of reassurance. Then, after waiting for the witness to be led into the courtroom in shackles and handcuffs, Klingbeil heard him sworn.

"You may proceed," stated Judge Pinkston.

"Thank you, your Honor," replied Klingbeil. And with that began what was expected to be the questioning of the defense's most powerful witness. It did not take Klingbeil long to dispense with the background questions that explained who this witness was and why he was important to the case. He then began the important task of eliciting the testimony that he hoped would overturn his client's conviction. "Mr. Walker, you just told us about your testimony at the trial."

"Yes, sir."

"And you just testified that at the trial you told the jury that Mr. Abramson here told you in the prison yard that he killed Ed Baker. Was that testimony true, Mr. Walker?"

Every eye in the courtroom was riveted on the witness as the man who had previously given the State the only independent, direct connection between Mark and Ed's death rocked slightly back and forth in the witness chair. Walker was obviously uncomfortable.

"Mr. Walker, do you need me to repeat the question?" asked Klingbeil.

"No, sir, I understand the question," answered the witness. "I was just thinking . . . no, the testimony I gave at trial was incorrect. Abramson never told me that he killed that man."

Amid the murmurs in the audience, Klingbeil, himself feeling somewhat relieved, continued the questioning. "Mr. Walker, did Mr. Abramson at any time say anything to you about using a knife to try to kill Mr. Baker?"

Then, catching everyone by surprise, Mark heard Judge Pinkston interrupt.

"Excuse me," boomed the judge's voice, "under the circumstances I think it would be wise to explain to this witness that he has certain constitutional rights. Mr. Smallwood, would you please so advise the witness?"

"Surely, your Honor," answered the prosecutor. "Mr. Walker, do you understand that the testimony that you just gave could subject you to perjury charges being filed against you by the State?"

"Yes, sir, I do," said Walker, his voice remaining strong.

"And do you understand that you have the constitutional right to remain silent and not to incriminate yourself?"

"What are you saying? That I don't have to answer these questions?"

"Yes, sir, that's what I'm saying. If you wish to have an attorney present with you, you're also entitled to that. Now, do you also understand that if you are charged and convicted with perjury you could be incarcerated for up to seven years?"

"Your Honor, I object!" interrupted Klingbeil. "This questioning is totally improper and designed to do nothing more than to prevent this witness from assisting in the defense's case."

"Overruled," snapped Pinkston. "The witness is entitled to know his constitutional rights. Continue, Mr. Smallwood."

"Do you understand the penalties associated with a perjury conviction, Mr. Walker?"

"I do."

"And do you understand that if you continue to testify in this fashion, the State of Florida will, in fact, charge you with perjury?"

As he squirmed in his chair Walker paused, then said, "I do."

"And do you wish to continue this testimony?" asked Smallwood.

"I do," shot back Walker.

As Smallwood sat down he glared at Klingbeil. "Your witness," was all that he could say under the circumstances.

"Mr. Walker, I will repeat my last question," continued Klingbeil. "Did Mr. Abramson at any time say anything to you about using a knife to try to kill Mr. Baker?"

"No. He did not."

"Why, Mr. Walker, did you testify as you did?"

"Well, at the time, see, I was in jail awaiting trial. And this detective came to me and told me that if I could get any information against Abramson they would do what they could to get the charges dropped." After a brief pause he continued. "Oh, yeah, and I would also have to testify against him at trial."

"And did the State make good on their promise to you?"

"Yeah. The charges were dismissed. They called it something weird."

"Nol Prosse?"

"Yeah, that's it."

"And when were the charges dismissed?"

"I don't know. A little while after I testified."

"Your Honor," Klingbeil addressed the court. "I have here a certified copy of the dismissal. I would like the record to reflect that Mr. Walker's charges were dismissed the day after Mr. Abramson was sentenced to death by the court."

"So noted," said Pinkston.

"I have no further questions, your Honor."

As Smallwood rose from his chair he stared at Walker in disgust. "Mr. Walker, you are incarcerated now, are you not?"

"Yes sir, I am."

"And what are you incarcerated for?"

"Burglary, but I haven't been to trial yet."

"Now, how did you come to sign this affidavit that you previously testified about?"

"Some investigator brought it to me to sign."

"And how did the investigator get the information to put in the affidavit?"

"I told him what to put in it."

"Why did you do that?"

"Because, I knew that what I said at the trial was wrong. I don't want this guy to go to the chair because of what I said."

"That's very kind of you, sir. So when did you become so charitable in your approach to mankind?"

"Objection," shouted Klingbeil.

"Sustained."

"Mr. Walker," continued Smallwood, "isn't it true that the facts in the affidavit were already in that affidavit when the investigator first met with you?"

"No."

"And isn't it true that they simply told you what they wanted you to say?"

"No, it isn't."

"When is your burglary trial scheduled in Miami?"

"Objection."

"Overruled," answered Pinkston. "The witness will answer."

"Sometime next month."

"And you're not lying now to gain favor with the court, are you?"

"No, sir."

"But you were lying then, is that correct?"

"Yeah, because that's what you wanted me to do."

"What I wanted you to do? How is that?" Smallwood put on a forced grin.

"Well, you all made it perfectly clear that I was supposed to bury Abramson, and that if I did then I'd walk out of here. Just like happened last night when you came back to see me. Same thing. You said that if I took back what I said in the affidavit that they would go easy in Miami this time."

Silence can be a powerful statement. It was silence that now spoke in the courtroom. Then there were muffled voices in the audience. It was disbelief, really. The question, though, was whom to believe and whom not to believe. No one wanted to believe the inmate who sat before them. After all, who would believe anything he had to say anyway. It was obvious that he was simply trying to save one of his own from getting his just punishment.

As Smallwood stood before the witness and pondered his next question, Judge Pinkston interrupted his thoughts. "Mr. Smallwood, we don't have all day. Do you have any further questions?"

"No, your Honor. I have no further questions for this witness."

"Any redirect?"

"No, your Honor," answered Klingbeil.

"Very well, then. Mr. Walker, you are excused. Call your next witness, Mr. Klingbeil."

"The defense calls Joel Cummings," announced Klingbeil, as he continued to present his client's case. The battle between Klingbeil and Cummings was painful for Mark to watch. Klingbeil began a systematic review of the trial attorney's investigation into the case and found fault with practically everything that Cummings had done. To Klingbeil's proper assertions that more witnesses should have been interviewed, Cummings agreed. But his funds and his time were limited. He'd done the best that he could with what he had. If he had been given more time he probably would have spoken with more people. But he doubted that his strategy would have changed. He felt then, and he felt now, that his client was innocent. Other than Walker and Langdon, there was no testimony or other evidence linking Mark to the crime.

Klingbeil questioned Cummings for hours and purposely concentrated on Cummings's handling of the penalty phase of Mark's trial. "Why didn't you interview his parents?" asked Klingbeil. "I did speak with them," replied Cummings, "but in my estimation there simply wasn't anything there." "Are you a psychiatrist?" asked Klingbeil. "No I'm not, and neither are you," came the answer. Klingbeil responded that such was the reason he had hired someone to evaluate his client and to show the court the reasons Mark should be spared from the electric chair.

After what seemed like an eternity Cummings was done. As he stepped from the witness stand he looked at Mark, shook his head, and vowed to himself never to handle one of these cases again.

"The defense calls Dr. Steven Goldfarb," Klingbeil next announced. As the doctor slowly entered the courtroom and walked to the stand, Klingbeil bent down to his client and whispered, "Mark, this testimony is going to be rough. If you don't think you can handle it you can go sit outside the courtroom." "I'll be okay," answered Mark. "I want to hear what he has to say."

Goldfarb's testimony began with an impressive recitation of his credentials, after which he was accepted by the court as an expert in his field. He told the Court that each of the tests he conducted substantiated his ultimate diagnosis that Mark suffered from a behavioral disorder – one that had been induced by significant abuse at the hands of his father. What passed for routine punishment in the Abramson household, the doctor advised the court, amounted to nothing less than child abuse. Mark was savagely beaten as a child and was then told over and over again that he was worthless as a human being. The ultimate effect was that he grew up frustrated, believing that he had little to contribute to this world. He nevertheless tried to better himself, only to be continuously knocked down by those around him. The final straw was being terminated by Ed Baker. Something snapped inside Mark, which resulted in the killing. Mark, as he had done when a child, had suppressed all memories of the event itself.

As Mark sat and listened to the doctor's testimony, he was in a state of disbelief. Where did they come up with this crap, he asked himself over and over. But his amazement culminated when he heard Goldfarb say that he had, in fact, committed the murder. This was not what he had understood would happen. And so, with little thought given to the consequences, Mark suddenly rose from his chair and addressed the court.

"Your Honor, may I say something?"

"No you may not, Mr. Abramson. Now sit back down."

"But your Honor, I did not commit this murder!" Mark exclaimed. "If this man is going to testify like this I don't want him. And I don't want this attorney representing me anymore."

"Your Honor," interjected Klingbeil, "if I might have a few minutes to consult with my client."

"Well, I'll tell you what, sir," said Pinkston. "It's getting late anyway. Why don't we take a five minute break then resume with this witness, finish him up, and break for today. The court will be in recess until 4:30."

As Klingbeil turned to look at Mark, he could see that his client was seething. "So that's why you wanted me out of the courtroom." He heard Mark say. "You didn't want me to hear what this man was going to say. You didn't want me to hear you sell me down the river. Well, I don't want any part of it! And I want you off the case! Do you hear me?"

"Now listen, Mark. That's not in your best interest."

"And how, exactly is it in my best interest to sit here and listen to my own damn lawyer tell the world that I killed Ed Baker? Huh? How is that in my best interest?"

"It could save you from the chair, Mark. That's how."

"So I get to live the rest of my life in a cage. Is that the idea? Is that in my best interest?"

"Yes, it is, for now."

"Well, answer me this, Klingbeil. Why hasn't anyone asked me about what I think is in my best interest? Or, don't I count?"

"All rise," Mark suddenly heard the bailiff announce. Court was back in session.

"Your Honor," Mark abruptly said, as Pinkston once more seated himself. "I want this attorney off of my case, and I want to stop this questioning of this doctor Goldfarb, or whoever he is."

"Your Honor," interjected Klingbeil, "as I am sure the court is aware the Florida Supreme Court has repeatedly held that our office is required to represent capital inmates such as Mr. Abramson. And while I can understand his position, I think, the fact of the matter is, he doesn't have the right to choose who will represent him, or to represent himself. What I would propose doing at this juncture is to have Mr. Abramson sit outside of the courtroom and monitor the proceedings via closed-circuit television, if possible. I regret any inconvenience that this might have caused the court."

"I'm inclined to agree with you, Mr. Klingbeil," replied Pinkston. "Mr. Abramson, for the duration of these proceedings you will observe the case from an anteroom. Should you change your mind about these proceedings your lawyer will so advise the court and you can return. Your request to fire your attorney is denied. Bailiff, take the prisoner away."

As Mark was led out of the courtroom, he turned to look out through the courtroom and heard Klingbeil continuing his questioning of the doctor. Mark then turned, hung his head, and slowly walked to the cell to watch the remainder of the proceedings by himself.

His point having been made, it did not take long for Klingbeil to dispense with the doctor. By the time the doctor's direct testimony was concluded, Mark's counsel had rather convincingly established Mark's abusive childhood and consequent behavioral disorder.

For its part, the prosecution's questioning of the esteemed doctor was limited to confirming that Mark had never told Goldfarb about the abuse. No one had. It was a deducement reached by the doctor based upon his experience in examining such patients.

As Mark sat in the cell and listened to the cross-examination of the witness, he was struck by the surrealistic nature of what had been laid out before him. The very people who were intent on putting him to death were now unknowingly supporting Mark's assertion to his attorney that the defense's expert was lying on the stand. At least it'll end soon, he thought to himself. At least it'll end soon.

But relief, as Mark learned the next day, was to be short lived. After being led back to his cell upon the conclusion of the first day's proceedings Mark had spent the next sixteen hours alone in his cell. No visitors. He really was not displeased by the lack of interest shown him, however, for he was in no mood to talk to anyone. Especially not Klingbeil or any of his cohorts. At least this way he could choose the matters that would occupy his time, thereby alleviating the pain that he had experienced as a result of seeing alleged details of his personal life laid bare before the people of St. Bartholomew to dissect. That pain returned the next day with a vengeance when Mark returned to the courtroom against the advice of his attorney.

Keith Abramson slowly walked to the witness stand after being called by his son's attorney. The preliminaries were quickly dispensed with. Everyone knew that Keith was Mark's father. The audience had not gathered to hear him talk about that fact. They wanted to hear the sordid details of the beatings that he had administered to his son -- beatings that, according to the defense, had created a monster.

The questioning of Keith Abramson had begun innocently enough. Klingbeil had been through the procedure countless times before. It was never easy for a parent to admit that he had abused his child. The job, as he saw it, was to reach down inside that parent and make him understand that his depraved actions were now little more than a past history that could finally be used to produce something good. In order to accomplish his task Klingbeil routinely allowed the parent to discuss those memories that had sustained the parent in the latter years of his miserable existence. Keith Abramson would be no different. He quite willingly told the court about Mark's childhood days, days which saw a happy boy, full of energy and enthusiasm for life. The seemingly endless days of buying new shoes because the pair he had worn for a month were now too small.

And there were sad days, as well, such as when Mark had struck out over and over in baseball to the point that his father had mercifully told him that he no longer needed to play if he didn't want to. But equally prevalent were the days of youth when Mark had seemed to be little more than a big question mark, always asking questions about anything and everything. Unbeknownst to the unwitting Keith Abramson, it was the reminiscing about those days that Klingbeil decided would provide the foot in the door to explore what he assumed would be the abuse that his client had suffered at the hands of this man.

"Now, Mr. Abramson," he began, "what kind of thoughts went through your mind when Mark would ask you those repeated questions?"

"Oh, I don't know. A lot of things, I guess."

"Well, I'm sure that you were happy that he was so inquisitive."

"Sure."

"But didn't there come a point in time when you just wanted to sit down and read the paper without being bothered by a four year old boy?"

"Sure, there were times like that. Everyone experiences that."

"And I bet that Mark was pretty much like any other four year old, wasn't he?"

"How do you mean?"

"Well, I bet that he didn't always shut up when you told him to, did he?"

"Nope. He sure didn't."

Klingbeil continued. "And there were times when you said to yourself, enough is enough, weren't there?"

"Oh, yeah."

"And I suppose every now and then you had to discipline Mark to get him to listen to him, didn't you?"

"Of course."

"And, Mr. Abramson, didn't you use corporal punishment on Mark?"

"Do you mean, did I spank him?"

"Yes. Did you spank him?"

"Sure did, when he deserved it."

"How often did that happen, Mr. Abramson? Once, twice a week?"

"Oh, I don't know. Whenever he needed it. Sometimes it was more often than others."

"But sometimes you spanked him a couple of times a week on average?"

"I guess so. Yeah."

"And when you say that you spanked Mark, what you really mean is that you hit him, isn't that true, Mr. Abramson?"

"Well, yeah. I mean, that's what spanking is, sir."

"And did he cry when you hit him?"

"Yes."

"But you spanked him anyway, didn't you?"

"Yes."

"And did there come a point in time when you were investigated by Child Services for using excessive force on your child, Mr. Abramson?"

"No."

"No, Mr. Abramson? I'll ask you again. Did there come a point in time when you were investigated by Child Services for using excessive force on your child?"

As Keith Abramson listened to the question he slowly turned his head and looked at his son. Mark, tears welling up in his eyes, returned the gaze with a blank but apologetic stare that tore at the very heart of his father's soul. "Yes, there was such a time," he heard his father say.

"Now, Mr. Abramson, they investigated you for a period of six months, didn't they?"

"I don't remember. It was about that long, I guess," Keith replied.

"Mark was four years old when that investigation began, wasn't he?"

"Yes, I guess."

"And after that investigation was concluded it was resumed two years later when your wife filed a complaint, correct?"

"Correct. It was resumed because we . . ."

"That's all we need to know, Mr. Abramson. And just so that the record is clear, you were investigated for child abuse, isn't that correct?"

"I don't know what you call it, sir," Keith answered.

"Well, let's put it in terms you do understand," Klingbeil snapped back. "Child Services came into your home to investigate complaints that you had repeatedly beaten Mark. Isn't that correct, sir?"

"Those were the allegations, yes."

"Thank you. No further questions."

As Smallwood now stood before Mark's father, he decided that the man had been through enough. "Mr. Abramson, I have only a few questions for you. To your knowledge were those allegations ever proven?"

"No they were not."

"Ever?"

"No."

"Did you ever use more force against your son than you needed to use in order to make him behave?"

"No, I did not."

"Did your son ever receive bruises because of these spankings?"

"No, he did not."

"Thank you, sir."

As Keith Abramson stepped down from the witness stand he slowly approached the defense table where his son and Klingbeil sat in silence. He received no recognition from either man that he was even present: for Mark it was due to embarrassment, for Klingbeil it was due to contempt.

As soon as Klingbeil saw Keith Abramson exit the courtroom, he rose again and announced that the next witness would be Shelby Abramson. All heads in the courtroom turned to watch the aging, former brunette walk into the courtroom and approach the witness stand. Upon being sworn in, Mark's petite mother sat down and awaited the questioning from her son's attorney. But unlike her husband, Shelby Abramson was not in a frame of mind to put up with Klingbeil's insinuations. When the point of critical mass was reached in her examination, she finally gave a response that she later punished herself with upon waking from sleep every morning.

"No, Mr. Klingbeil," she said in a tearful, quaking voice, "my husband never, ever, did anything more than spank my son on the few occasions that he needed it. We taught him right from wrong, and I believe that we raised a good boy. I've heard your psychiatrist make all sorts of statements about how my husband abused our boy. I don't know where you got that man, but as far as I'm concerned he's nothing but trash. And if you weren't representing Mark right now, I'd be inclined to think the same thing about you!"

With that having been said, Klingbeil terminated the questioning of Shelby Abramson. Smallwood, realizing that there was no way he could improve upon the testimony thus far submitted, graciously announced that he had no questions to pose to Mrs. Abramson. She, like her husband before her, walked quickly past the piercing eyes of the thrill-seekers in the audience. As she opened the door to leave she looked back at her son, who sat with his head in his shackled hands, and began to join him in experiencing a pain that neither would ever forget as long as they lived.

With Shelby out of the courtroom, Klingbeil dutifully examined his notes as if to ensure himself that he had done all that he could for his client. Then, as he rose from his chair, he addressed the court. "Your Honor, the defense rests its case."

"Very well," Pinkston said. "Mr. Smallwood, is the State prepared to present its case?"

"Your Honor, in light of the rather unconvincing evidence presented by the defense, I really do not believe that the State needs to present any evidence. It is clear that the conviction and sentence were appropriate in this case, and we therefore rest our case at this time."

"Very well," said Pinkston. "The court will therefore take this matter under advisement. I will advise you gentlemen of my decision at a later date. Court is adjourned. Guards, you may transport the defendant back to State prison at this time."

Then, in what seemed to be an instant, the judge was gone and Mark was escorted from the courtroom to await the return to his prison cell.

Not long after returning to his jail cell, Mark began gathering together what few belongings he had in anticipation of the drive back to Raiford. Lost in his thoughts as he slowly arranged his possessions in his small bag, he didn't hear the guard calling him out for a visit. "Whadda ya mean I have a visitor?" Mark asked. "I thought I was supposed to be leaving here tonight."

"Yep, you are," said the guard, "but this guy wants to see you, and I figured, why not. Hard to say when you'll get back here."

"Guess you're right about that," said Mark. "What the heck, I don't have nothin' else to do anyway."

But a few minutes later, as he was undergoing the mandatory strip search, Mark asked himself why he had bothered. "Hello," he nevertheless said to the unfamiliar face that looked up at him. "Do I know you?"

"Mr. Abramson, you don't know me. My name is Steven Morada. I didn't know if they'd let me in to see you, but I wanted to try."

Mark looked down at the kid standing in front of him. This kid's petrified, he thought to himself. "Okay. So would you tell me why you wanted to see me?"

"Mr. Abramson, I said that you don't know me. Well, I guess you don't. But I've been reading about your case in the papers. And when . . ."

"Now wait a minute kid. I don't know how you managed to get in here, but I don't feel like being put on display like . . ."

"No, Mr. Abramson, it's not like that at all. Honest." the boy urged the inmate.

"Just hear me out. That's all I ask."

"Okay. I'll hear you out. Got nothin' else to do anyway."

As Mark sat down at the table he noticed that the boy's hands were shaking. From fear, he supposed. Fear of being in the same room with a murderer. "Mr. Abramson, you're from around here, aren't you?"

"Yes. My wife and I lived here. Why?"

"Well, do you go to Lone Pine Island?" Then, in embarrassment, the boy quickly added, "I mean before you got arrested."

"Yes. We used to go there a lot. It's beautiful there."

"Okay. Did you used to go there by yourself?"

"Sure. I used to do that a lot. Used to go there to think."

"About five years or so ago?"

"Yeah. But why? Is there a point to any of this?"

"Yeah, I'm getting to it. Was there ever a time when you were sitting on the beach alone and a boy came up to you and started talking to you? It would have been about five years ago."

Mark ran his fingers through his hair and tried to think. While he enjoyed talking about something other than the case he wasn't sure that he was thrilled about being reminded about those days spent on the beach. But after looking at his visitor's inquisitive expression he decided to humor him and at least try to recall whatever it was that the boy seemed so interested in discussing. And then, to his surprise, his mind did yield a memory of a sunny day spent on the island -- a time when he was at the end of his rope. Almost suicidal, he recalled. It was just after he'd been fired from Bluestone. "Are you that little boy that came up and sat down next to me on the beach?" Mark suddenly asked in astonishment. "The little boy with his parents?"

"So it *was* you," Steve said confidently. "I knew it. I knew it all along." A big grin began to overtake his face.

"But how in the world did you remember that?" Mark asked while shaking his head in disbelief. "I mean, you weren't there more than a couple of minutes."

"Yep. That's right. But I guess at the time I was just kinda surprised that you let me sit there with you. You were pretty nice and all, and then my parents got real mad at me for talking to you. . . . I don't know. I just remembered it, that's all. . . . I guess it wasn't that long after that that you got arrested. I saw your picture in the paper."

"Yeah. You're right," answered Mark. "It wasn't but a few days later that I wound up in jail. . . . Gosh I wish I could go back to that island." As he sat at the table Mark's eyes began to glaze over, betraying the fact that his mind had drifted back to places he had known in better times. Then, when the journey ended, he looked back at the boy sitting in front of him and asked, "But how in the world did you manage to get in here to see me? They never let kids in places like this unless their parents are with them. And not always then."

"Oh, it wasn't too hard," Steve said. "I have a friend whose father works at the State prison up the road here. And the father's brother works here at the jail. After a while they got tired of me griping at them, and they told me I could come in to see you for a few minutes. But they're gonna be coming to get me real soon they said. My parents don't know I'm here. I guess I could get in trouble if they knew I were here."

"My gosh. I don't believe it," said Mark. "I just don't believe it." He couldn't keep from shaking his head. "Well, I'm glad you came by to see me. . . . what did you say your name was?"

"Steve. Steven's my real name. Steven Morada."

"Well, Steve. I'm real glad you came by. But I don't know what to say."

"Yeah. I don't know either," said Steve. "But can I ask you something?"

"Sure. I guess."

"Would it be all right if I write to you? And maybe you could write to me?"

"Sure. . . . I'd like that. I'd like that very much," answered Mark. He wrote down his own address on the piece of paper Steve handed him. Still in disbelief but very happy at finding someone on the outside who wanted to communicate with him, he looked at his visitor and asked, "So, do you have an address?"

"Yep. But I'd better work it out with my folks first. Like I said, they don't know I'm here. I'll have to let you know." No sooner had Steve finished his statement than the door to the visiting room opened and the guard motioned for him to leave.

"Well, gotta go," Steve said to his newfound friend. "Take care of yourself, Mr. Abramson."

"Mark. Call me Mark," was the inmate's reply as he extended his arm to shake hands with his small visitor. "It was really good to meet you. I look forward to getting your letters. I look forward to it a lot. Don't get much mail where I'm at."

"Okay . . . Mark," said Steve, hesitating to say the man's first name. "It was good to meet you, too. Gotta go, I guess."

With that the boy walked out of the door and into a world unknown to Mark for many years now. As he walked back to his cell Mark couldn't help shaking his head.

Imagine that, he thought to himself. Remembering me after all those years. Imagine that.

CHAPTER XXIII

Summers in Florida are difficult for many people to endure. The state does an admirable job in selling its image -- warm sandy beaches that offer rest and relaxation to distressed souls who are tired and weary of the endless gray skies that blanket their northern towns in the winter. It is hardly false advertisement, for there are few people who would question the benefit conferred upon a spirit who, after enduring months of sub-freezing temperatures, is able after a three-hour plane ride to walk beside warm, clear waters in a bathing suit.

But summers are different for those who don't live on the coast. There is sweltering humidity, which feeds tiny insects, many of whom have hypodermic needles for beaks. And for such locales there is no breeze to mitigate the daily hundred-degree heat. Raiford is such a locale. And for Mark, sitting in a cell that seemed more like a sauna, summer was unbearable. It was unbearable because this had always been his favorite time of the year. In St. Bartholomew he had always been able to find relief from the heat, either with a welcomed breeze or by choosing to forget about all cares and going for a swim in the Gulf. Raiford allowed for none of that, for obvious reasons.

This particular summer was no different from the rest. Mark passed each day no differently from the one before. It was with some relief then, that he one day received the long-awaited letter from Klingbeil informing him of Judge Pinkston's decision. At least it broke the monotony.

Sitting alone in his cell, Mark's trembling hands opened the envelope. It had been four months since his hearing had been held in St. Bartholomew. Four empty months.

Now, as he unfolded the letter and judge's opinion, Mark realized that the apprehension he had experienced during the hearing was returning with a vengeance. "Dear Mark," the letter began. And then the dreaded introduction, "I am sorry to inform you that Judge Pinkston has denied your Motion for Postconviction Relief. I am enclosing his decision for your files, and as you will see when you read it, he has determined that none of your claims for relief have any merit. We are in the process of working on the appeal to the Florida Supreme Court. Again, I am sorry that the news is bad for you. Sincerely, Judd Klingbeil."

Mark sat in his cell holding Klingbeil's letter for a few minutes and then, without reading Pinkston's decision, he put the contents back in the envelope and lay down on his bunk. As the memories of the hearing returned and then mixed with the news from the Group, the tears began to escape from the depths of his soul. Slowly, ever so slowly, they became a river unto themselves. Then, as the tears became uncontrollable, Mark's muffled cries turned to sobs, which lasted for hours on end.

Returning to his cell from his weekly visit to the yard, Frederico heard the unmistakable sign that his friend and neighbor of the past five years had just received the news that every man on the row dreaded. "Hey, Blondie, what's goin' on over there?" he asked. "Did it come?"

"Yeah, it came," Mark said after struggling for a few minutes to find the means with which to talk. "The bastard denied all relief, man. Everything. I'm dead, man. I'm dead. . . . And Klingbeil told me that he thought the claims stood a high likelihood of success."

"So what's he say now?" asked Frederico. "How does it look for the appeal?"

"I don't know. I haven't read it yet. Don't make any difference anyhow, does it?"

"Maybe, maybe not."

"Well, put it like this. Unless he really screwed up, this thing will be rubber-stamped. You told me that yourself when I first got here, Billygoat."

"So, did he screw up or not?"

"I don't know, man. Here." Mark fumbled through the envelope and retrieved the judge's decision with his now trembling hands. "Would you read it to me, man? I'm too nervous."

As Frederico reached out through the bars and took the opinion from his neighbor he unfolded it, skimmed it briefly, and then began reading it aloud. The more he read, the more it became apparent to both men that, for whatever reason, Pinkston had decided that Mark Abramson would not escape his conviction and sentence. The opinion was heavily laden with facts that the judge said supported his decision that Mark was entitled to no relief. Walker, the court found, was telling the truth about his previous lies at trial. It was evident that he had testified against Mark simply to get a deal from the State. However, Pinkston held that even if Walker's testimony were wholly stricken from the trial record there was still abundant evidence to support the conviction and sentence. He then launched into a recitation of the incriminating evidence that tied Mark to the murder of Ed Baker. In short, the error was harmless, according to the court. As Mark listened to the opinion he was incredulous. "No. He can't do that," he mumbled to himself. "He can't do that."

"Do you want me to go on?" Billygoat mercifully asked.

"Yeah. I might as well hear it all," came the tearful voice through the wall.

And so he continued. Even though, in the court's opinion, Joel Cummings had failed to conduct a proper investigation, there was no reason to believe that a more thorough investigation would have changed the outcome of the trial. Again the court found that the errors committed were harmless.

Billygoat then reached the final part of the opinion. "You sure you want me to read this?"

"Yes. Read it," was the only response.

"Well, what it says is, quote: 'As for the evidence presented in support of mitigation, this court finds that the defense proved its case that the Defendant was abused as a child by his father. This evidence therefore supports Dr. Goldfarb's opinion that the

Defendant suffered from a mental disorder at the trial, and that he acted under extreme emotional distress. However, the court is also cognizant of the jury vote in this case, which was twelve to zero in favor of a sentence of death. In light of that decision it is beyond question that this additional evidence, even if it had been introduced at trial, would not have altered the outcome of the Defendant's sentence. Further, this court would not have changed its decision to sentence the Defendant to death, based on the evidence presented. Therefore, while it is accepted that defense counsel's performance in failing to present this evidence was deficient, it is further clear to this court beyond a reasonable doubt that the error in failing to present the evidence was harmless and that it would have had no impact on the jury's decision.'"

"Is that all?" asked Mark.

"Yeah, that's about it. Just some closing stuff about denying the motion and then telling you about the right to appeal. . . . I'm sorry, man. It's vicious."

"Whadda ya think? How bad is it, Billygoat?"

"The truth?"

"Yeah. The truth."

"Real bad. This guy's making it look like he's real impartial and that he's agreeing with you, only to turn around and say that based on what he observed at trial it wouldn't have made any difference. He did help you a little bit though. I think the harmless error rulings are legal determinations. So he can be reversed on that. But the guy's tried to write a decision that will stand up. That's for sure."

"That's what I thought. I wonder what the jurors would think now if they saw that their opinion really was what counted after all? It's sick, man. Hey Billygoat, thanks for giving it to me straight. That's more than I'd get from Klingbeil."

"No sweat. I'm sorry, man. I'm real sorry. But look at it like this, there's plenty of more appeals left. You've got more chances, and more time."

As he sat alone on his bunk Mark read and reread the letter and the decision. Klingbeil, how could you tell the world that my father abused me as a child, he thought to himself. It was a lie, you know it was a lie. And now my father's branded for life. Why should he have to suffer for this? He did nothing.

The night mercifully overtook the sun on that hot summer day. But while it provided relief from the heat it could not provide relief from the pain that had invaded the very core of Mark's being. The tears flowed relentlessly that night. The river that they formed did little however, to provide sustenance to Mark. Instead, this river continued to rise until it threatened to drown the inmate, perhaps compassionately, lest his suffering be prolonged by forces beyond his control.

PART FOUR

CHAPTER XXIV

L ooking back on his years on the row, Mark Abramson had come to see himself and his friends on the row as almost heroic for being able to endure the endless waiting that pervaded each new day. It wasn't an excuse for what he knew many of them had done. It was understanding. Understanding that the system that had tried them had become hopelessly corrupted to the point that the truth no longer mattered in the final outcome.

The days had passed slowly in a way. But in another way Mark now felt that each day, indeed each hour, was more precious than the last. It had now been ten years since he had been sentenced to death, and five years since Judge Pinkston had denied his postconviction case. His case had been presented to, and denied by, the Florida Supreme Court. His lawyers had then filed a federal petition for a writ of habeas corpus in the United States District Court asking that court to review the constitutional violations that had been presented to Judge Pinkston so long ago. That court, like the two before it, had concluded that the State had withheld evidence from Joel Cummings prior to and during the trial -- that is, that Walker had been lying when he testified about Mark's alleged confession. Nevertheless, the federal court, like its State counterparts, had concluded that there was no reasonable probability that the outcome would have been different if the jury had not been lied to. The same was true for the claim that Bennett's performance had been deficient. The bottom line was that the federal court intended to look the other way. The errors were all harmless. On appeal to the federal Eleventh Circuit Court of Appeals, the outcome was identical. And with a two-paragraph decision the United States Supreme Court had decided not to review the case of the State of Florida versus Mark Abramson. With the issuance of that last opinion, Mark's conviction and sentence were now all but certain to remain intact. It was all quite legal. It meant that the days for Mark Abramson had become even more precious than before.

Sitting alone now in his cell, Mark's thoughts were quietly interrupted by the sound of one of the few people he now considered trustworthy enough to be a true friend. "Mark, it's me, Brian Connors," the lay minister said to Mark. "How are you doing today?"

"Oh, about the same, I guess," answered the inmate. "Not much going on right now. How about you?"

"'Bout the same as you, I suppose," chuckled Brian. "Seems kinda slow for some reason. So how've you been doing, Mark? Keeping the spirits up?"

"Yeah, I guess so," came the now standard response. "I decided today, though, that I'd better start getting ready for Christmas. It's only about a month away, you know. I've got to get my cards in the mail. How about you, Brian?"

"Well, you know me," said Connors. "I'm always late. But I guess I'll get started soon. Before you know it'll be time for Christmas Eve services. It's amazing how fast the days fly by this time of the year. How are you doing with cards. Do you need anything?"

"Yeah, actually I do," said Mark after some thought. "You know that guy I told you about? Steve Morada? I'd like to get something for him this year. Something special. You know, Brian, besides you and Steve I ain't got nobody hardly."

"You've got the Lord, Mark. Don't forget about him," said Brian. "You know, I'm really glad that you became a Christian, Mark. It's more important than anything else. And you wouldn't believe how much different you are now. . . . But anyway, Mark. What did you want to do for him?"

"I don't know. I don't have hardly any money, but I did want to at least get him a real nice card this year. Can you handle it for me, Brian? It'd mean a lot."

"Sure, I'd be glad to," answered the soft-spoken friend. "Besides, it'll prompt me to get started on my cards this year." Brian smiled as he looked at Mark, who was obviously very pleased that he would be able to do something for his friend for the holidays.

"You know, Brian. You know what you said about the Lord?"

"Yeah."

"Well, you're right. It does help. It's pretty sad, I guess, that I had to get to the point where I had nothing, to be able to see that all I really needed was God. Never could have convinced me of that when I was on the outside. Kinda funny how that works. Anyway, thanks for your help, man. I don't know what I'd do without you."

"Sure. Glad to help, Mark. It's what I'm here for," said Brian as he smiled and stood up to leave. "I've got to go for now, but I'll see you again real soon. Take care of yourself, Mark. You'll be in my prayers."

Mark returned to his thoughts. It would be a day worth remembering, he told himself. It was always good to see Brian. He always felt so at peace with himself after such visits. They reminded him of what was really important in life. He felt so much richer being reminded that his trust and faith were in someone other than himself. It made each day worthwhile.

At five minutes after ten o'clock on Tuesday morning after Brian's visit the day before, Mark awoke from a half-sleep to hear his name being called. "Abramson, we need to speak with you," boomed the guard's voice.

"Yeah, what about?" asked Mark.

"I'm not sure," one of the guards replied. "You just need to come with us."

Rising to do as he was told, Mark watched as his cell door opened. He stepped outside where his feet and hands were grasped by the familiar cold steel of the cuffs that every prisoner knew all too well. "Where are we going?" Mark asked again.

"You just got a call out. No big deal," was the only response, as Mark began to walk with his escorts.

Ten minutes later, after being placed in a prison van and driven to the adjoining Florida State Prison, or FSP was it was known, Mark was led into the superintendent's office. He was met by the superintendent and two men dressed in gray business suits. As Mark was placed in front of the superintendent's massive oak desk, he watched as the equally massive superintendent rose from the other side.

"Mark Abramson," superintendent John Tubbman began, "I have the duty to read this document to you. I received it just now." As the superintendent reached for an official-looking paper, it dawned on Mark what was about to happen.

> "Mark Abramson, inasmuch as you were previously tried and convicted of the crime of the heinous first-degree murder of Ed Baker, and sentenced to death as punishment therefore, you are hereby advised that I, as Governor of the Great State of Florida, do hereby order that you be delivered to the Florida State Prison to await the execution of said sentence by electrocution, said execution to be held during the week beginning December 24, 1995, at a time set by the Honorable Superintendent of the Florida State Prison. May God have mercy on your soul. Signed Harold S. Chalmers, Governor."

As he stood before the superintendent Mark felt as though he were experiencing a bad dream. Realizing, however, that such was not the case, he began to shake and felt his knees begin to buckle. Seeing what was about to happen, however, the guards quickly responded to prevent the inmate from falling to the floor.

"Mr. Abramson, please be assured that we will do everything in our power to carry out your sentence in a courteous and considerate manner," continued the superintendent, as he handed Mark the death warrant that had just been read to him. "You will now be taken to a holding cell here at the prison to await your execution, which has been set for 7:01 A.M., on Wednesday, December 26th. Gentlemen, you may now take Mr. Abramson to his cell."

Mark leaned on the guards and slowly shuffled out the door. "We got us another one," he heard one of the gray-suited men say. "The Governor's been wanting another one before the end of the year." As Mark slowly regained his composure and followed the grim-faced guards, he began counting the days in his head. If the Governor had his way, Mark had exactly twenty-nine days left to live.

The location was appropriately called death watch. The cell was surprisingly large, ten feet by ten feet, over fifty square feet larger than the cell that Mark had called home for over ten years of his life. As he walked into the cell for the first time, Mark thought to himself how odd it was that in what could possibly be the last few days of his life he should be given more space in which to move around. Pretty sadistic, really. Like showing ice cream to a small child but not letting him eat it. I guess it's all designed to make them feel better about themselves before they kill me, Mark thought.

Over the years he had heard about death watch. It was a place of almost mythical proportions. Although in the early years many of the residents of death watch returned to their cells in other parts of the prison, their executions having been stayed by the courts, in later years there had been few to leave its confines alive.

Mark wondered in which group he would fall.

The cell was sparsely appointed, with only a cot, sink, and toilet. The front of the cell was lined with bars, while the other three sides were solid concrete walls painted a putrid apricot color. The cell was lit by two incandescent bulbs. Together, they seemed to shine brighter than a bright sunny day. There was nowhere to hide.

Mark looked at the floor and saw a box that contained all of his belongings, few though they were. Without thinking he picked up the box, put it on his cot, and began slowly removing each item and placing it in its own, carefully chosen spot in the cell. Reaching the end of the box he realized that his collection of pens and pencils was missing. What in the world have they done with that, he asked himself. "Hey, guard. Come here a second," he yelled to the guard who was stationed at the end of the hall outside his cell.

"Yes, sir," said the guard as he began walking over to the cell. "What do you need?"

"I need my pens and pencils. Where are they?"

"Pens and pencils?"

"Yeah. I had them before I was taken to the superintendent's office. Where are they?"

"I imagine they're in the property room."

"Well, I need them. I need to write some letters."

"Okay. No problem for you to write. But you can't have pens and pencils in your cell all the time."

"Well, how am I supposed to write to anybody then?"

"Just let me know when you need to use one and I'll get it for you," came the guard's cautioned reply.

"Why can't I just keep them in here with me?" asked Mark as insistently as he could muster under the circumstances. "Like I said, I had them in my other cell. It's not like they're contraband or anything."

"Well, yes and no," the guard answered.

"Now that makes a lot of sense. Either I can have them or I can't. And I'd like to have them."

"Well, you can't," came the response. "It's for your own protection."

As he absorbed the answer the import finally dawned on Mark. "You mean I might hurt myself with them, don't you?"

The guard stared at him.

"Don't you!" yelled Mark suddenly.

"Mr. Abramson, I didn't make the rules. I just have to enforce them, that's all. Please understand. I'm only doing my job."

"I don't believe it, man," Mark said. "You all are afraid I might kill myself before you get the chance. Man, you people are sick! Well, I'll tell you what. I'll be a good boy. You can kill me real legal-like and all. Okay? Now, give me my damn pens."

"Mr. Abramson, I can't. I'm sorry." The guard's voice seemed to substantiate the apology. It was not an easy position for anyone to be in. It was these moments that the guard had come to despise.

Sensing that it was futile to press the issue further, Mark elected to back off. "All right," he said. "Forget it." The battle having been engaged and quickly brought to an end, the prisoner turned and completed the task of rearranging the rest of his belongings. In the days to come he would rearrange each item almost incessantly. It's all I have any control over, he thought to himself. Might as well do what I can.

It was but a few short hours later that the guard answered a nearby telephone and, after almost whispering into the mouthpiece for what seemed like minutes, slowly walked over to Mark's cell with the phone and advised his charge that he had a legal call. The guard set the phone on a stool placed outside of the cell and handed the receiver to Mark. Then he walked to his gray metal desk, which was placed perpendicular to the wall across from Mark's cell.

"Hello?" Mark said as he placed the receiver to his ear.

"Hello, Mark," he heard Judd Klingbeil say on the other end. "This is Judd. Listen, we were just provided with a copy of your warrant. I wanted to call you and let you know that we have it and that we are beginning to work on it now. Mark, we have everyone in the office on this."

"Thanks, Mr. Klingbeil."

"Another thing, Mark. This is your first warrant. I can't make any guarantees, but I feel pretty confident that we'll get a stay. Okay?"

"How confident?"

"Very confident, Mark. But now listen. It may take awhile. It could be that it won't happen until well into the warrant. So you gotta do me a favor and stay calm, okay?"

"Okay. But how far into the warrant?"

"Depends. I'll have someone out to talk to you about it soon. That person can give you more specifics. But for now you just need to remember that we're doing everything that we can on this end. All right?"

"Yeah. All right."

"Mark, I've gotta go for now. Take care of yourself. We'll be in touch."

"Well, you know where to find me," was the only response Mark could think of. He was proud of his attempt at humor under the circumstances.

"Sure. Okay. I've gotta run, Mark. I'll talk to you later. Good-bye."

As Mark heard the click on the other end of the line he felt as though his only connection to a lifeline had been severed. "Guard, I'm through with the phone," he instinctively yelled to the guard.

It was now one o'clock in the afternoon. In the past three hours, what for the past ten years had been Mark's life had been severely altered. And as much as he had hated that life, he now marveled at how much he would give to have that "life" back. But that was the past, and he had long since learned that the past could not be relived. He now had twenty-nine days left to put the rest of his affairs in order, regardless of his lawyer's feeble attempts to convince him otherwise.

Fourteen days. Three hundred and thirty-six hours left to live.

In the past fifteen days Mark had heard nothing from the Group. It was with some surprise then, when Mark learned of a legal visit that he was to receive from John Winston. The investigator, to Mark's surprise, was still assigned to his case. Ten minutes later he was led into a visiting room to meet the man he'd hardly heard from in the years since the hearing on his 3.850 motion in St. Bartholomew.

"Mr. Abramson, it's good to see you," Winston said to Mark as he walked through the door. "How are you doing?"

"Doin' okay for someone who only has fourteen days left to live. Doin' especially well for somebody who don't know whether or not his lawyers are working on his case."

Mark didn't feel like being particularly hospitable to this man, in spite of the fact that he'd driven over three hours to see him. "If I'd have known you were coming I'd have dressed up or something. Might've even shaved."

"Mr. Abramson, I know you're upset. I guess anyone in your position would be very upset right now. But believe me, we've been working around the clock on your case. The reason I came here today was to let you know that we have concluded our investigation in your case and have found some incredible new evidence that I think you're going to be very pleased with. We have written a new 3.850 that needs to be filed tomorrow. I have it with me and I need you to sign it so that it can be filed." Winston looked at Mark with a look that conveyed a strong sense of urgency, as well as hope that Mark would cooperate.

"So, what's this new evidence that's so incredible?"

"Mr. Abramson," Winston began. He looked around to be sure that he could not be overheard, and then lowered his voice to a whisper. "We have discovered new evidence that we believe strongly supports your claim of innocence! After the warrant was signed on you we received a call from a guy named Eddy . . . oh, what was his last name?"

"Hinson. Eddy Hinson," said Mark.

"Yeah. Eddy Hinson. Anyway, Hinson informed us about a conversation that he overheard some years ago between a couple of guys that worked at Bluestone Construction. It was an Al Stempson and Randy Collier. Anyway, it seems that Eddy heard this guy Randy telling Stempson that he was real uncomfortable about you taking the heat for something you didn't do. Well, Eddy said that Al was getting real mad at Randy about the whole thing and it was obvious to Eddy that Al knew a lot more about the crime than he would have gotten from reading the papers, if you know what I mean."

"Winston, I like what I'm hearing, but this isn't exactly news to me. I told you people about this years ago."

"I know, I know," Winston said. "But anyway, according to what Eddy tells us, Randy and Al didn't know that Eddy overheard them. So a few days later Eddy manages to get Randy off to the side and makes a little small talk, you know? One thing leads to another and they decide to go to a bar for some drinks. Eddy gets Randy pretty soused . . ."

"I can see Eddy doing that," Mark interrupted. "He's just the type person who likes to play private eye, you know?"

"Yeah, I can believe it," chuckled Winston. "But get this. He gets Randy tanked up and manages to work the conversation around to your execution. Tells Randy how he thinks you got a raw deal. Then Randy blurts out that he knows you got a raw deal because you didn't commit the crime! According to Eddy, Randy goes further and tells him that he always thought it was funny that the cops pinned it on you so fast and that it made some other people real relieved when it happened."

"You're kidding me? What else did he say?" asked Mark, whose eyes had suddenly widened in disbelief at what he was hearing.

"He didn't say much more than that," said Winston. "Supposedly when Eddy tried to push Randy a little further he clammed up. But get this, he told Eddy he wasn't saying anything more, because he had no intention of trading places with you! . . . Pretty good stuff, huh?" As Winston concluded his recitation of Eddy's comments Mark could tell that he was obviously very pleased with himself.

"So what happens next?" Mark asked.

273

"Well, that's why I'm here. Eddy has given us an affidavit, Mark. The affidavit sets out everything I've just mentioned. We've drafted a new 3.850 to be filed tomorrow in the circuit court. I've brought the original with me and I have a copy for you." As Winston retrieved the two lengthy pleadings from his worn-out leather satchel, he continued with his instructions. "I need you to sign the original and then I can get back to Tallahassee so that we can finalize getting it filed. We're asking the court to give you a new trial, of course. But before that can happen you need an evidentiary hearing on this new evidence. It'll be like the last one we had."

"And all of this is going to happen when?" asked Mark. "I don't have a long time to wait."

"No problem," said Winston. "We also are asking for an indefinite stay of execution, so that the courts can properly review these claims. I don't think there will be a problem getting it. . . . It's pretty much a formality at this point, Mark. So you need to relax, okay?"

"Easier said than done," Mark said. "But with what you've given me today it should be quite a bit easier."

"Good enough, man. Here's the pleading. Just sign it here on the last page and I'll be on my way. One other thing. If there is an evidentiary hearing held, it's possible you could be transported back to St. Bartholomew real soon. I just wanted you to know in case they come to take you. That's what it'll be about."

It was with a strong sense of relief that Mark signed the pleading that he hoped would finally shed some light on what had happened to him. As he said good-bye to Winston and watched him walk out the door he couldn't help but begin to cry. Maybe. Just maybe, he thought to himself. Maybe this time things will finally be different.

Upon returning to his cell and hearing the heavy iron bars close shut behind him, Mark walked to his cot, sat down, closed his eyes, and for the first time in years began to contemplate the possibility that he could one day return to life on the outside. Perhaps it wouldn't be the same as before, but it would still be a resumption of the ability to taste freedom once more. He hadn't been able to do that in over a decade. Now he didn't know if he could handle it if the opportunity were handed to him. But that was not something he had to deal with right away. For now he simply had to continue to survive within the confines of what he hoped would be a temporary cell in the bowels of Florida State Prison.

The first step toward Mark's new life began in the form of an order issued by Judge Pinkston. The order informed both the defense and the State that the court intended to hold a hearing on the 3.850 filed by Mark. The hearing was to be held three days from the date that the motion was filed. No evidence would be allowed to be presented--at least not for now. The court wanted to inquire further into the specifics of the motion filed by Mark's attorneys. The court reserved one hour for the hearing. Mark's presence, it ruled, would not be required.

At seven P.M. on that Monday evening, with just over nine days before Mark's scheduled execution, Judge Pinkston entered the courtroom. His entrance was duly announced by the bailiff in a voice that was calculated to summon the attention of every living soul within earshot of the judge's bench. As he approached his seat behind the bench, Judge Pinkston surveyed the surprisingly packed courtroom that awaited the beginning of the proceedings. "Be seated," the judge matter-of-factly commanded from his position high above the crowd.

"Once again we have the case of the State of Florida versus Mark Abramson, case number CF-19A61. I see that Mr. Klingbeil is present on behalf of the defendant, Mark Abramson. Mr. Smallwood is present on behalf of the people of the State of Florida. Are you gentlemen ready to proceed?"

"The defense is ready, your Honor," announced Klingbeil.

"The State is ready, your Honor," announced Smallwood.

"Very well, then," said Pinkston. "Mr. Klingbeil, you may begin. I would tell you up front that I have reviewed your motion and am generally familiar with the allegations that are made therein. The question that I have, and the reason I wanted this hearing, is whether or not we should hold an evidentiary hearing. I note that you have requested such a hearing."

"That is correct, your Honor," began Klingbeil. "We believe that Mr. Hinson's affidavit clearly presents the court with facts that, if proven, would entitle our client to a new trial. The allegations contained in that affidavit are serious. If proven, they provide this court, and a new jury, with evidence that Mark Abramson was arrested, convicted, and sentenced to death for a crime that he did not commit. This evidence consists of admissions made by a Randy Collier that he was involved in the murder of Ed Baker. Mark Abramson had nothing to do with it." Feeling a rising sense of grandiosity, Klingbeil continued. "Your Honor, in the interest of fairness, in the interest of justice, and last but not least in accordance with the Rules of Criminal Procedure, it is beyond question that Mr. Abramson is entitled to an evidentiary hearing on these matters. He is facing execution, your Honor!"

"I'm well aware of that, Mr. Klingbeil. Why do you think I scheduled this hearing within three days of receiving your motion. And why do you think I scheduled it for this late hour? Does the State object to an evidentiary hearing, Mr. Smallwood?"

"The State most certainly does object, your Honor," began the prosecutor. "We feel that these allegations, even if proven, would not alter the outcome of this case. There's nothing conclusive here, your Honor. It's nothing more than another death-row inmate trying to forestall his rightful appointment with justice. But there's something more compelling than that, your Honor. The State contends that the allegations, even if proven, and even if they pointed to someone else, which I might add we in no way concede, would nevertheless be time barred because they are being raised too late." As he finished his sentence Smallwood smugly glanced over in Klingbeil's direction to see if the point hit home.

"Your Honor, how could this claim possibly be time barred?" asked Klingbeil. "We raised the claim as soon as we had the facts."

"We disagree with that statement, your Honor," interjected Smallwood. "And in anticipation of this moment we are prepared to present testimony on this point tonight."

"What sort of testimony, Mr. Smallwood?" asked Judge Pinkston.

"We would be prepared to present the testimony of Eddy Hinson, your Honor. He's the man that gave the affidavit to the defense."

"Your Honor, this is highly irregular. We have had no notice of this. This is nothing more than trial by ambush, and I don't appreciate it! If we are to have an evidentiary hearing, then fine. Let us put Mr. Hinson on the stand and get to all of the evidence. But let's do it in a civilized fashion."

"Mr. Klingbeil," answered Judge Pinkston, "I am faced with a death warrant that expires in nine days. I have a Supreme Court calling me wanting to know when I'll have a ruling. I am not inclined to put off an evidentiary hearing. It seems to me that from your motion there's one principal witness, and that's Mr. Hinson. Now I don't see why we can't hear from him tonight and clear this all up. . . . Mr. Smallwood, is Mr. Hinson here?"

"He is your Honor."

"Then let's bring him in," Pinkston said.

"Your Honor, may I at least have some time to interview him and find out what he's going to say?" asked Klingbeil, trying hard to suppress the anger.

"I believe that would be in order, Mr. Klingbeil," responded the judge. "Court will recess for fifteen minutes, after which we will begin with the evidentiary hearing." As Pinkston rose from the bench, he glanced down at Klingbeil as if to warn him to restrain himself in the future. With that the stern-faced jurist exited the courtroom.

The fifteen minutes flew by. Judge Pinkston, not one to tarry, thereupon re-entered the courtroom and rose to the bench. Upon calling court to order once more, Pinkston began. "Mr. Smallwood, before we recessed you indicated that it is the State's position that the defendant's claim is procedurally barred. What is your basis for your position?"

"Your Honor, in support of our claim the State would call Eddy Hinson, the affiant, to testify regarding the sole issue of when he became aware of this alleged knowledge."

"Very well. I think we should hear from Mr. Hinson. Bailiff, bring in the witness."

"Your Honor, I once again object to this testimony," announced Klingbeil. "We have had no time to prepare for this hearing. In addition to that, my client is not present, although his presence is clearly required."

"Mr. Klingbeil," replied the judge, barely restraining his anger, "this man is your witness. I would assume that you spoke with him prior to coming to court this evening. Your client, Mr. Klingbeil, is awaiting execution. What did you expect to find here this evening? A tea party? I'm going to hear from this witness."

Eddy Hinson slowly approached the witness stand, quickly glancing over to Klingbeil as if to signal his intent to help his long-time friend who was in so much trouble. As the short, stocky, and now-balding witness took his seat, it was evident to most in the courtroom that the man was viewed by both sides as a very important witness. It was not unexpected that the courtroom grew silent as all ears awaited the testimony of the man in the witness chair.

"Mr. Hinson, please state your full name for the record," began Smallwood.

"Edward Hinson. But people call me Eddy."

"Mr. Hinson," continued Smallwood, being formal in spite of the invitation to lower the tension in the courtroom, "do you recognize this document that I am handing you?"

"Yes, I do. It's an affidavit that I gave Mr. Klingbeil."

"Is the date accurate on the affidavit?"

"Yes, it is."

"Mr. Hinson, when did you first learn the information contained in the affidavit?" asked Smallwood.

"Oh, it was years ago."

"Five years?"

"More than five years," answered Eddy. "Probably closer to eight years or so ago."

"And what did you do when you learned about it?"

"Well, I thought to myself that this was some pretty important stuff. I mean, it sounded to me like Mark, I mean Mr. Abramson, was probably not guilty of killing Mr. Baker. So anyway, I called Mark's wife, Susan, and told her about it."

"And what did she do?"

"I don't know. She thanked me for telling her. I guess she told Mr. Klingbeil about it sometime, because he got in touch with me about it."

"And when did he get in touch with you, Mr. Hinson?" pushed Smallwood.

"Oh, probably about four years or so ago. . . . It was a good while ago."

"Would you say that it was at least more than two years ago?"

"Oh, definitely."

"And what did you tell him, when he first talked with you?"

"I told him what's in the affidavit."

"All of it?"

"Yes."

"Thank you, Mr. Hinson. I have no further questions," Smallwood said as he took his seat.

Judd Klingbeil slowly rose and looked at Eddy. "Mr. Hinson, what information did you learn about that you told my office?"

"Objection!" shouted Smallwood. "This hearing is not about the nature of the information. It's about when the defendant learned about it."

"Sustained," said Pinkston matter-of-factly. "Mr. Klingbeil, please restrict your questions to that issue."

"Mr. Hinson," Klingbeil continued, "are you certain about the date that you advised my office about this information?"

"Not about the date, no sir."

"Your Honor I would like nevertheless to proffer his testimony for the record."

"All right, Mr. Klingbeil," replied an obviously perturbed judge.

"Mr. Hinson, tell me what information you acquired."

"You mean, what did I hear?"

"Yes, sir."

"Well, it was years ago, after Mr. Baker's murder. I heard this guy, Randy Collier, telling another guy, Al Stempson, how he didn't like the fact that Mark took the heat for the murder. Anyway, this guy Stempson told him to shut up and never discuss it anymore."

"Who were these two men, Eddy?"

"They were employees of Bluestone Construction. They worked for Mr. Baker."

"Did you hear anything else?"

"Yeah. A few days later I was in this bar, The Spotted Seagull. Anyway, I sees this guy Randy in there and we start talking. Randy was pretty loaded, and he got pretty loose. Anyway, we got to talking about Mark being executed and all and he was laughing about it, you know? He said that a lot of people would be better off when it was over. And I asked him what he meant, and he said that Mark didn't kill nobody, or know anything about it! I guess that I got kinda shocked when I heard it. I mean, I never thought Mark did nothing like that, but you know, to hear somebody say something like that, it kinda shocked me. Anyway, I asked him what he meant by that and he said that he wasn't going to say anything more, because he didn't want to go to no electric chair."

"And what did you understand that to mean?"

"Well, the way he said it and all it was pretty clear to me that he was involved in the murder."

"Thank you, Mr. Hinson. I have no further questions."

Andrew Smallwood, remaining seated at his wooden table, looked at Hinson and, after a few moments of silence, asked the nervous witness, "Mr. Hinson, you say that all of that information was communicated to Mr. Klingbeil over two years ago?"

"Yeah. I guess it kinda surprised me that I was just now being asked about it," answered Eddy.

"Now, when he asked you about the exact date, you said you weren't sure."

"Yes, sir."

"But that didn't mean that you had any doubts that it was over two years ago, did it?"

"No, sir. I know it was longer than that."

"Thank you, Mr. Hinson." As he turned to look at Pinkston, Smallwood quickly announced that he was through with the witness.

As Eddy stood down from the witness stand he walked past Klingbeil and nodded, as if to let him know that he had done the best he could.

"Your Honor," continued Smallwood, "in light of the witness' testimony, the State submits that this claim, even if it had any merit, is *clearly* procedurally barred. For that reason, the State has no further witnesses, and would simply ask the court to impose the bar at this time."

"Your Honor," said Klingbeil, "I again object to the manner in which this hearing is being held. But the evidence has been taken. We submit that Mr. Hinson's memory is faulty on the issue of how long this information has been known. I would again remind this court that Mr. Abramson's life is at stake here. If you impose a procedural bar the claim is over. I suggest that justice demands that this information be heard by way of a formal evidentiary hearing."

"Mr. Klingbeil," began Judge Pinkston, "I agree with you that the witness' testimony is serious. However, I am also struck by the testimony that he told your office about this matter several years ago. If, as you say, the testimony would change the nature of the trial, then why . . . well, let me do this -- the court will take the matter under advisement and issue its order at a later date. Court is adjourned." The judge then rose from the bench and abruptly exited the courtroom.

As Judge Pinkston walked through the heavy wooden door into his chambers, the courtroom suddenly came to life with sounds of disbelief on both sides of the isle.

Whispers gained intensity and became excited expressions of suspense at what the judge would do with the case. As the reporters began to gather around Klingbeil and his crew, Andrew Smallwood watched and began to shake his head at the outrage being expressed by the defense attorney who was openly pleading for his client's life. This system is sick, Smallwood thought to himself. It's really sick.

Two hours later Mark rose from his cot in his cell and walked to the cell door to receive the anticipated call from his attorney. "Hello? Mr. Klingbeil? How'd it go?" he asked, eagerly awaiting the response.

"It went pretty well, Mark," Klingbeil began. "Eddy testified as expected. I think the judge was very concerned about the claim. All we can do now is wait for his ruling."

"How long do you think it'll take?" asked Mark.

"I don't know, Mark. Not too long, I believe. I'll let you know as soon as I hear something. How are you holding up?"

"Pretty well, I guess. Actually I'm pretty happy considering Eddy's testimony and all. I feel real good about everything."

"Good. You just keep your spirits up and I'll let you know as soon as I hear something. Good-bye Mark."

"Good-bye." As Mark handed the receiver back through the bars of the cell door he returned to his cot. It's finally gonna work out, he thought to himself. It wasn't long before he dozed off into a restful sleep such as he had not had for many weeks.

Judge Pinkston's order would see to it that Mark's few nights of restful sleep would come to an end. Judd Klingbeil sat in his office and read the order that was faxed to his office. It was issued four days after the hearing. Five days before he scheduled execution. As Klingbeil read the order he admitted to himself that he wasn't surprised. The last paragraph said it all. "Inasmuch as the evidence is uncontroverted that the Defendant knew of the facts now alleged, in excess of two years prior to filing the instant motion, his claim is procedurally barred from consideration by this court. Accordingly, the court does not reach the merits of the Defendant's allegations."

The court, as expected by Klingbeil, had decided not to consider whether or not Eddy's testimony about Mark's innocence should be heard. Since the claim had been raised too late it could not be considered now. "Hey guys, we'd better get this brief finished!" Klingbeil yelled out to his colleagues. "Pinkston just denied us. He says we're barred!"

Minutes later, Mark was in a state of disbelief as he listened to his lawyer's words. "How could he do that?" he asked Klingbeil over the phone. "I mean, I thought you said this was airtight. From what you just read, it sounds like he won't consider it because you guys didn't file the claim in time. Is that it?"

"Mark, that's what it says. Yes. But I think. . . . Look, I think Eddy lied to the court about all of that. We're looking at our files right now. . . . I think . . ."

"You think what, man? Right now I don't care what you think! Eddy didn't lie to no court and you know it!" Mark yelled into the phone. You knew about these facts years ago and you did nothing! NOTHING! Now *I'm* gonna pay for it!" After he slammed the receiver down Mark began to pace around the inner perimeters of his cell. Around and around. It wasn't long before the tears began to flow as if a spigot had just been opened.

I've got five days to live, he thought to himself. They're really gonna do it!

CHAPTER XXV

"**L**adies and Gentlemen, this past week we saw the workings of evil in our humble county. Many of you have no doubt heard accounts of what happened in our courts during the week. Many of you may have even been present to witness what occurred. And if you don't know by now, what I am referring to is the efforts of a convicted murderer to escape the punishment that has been rightfully imposed upon him by a judge and jury of his peers. It is just this sort of behavior that I want to consider with you this morning." And so began the minister's sermon to the congregation of Steven Morada's church in Shelbyville.

"I tell you good folks that it is time for us to demand that the members of our community accept responsibility for our actions. That means all of us. And it also means that we must accept the punishment that is rightfully handed down to us when we go astray. The Bible commands it and we can do no less if we expect to live as the Bible teaches that we should.

"Now let us look at this *murderer.*" In order to heighten the effect that it would have on the congregation, the minister allowed the despised word to roll slowly off of his tongue, like honey falling from a spoon. "Here is a man who was caught within days of butchering poor Ed Baker. And even though he was caught red-handed, has he ever been man enough to look at his fellow citizens and admit his guilt and ask for forgiveness? No. That has never happened. And what is worse, ladies and gentlemen, is that there are those in this community who have befriended this man and encouraged this behavior." As the minister made the point he looked directly at Steven. "I tell you, no good can come from the encouragement of such wicked behavior!"

There are times when enough is enough, and for Steven Morada such a time had now come. It was with little thought, but dogged determination, that he rose from his seat in the middle of the congregation, looked at the man who denounced his behavior, and turned to leave the sanctuary. His parents slowly bowed their heads, hoping that somehow no one would remember that this was their son.

"You cannot run from the truth, young man," the minister persisted.

As he heard the words of the man whom he for years had counted as one of his friends, Steven stopped, turned back to face the podium, and began to respond in a voice that shook through every ounce of his being. "Sir, I am amazed to hear you claim to be a man of God," the young man intoned. "You speak about a man whom you know nothing about, except for what you read in the papers. You've never met the man, nor have you spoken with any of the people who believe him to be innocent. Instead, you continue to denounce him and call for his death in order to feed the venom that your people want to hear. I wonder if you care about the *truth* in all of this, sir? And where is the mercy that I also recall reading about in the Bible? Where is that? All I see is hatred. Well, I'll tell you what. I'll pray for your soul today and from now on! In the meantime, I'm sure that if you get up bright and early in the morning you can go down to the local quarry and buy some real nice rocks to throw at Mr. Abramson next Wednesday. I'm sure that it'll go *real* nice, especially since it'll be the day after Christmas! By the way, quite a Christmas message you have for us today, sir."

As Steven Morada walked out of the sanctuary he turned and looked one last time at the room that for most of his life had occupied much of his time. When he finally turned to exit the building he determined never again to set foot in the church that he had known all of his life.

Three hours later Steven Morada parked his car in the Florida State Prison parking lot. It had been a long drive, but it had also been a cathartic time that was greatly needed by the young man.

285

Now, as he walked toward the prison entrance, he began to realize that these trips might be coming to an abrupt end. He began to shiver at the thought of what was to come.

"Mr. Morada, since you're on the short list that Mr. Abramson gave us, we'll allow the visit; however, it will have to be limited to fifteen minutes today. Also, it will be a non-contact visit, and will be in the first room to your right after we get through the metal-detection process. Do you have any questions?"

"No, sir," Steven replied.

"Good," the guard said. The smile on the guard's face indicated to Steven that the man sympathized with his plight.

Later, upon entering the visitors' room, Steven was struck by the smallness of the room itself. There was little room to move around. It was painted a sickly orange and contained only a metal stool of sorts, which was bolted to the floor and which stood in front of a small shelf. The shelf was only a foot or so wide itself and joined an inch-thick piece of clear glass, the center of which contained a circle of wire mesh for speaking through.

No sooner had Steven entered the room when a door opened on the other side of the glass and Mark was escorted into his side of the visiting area. As he sat down across from Steven, the guard, in a gesture of kindness, decided to remove the shackles from his wrists, thus allowing some freedom during the visit.

"Steven, thanks for coming by," Mark said to his friend. "How was your trip?"

"It was okay, I guess," answered Steven. "Under the circumstances. How're you holding up, Mark?"

"Oh, you know me. One party after another," Mark chuckled, though it was devoid of levity. "I'm glad you came, Steven. There's some things I want to talk about."

"Sure. But we've only got fifteen minutes. At least that's what they said."

"Okay. I'll get right to the point then. Look, I don't know if you know or not, but I'm allowed to have a witness when they do it."

"Mark, there's nothing saying it's going to happen. There's still appeals left." Steven felt his eyes beginning to water.

"It's going to happen, Steven," answered Mark. "I've heard about the appeal thing. Frankly I don't have any faith in those courts. They couldn't care less about truth. They just want to process the case. The only way this will stop is if God puts an end to it. That's the only way. . . . Now listen to me."

"Sure."

"Look, from what I hear I'm normally allowed to have either my lawyer or a minister witness it. I sure don't want that lawyer in there. Not after what he did to me. Brian's a real nice guy and a real friend, but I don't know if he could handle it, you know."

"Well, I imagine he's pretty upset about now," responded Steven.

Mark continued, "That's why I want you to be there, Steven."

"*What?*" said Steven. Although it should have been obvious what Mark was leading up to, he had utterly failed to grasp the man's line of thinking. "You want me to witness it? Mark, I don't know if I . . ."

"Will you at least think about it, Steven? It would mean a lot to me."

"If it's what you want, Mark, then I'll do it," Steven responded before realizing what he was going to say. "I'll be there for you. You know that."

"I knew I could count on you," said Mark. "I never had any doubts." He suddenly began to smile. "Now you cheer up. I hear you'll get a free breakfast, compliments of the State of Florida."

"Just what I always wanted," replied Steven. "Oh, by the way. I was at that hearing."

"Good. I knew you'd be there. Tell me one thing, Steven: what did Eddy really say?"

"He told them that that guy Randy had basically confessed to the crime and that it was obvious to him that you had had nothing to do with it. Then they started asking him about when he had told people about it, and he told them that he had told the Group about it at least a few years ago."

"That's what I thought. How did he sound?"

"He sounded real good," replied Eddy. "The thing is, he sounded like he was real mad at the Group for not doing anything. But I don't think he knew the effect of them not doing anything until now."

"He wouldn't know," said Mark, as he nodded his head. "Eddy's a really good guy. I think a lot of him. At least he did what he could."

"Yeah, I think he tried, Mark. He was pretty nervous up there. But he got . . ."

"Abramson, gotta go," a guard's voice interrupted as the door to Mark's side of the room opened. "Time's up."

"Anyway, he got it all out," said Steven as they got up to go. "Take care of yourself, Mark. I'll be praying for you."

"Hey, I'll be praying for you," said Mark, as he turned and walked out the door.

"Take care of yourself. I'll see you later."

After Mark walked out of sight, Steven sat back down on the stool, put his head in his hands, and quietly began to cry. How can I watch this man die, he asked himself.

At nine o'clock the next morning the Florida Supreme Court denied all relief in the State of Florida versus Mark Abramson. Mark's claim, the court held, was procedurally barred since his attorneys had failed to raise it sooner. And just for added security, the court looked at the testimony given by Eddy at the hearing and found that even if true, there was no probability that the outcome of the trial would have been different. To the extent that there was error, the court said, the error was harmless. The execution would be carried out in forty-six hours.

The denial of Mark's appeal in the State courts was not particularly unexpected in Judd Klingbeil's office. In fact, the only significant unanswered questions were when the denial would come, and on what grounds it would be premised. Of the two, Klingbeil had more uncertainty over the first. It was assumed that the Florida Supreme Court would uphold the bar imposed by the trial court. Such minimal uncertainty nevertheless provided the defense team with the dubious benefit of being able to proceed with writing the petition for habeas corpus, which would be filed with the federal district court. Since the State court's decision was largely as predicted the habeas petition was completed and filed by lunchtime on Christmas Eve. It sought a stay of execution to allow the courts an opportunity to address Mark's claim of innocence. There was little to do now except to wait. Given the generally accepted view that Mark's chances of success were minimal, the defense team had already prepared the papers to be filed with the Eleventh Circuit Court of Appeals in the event that Mark was turned down by the federal district court.

Mark received the news of the district court's decision by five o'clock on Christmas Eve. It had taken Klingbeil thirty minutes to get his client on the phone, an interminable delay under the circumstances. "Mark, this is Judd," the attorney began.

"Listen, Mark, the district court has granted our request to stay the execution!"

"Whew," was the only thing Mark could think of to say. "That's great!"

"Yes, it is," continued Klingbeil, "but Mark, the court stayed it for only twenty-four hours, apparently in order to give the court time to consider the issues."

"You mean because it didn't want to deal with it on Christmas? Isn't that the real reason?" asked Mark.

"Who knows what the real reason is," answered Klingbeil. "I suspect that you're right, but at least we bought the twenty-four hours. Listen, we're all doing everything that we can, Mark."

"Yeah. Too bad you couldn't have been doing that years ago, when Eddy came to you and asked you to look into all of this. As I recall I asked you to look into it then, too. You remember that, Judd?"

"Mark, we're doing all we can," responded the attorney.

"Just as I thought. Don't admit to anything. We wouldn't want you to have a guilty conscience now, would we? Well, I hope you have a real merry Christmas, Klingbeil!" yelled Mark. With that he slammed the receiver down. Enough of that, he thought to himself. Those jerks have already hurt me enough.

"Jimmy," he said to the guard sitting outside his cell, "I really don't want to talk to any of those people for a while if it's okay."

"Sure. It's your decision," said the guard. "I think I'd be doing the same thing if I was in your shoes right now."

"Yeah, but you're not," came the prisoner's terse reply. "I'm the only one wearing these shoes now. And they don't fit too good." As he lay back down on his cot, Mark stared first at the ceiling and then at the clock, which unmercifully hung on the wall outside his cell. It was now seven-thirty, Christmas Eve night. As he closed his eyes, the pain that came with the recurrent knowledge that this would be his last Christmas Eve and Christmas grew to proportions beyond anything that he had experienced to that point in his life. And yet, as painful as it was, he determined to stay awake as long as he could lest he miss even a second of what for him used to be his most memorable and joyous time of year.

CHAPTER XXVI

Until now Mark had not spent a night as long as that Christmas Eve. Every hour and every minute of every hour had suddenly become more precious than the last. It was a feeling that at that moment in time only he could experience. And with it came a loneliness equally as unique. For the first time since he had been incarcerated for Ed Baker's murder, Mark now allowed himself to remember life as it had been when he was a free man. It was difficult at first, but eventually the memories began to flood his consciousness to the point that he could not have fallen to sleep had he tried. On this most holy of nights he recalled the times when his family had gathered together for a special dinner on Christmas Eve. It was a family gathering that he could depend on. Indeed, he could not remember ever spending Christmas Eve anywhere else. Even after he and Susan had married they still had gone to his parents' house for that special dinner.

Once everyone had arrived the family would sit down to what by anyone's standards would have been a feast. The glazed ham, topped with pineapple and cloves and then covered with a sticky-sweet glaze, was always accompanied by sweet potatoes and a host of other vegetables. No one felt left out of the opportunity to enjoy his favorite dish. Dinner would then be completed by fresh coffee and his mother's four-layer coconut cake, always made with fresh coconut at his father's insistence. The family would then attend the Christmas Eve services at their local church.

Now, sitting alone in his cell for what he expected would be his last Christmas Eve on earth, he thought about those services and considered how ironic it was that his incarceration had caused him to appreciate more fully the meaning of those services. He only wished that he would be given an opportunity to participate in them once more. It was those thoughts that accompanied Mark into sleep on that night. It was those thoughts that shielded him from the otherwise recurring vision of the manner in which he expected eventually to die.

Christmas morning came all too soon for death-row inmate number G904892. Never entitled to have sleep allow him to escape his confinement for more than a brief period, Mark was awakened by the guard at five o'clock in the morning. In all of his years of incarceration, Mark had never understood why it was necessary for the guards to awaken inmates at such early hours when those same inmates would be required to spend at least twenty-three hours a day in their cells. But such was life, and it obviously made no difference that he was now just forty-eight hours away from being killed. Rules must be followed.

As Mark awoke on that Christmas morning the thought entered his mind that on this day he would be free from having to deal with his lawyers. The courts would be closed. Indeed, it would almost be as if life were normal for one day. On top of that he'd probably get a special Christmas dinner, to the extent that what he was given was classified as food.

"Hey, Jimmy," Mark said to the guard who was sitting outside of his cell.

"What're they gonna give us today to eat?"

"Oh, I don't know," replied the guard, who seemed to be glad to have the opportunity to talk. "You probably won't like it, whatever it is."

"And you will?" asked Mark. "I've seen what you guys get and it don't look much better to me."

"It's not. But we get it for free, so I guess I won't complain." As the guard began to yawn Mark realized that the man had been there for the better part of sixteen hours.

"How long are you gonna sit out there before you collapse?" Mark asked Jimmy. "You've been sittin' out there a good while."

"Yeah, well I was supposed to go home last night, but my replacement didn't show. I decided to stick around since things have been pretty quiet. . . . I did get some sleep last night though, when they relieved me for a couple of hours."

"Guess they wouldn't dare leave me unattended now, would they?" said Mark. "After all, I might do something."

"They just want to be sure that everything goes smooth I guess," Jimmy replied.

"Well now, we wouldn't want anything to spoil their party now would we?" chuckled Mark. "Tell me, Jimmy, what's it like? I mean, it seems kinda screwy that I'd have a bigger cell on the watch than I did on the row. Everything is so different."

Jimmy looked at the prisoner and shook his head. "I know. It's pretty weird in a way. I don't know how come I got assigned to this duty, but it's really bizarre if you ask me. Everybody has to be real nice to the guy toward the end. It's the same guy they treated like garbage for all the years on the row. But now that they're gonna kill 'em it's a different matter. It seems to unnerve everybody. I think the people who run this place get to feelin' guilty about what they're gonna do. This is the only way they can ease their consciences."

"Yeah, that's what it feels like on this end," Mark continued the conversation. "You know, I've always wondered what it would be like. I never thought it'd be like this. . . . How did the others act when they were here?"

"'Bout the same as you," answered Jimmy. "You know, by this time everybody seems to be pretty resigned to it all. Sometimes I think that some of the guards are more upset than the inmates. I mean, I know that's not the case, but really man, some of us don't like this one bit."

"But you're still helping out, aren't you?" said Mark in an unexpectedly terse voice. "Sorry man," he continued. "It's just that on this end all I see is everybody outside of these bars working to help kill me. It don't feel too good. Believe me, it don't."

"I guess not. And if I didn't have a family to feed I wouldn't be a part of this. But at the same time, I guess I kinda thought that at least I could show you guys some respect in your last days. Maybe that's why I haven't really tried to get taken off this detail. I don't know."

The words hung in the air between the two men. Suddenly neither felt like talking any more.

"Well, Merry Christmas anyway," Mark suddenly found himself saying.

"Same to you," said Jimmy. "Same to you."

As the hours passed by Mark found himself looking more and more at the clock on the wall. It wasn't long before it was ten o'clock. Lunchtime for the row. Mark would receive his meal a half-hour or so later. Today was no different. But this time the meal was edible. A roast beef sandwich, potato chips, Jell-O, and milk. What he wouldn't give for a nice hot cup of hot chocolate! He nevertheless decided that it would be better to eat what he had. No point in returning it as he sometimes did on the row. Protesting at this point would hurt no one but himself.

Upon finishing the meal Mark once again lay down on his cot and began to recall his life before this nightmare beset him. It had been a good life, he decided. Although he had wanted for many things he had also gained a lot. His life with Susan had been wonderful -- in spite of the fights that sometimes divided them. He thought back to those years when he had been young and impetuous -- hot headed. He remembered the time that he had been fired from the job at the car wash and how he had gotten in his car and driven as far and as fast as he could. No destination intended. He just wanted to drive. I'd sure like to be able to do that now, he thought to himself. If I got outta here the State of Florida would never see me again.

Thoughts of Susan. I wonder where she is and what she's doing, Mark asked himself. He posed the question over and over. There was never an answer.

The clock continued its progression through the day. It was now four o'clock, time for the Christmas dinner.

"Hey, guard," Mark asked, " where's Jimmy?"

"He left to go back home. He said to tell you he'd see you tomorrow. You had dozed off when he left."

"What's your name?"

"Sidney."

"Good to know you, Sidney. . . . Hey, can you tell me something? What's the weather like? I hate it in here with no windows."

"It's pretty nice out," said Sidney. "It's sunny, but it's also cold. High of fifty today."

"Thanks."

As he broke off the conversation Mark watched another guard bring his dinner. Turkey with something they called dressing, mashed potatoes, and peas. My gosh, he thought to himself, I must be special because I even got a piece of cake.

He ate the dinner ever so slowly. Not because it tasted so good. It was just that he wanted to do everything he could to keep the holiday alive for as long as possible.

Having completed his dinner, Mark began the task that he had often hoped to avoid. But it was time to face reality, and reality dictated that he pay his final respects to his friends. There weren't many, but those did deserve to hear from him one last time. And though he knew it would be hard, it was time to write to them and say good-bye. In a way it would be more special that he was writing to them on Christmas. Besides, tomorrow would be a busy day with no time to think.

The letters, Mark soon discovered, would take the rest of the evening to write.

The first one was to Susan. He quickly discovered that for someone in his position it was not easy to tell someone good-bye. But then again, at least he had the chance. As he wrote he couldn't help but think that Ed Baker had never had that chance. As he wrote he couldn't get that thought out of his mind.

The letter to Susan was difficult. Very difficult. So were the letters to his family and to Joel Cummings. He decided to write to Joel and let him know that it was the Group's idea to go after him. It was not an easy letter to write, but he needed to let the man know how he felt. He even decided to write to Jim Raulerson. "Jim, I just wanted to let you know how much I appreciated your friendship during those years. Don't ever let yourself get in the shape I'm in. It's not worth it." Mark didn't even know Jim's address, but perhaps someone could find him and give him the letter.

To his surprise Mark found that the letter to Eddy was the most difficult. Eddy had gone out on a limb for Mark. So much so that his own life could be in jeopardy depending upon Al's reaction to his testimony. Then again, with Mark's death Al would most likely feel that he was beyond the reach of the law. He would probably be right.

Nevertheless, in many respects Eddy had acted more selflessly than anyone Mark had ever known in his life. He would never forget it. "I only wish that I had some way to repay you for what you've done for me," Mark wrote. "It is knowing that at least someone out there cared enough to try and get to the truth that has especially helped me to get through these past few weeks. I'll be waiting for you on the other side. Your friend, Mark." Unless he received a stay the letter would be the last that he would write.

As he finished it he looked at the clock. It was one-thirty in the morning. The last full day of his life had begun.

It began like any other day. Five o'clock arrived and Mark was awakened.

Breakfast was served and the rest of the day began. So far so good, Mark thought to himself.

Not long after the meal was over, Mark was surprised to find John Tubbman, the prison superintendent, come down the hall to his cell.

"Mr. Abramson, I just wanted to stop by and fill you in on the events that will be taking place if the stay is lifted by the district court. As I believe you know, you will be entitled to a little more leeway on your visits today. I believe that there will be a number of them. We do not allow contact, except at the close of the visit. After normal visiting hours are over you will be given your dinner. I believe you've already given us your request for that, and we're doing everything we can to accommodate that.

"After your dinner you will be allowed continual visitation with your spiritual advisor, Brian Connors. Also, should your attorneys wish to meet with you, we will, of course, allow that. At approximately three o'clock tomorrow morning we will need to prepare you for the procedure. That means that . . ."

"Wait a minute," interrupted Mark. "Procedure . . . procedure? You mean where they kill me, don't you?"

"Well, . . ."

"You can't even say it, can you?"

"Mr. Abramson, I was trying to be considerate."

"Oh, and I do appreciate it. It means so much that you-all will kill me in a friendly manner. It really does mean a lot."

"Anyway," continued Tubbman, "at about three o'clock tomorrow morning the prison team will arrive to prepare you for the procedure. That means they will have to shave part of your head and your leg. They will also give you a new pair of pants and a white shirt, which you will need to put on by six o'clock. At five minutes to seven o'clock the prison team will come to escort you to the room down the hall there. That is where the chair is. You will be escorted to the chair and helped to sit in it. At that point you will be strapped in. We will try to make it as comfortable as possible. You will then be given an opportunity to make a final statement. We ask that the statement be kept to a reasonable length. After the statement the procedure will begin, assuming of course that there is no reprieve from the Governor, who will be continuously available by phone. Do you have any questions?"

"No," replied Mark.

"Okay then. I wish you the best of luck, son. I'll be checking up on you a little later in the day."

Mark watched as the superintendent turned and walked down the hall and out the door. "Jimmy," Mark said to the guard, "do you think the man enjoys his job?"

"Between you and me," said Jimmy, "I think he hates this stuff. You know, when he first got here he liked to talk tough about it, but after his first one he started changing. He rarely talks about it anymore. He doesn't act like a man who's proud of himself."

"He's just earning a living, is that the deal?" asked Mark.

"Yeah, I think that's about the size of it."

"Well, I think that's a cop-out," Mark shot back. "The man doesn't have any convictions. He's just using the money for an excuse." As he stepped back from the bars on his cell Mark looked at the clock. It was seven A.M. He had exactly twenty-four hours to live.

Eleven A.M. Twenty hours remaining. When the phone rang Mark quickly raised up on his cot and watched as Jimmy answered. The guard's whispered voice made it clear that Mark was being discussed. Then, as if he had no choice in the matter, he stood and walked over to Mark's cell and handed him the receiver. "It's for you, Mark."

"Who is it?"

"Your lawyer."

Mark slowly reached his arm through the bars and took the receiver. "Hello," he whispered, "is that you Judd?"

"Yes, it's me, Mark. Listen, I have some bad news. The district court just denied your federal habeas."

"Well, we go to the Eleventh Circuit now, don't we?"

"We'll try, Mark. The bad thing is this," the attorney continued. "The judge denied a CPC."

"What's that? I've never heard of that?"

"It's what we call a certificate of probable cause. You have to have it in order to appeal to the next highest level. When the judge denied it he was saying that there's no merit to your claim. He's saying it's frivolous, in other words."

"How can he say that!" Mark shouted into the receiver. "How can the jerk say it's frivolous. The issue is whether or not I even did the crime, for crying out loud!"

"Mark, listen to me. It's not fair. We all know that. But the man almost has immunity to do anything he wants. We're filing the appeal anyway. It'll probably be filed within the next few hours. So just bear with us. We're not done yet." When Klingbeil got no response he finally asked, "Are you okay, Mark?"

"Yeah, I'm fine," came the delayed response. "Look, I've gotta go. Thanks for all you're doing."

"You're welcome, Mark. Now don't give up. You hear?"

"Sure. . . . Hey Jimmy," Mark shouted over to the guard, "I'm done here."

Once more Jimmy retrieved the phone from the prisoner. He watched as Mark again returned to the cot, lay down, and seemed to stare out into space. "You gonna be all right?" he asked. "I can maybe get you something if you need it."

"Naw, man. I'm okay, I think. But thanks anyway."

"No problem. All you gotta do is ask." As Jimmy turned back to look at some papers on his desk, he couldn't help but notice that Mark's voice was betraying a pronounced degree of despondency. It had to happen sooner or later, he thought to himself. He knew from past experience that reality was beginning to sink in on the prisoner. The next hours were likely to be more difficult yet.

As the door at the end of the hall opened Mark saw another guard walk through and approach Jimmy. There was a short conversation and then both men walked over to his cell. "Mr. Abramson," the guard said, "you have some visitors. It's your parents. Would you like to see them?"

"Sure I want to see them," answered Mark.

Fifteen minutes later Mark entered the visiting room where he sat across a table from his parents. The room was larger than the normal visiting rooms, fifteen by fifteen feet, but it was still a prison visiting room. Everything was metal and bolted to the floor. The drab orange-pink paint didn't help at all.

"Mom. Dad. How are you?" Mark smiled as he looked directly into his parents' eyes.

"We're doing okay," his mother lied. "But what's important is how you are doing, son."

"I'm okay, too," Mark lied back. "I just heard from my attorneys that the federal judge denied my appeal. We're now appealing to the Eleventh Circuit."

"When do you expect to hear from them?" his father interjected.

"No idea. Could be soon. Could be late into the night from what I understand. But I really don't think it'll make a difference."

"Now son, you can't talk like that," Shelby replied. "You have to think positive."

"Mom," the word sounded funny to him -- he hadn't said it in so long, "you've got to understand something. These people don't care about the truth. That goes for the attorneys, the judges, the guards here, everyone. The truth just doesn't matter anymore. I'm nothing more than a number to these people. A number to be processed. If the truth mattered I'd be a free man by now."

"The truth matters to some people, Mark. Honestly it does. And it's just a matter of finding that person. That's all. You just wait and see. It'll happen."

"Mom. Listen to me," Mark said as he suddenly reached over and took her hand.

"In seventeen hours they're gonna kill me. It's gonna happen. The only way it won't is if God decides that He doesn't want it to. And so far it doesn't look like that's what He has in mind."

"Look, why don't we get off this subject," said Keith. "At least for a little while. Whadda you say?"

The suggestion was well taken by mother and son, and soon they were all engaged in recollections of better times. Times when Mark was still a boy growing up along the coast. He had loved the water from his earliest days. So much so, Keith reminded them, that the overly concerned parents had been very reluctant to send their young child to school because they were afraid that he would run off and go exploring, as he seemed to do with every waking moment of his life. Those days had been good days for everyone in the Abramson household. And today, for the duration of the visit, the three family members forgot about the more unpleasant teenage years when their son had become a person that neither parent could recognize. No, those regrets would linger forever. There was no need to dwell on them now.

But eventually the conversation always turned back to the present. Each of the three could sense when it was about to happen. It was almost uncanny how suddenly none of them would have anything to talk about. And then reality would steal back into the conversation. And reality was unforgiving and relentless, unmerciful. And each of them knew it to the depths of his souls.

And so, father, mother, and son did the best they could under the circumstances.

And when they had said all that could be said, the time came that each had dreaded. As he stood from his seat, Mark once more looked at the two people who together had given him life. They were now here to help him give it back. And with that recognition the man broke. The tears came and continued to flow until he was sure there were no more left.

"Mom. You've always been there for me. I know I didn't let you know it, but I felt it. Deep down, I felt it. . . Thanks. . . I love you." Mark's voice trembled. "And I love you too, Dad. In spite of everything. You were just looking out for me."

The three occupants of that cold, isolated but still so public room then embraced for what each expected would be the last time. And for a single second each felt as though he had been somehow removed from that place.

But reality returned in the form of a prison guard. "I'm sorry folks, but time's up. I have to get Mr. Abramson back to his cell." The man seemingly had no mercy. His voice betrayed his inner thoughts.

As Mark slowly stepped back from his parents he looked at each of them once more. "Pray for me," is all he could think to say as he motioned to the guard and walked back out the door. It was another twenty minutes before his mother would be in a condition to leave the room.

It was barely an hour later that Mark found himself back in the same room staring at two more visitors. One he expected. His ex-wife he did not.

"Susan, what are you doing here?" he almost shouted in surprise. "How on earth did you get in to see me?"

"Well, let's just say that Steven here apparently has some friends in low places," said Susan. "I get this call one evening last week and here I am. We wanted to surprise you."

"You did. You did," Mark replied with a smile. "You don't know how good it is to see you, Susan. And you too, Steven."

"How're you doing, Mark?" asked Steven. "I hear the news hasn't been that great."

"No. The news has been terrible. I've got to quit reading the paper." Mark's attempt at humor fell flat. "But I'm doing about as well as can be expected."

"Have you heard anything from the Eleventh Circuit?" continued Steven.

"Nope. Not yet. But I've got fourteen or so hours left. So there's time, I guess."

It wasn't long before this visit, like the one before, moved on to reminiscing about times past. For Steven it meant that he was to become a spectator for awhile. But that was all right. In bringing Mark and Susan back together one last time he had accomplished what he had set out to do. This was to be their time together. At least for now.

"Susan, whadda you say that we head back down to the island and stay in Eddy's cottage for the night? I seem to remember a vacation we took there some years ago. Pretty nice time, don't you think?"

"Mark, you know, Steven is sitting right here. Don't you think we should talk about something else?"

"Nope. Right now I like the idea of being back on that island. Just you, me and nature. What I wouldn't give to be able to go back there. . . . Maybe tomorrow, huh?"

He tried to chuckle as he said it.

"Yeah, maybe tomorrow," answered Susan. "Listen, Mark. There's something I've wanted to tell you, but I just never knew how. I'm sorry about how everything . . ."

"Stop. Stop right now!" interrupted Mark. "Now you listen to me Susan. You did what you had to do. And it's real clear right now that you did the right thing. I understand. Do you hear me?" As he looked at her Mark watched as she hung her head as though it were being pulled down by the cumulative weights of years of guilt. "Do you hear me?" he asked again.

"Yes. I hear you. But I still feel guilty, Mark."

"Well, don't. When you leave here you don't look back. You go forward and you live your life and you live every day like it's the last you're gonna have. 'Cause you have no idea how precious life is." As he looked at Susan, Mark could tell that the pressure was becoming too much for her. After all these years apart he could still sense it. "Tell you what," he continued, "I need to talk to Steven for a minute, and they're gonna be coming soon to pull you guys outta here. Would you mind if we said good-bye now so I can talk to this fool who brought you over here?" Mark smiled as he encouraged her to make it easy on both of them.

"Sure, Mark. Now listen. You take care of yourself, you hear? And you know that you're in my thoughts. Always in my thoughts. I still love you Mark. Honest I do."

"I love you, too, Susan."

As the two of them embraced for the first time in over fifteen years it was more than either could stand. "You'd better be gettin' outta here," Mark finally said. "I love you, Susan."

"I love you, too. I always have." Susan's last words seemed to trail behind her as she slowly walked sideways out of the room-- refusing to look away from her former husband.

"Now, Steven, are you sure that you're up to this tomorrow morning?"

"I told you I was, didn't I?" said Steven. "I wouldn't have said that I was unless I meant it."

"Well, you don't know how much it means to me, man. I'll never forget you for it. And by the way, how did you pull that off with Susan?"

"Like I said," said Steven, "I've got friends."

"Yeah, well you must, 'cause from what Jimmy tells me they never bend the rules on these things. Never. I owe you man. I really do."

303

"No problem," said Steven. "Are you doing okay? How're you holdin' up?"

"Oh, so-so, I guess. I don't know how I'm supposed to be doin'. How are you supposed to act when you know you're gonna die in a few hours?" Mark looked at the boy in front of him. Both of them realized there was simply nothing left to say. "Steven,"

Mark finally managed a word, "you look at me. Don't you ever do anything to get yourself put in the position I'm in. Watch who you hang around. You never know how it'll come back on you. Okay?"

"Okay, *dad*." quipped Steven, while trying without success to smile. "I see the guard is coming. So . . ." as he took a deep breath he continued, "you take care of yourself, Mark. We're all praying for you. You know that. We'll all be there for you."

The final hug between the two men was short but poignant. Suddenly Mark was watching his friend walk out of the door toward his former wife. As the two of them waited for the iron gate to open so they could exit they both stood and muttered unintelligible words to a man who both knew they would never speak to again. When the gate finally opened it was with measured relief that they turned and began their return to the outside world.

Mark had been in his cell little more than a half an hour when he saw the door at the end of the hall open and the guard walk toward him carrying a tray with what he assumed was to be his last meal. The aroma was unmistakable as the cell door opened.

"You're in luck," Jimmy said, as the guard placed the tray on Mark's cot. "The cook really knows how to fry fish. He grew up on the coast and used to work in a restaurant over in St. Pete."

"Jimmy, right now I could stand some good news like that. You wouldn't happen to have any more would you?"

Jimmy looked at the prisoner. Although he could sense that Mark was trying to keep a stiff upper lip by being funny, he could tell that the pressure was starting to get to him. Humor seemed to be the best way for this prisoner to deal with it. They all reacted differently for a while. But sooner or later reality set in for good. And when that happened most seemed to be inconsolable. "No, Mark. I don't have any other good news," Jimmy finally said. "I wish I did. I really do."

As the guard lifted the cover on the tray Mark looked at the plate. Fried snapper, cheese grits, fries, and hush puppies. Sweet tea to drink. Mark hadn't seen a meal like this since before he was arrested in what he had come to think of as his prior life. This meal would be one worth remembering, he thought to himself. Realizing the significance of the moment, both guards walked away from the cell as they heard the prisoner asking the Lord to bless the food that had been placed before him that night.

Upon finishing his meal Mark sat on his cot and once again allowed himself to reflect upon his past. Upon Susan. What a life they could have had together. For the first time in years he allowed himself to think back to those first few months that he had spent on the job at Bluestone. It had been difficult at first, what with just getting out of prison and then starting a new job. But he and Susan had made it through. It mattered little back then that they didn't have the best of everything. They'd had each other, and that was all they'd needed.

And there were the times that the couple had spent on Lone Pine Island. Just the two of them for hours upon hours. It had all seemed to come together with that weekend trip to Eddy's cottage on the island. Those walks on the beach had brought the two of them together in ways that neither would ever forget. But what stood out most in Mark's memory on this cold, fateful night was their walk on the beach that first night. The sun, Mark remembered, had ever so slowly descended below the horizon as it had painted the sky with multiple shades of orange and red. The entire landscape was highlighted, he recalled, by the silhouette of that lone pelican, which had lazily patrolled the Gulf in its final search for food. So peaceful. So perfect. On that night it had seemed as though nothing would ever go wrong for the two of them ever again. It was all so distant from where he now found himself.

It won't be long before I'll be free once more, he thought to himself. It won't be long at all.

CHAPTER XXVII

Seven P.M. Twelve hours remaining and still no call. The clock still hung on the wall, its hands continuously moving. Mark's life expectancy lessened with each slight movement. It did not go unnoticed.

Once more the door opened. This time Mark saw Brian Connors walk into the hallway and over to his cell. Brian's presence was bittersweet for the recipient of the visit. It signaled that the final hours were about to begin. Both men were now painfully cognizant of that fact.

"How're you doing, Mark?" asked Brian, not realizing that by now Mark was growing tired of being asked that question.

"Well, let me see. Not as good as yesterday, but probably a lot better than tomorrow. Does that make any sense?"

"Yeah, I guess it does," replied Brian. "Is there anything I can get for you, Mark?" he asked.

"Well, maybe a key and a real fast car," chuckled the inmate nervously. "Naw, nothin' I can think of right now. I'm okay."

"Honest?"

"Honest."

"The guards said that Susan came by to see you earlier today. I bet you were real surprised about that."

"Yeah, I was. You know, in a way she was the last person I expected to see. But it sure was nice of her to come."

"And Steven was with her?"

"Sure was. That kid's really somethin'. I don't know why he's doing all of this. But he seems to be really genuine about it. In a way he's done more for me than my own family has."

"Maybe so, but your folks really love you, Mark. Don't think for a minute that they don't."

307

"Then why didn't they come to see me all these years, huh? Tell me that."

"Because I suspect they couldn't bear to see you in here. It's no excuse, but you know, not everyone's strong enough to take this. Don't get me wrong, there's nowhere else I'd be right now. But at the same time it's hard enough coming in here to see people you *aren't* related to. I can't imagine how it would be to come see your own son. How many inmates do you know who regularly see their relatives?"

"None, really."

"That's right. So don't think your parents are unusual. They're not."

Mark suddenly seemed to drift away, as if he weren't even in the cell. Then a few seconds later he returned. "Brian, would you do me a favor?"

"Sure, what?"

"I never got to say good-bye to Billygoat. When they came and got me I didn't know what was going on. Would you tell him good-bye for me?"

"Of course I will, Mark. I'm sure he understands."

"And last night I wrote up this will. What I've got ain't worth nothin', but I want him to have what's mine. I think he'd appreciate it. He doesn't have anyone to look out after him. Anyway, if you could see to it that it gets it."

"Sure. No problem. But you'd better get someone in here to notarize and witness it, you know."

"Already done. All's you need to do is to carry it out."

It wasn't long before the cell once again grew silent. Brian noticed that Mark seemed to be doing this more and more. It was as if he were drawing into himself, preparing himself for what was to come. Preparing himself to leave. Brian decided that it was best to give him the space that he needed. "I'll be right outside if you need me, Mark."

"Oh, okay. Thanks."

As Jimmy moved over and opened the door to the cell, Brian looked back at his friend. It was hard to believe that in just a few hours his life would be ended. For now, however, there seemed to be nothing he could do. So he and Jimmy sat together outside of Mark's cell and waited. The wait, Brian later decided, was both the longest and the shortest that he had ever experienced in his life.

One o'clock in the morning. Jimmy, who had dozed off, was suddenly awakened by the phone. "Brian, it's for Abramson," he said. "It's his lawyer."

"Let me take it," said Brian. As he took the phone from Jimmy he began the conversation that he knew he didn't even want to acknowledge. "This is Brian Connors, may I help you?"

"Brian, this is Judd Klingbeil. Listen, the Eleventh Circuit has denied Mark's appeal. They've also denied a stay. We took it to the U.S. Supreme Court and they also denied it within thirty minutes. It's over, Brian. We waited to call, because we wanted to hear from the Supreme Court first. I guess I need to talk to Mark."

"Tell you what, let me do it," said Brian. "It might be better coming from me."

"Okay. Thanks a lot. Good luck. Tell Mark we're sorry and that we're on our way out to the prison now. Should be there in about three hours."

As he hung up the phone Brian looked over at Mark, who by now had realized that something was going on and was anxiously waiting to find out what it was. "Mark, that was Judd Klingbeil," Brian began as Jimmy let him into the cell. "Mark, the Eleventh Circuit has denied your appeal."

"Well, it's not a surprise. But we have the Supreme Court left."

"No, we don't. The Supreme Court has already refused to hear the case. Klingbeil wanted to get the word from both courts before he called."

"So it's over then, isn't it?" It was more of a statement than a question. "They're really gonna do it."

"It would seem so, Mark. I'm terribly sorry. You know that."

"Yeah, I know. It's just a shame that the Group couldn't have thought about this years ago when I was trying to get them to do something on this case. But they were too busy, weren't they?"

"Mark, that won't do you any good."

"Maybe not, but it's the truth. You know, the bottom line is that they were just playing games with my life. I was nothing but a pawn all along. As far as I'm concerned they're doing this as much as the guy that pulls the switch. Sorry, but that's the way I feel."

"And I don't blame you, Mark. But why don't we try to forget about them. They're not worth it."

"No argument from me there." Mark once again grew silent. Back into his own world.

The silence was broken at three o'clock. As three men walked through the hall door Mark looked up. Then his eyes moved to the clock. It was beginning.

"Hello, Mark," the largest of the men said. "We're here to prepare you for later on. We'll make this as quick as we can so as to inconvenience you as little as possible."

Mark just looked at them.

"Okay, son?"

"Okay."

The procedure didn't take long. Fifteen minutes to shave Mark's head and left leg. Mark would remember little more than the fact that the straightedge razor felt cold on his scalp. When they were done they left a pair of pants and white shirt lying beside Mark on the cot.

"About six o'clock you'll need to put those on, sir," the big man indicated to the prisoner. "We'll be back in at about six forty-five for the final preparations. Thank you."

As quickly as they had come in they were gone. The procedure had begun.

Then hours of prayer. Continual prayer in that cold, brightly lit cell. Brian would later recall that during the entire time he felt as though the two of them were on display.

Every fifteen minutes or so Jimmy had begun to make notes in a spiral binder. When asked about it later he replied that he was required to make continual notes of the prisoner's condition during these final hours in case the family later claimed that he had been abused.

In spite of the macabre atmosphere, Brian would also remember feeling closer to God than at any other time in his life. "You know, it's true what they say, Mark," he once told his friend, "God can penetrate even the darkest places on this earth. He's here with us now. He's with you, Mark."

"I know it, man. I know it. There's no other way I could get through all of this."

Brian noticed that between the prayers, Mark was now repeatedly watching the clock. His mind was beginning to focus. How unfortunate, Brian thought to himself.

Five thirty. An hour and a half to go. The hall door opened once again. As John Tubbman walked in Mark looked at him. He was carrying a bottle of Jack Daniels.

"Mr. Abramson," Tubbman said to the inmate. "I thought that if you'd like we could have a drink together. I don't know if you're a drinking man or not, but it might help you get through the next couple of hours."

Mark couldn't believe what he was hearing. "You want to have a drink with me?" he asked.

"If you'd like. It's sort of customary."

"Well, I'll tell you what. I'm not much for custom. Especially right now. So I think I'll have to decline. Maybe this afternoon, huh?" Mark smiled as his voice turned sarcastic.

"Okay. Whatever you want, sir." And with that Tubbman walked back down the hall and out the door.

"I don't believe the nerve of that man," Mark said to Brian. "All he wants to do is make himself feel better about all of this. That's all it is."

"They've been doing it for years," Jimmy interrupted. "It was stopped for a while because some group got upset that it might lessen the pain of the inmate. But Tubbman decided he was going to do it anyway. Pretty sick if you ask me."

"The whole thing's unreal," Brian added. "I don't know how you deal with it all the time."

Six o'clock. The door opened once more. In walked the same three men. "Mr. Abramson, we need to apply this gel to your head and leg. It won't take but a minute."

The big man was true to his word. Moments later they were done.

"Now please, sir, don't wipe that off. It helps the current run through the body, which makes everything go smoother. It'll ensure that you don't feel anything."

"But you haven't tried it out, have you?" Mark asked sarcastically. The men simply turned and walked away.

On the other side of the prison Steven Morada had cleared the security check-points. He and the other witnesses were escorted into a waiting room and given instructions. The main point of it all was that they were to be quiet and solemn during the entire procedure. The dignity of the prisoner was to be observed at all times. At six forty-five they were finally herded out into a waiting prison van and driven to the opposite end of the prison to wait for Mark Abramson to be put to death.

With fifteen minutes left to live Mark slowly began changing his clothes. It felt odd putting on the street clothes. He hadn't worn anything but prison clothes since his trial. He had asked to be allowed to wear a suit for his other hearings before Judge Pinkston; however the judge had denied the request. Now, as he began to leave behind forever the uniform that he'd grown accustomed to, he began to tremble. I don't know if I can do this, he said to himself. I just don't know.

Seeing what was happening, Brian received permission from Jimmy to help his friend. Together the two men slowly began final preparations for Mark's death. Both men found themselves shaking with fear. Both men prayed continuously. There was nothing more that could be done.

At five minutes to seven Mark suddenly heard the hall door open. Out of reflex his head swiftly turned to look at the clock. It was about to end.

"NO! YOU CAN'T DO THAT! PLEASE, DON'T! PLEASE MISTER, NO!"

The voice returned to Mark's memory. "NO! YOU CAN'T DO THAT! PLEASE, DON'T! PLEASE MISTER, NO!"

"Mr. Abramson, it's time to go." A guard twice the size of Mark slowly opened the door to the cell and walked inside.

"Mark, I love you. You're gonna be okay. I'm praying for you." Brian could think of nothing else to say. His friend was now sweating profusely and visibly shaking with fear.

"I love you too, Brian," Mark's trembling voice responded. "Thank you for all you've done for me."

"May God be with you, son. In a few minutes you'll be in a much better place."

Brian watched as the guards surrounded the prisoner and slowly walked him out of the cell and down the opposite end of the hall to a door thirty feet away. Brian followed but was unable to say a word. As the door opened and Mark began to walk into a brightly lit room, the two glanced at each other ever so briefly. With that Mark was gone--the door quickly shut behind him.

Upon entering the execution chamber Mark was stunned by the lights. The room itself was sparse. Two phones hung on the wall. Tubbman was standing by them. The electric chair sat in the middle of the room on a pedestal of sorts. After briefly stopping, the guards resumed their pace. By now they were practically carrying their prisoner – his legs having lost their ability to discharge their function. Mark, remembering what Steven had told him, quickly looked into the room on the other side of the chamber. Steven sat on the front row in the middle. The two of them found each other's eyes and smiled at each other.

As Mark sat in the chair the guards moved with uncanny speed and precision to finish their task. First the left leg was strapped to the chair. Then the right leg.

313

Simultaneously Mark's arms were strapped to the chair's arms. Another leather strap was tightened against his chest. All straps in place. He could barely move. Finally, his head was secured to the back of the chair itself. During the entire process the prisoner gazed upon his friend.

It was at this juncture that Mark managed to look down and see a guard connecting a wire to an electrode on his left leg. Then he felt a cold metal cap sitting on his head and heard something being done to it, as if metal were joining metal.

"Mark Abramson," Tubbman suddenly began. "By order of the Governor of the State of Florida, after being tried and found guilty of the murder of Mr. Ed Baker and then being sentenced to death, you are now to be put to death. Do you have any final words?"

As a small microphone was placed in front of his mouth, Mark realized that he hadn't given any thought to what he would say at this moment.

"Sir, do you have any last words?" Tubbman repeated.

"Just that I didn't do it."

"Very well," responded Tubbman. Then, out of the corner of his eye Mark watched as another guard moved toward him and lowered a leather mask over his face.

Dear Lord, please be with me, Mark said to himself.

Steven would forever remember the sight of Mark's body surging when hit by the first jolt of electricity. The condemned man's fingers curled into clenched fists as his body seemed to convulse uncontrollably. A wisp of smoke rose from his friend's head and leg.

It was five minutes after seven. Ten minutes later, after two more surges of electricity were pumped into Mark's body, a doctor pronounced Mark Abramson dead.

"The sentence of the State of Florida has been carried out," Tubbman finally stated. "The witnesses may leave."

Steven took one last look at his friend's lifeless body sitting in the chair. Then, as blinds were lowered to prevent any further viewing he turned and hurriedly walked out of the door.

Standing outside of the death house Steven looked over and saw Brian leaning against a wall. When the two men saw each other they both finally broke down into tears.

Nothing was said. Nothing could be said. The two stood together, holding each other up until at last they felt that their legs would move them forward. As they began walking toward the parking lot they watched as a white hearse pulled from behind the prison and slowly bore Mark's body away.

"He's in a better place," was all Brian could think to say.

"I know," Steven confirmed. "I know."

Then Brian looked toward the parking lot. "Look over there," he said to Steven. "Isn't that Klingbeil?"

"Yeah, it is. I wonder what he's telling those reporters?"

Moving closer to the small group of reporters, the two men listened as Klingbeil read from a prepared script. "Today the State of Florida has killed an innocent man. This is murder by anyone's definition! Every court in the state refused to hear Mark Abramson's version of what happened. Every court turned a deaf ear. The Governor didn't have the courage to intervene. Now, as a result, this man is dead."

"Steven, did Klingbeil ever go to the Governor on this case?" Brian whispered to his friend.

"Not that I know of," answered Steven. "Probably wouldn't have made a difference though. No one on the row has been granted clemency in over ten years. But this guy's still pathetic."

"He's scary is what he is," continued Brian. "Makes me wonder why they waited so long to bring out that evidence."

"You probably don't want to know, my friend. Neither one of us really wants to know, I suspect."

As the two men walked away from the hastily called press conference, they hugged once more and then departed that place. The sun had just risen over the back of the prison and was slowly dispersing the haze and fog that had settled in over the fields that surrounded it. The egrets slowly walked behind the cattle that grazed nearby. As he drove past the prison Steven couldn't help but think how peaceful the place seemed at this time of day. It was in stark contrast to what he had witnessed little more than an hour earlier. Then, as he slowed his car, his eye caught sight of an object in the sky. As the object drew nearer Steven realized that it was a small, twin-engine plane. In his rearview mirror Steven saw the plane circle the prison and then land in the field next to the administration building. As the two men stepped out of the plane wearing suits and carrying briefcases Steven realized that he had stopped his car in the middle of the road.

Time to get out of here, he thought to himself as his foot pressed the accelerator and he headed home.

EPILOGUE

Walking down the beach that Sunday afternoon Steven was glad to be by himself. It was cold out. Fifty-five degrees and windy. But it was also sunny. Not a cloud in the sky. It was low tide. The waves slowly lapped at the shore as the sandpipers ran haphazardly along the beach trying to avoid the water but also trying to find small treasures left behind by every wave.

It had been a month since Mark was killed. Steven had moved on with his life, but it had been difficult. Everywhere he went, it seemed, people wanted to know what it had been like in that room when it happened. He had truly grown weary of avoiding those questions. Likewise, he was tired of hearing community leaders take credit for bringing another murderer to justice. That would go on for a while, he thought to himself. Politicians love this stuff.

As he walked down the beach, however, Steven was finally alone -- away from everything. It's amazing how so much evil can occur in a place this beautiful, he thought. It really is. Walking a bit further, however, his mind finally allowed him to drift off to worlds unknown. He had been waiting for this moment. He knew that he would eventually find it on this island. So it was with final simple joy that he sat down on the sand, pulled his legs up to his chest and stared out at the Gulf ahead of him. The sun was beginning to set amidst the patchy clouds over the water.

"Whatcha" doin'?" the little boy suddenly asked him.

"Nothin' much. Just looking out at the water," Steven responded. "How'd you like to sit here with me?"

"Sure, mister," the little boy replied as he pulled up beside him. "How long you been here?"

"Not long enough, son. Not long enough."

The two sat and talked until the little boy's parents appeared and asked the child to come with them. "You don't just walk up to strangers like that son," Steven heard the boy's father say to his son.

"That's right," Steven mumbled to himself, as the little boy began to resume his walk down the beach. "Hard to tell what you might get yourself into, talking to strangers on this beach."

ABOUT THE AUTHOR

Jerrel E. Phillips has lived most of his life in Florida. He graduated from Florida State University with a B.A. in German, Cum Laude in 1977. He is a member of Phi Beta Kappa. He later attended the University of Maryland, School of Law in Baltimore, Maryland. There he earned his Juris Doctor degree in 1987. He has represented Florida's death row inmates in post-conviction proceedings in Florida. He is also an advocate of progressive environmental policies that would protect Florida's fragile ecosystem, devoting much of his current efforts to that cause. He and his family currently live in Florida.

Made in the USA
Charleston, SC
22 October 2012